COLLECTED SHORT STORIES

BY

ANTHONY TROLLOPE

EDITED AND INTRODUCED BY
JOHN HAMPDEN

WOOD ENGRAVINGS BY
JOAN HASSALL

DOVER PUBLICATIONS, INC.
NEW YORK

This Dover edition, first published in 1987,
contains the unabridged texts of the following
short story collections by Anthony Trollope:

The Parson's Daughter and Other Stories,
as published by The Folio Society, London, in 1949.

Mary Gresley and Other Stories,
as published by The Folio Society, London, in 1951.

Manufactured in the United States of America
Dover Publications, Inc., 31 East 2nd Street, Mineola, N.Y. 11501

Library of Congress Cataloging-in-Publication Data

Trollope, Anthony, 1815–1882.
Collected short stories.

I. Hampden, John, 1898–   II. Title.
PR5682.H36   1987   823′.8   87-15464
ISBN 0-486-25484-4 (pbk.)

CONTENTS

THE PARSON'S DAUGHTER
AND OTHER STORIES

NOTE

Anthony Trollope was born on April 24th, 1815, at 6 Keppel Street, Russell Square, London. He was educated, and was profoundly miserable, at Harrow and Winchester. He served in the General Post Office from 1834 until 1867, inventing the pillar-box and making substantial improvements in postal services at home and overseas. He died at 34 Welbeck Street, London, on December 6th, 1882.

La Mère Bauche was sold to "Harper's New Monthly Magazine" (U.S.A.) early in 1860, but apparently never used, and appeared in "Tales of All Countries", November, 1861. The Parson's Daughter of Oxney Colne was published in "The London Review", March 2nd, 1861, and "Tales of All Countries, Second Series", February, 1863: Father Giles of Ballymoy in "The Argosy", May, 1866, and "Lotta Schmidt and Other Stories", August, 1867: The Spotted Dog in "St. Paul's Magazine", in two instalments, March and April, 1870, and "An Editor's Tales", May, 1870: Alice Dugdale in "Good Cheer", the Christmas Number of "Good Words", 1878, and "Why Frau Frohmann raised her prices", December, 1881. For these data the editor is indebted to Trollope: a Bibliography, by Michael Sadleir, to whom all lovers of Trollope owe a major debt of gratitude. The tales are here reprinted from the London Library's copies of the first editions.

NOTE: The original Editor's Note and Introduction concerning the stories in the second half of this volume appear following page 229.

INTRODUCTION

"I WAS once told", said Anthony Trollope, "that the surest aid to the writing of a book was a piece of cobbler's wax on my chair", and he went on to demonstrate—being neither mock-modest nor conceited—that at least he never ran out of wax. Indeed his industry was prodigious, and the list of his works would be surprising even if he had done nothing in his life but write. When it is remembered that for twenty-six years he was an energetic and efficient civil servant, and for seven years before that an inefficient one, that he travelled many thousands of miles on horseback and by ship and train, and that he lived a very full social life, the quantity of his work is surprising and the quality of a great deal of it astonishing.

It has often been said that he wrote too much, though he always firmly maintained that writing less would not have enabled him to write any better, and "that the work which has been done the quickest has been done the best". Whether he was mistaken in this or not the spaciousness of his canvas is a considerable element in his greatness. No other novelist has added an entire county to the literary map of England, and many would have rested content with having done so, but Trollope travels far beyond the borders of Barsetshire. His later novels, which have not even now secured the public they deserve, deal with many aspects of London life, in political circles, aristocratic society, the civil service, boarding houses and slums, and he journeys into most of the English counties and to many countries overseas. He produced a *comédie humaine* which can be compared only with Balzac's, and a picture of Victorian England which is unequalled, in comprehensiveness and truth, in the work of any other novelist.

Copiousness has its drawbacks, however. One result is that there has never been a Collected Edition of Anthony Trollope; he probably wrote more than Dickens and Thackeray put together. Another result is that a good deal of his work, some of it little short of his best, is now almost completely unknown, and this is particularly true of his short stories and *nouvelles*.

He wrote over forty of them, and all but a dozen or so have been out of print since the end of the nineteenth century. The present volume, long overdue, recovers four of those which have least deserved their oblivion, and includes also one of his more familiar stories, *La Mère Bauche*.

The five tales reprinted here were written at intervals over a period of eighteen or nineteen years, the central period of Trollope's career as an author. When he began work on the earliest of them, *La Mère Bauche*, at the end of 1859 or beginning of 1860, he was by no means fully established, though *Barchester Towers*, *Doctor Thorne* and the first of his travel books, *The West Indies and the Spanish Main*, had attracted a good deal of notice. But before *La Mère Bauche* was published in November, 1861, *Framley Parsonage* had made him one of the most famous novelists of the day and, indeed, of the century. The latest of these tales, *Alice Dugdale*, appeared in sadly different circumstances in 1878. By that time Trollope had outstayed his contemporary welcome, and when he died, in 1882, not only his novels but his whole attitude to life and literature were outmoded for a generation which was learning to appreciate Henry James, George Meredith, Stevenson, Hardy, Pater and Oscar Wilde. The bluff ingenuous old mid-Victorian novelist, with his love of good living, whist and fox-hunting, his solid bourgeois virtues and corresponding limitations, had become an anachronism, and his work was derided for the qualities which constitute much of its appeal to the twentieth-century reader.

Trollope's short stories and *nouvelles* are more autobiographical than the lengthy novels on which his reputation rightly depends, and they reflect more definitely his travels about Europe and around the world. Many of them have foreign settings, in Ireland, France, Spain, Italy, Egypt, Palestine, the West Indies, the United States and other countries. While some merely use "local colour" to decorate a threadbare theme, there are others in which character and incident are native to their setting, and derive their vitality from it. Presumably he found the germ of *La Mère Bauche*, or perhaps the whole story waiting to be written, at Vernet during his holiday in Pyrénées-Orientales in 1859, but it is not hasty *reportage*; it is one of the most powerfully convincing of his stories.

Ballymoy and Pat Kirwan's "hotel" are as thoroughly Irish as Vernet and the Hôtel Bauche are French. "Some adventures I had [in Connaught]" says Trollope in his *Autobiography*, "two of which I told in the *Tales of All Countries* under the names of *The O'Conors of Castle Conor* and *Father Giles of Ballymoy*. I will not swear to every detail in those stories, but the main purport of each is true." Ballymoy may not be identifiable. Archibald Green is undoubtedly Anthony Trollope, the raw young man of twenty-six who landed in Dublin in 1841, a failure and almost an outcast, but found in Ireland with surprising rapidity the beginnings of his happiness as a man, a writer and a civil servant.

When he was transferred to Western England in 1851 he had been seven years happily married and six years a Post Office Surveyor, and the publication of his first three novels, though they were complete failures, had determined him to follow his mother's highly successful career as a novelist. He had reorganised the rural letter services of his Irish district so well that he was commissioned to do the same for a large area of England. "I spent two of the happiest years of my life at the task", his *Autobiography* records. "I began in Devonshire and visited, I think I may say, every nook in that county, in Cornwall, Somersetshire, the greater part of Dorsetshire, the Channel Islands, part of Oxfordshire, Wiltshire, Gloucestershire, Worcestershire, Herefordshire, Monmouthshire, and the six southern Welsh counties. . . . All this I did on horseback, riding on an average forty miles a day. . . ." It was during these rural rides that the towers of Barchester rose in his imagination, although pressure of official work prevented his finishing *The Warden* until 1853, and the village of Oxney Colne (which is apparently not to be found on the map) may well be a reminiscence of the same period. *The Spotted Dog* was written some fifteen years later, when

Trollope was editing *St. Paul's Magazine*, not at all successfully. He had resigned from the Post Office by that time; he had written *The Last Chronicle of Barset* and passed the peak of his popularity though not of his literary powers. "*An Editor's Tales*", says the *Autobiography*, "professed to give an editor's experiences of his dealing with contributors. I do not think that there is a single incident in the book which could bring back to anyone concerned the memory of a past event. And yet there is not an incident in it the outline of which was not presented to my mind by the remembrance of some fact. . . . How terrible was the tragedy of a poor drunkard who, with infinite learning at his command, made one sad final effort to reclaim himself and perished while he was making it. . . . Of these stories, *The Spotted Dog* . . . is the best." *Alice Dugdale* he might also have put among his shorter best, but the *Autobiography* was written before the *nouvelle*. It may well have lacked any exact basis in personal experience, however. Even if Beetham is not in Barsetshire, it must be very near the border, for this is evidently not the real Beetham of Westmorland.

Trollope's shorter tales are very like segments of his long novels. No one would rank him with the great writers of the short story, who have brought it, by tautness and concentration, nearer to poetic drama than prose narrative. The short story in this sense is a new thing of which Trollope, even if he had seen its possibilities, would have been incapable. He was essentially a prose novelist, with no distinction of style, no strong sense of form and no profound imaginative insight. He wrote more or less as he rode to hounds, with a rather short-sighted and lumbering but indomitable persistence. But his limitations were never those of insincerity or of narrow ignorance. Indeed he had a wider experience of life than any other Victorian novelist, or perhaps any English novelist whatever, and though he did not plumb any psychological abysses, he was a very shrewd observer of behaviour and motive in London slums and drawing-rooms, the cathedral close and the remote cottage, a French village, a Czech ghetto or an Australian gold-field.

In one respect, however, he surpasses even his greatest contemporaries: it is a commonplace criticism that his women are more convincingly drawn than those of any other Victorian novelist. As Henry James pointed out, he had fallen in love with the English miss; his weakness for the pretty young landlady of "The Spotted Dog", for example, is amusingly obvious. But his heroines are never idealized or falsified. He sees them as human beings, with a genuine respect of which Dickens (though a greater artist) was quite incapable. So we believe in Patience Woolsworthy and Alice Dugdale and their problems. The "triangle" in which Alice is involved, Trollope used far too often, yet he redeems it repeatedly, as he does here, by his delicate sympathetic understanding of young lovers and his perception of the pressures which a community exerts upon its members. His genial sense of social comedy is poorly illustrated in his short stories: *Father Giles* is almost the only humorous story worth reprinting, and this owes its interest mainly to its Irish background. But his clear, objective vision of life, his power to render pathos and tragedy unfalsified by sentimentality or melodrama are shown not so very far short off their best in *The Parson's Daughter of Oxney Colne*, *The Spotted Dog*, and *La Mère Bauche*. He is a realist, as he claimed to be, in the true sense of that much misused word. He makes his stories of the most matter-of-fact materials, yet invests them with fascination and emotional significance. He is at his greatest when dealing with commonplace suffering, for then the pedestrian movement of his prose, the slow accumulation of his circumstantial detail, take on the terrible, inevitable movement of life itself: we hear the Fates closing in upon Marie Clavert and we know that nothing can save her. And if in much of Trollope's work, as in *Alice Dugdale*, it is the sense of escape into a lost age of security which attracts many of his readers, they escape into a real world, for though there have been greater English novelists, there has been none more intent upon discovering the truth about his men and women and telling it as honestly as he could.   JOHN HAMPDEN

THE PARSON'S DAUGHTER
OF OXNEY COLNE

THE PRETTIEST SCENERY IN ALL ENGLAND—
and if I am contradicted in that assertion, I will say in all Europe
—is in Devonshire, on the southern and south-eastern skirts
of Dartmoor, where the rivers Dart, and Avon, and Teign
form themselves, and where the broken moor is half culti-
vated, and the wild-looking upland fields are half moor. In
making this assertion I am often met with much doubt, but
it is by persons who do not really know the locality. Men
and women talk to me on the matter, who have travelled
down the line of railway from Exeter to Plymouth, who
have spent a fortnight at Torquay, and perhaps made an
excursion from Tavistock to the convict prison on Dartmoor.
But who knows the glories of Chagford? Who has walked
through the parish of Manaton? Who is conversant with
Lustleigh Cleeves and Withycombe in the moor? Who has
explored Holne Chase? Gentle reader, believe me that you
will be rash in contradicting me, unless you have done these
things.

There or thereabouts—I will not say by the waters of which
little river it is washed—is the parish of Oxney Colne. And
for those who would wish to see all the beauties of this lovely

country, a sojourn in Oxney Colne would be most desirable, seeing that the sojourner would then be brought nearer to all that he would wish to visit, than at any other spot in the country. But there is an objection to any such arrangement. There are only two decent houses in the whole parish, and these are—or were when I knew the locality—small and fully occupied by their possessors. The larger and better is the parsonage, in which lived the parson and his daughter; and the smaller is the freehold residence of a certain Miss Le Smyrger, who owned a farm of a hundred acres, which was rented by one Farmer Cloysey, and who also possessed some thirty acres round her own house, which she managed herself, regarding herself to be quite as great in cream as Mr. Cloysey, and altogether superior to him in the article of cider. "But yeu has to pay no rent, Miss", Farmer Cloysey would say, when Miss Le Smyrger expressed this opinion of her art in a manner too defiant. "Yeu pays no rent, or yeu couldn't do it." Miss Le Smyrger was an old maid, with a pedigree and blood of her own, a hundred and thirty acres of fee-simple land on the borders of Dartmoor, fifty years of age, a constitution of iron, and an opinion of her own on every subject under the sun.

And now for the parson and his daughter. The parson's name was Woolsworthy—or Woolathy as it was pronounced by all those who lived around him—the Rev. Saul Woolsworthy; and his daughter was Patience Woolsworthy, or Miss Patty, as she was known to the Devonshire world of those parts. That name of Patience had not been well chosen for her, for she was a hot-tempered damsel, warm in her convictions, and inclined to express them freely. She had but two closely intimate friends in the world, and by both of them this freedom of expression had now been fully permitted to her since she was a child. Miss Le Smyrger and her father were well accustomed to her ways, and on the whole well satisfied with them. The former was equally free and equally warm-tempered as herself, and as Mr. Woolsworthy was allowed by his daughter to be quite paramount on his own subject—for he had a subject—he did not object to his daughter being paramount on all others. A pretty girl was Patience Woolsworthy at the time of which I am writing, and one who possessed much that was worthy of remark and admiration, had she lived where beauty meets with admiration, or where force of character is remarked. But at Oxney Colne, on the borders of Dartmoor, there were few to appreciate her, and it seemed as though she herself had but little idea of carrying her talent further afield, so that it might not remain for ever wrapped in a blanket.

She was a pretty girl, tall and slender, with dark eyes and black hair. Her eyes were perhaps too round for regular beauty, and her hair was perhaps too crisp; her mouth was large and expressive; her nose was finely formed, though a critic in female form might have declared it to be somewhat broad. But her countenance altogether was wonderfully attractive—if only it might be seen without that resolution for dominion which occasionally marred it, though sometimes it even added to her attractions.

It must be confessed on behalf of Patience Woolsworthy, that the circumstances of her life had peremptorily called upon her to exercise dominion. She had lost her mother when she was sixteen, and had had neither brother nor sister. She had no neighbours near her fit either from education or rank to interfere in the conduct of her life, excepting always Miss Le Smyrger. Miss Le Smyrger would have done anything for her, including the whole management of her morals and of the parsonage household, had Patience been content with such an arrangement. But much as Patience had ever loved Miss Le Smyrger, she was not content with this, and therefore she had been called on to put forth a strong hand of her own. She had put forth this strong hand early, and hence had come the character which I am attempting to describe. But I must say on behalf of this girl, that it was not only over others that she thus exercised dominion. In acquiring that power she had also acquired the much greater power of exercising rule over herself.

But why should her father have been ignored in these family arrangements? Perhaps it may almost suffice to say, that of all living men her father was the man best conversant with the antiquities of the county in which he lived. He was the Jonathan Oldbuck of Devonshire, and especially of Dartmoor, without that decision of character which enabled Oldbuck to keep his womenkind in some kind of subjection, and probably enabled him also to see that his weekly bills did not pass their proper limits. Our Mr. Oldbuck, of Oxney Colne, was sadly deficient in these. As a parish pastor with but a small cure, he did his duty with sufficient energy to keep him, at any rate, from reproach. He was kind and charitable to the poor, punctual in his services, forbearing with the farmers around him, mild with his brother clergymen, and indifferent to aught that bishop or archdeacon might think or say of him. I do not name this latter attribute as a virtue, but as a fact. But all these points were as nothing in the known character of Mr. Woolsworthy, of Oxney Colne. He was the antiquarian of Dartmoor. That was his line of life. It was in that capacity that he was known to the Devonshire world; it was as such that he journeyed about with his humble carpet-bag, staying away from his parsonage a night or two at a time; it was in that character that he received now and again stray visitors in the single spare bedroom—not friends asked to see him and his girl because of their friendship—but men who knew something as to this buried stone, or that old land-mark. In all these things his daughter let him have his own way, assisting and encouraging him. That was his line of life, and therefore she respected it. But in all other matters she chose to be paramount at the parsonage.

Mr. Woolsworthy was a little man, who always wore, except on Sundays, grey clothes—clothes of so light a grey that they would hardly have been regarded as clerical in a district less remote. He had now reached a goodly age, being full seventy years old; but still he was wiry and active, and showed but few symptoms of decay. His head was bald, and the few remaining locks that surrounded it were nearly white. But there was a look of energy about his mouth, and a humour in his light grey eye, which forbade those who knew him to regard him altogether as an old man. As it was, he could walk from Oxney Colne to Priestown, fifteen long Devonshire miles across the moor; and he who could do that could hardly be regarded as too old for work.

But our present story will have more to do with his daughter than with him. A pretty girl, I have said, was Patience Woolsworthy; and one, too, in many ways remarkable. She had taken her outlook into life, weighing the things which she had and those which she had not, in a manner very unusual, and, as a rule, not always desirable for a young lady. The things which she had not were very many. She had not society; she had not a fortune; she had not any assurance of future means of livelihood; she had not high hope of procuring for herself a position in life by marriage; she had not that excitement and pleasure in life which she read of in such books as found their way down to Oxney Colne parsonage. It would be easy to add to the list of the things which she had not; and this list against herself she made out with the utmost vigour. The things which she had, or those rather which she assured herself of having, were much more easily counted. She had the birth and education of a lady, the strength of a healthy woman, and a will of her own. Such was the list as she made it out for herself, and I protest that I assert no more than the truth in saying that she never added to it either beauty, wit, or talent.

I began these descriptions by saying that Oxney Colne would, of all places, be the best spot from which a tourist could visit those parts of Devonshire, but for the fact that he could obtain there none of the accommodation which tourists require. A brother antiquarian might, perhaps, in those days have done so, seeing that there was, as I have said, a spare

bedroom at the parsonage. Any intimate friend of Miss
Le Smyrger's might be as fortunate, for she was equally well
provided at Oxney Combe, by which name her house was
known. But Miss Le Smyrger was not given to extensive
hospitality, and it was only to those who were bound to her,
either by ties of blood or of very old friendship, that she
delighted to open her doors. As her old friends were very
few in number, as those few lived at a distance, and as her
nearest relations were higher in the world than she was, and
were said by herself to look down upon her, the visits made to
Oxney Combe were few and far between.

But now, at the period of which I am writing, such a visit
was about to be made. Miss Le Smyrger had a younger
sister, who had inherited a property in the parish of Oxney
Colne equal to that of the lady who now lived there; but
this the younger sister had inherited beauty also, and she
therefore, in early life, had found sundry lovers, one of
whom became her husband. She had married a man even
then well-to-do in the world, but now rich and almost
mighty; a Member of Parliament, a Lord of this and that
board, a man who had a house in Eaton Square, and a park
in the north of England; and in this way her course of life
had been very much divided from that of our Miss Le Smyrger.
But the Lord of the Government Board had been blessed with
various children; and perhaps it was now thought expedient
to look after Aunt Penelope's Devonshire acres. Aunt Penelope
was empowered to leave them to whom she pleased; and
though it was thought in Eaton-square that she must, as a
matter of course, leave them to one of the family, nevertheless
a little cousinly intercourse might make the thing more
certain. I will not say that this was the sole cause for such a
visit, but in these days a visit was to be made by Captain
Broughton to his aunt. Now Captain John Broughton was
the second son of Alfonso Broughton, of Clapham Park and
Eaton-square, Member of Parliament, and Lord of the
aforesaid Government Board.

"And what do you mean to do with him?" Patience Woolsworthy asked of Miss Le Smyrger when that lady walked over from the Combe to say that her nephew John was to arrive on the following morning.

"Do with him? Why, I shall bring him over here to talk to your father."

"He'll be too fashionable for that, and papa won't trouble his head about him if he finds that he doesn't care for Dartmoor."

"Then he may fall in love with you, my dear."

"Well, yes; there's that resource at any rate, and for your sake I dare say I should be more civil to him than papa. But he'll soon get tired of making love, and what you'll do then I cannot imagine."

That Miss Woolsworthy felt no interest in the coming of the Captain I will not pretend to say. The advent of any stranger with whom she would be called on to associate must be matter of interest to her in that secluded place; and she was not so absolutely unlike other young ladies that the arrival of an unmarried young man would be the same to her as the advent of some patriarchal paterfamilias. In taking that outlook into life of which I have spoken she had never said to herself that she despised those things from which other girls received the excitement, the joys, and the disappointment of their lives. She had simply given herself to understand that very little of such things would come her way, and that it behoved her to live—to live happily if such might be possible—without experiencing the need of them. She had heard, when there was no thought of any such visit to Oxney Colne, that John Broughton was a handsome, clever man—one who thought much of himself, and was thought much of by others—that there had been some talk of his marrying a great heiress, which marriage, however, had not taken place through unwillingness on his part, and that he was on the whole a man of more mark in the world than the ordinary captain of ordinary regiments.

Captain Broughton came to Oxney Combe, stayed there a fortnight—the intended period for his projected visit having been fixed at three or four days—and then went his way. He went his way back to his London haunts, the time of the year then being the close of the Easter holydays; but as he did so he told his aunt that he should assuredly return to her in the autumn.

"And assuredly I shall be happy to see you, John—if you come with a certain purpose. If you have no such purpose, you had better remain away."

"I shall assuredly come", the Captain had replied, and then he had gone on his journey.

The summer passed rapidly by, and very little was said between Miss Le Smyrger and Miss Woolsworthy about Captain Broughton. In many respects—nay, I may say, as to all ordinary matters, no two women could well be more intimate with each other than they were—and more than that, they had the courage each to talk to the other with absolute truth as to things concerning themselves—a courage in which dear friends often fail. But, nevertheless, very little was said between them about Captain John Broughton. All that was said may be here repeated.

"John says that he shall return here in August", Miss Le Smyrger said, as Patience was sitting with her in the parlour at Oxney Combe, on the morning after that gentleman's departure.

"He told me so himself", said Patience; and as she spoke her round dark eyes assumed a look of more than ordinary self-will. If Miss Le Smyrger had intended to carry the conversation any further, she changed her mind as she looked at her companion. Then, as I said, the summer ran by, and towards the close of the warm days of July, Miss Le Smyrger, sitting in the same chair in the same room, again took up the conversation.

"I got a letter from John this morning. He says that he shall be here on the third."

"Does he?"

"He is very punctual to the time he named."

"Yes; I fancy that he is a punctual man", said Patience.

"I hope that you will be glad to see him", said Miss Le Smyrger.

"Very glad to see him", said Patience, with a bold clear voice; and then the conversation was again dropped, and nothing further was said till after Captain Broughton's second arrival in the parish.

Four months had then passed since his departure, and during that time Miss Woolsworthy had performed all her usual daily duties in their accustomed course. No one could discover that she had been less careful in her household matters than had been her wont, less willing to go among her poor neighbours, or less assiduous in her attentions to her father. But not the less was there a feeling in the minds of those around her that some great change had come upon her. She would sit during the long summer evenings on a certain spot outside the parsonage orchard, at the top of a small sloping field in which their solitary cow was always pastured, with a book on her knees before her, but rarely reading. There she would sit, with the beautiful view down to the winding river below her, watching the setting sun, and thinking, thinking, thinking —thinking of something of which she had never spoken. Often would Miss Le Smyrger come upon her there, and sometimes would pass by her even without a word; but never—never once did she dare to ask her of the matter of her thoughts. But she knew the matter well enough. No confession was necessary to inform her that Patience Woolsworthy was in love with John Broughton—ay, in love, to the full and entire loss of her whole heart.

On one evening she was so sitting till the July sun had fallen and hidden himself for the night, when her father came upon her as he returned from one of his rambles on the moor. "Patty", he said, "you are always sitting there now. Is it not late? Will you not be cold?"

"No, papa", she said, "I shall not be cold."

"But won't you come to the house? I miss you when you come in so late that there's no time to say a word before we go to bed."

She got up and followed him into the parsonage, and when they were in the sitting-room together, and the door was closed, she came up to him and kissed him. "Papa", she said, "would it make you very unhappy if I were to leave you?"

"Leave me!" he said, startled by the serious and almost solemn tone of her voice. "Do you mean for always?"

"If I were to marry, papa?"

"Oh, marry! No; that would not make me unhappy. It would make me very happy, Patty, to see you married to a man you would love—very, very happy; though my days would be desolate without you."

"That is it, papa. What would you do if I went from you?"

"What would it matter, Patty? I should be free, at any rate, from a load which often presses heavy on me now. What will you do when I shall leave you? A few more years and all will be over with me. But who is it, love? Has anybody said anything to you?"

"It was only an idea, papa. I don't often think of such a thing; but I did think of it then." And so the subject was allowed to pass by. This had happened before the day of the second arrival had been absolutely fixed and made known to Miss Woolsworthy.

And then that second arrival took place. The reader may have understood from the words with which Miss Le Smyrger authorized her nephew to make his second visit to Oxney Combe that Miss Woolsworthy's passion was not altogether unauthorized. Captain Broughton had been told that he was not to come unless he came with a certain purpose; and having been so told, he still persisted in coming. There can be no doubt but that he well understood the purport to which his aunt alluded. "I shall assuredly come", he had said. And true to his word, he was now there.

Patience knew exactly the hour at which he must arrive at the station at Newton Abbot, and the time also which it would take to travel over those twelve uphill miles from the station to Oxney. It need hardly be said that she paid no visit to Miss Le Smyrger's house on that afternoon; but she might have known something of Captain Broughton's approach without going thither. His road to the Combe passed by the parsonage gate, and had Patience sat even at her bedroom window she must have seen him. But on such a morning she would not sit at her bedroom window —she would do nothing which would force her to accuse herself of a restless longing for her lover's coming. It was for him to seek her. If he chose to do so, he knew the way to the parsonage.

Miss Le Smyrger—good, dear, honest, hearty Miss Le Smyrger, was in a fever of anxiety on behalf of her friend. It was not that she wished her nephew to marry Patience— or rather that she had entertained any such wish when he first came among them. She was not given to match-making, and moreover thought, or had thought within herself, that they of Oxney Colne could do very well without any admixture from Eaton-square. Her plan of life had been that, when old Mr. Woolsworthy was taken away from Dartmoor, Patience should live with her; and that when she also shuffled off her coil, then Patience Woolsworthy should be the maiden mistress of Oxney Combe—of Oxney Combe and Mr. Cloysey's farm—to the utter detriment of all the Broughtons. Such had been her plan before nephew John had come among them—a plan not to be spoken of till the coming of that dark day which should make Patience an orphan. But now her nephew had been there, and all was to be altered. Miss Le Smyrger's plan would have provided a companion for her old age; but that had not been her chief object. She had thought more of Patience than of herself, and now it seemed that a prospect of a higher happiness was opening for her friend.

"John", she said, as soon as the first greetings were over, "do you remember the last words that I said to you before you went away?" Now, for myself, I much admire Miss Le Smyrger's heartiness, but I do not think much of her discretion. It would have been better, perhaps, had she allowed things to take their course.

"I can't say that I do", said the Captain. At the same time the Captain did remember very well what those last words had been.

"I am so glad to see you, so delighted to see you, if—if—if—", and then she paused, for with all her courage she hardly dared to ask her nephew whether he had come there with the express purpose of asking Miss Woolsworthy to marry him.

To tell the truth—for there is no room for mystery within the limits of this short story—to tell, I say, at a word the plain and simple truth, Captain Broughton had already asked that question. On the day before he left Oxney Colne, he had in set terms proposed to the parson's daughter, and indeed the words, the hot and frequent words, which previously to that had fallen like sweetest honey into the ears of Patience Woolsworthy, had made it imperative on him to do so. When a man in such a place as that has talked to a girl of love day after day, must not he talk of it to some definite purpose on the day on which he leaves her? Or if he do not, must he not submit to be regarded as false, selfish, and almost fraudulent? Captain Broughton, however, had asked the question honestly and truly. He had done so honestly and truly, but in words, or, perhaps, simply with a tone, that had hardly sufficed to satisfy the proud spirit of the girl he loved. She by that time had confessed to herself that she loved him with all her heart; but she had made no such confession to him. To him she had spoken no word, granted no favour, that any lover might rightfully regard as a token of love returned. She had listened to him as he spoke, and bade him keep such sayings for the drawing-rooms of his fashionable friends. Then he had spoken out and had asked for that hand—not, perhaps, as a suitor tremulous with hope—but as a rich man who knows that he can command that which he desires to purchase.

"You should think more of this", she had said to him at last. "If you would really have me for your wife, it will not be much to you to return here again when time for thinking of it shall have passed by." With these words she had dismissed him, and now he had again come back to Oxney Colne. But still she would not place herself at the window to look for him, nor dress herself in other than her simple morning country dress, nor omit one item of her daily work. If he wished to take her at all, he should wish to take her as she really was, in her plain country life, but he should take her also with full observance of all those privileges which maidens are allowed to claim from their lovers. He should contract no ceremonious observance because she was the daughter of a poor country parson who would come to him without a shilling, whereas he stood high in the world's books. He had asked her to give him all that she had, and that all she was ready to give, without stint. But the gift must be valued before it could be given or received. He also was to give her as much, and she would accept it as being beyond all price. But she would not allow that that which was offered to her was in any degree the more precious because of his outward worldly standing.

She would not pretend to herself that she thought he would come to her that day, and therefore she busied herself in the kitchen and about the house, giving directions to her two maids as though the afternoon would pass as all other days did pass in that household. They usually dined at four, and she rarely, in these summer months, went far from the house before that hour. At four precisely she sat down with her father, and then said that she was going up as far as Helpholme

after dinner. Helpholme was a solitary farmhouse in another
parish, on the border of the moor, and Mr. Woolsworthy
asked her whether he should accompany her.

"Do, papa", she said, "if you are not too tired." And yet
she had thought how probable it might be that she should
meet John Broughton on her walk. And so it was arranged;
but, just as dinner was over, Mr. Woolsworthy remembered
himself.

"Gracious me", he said, "how my memory is going.
Gribbles, from Ivybridge, and old John Poulter, from Bovey,
are coming to meet here by appointment. You can't put
Helpholme off till to-morrow?"

Patience, however, never put off anything, and therefore
at six o'clock, when her father had finished his slender
modicum of toddy, she tied on her hat and went on her
walk. She started forth with a quick step, and left no word
to say by which route she would go. As she passed up along
the little lane which led towards Oxney Combe, she would
not even look to see if he was coming towards her; and
when she left the road, passing over a stone stile into a little
path which ran first through the upland fields, and then
across the moor ground towards Helpholme, she did not
look back once, or listen for his coming step.

She paid her visit, remaining upwards of an hour with
the old bedridden mother of the tenant of Helpholme. "God
bless you, my darling!" said the old woman as she left her;
"and send you some one to make your path bright and
happy through the world." These words were still ringing
in her ears with all their significance as she saw John Broughton
waiting for her at the first stile which she had to pass after
leaving the farmer's haggard.

"Patty", he said, as he took her hand, and held it close
within both his own, "what a chase I have had after you!"

"And who asked you, Captain Broughton?" she answered,
smiling. "If the journey was too much for your poor London
strength, could you not have waited till to-morrow morning,

when you would have found me at the parsonage?" But
she did not draw her hand away from him, or in any way
pretend that he had not a right to accost her as a lover.

"No, I could not wait. I am more eager to see those I
love than you seem to be."

"How do you know whom I love, or how eager I might
be to see them? There is an old woman there whom I love,
and I have thought nothing of this walk with the object of
seeing her." And now, slowly drawing her hand away from
him, she pointed to the farmhouse which she had left.

"Patty", he said, after a minute's pause, during which she
had looked full into his face with all the force of her bright
eyes; "I have come from London to-day, straight down here
to Oxney, and from my aunt's house close upon your footsteps after you, to ask you that one question. Do you love
me?"

"What a Hercules!" she said, again laughing. "Do you
really mean that you left London only this morning? Why,
you must have been five hours in a railway carriage and
two in a postchaise, not to talk of the walk afterwards. You
ought to take more care of yourself, Captain Broughton!"

He would have been angry with her—for he did not like
to be quizzed—had she not put her hand on his arm as she
spoke, and the softness of her touch had redeemed the offence
of her words.

"All that have I done", said he, "that I may hear one
word from you."

"That any word of mine should have such potency! But
let us walk on, or my father will take us for some of the
standing stones of the moor. How have you found your
aunt? If you only knew the cares that have sat on her dear
shoulders for the last week past, in order that your high
mightiness might have a sufficiency to eat and drink in these
desolate half-starved regions."

"She might have saved herself such anxiety. No one can
care less for such things than I do."

"And yet I think I have heard you boast of the cook of your club." And then again there was silence for a minute or two.

"Patty", said he, stopping again in the path; "answer my question. I have a right to demand an answer. Do you love me?"

"And what if I do? What if I have been so silly as to allow your perfections to be too many for my weak heart? What then, Captain Broughton?"

"It cannot be that you love me, or you would not joke now."

"Perhaps not, indeed", she said. It seemed as though she were resolved not to yield an inch in her own humour. And then again they walked on.

"Patty", he said once more, "I shall get an answer from you to-night—this evening; now, during this walk, or I shall return to-morrow, and never revisit this spot again."

"Oh, Captain Broughton, how should we ever manage to live without you?"

"Very well", he said; "up to the end of this walk I can bear it all—and one word spoken then will mend it all."

During the whole of this time she felt that she was ill-using him. She knew that she loved him with all her heart; that it would nearly kill her to part with him; that she had heard his renewed offer with an ecstasy of joy. She acknowledged to herself that he was giving proof of his devotion as strong as any which a girl could receive from her lover. And yet she could hardly bring herself to say the word he longed to hear. That word once said, and then she knew that she must succumb to her love for ever! That word once said, and there would be nothing for her but to spoil him with her idolatry! That word once said, and she must continue to repeat it into his ears, till perhaps he might be tired of hearing it! And now he had threatened her, and how could she speak it after that? She certainly would not speak it unless

he asked her again without such threat. And so they walked
on again in silence.

"Patty", he said at last. "By the heavens above us you
shall answer me. Do you love me?"

She now stood still, and almost trembled as she looked
up into his face. She stood opposite to him for a moment,
and then placing her two hands on his shoulders, she answered
him. "I do, I do, I do", she said, "with all my heart; with all
my heart—with all my heart and strength." And then her
head fell upon his breast.

———

Captain Broughton was almost as much surprised as
delighted by the warmth of the acknowledgment made by
the eager-hearted passionate girl whom he now held within
his arms. She had said it now; the words had been spoken;
and there was nothing for her but to swear to him over and
over again with her sweetest oaths, that those words were
true—true as her soul. And very sweet was the walk down
from thence to the parsonage gate. He spoke no more of
the distance of the ground, or the length of his day's
journey. But he stopped her at every turn that he might
press her arm the closer to his own, that he might look into
the brightness of her eyes, and prolong his hour of delight.
There were no more gibes now on her tongue, no raillery at
his London finery, no laughing comments on his coming
and going. With downright honesty she told him everything:
how she had loved him before her heart was warranted in
such a passion; how, with much thinking, she had resolved
that it would be unwise to take him at his first word, and had
thought it better that he should return to London, and then
think over it; how she had almost repented of her courage
when she had feared, during those long summer days, that
he would forget her; and how her heart had leapt for joy
when her old friend had told her that he was coming.

"And yet", said he, "you were not glad to see me!"

"Oh, was I not glad? You cannot understand the feelings

of a girl who has lived secluded as I have done. Glad is no
word for the joy I felt. But it was not seeing you that I cared
for so much. It was the knowledge that you were near me
once again. I almost wish now that I had not seen you till
to-morrow." But as she spoke she pressed his arm, and this
caress gave the lie to her last words.

"No, do not come in to-night", she said, when she reached
the little wicket that led up to the parsonage. "Indeed, you
shall not. I could not behave myself properly if you did."

"But I don't want you to behave properly."

"Oh! I am to keep that for London, am I? But, nevertheless, Captain Broughton, I will not invite you either to tea
or to supper to-night."

"Surely I may shake hands with your father."

"Not to-night—not till—— John, I may tell him, may I
not? I must tell him at once."

"Certainly", said he.

"And then you shall see him to-morrow. Let me see—at
what hour shall I bid you come?"

"To breakfast."

"No, indeed. What on earth would your aunt do with
her broiled turkey and the cold pie? I have got no cold pie
for you."

"I hate cold pie."

"What a pity! But, John, I should be forced to have you
directly after breakfast. Come down—come down at two, or
three; and then I will go back with you to Aunt Penelope.
I must see her to-morrow"; and so at last the matter was
settled, and the happy Captain, as he left her, was hardly
resisted in his attempt to press her lips to his own.

When she entered the parlour in which her father was
sitting, there still were Gribbles and Poulter discussing some
knotty point of Devon lore. So Patience took off her hat,
and sat herself down, waiting till they should go. For full an
hour she had to wait, and then Gribbles and Poulter did go.
But it was not in such matters as this that Patience Wools-

worthy was impatient. She could wait, and wait, and wait, curbing herself for weeks and months, while the thing waited for was in her eyes good; but she could not curb her hot thoughts or her hot words when things came to be discussed which she did not think to be good.

"Papa", she said, when Gribbles' long-drawn last word had been spoken at the door. "Do you remember how I asked you the other day what you would say if I were to leave you?"

"Yes, surely", he replied, looking up at her in astonishment.

"I am going to leave you now", she said. "Dear, dearest father, how am I to go from you?"

"Going to leave me", said he, thinking of her visit to Helpholme, and thinking of nothing else.

Now, there had been a story about Helpholme. That bedridden old lady there had a stalwart son, who was now the owner of the Helpholme pastures. But though owner in fee of all those wild acres, and of the cattle which they supported, he was not much above the farmers around him, either in manners or education. He had his merits, however; for he was honest, well-to-do in the world, and modest withal. How strong love had grown up, springing from neighbourly kindness, between our Patience and his mother, it needs not here to tell; but rising from it had come another love—or an ambition which might have grown to love. The young man, after much thought, had not dared to speak to Miss Woolsworthy, but he had sent a message by Miss Le Smyrger. If there could be any hope for him, he would present himself as a suitor—on trial. He did not owe a shilling in the world, and had money by him—saved. He wouldn't ask the parson for a shilling of fortune. Such had been the tenor of his message, and Miss Le Smyrger had delivered it faithfully. "He does not mean it", Patience had said with her stern voice. "Indeed he does, my dear. You may be sure he is in earnest", Miss Le Smyrger had replied; "and there is not an honester man in these parts."

"Tell him", said Patience, not attending to the latter portion of her friend's last speech, "that it cannot be—make him understand, you know—and tell him also that the matter shall be thought of no more." The matter had, at any rate, been spoken of no more, but the young farmer still remained a bachelor, and Helpholme still wanted a mistress. But all this came back upon the parson's mind when his daughter told him that she was about to leave him.

"Yes, dearest", she said; and as she spoke she now knelt at his knees. "I have been asked in marriage, and I have given myself away."

"Well, my love, if you will be happy——".

"I hope I shall; I think I shall. But you, papa?"

"You will not be far from us."

"Oh, yes; in London."

"In London?"

"Captain Broughton lives in London generally."

"And has Captain Broughton asked you to marry him?"

"Yes, papa—who else? Is he not good? Will you not love him? Oh, papa, do not say that I am wrong to love him?"

He never told her his mistake, or explained to her that he had not thought it possible that the high-placed son of the London great man should have fallen in love with his undowered daughter; but he embraced her, and told her, with all his enthusiasm, that he rejoiced in her joy, and would be happy in her happiness. "My own Patty", he said, "I have ever known that you were too good for this life of ours here." And then the evening wore away into the night, with many tears, but still with much happiness.

Captain Broughton, as he walked back to Oxney Combe, made up his mind that he would say nothing on the matter to his aunt till the next morning. He wanted to think over it all, and to think it over, if possible, by himself. He had taken a step in life, the most important that a man is ever called on to take, and he had to reflect whether or no he had taken it with wisdom.

"Have you seen her?" said Miss Le Smyrger, very anxiously, when he came into the drawing-room.

"Miss Woolsworthy you mean", said he. "Yes, I've seen her. As I found her out, I took a long walk, and happened to meet her. Do you know, aunt, I think I'll go to bed; I was up at five this morning, and have been on the move ever since."

Miss Le Smyrger perceived that she was to hear nothing that evening, so she handed him his candlestick and allowed him to go to his room.

But Captain Broughton did not immediately retire to bed, nor when he did so was he able to sleep at once. Had this step that he had taken been a wise one? He was not a man who, in worldly matters, had allowed things to arrange themselves for him, as is the case with so many men. He had formed views for himself, and had a theory of life. Money for money's sake he had declared to himself to be bad. Money, as a concomitant to things which were in themselves good, he had declared to himself to be good also. That concomitant in this affair of his marriage, he had now missed. Well; he had made up his mind to that, and would put up with the loss. He had means of living of his own, the means not so extensive as might have been desirable. That it would be well for him to become a married man, looking merely to that state of life as opposed to his present state, he had fully resolved. On that point, therefore, there was nothing to repent. That Patty Woolsworthy was good, affectionate, clever, and beautiful he was sufficiently satisfied. It would be odd indeed if he were not so satisfied now, seeing that for the last four months he had so declared to himself daily with many inward asseverations. And yet, though he repeated now again that he was satisfied, I do not think that he was so fully satisfied of it as he had been throughout the whole of those four months. It is sad to say so, but I fear—I fear that such was the case. When you have your plaything, how much of the anticipated pleasure vanishes, especially if it be won easily.

He had told none of his family what were his intentions in this second visit to Devonshire, and now he had to bethink himself whether they would be satisfied. What would his sister say, she who had married the Honourable Augustus Gumbleton, gold-stick-in-waiting to Her Majesty's Privy Council? Would she receive Patience with open arms, and make much of her about London? And then how far would London suit Patience, or would Patience suit London? There would be much for him to do in teaching her, and it would be well for him to set about the lesson without loss of time. So far he got that night, but when the morning came he went a step further, and began mentally to criticize her manner to himself. It had been very sweet, that warm, that full, that ready declaration of love. Yes; it had been very sweet; but—but—; when, after her little jokes, she did confess her love, had she not been a little too free for feminine excellence? A man likes to be told that he is loved, but he hardly wishes that the girl he is to marry should fling herself at his head!

Ah me! yes; it was thus he argued to himself as on that morning he went through the arrangements of his toilet. "Then he was a brute", you say, my pretty reader. I have never said that he was not a brute. But this I remark, that many such brutes are to be met with in the beaten paths of the world's high highway. When Patience Woolsworthy had answered him coldly, bidding him go back to London and think over his love; while it seemed from her manner that at any rate as yet she did not care for him; while he was absent from her, and, therefore, longing for her, the possession of her charms, her talent and bright honesty of purpose had seemed to him a thing most desirable. Now they were his own. They had, in fact, been his own from the first. The heart of this country-bred girl had fallen at the first word from his mouth. Had she not so confessed to him? She was very nice—very nice indeed. He loved her dearly. But had he not sold himself too cheaply?

I by no means say that he was not a brute. But whether brute or no he was an honest man, and had no remotest dream—either then, on that morning, or during the following days on which such thoughts pressed more thickly on his mind—of breaking away from his pledged word. At breakfast on that morning he told all to Miss Le Smyrger, and that lady, with warm and gracious intentions, confided to him her purpose regarding her property. "I have always regarded Patience as my heir", she said, "and shall do so still."

"Oh, indeed", said Captain Broughton.

"But it is a great, great pleasure to me to think that she will give back the little property to my sister's child. You will have your mother's, and thus it will all come together again."

"Ah!" said Captain Broughton. He had his own ideas about property, and did not, even under existing circumstances, like to hear that his aunt considered herself at liberty to leave the acres away to one who was by blood quite a stranger to the family.

"Does Patience know of this?" he asked.

"Not a word", said Miss Le Smyrger. And then nothing more was said upon the subject.

On that afternoon he went down and received the parson's benediction and congratulations with a good grace. Patience said very little on the occasion, and indeed was absent during the greater part of the interview. The two lovers then walked up to Oxney Combe, and there were more benedictions and more congratulations. "All went merry as a marriage bell", at any rate as far as Patience was concerned. Not a word had yet fallen from that dear mouth, not a look had yet come over that handsome face, which tended in any way to mar her bliss. Her first day of acknowledged love was a day altogether happy, and when she prayed for him as she knelt beside her bed there was no feeling in her mind that any fear need disturb her joy.

I will pass over the next three or four days very quickly, merely saying that Patience did not find them so pleasant as

that first day after her engagement. There was something
in her lover's manner—something which at first she could
not define—which by degrees seemed to grate against her
feelings. He was sufficiently affectionate, that being a matter
on which she did not require much demonstration; but
joined to his affection there seemed to be——; she hardly
liked to suggest to herself a harsh word, but could it be
possible that he was beginning to think that she was not
good enough for him? And then she asked herself the question
—was she good enough for him? If there were doubt about
that, the match should be broken off, though she tore her
own heart out in the struggle. The truth, however, was this
—that he had begun that teaching which he had already
found to be so necessary. Now, had any one essayed to
teach Patience German or mathematics, with that young
lady's free consent, I believe that she would have been found
a meek scholar. But it was not probable that she would
be meek when she found a self-appointed tutor teaching her
manners and conduct without her consent.

So matters went on for four or five days, and on the evening
of the fifth day, Captain Broughton and his aunt drank tea
at the parsonage. Nothing very especial occurred; but as the
parson and Miss Le Smyrger insisted on playing backgammon
with devoted perseverance during the whole evening,
Broughton had a good opportunity of saying a word or two
about those changes in his lady-love which a life in London
would require—and some word he said also—some single
slight word as to the higher station in life to which he would
exalt his bride. Patience bore it—for her father and Miss Le
Smyrger were in the room—she bore it well, speaking no
syllable of anger, and enduring, for the moment, the implied
scorn of the old parsonage. Then the evening broke up, and
Captain Broughton walked back to Oxney Combe with his
aunt. "Patty", her father said to her before they went to bed,
"he seems to me to be a most excellent young man." "Dear
papa", she answered, kissing him. "And terribly deep in

love", said Mr. Woolsworthy. "Oh, I don't know about that", she answered, as she left him with her sweetest smile. But though she could thus smile at her father's joke, she had already made up her mind that there was still something to be learned as to her promised husband before she could place herself altogether in his hands. She would ask him whether he thought himself liable to injury from this proposed marriage; and though he should deny any such thought, she would know from the manner of his denial what his true feelings were.

And he, too, on that night, during his silent walk with Miss Le Smyrger, had entertained some similar thoughts. "I fear she is obstinate", he had said to himself, and then he had half accused her of being sullen also. "If that be her temper, what a life of misery I have before me!"

"Have you fixed a day yet?" his aunt asked him as they came near to her house.

"No, not yet: I don't know whether it will suit me to fix it before I leave."

"Why, it was but the other day you were in such a hurry."

"Ah—yes—I have thought more about it since then."

"I should have imagined that this would depend on what Patty thinks", said Miss Le Smyrger, standing up for the privileges of her sex. "It is presumed that the gentleman is always ready as soon as the lady will consent."

"Yes, in ordinary cases it is so; but when a girl is taken out of her own sphere—"

"Her own sphere! Let me caution you, Master John, not to talk to Patty about her own sphere."

"Aunt Penelope, as Patience is to be my wife and not yours, I must claim permission to speak to her on such subjects as may seem suitable to me." And then they parted—not in the best humour with each other.

On the following day Captain Broughton and Miss Woolsworthy did not meet till the evening. She had said, before those few ill-omened words had passed her lover's lips, that she would probably be at Miss Le Smyrger's house on the following morning. Those ill-omened words did pass her lover's lips, and then she remained at home. This did not come from sullenness, nor even from anger, but from a conviction that it would be well that she should think much before she met him again. Nor was he anxious to hurry a meeting. His thought—his base thought—was this; that she would be sure to come up to the Combe after him; but she did not come, and therefore in the evening he went down to her, and asked her to walk with him.

They went away by the path that led to Helpholme, and little was said between them till they had walked some mile together. Patience, as she went along the path, remembered almost to the letter the sweet words which had greeted her ears as she came down that way with him on the night of his arrival; but he remembered nothing of that sweetness then. Had he not made an ass of himself during these last six months? That was the thought which very much had possession of his mind.

"Patience", he said at last, having hitherto spoken only an indifferent word now and again since they had left the parsonage, "Patience, I hope you realize the importance of the step which you and I are about to take?"

"Of course I do", she answered: "what an odd question that is for you to ask!"

"Because", said he, "sometimes I almost doubt it. It seems to me as though you thought you could remove yourself from here to your new home with no more trouble than when you go from home up to the Combe."

"Is that meant for a reproach, John?"

"No, not for a reproach, but for advice. Certainly not for a reproach."

"I am glad of that."

"But I should wish to make you think how great is the leap in the world which you are about to take." Then again they walked on for many steps before she answered him.

"Tell me then, John", she said, when she had sufficiently considered what words she would speak; and as she spoke a bright colour suffused her face, and her eyes flashed almost with anger. "What leap do you mean? Do you mean a leap upwards?"

"Well, yes; I hope it will be so."

"In one sense, certainly, it would be a leap upwards. To be the wife of the man I loved; to have the privilege of holding his happiness in my hand; to know that I was his own—the companion whom he had chosen out of all the world—that would, indeed, be a leap upwards; a leap almost to heaven, if all that were so. But if you mean upwards in any other sense——"

"I was thinking of the social scale."

"Then, Captain Broughton, your thoughts were doing me dishonour."

"Doing you dishonour!"

"Yes, doing me dishonour. That your father is, in the world's esteem, a greater man than mine is doubtless true enough. That you, as a man, are richer than I am as a woman, is doubtless also true. But you dishonour me, and yourself also, if these things can weigh with you now."

"Patience—I think you can hardly know what words you are saying to me."

"Pardon me, but I think I do. Nothing that you can give me—no gifts of that description—can weigh aught against that which I am giving you. If you had all the wealth and rank of the greatest lord in the land, it would count as nothing in such a scale. If—as I have not doubted—if in return for my heart you have given me yours, then—then—then you have paid me fully. But when gifts such as those are going, nothing else can count even as a make-weight."

"I do not quite understand you", he answered, after a pause. "I fear you are a little high-flown." And then, while the evening was still early, they walked back to the parsonage almost without another word.

Captain Broughton at this time had only one full day more to remain at Oxney Colne. On the afternoon following that he was to go as far as Exeter, and thence return to London. Of course, it was to be expected that the wedding day would be fixed before he went, and much had been said about it during the first day or two of his engagement. Then he had pressed for an early time, and Patience, with a girl's usual diffidence, had asked for some little delay. But now nothing was said on the subject; and how was it probable that such a matter could be settled after such a conversation as that which I have related? That evening, Miss Le Smyrger asked whether the day had been fixed. "No", said Captain Broughton harshly; "nothing has been fixed." "But it will be arranged before you go." "Probably not", he said; and then the subject was dropped for the time.

"John", she said, just before she went to bed, "if there be anything wrong between you and Patience, I conjure you to tell me." "You had better ask her", he replied. "I can tell you nothing."

On the following morning he was much surprised by seeing Patience on the gravel path before Miss Le Smyrger's gate immediately after breakfast. He went to the door to open it for her, and she, as she gave him her hand, told him that she came up to speak to him. There was no hesitation in her manner, nor any look of anger in her face. But there was in her gait and form, in her voice and countenance, a fixedness of purpose which he had never seen before, or at any rate had never acknowledged.

"Certainly", said he. "Shall I come out with you, or will you come upstairs?"

"We can sit down in the summer-house", she said; and thither they both went.

"Captain Broughton", she said—and she began her task the moment that they were both seated—"You and I have engaged ourselves as man and wife, but perhaps we have been over rash."

"How so?" said he.

"It may be—and indeed I will say more—it is the case that we have made this engagement without knowing enough of each other's character."

"I have not thought so."

"The time will perhaps come when you will so think, but for the sake of all that we most value, let it come before it is too late. What would be our fate—how terrible would be our misery—if such a thought should come to either of us after we have linked our lots together."

There was a solemnity about her as she thus spoke which almost repressed him—which for a time did prevent him from taking that tone of authority which on such a subject he would choose to adopt. But he recovered himself. "I hardly think that this comes well from you", he said.

"From whom else should it come? Who else can fight my battle for me; and, John, who else can fight that same battle on your behalf? I tell you this, that with your mind standing towards me as it does stand at present, you could not give me your hand at the altar with true words and a happy conscience. Am I not true? You have half repented of your bargain already. Is it not so?"

He did not answer her; but getting up from his seat walked to the front of the summer-house, and stood there with his back turned upon her. It was not that he meant to be ungracious, but in truth he did not know how to answer her. He had half repented of his bargain.

"John", she said, getting up and following him, so that she could put her hand upon his arm, "I have been very angry with you."

"Angry with me!" he said, turning sharp upon her.

"Yes, angry with you. You would have treated me like a child. But that feeling has gone now. I am not angry now. There is my hand—the hand of a friend. Let the words that have been spoken between us be as though they had not been spoken. Let us both be free."

"Do you mean it?" he asked.

"Certainly I mean it." As she spoke these words her eyes were filled with tears, in spite of all the efforts she could make; but he was not looking at her, and her efforts had sufficed to prevent any sob from being audible.

"With all my heart", he said; and it was manifest from his tone that he had no thought of her happiness as he spoke. It was true that she had been angry with him—angry, as she had herself declared; but nevertheless, in what she had said and what she had done, she had thought more of his happiness than of her own. Now she was angry once again.

"With all your heart, Captain Broughton! Well, so be it. If with all your heart, then is the necessity so much the greater. You go to-morrow. Shall we say farewell now?"

"Patience, I am not going to be lectured."

"Certainly not by me. Shall we say farewell now?"

"Yes, if you are determined."

"I am determined. Farewell, Captain Broughton. You have all my wishes for your happiness." And she held out her hand to him.

"Patience!" he said. And he looked at her with a dark frown, as though he would strive to frighten her into submission. If so, he might have saved himself any such attempt.

"Farewell, Captain Broughton. Give me your hand, for I cannot stay." He gave her his hand, hardly knowing why he did so. She lifted it to her lips and kissed it, and then, leaving him, passed from the summer-house down through the wicket-gate, and straight home to the parsonage.

During the whole of that day she said no word to any one of what had occurred. When she was once more at home she went about her household affairs as she had done on that day of his arrival. When she sat down to dinner with her father he observed nothing to make him think that she was unhappy; nor during the evening was there any expression in her face, or any tone in her voice, which excited his attention. On the following morning Captain Broughton called at the parsonage, and the servant-girl brought word to her mistress that he was in the parlour. But she would not see him. "Laws, miss, you ain't a quarrelled with your beau?" the poor girl said. "No, not quarrelled", she said; "but give him that." It was a scrap of paper, containing a word or two in pencil. "It is better that we should not meet again. God bless you." And from that day to this, now more than ten years, they never have met.

"Papa", she said to her father that afternoon, "dear papa, do not be angry with me. It is all over between me and John Broughton. Dearest, you and I will not be separated."

It would be useless here to tell how great was the old man's surprise and how true his sorrow. As the tale was told to him no cause was given for anger with anyone. Not a word was spoken against the suitor who had on that day returned to London with a full conviction that now at least he was relieved from his engagement. "Patty, my darling child", he said, "may God grant that it be for the best!"

"It is for the best", she answered stoutly. "For this place I am fit; and I much doubt whether I am fit for any other."

On that day she did not see Miss Le Smyrger, but on the following morning, knowing that Captain Broughton had gone off, having heard the wheels of the carriage as they passed by the parsonage gate on his way to the station—she walked up to the Combe.

"He has told you, I suppose?" said she.

"Yes", said Miss Le Smyrger. "And I will never see him again unless he asks your pardon on his knees. I have told him so. I would not even give him my hand as he went."

"But why so, thou kindest one? The fault was mine more than his."

"I understand. I have eyes in my head", said the old maid. "I have watched him for the last four or five days. If you could have kept the truth to yourself and bade him keep off from you, he would have been at your feet now, licking the dust from your shoes."

"But, dear friend, I do not want a man to lick dust from my shoes."

"Ah, you are a fool. You do not know the value of your own wealth."

"True; I have been a fool. I was a fool to think that one coming from such a life as he has led could be happy with such as I am. I know the truth now. I have bought the lesson dearly—but perhaps not too dearly, seeing that it will never be forgotten."

There was but little more said about the matter between our three friends at Oxney Colne. What, indeed, could be said? Miss Le Smyrger for a year or two still expected that her nephew would return and claim his bride; but he has never done so, nor has there been any correspondence between them. Patience Woolsworthy had learned her lesson dearly. She had given her whole heart to the man; and, though she so bore herself that no one was aware of the violence of the struggle, nevertheless the struggle within her bosom was very violent. She never told herself that she had done wrong; she never regretted her loss; but yet— yet!—the loss was very hard to bear. He also had loved her, but he was not capable of a love which could much injure his daily peace. Her daily peace was gone for many a day to come.

Her father is still living; but there is a curate now in the parish. In conjunction with him and with Miss Le Smyrger she spends her time in the concerns of the parish. In her own eyes she is a confirmed old maid; and such is my opinion also. The romance of her life was played out in that summer. She never sits now lonely on the hill-side thinking how much she might do for one whom she really loved. But with a large heart she loves many, and, with no romance, she works hard to lighten the burdens of those she loves.

As for Captain Broughton, all the world knows that he did marry that great heiress with whom his name was once before connected, and that he is now a useful Member of Parliament, working on committees three or four days a week with a zeal that is indefatigable. Sometimes, not often, as he thinks of Patience Woolsworthy, a gratified smile comes across his face.

LA MÈRE BAUCHE

THE PYRENEEAN VALLEY IN WHICH THE BATHS
of Vernet are situated is not much known to English, or
indeed to any travellers. Tourists in search of good hotels
and picturesque beauty combined, do not generally extend
their journeys to the Eastern Pyrenees. They rarely go beyond
Luchon; and in this they are right, as they thus end their
peregrinations at the most lovely spot among these mountains;
and are as a rule so deceived, imposed on, and bewildered
by guides, innkeepers, and horse-owners at this otherwise
delightful place as to become undesirous of further travel.
Nor do invalids from distant parts frequent Vernet. People
of fashion go to the Eaux Bonnes and to Luchon, and people
who are really ill to Baréges and Cauterets. It is at these
places that one meets crowds of Parisians, and the daughters
and wives of rich merchants from Bordeaux, with an admixture, now by no means inconsiderable, of Englishmen and
Englishwomen. But the Eastern Pyrenees are still unfrequented. And probably they will remain so; for though there
are among them lovely valleys—and of all such the valley of
Vernet is perhaps the most lovely—they cannot compete
with the mountain scenery of other tourists-loved regions in

Europe. At the Port de Venasquez and the Brèche de Roland
in the Western Pyrenees, or rather, to speak more truly, at
spots in the close vicinity of these famous mountain entrances
from France into Spain, one can make comparisons with
Switzerland, Northern Italy, the Tyrol, and Ireland, which
will not be injurious to the scenes then under view. But
among the eastern mountains this can rarely be done. The
hills do not stand thickly together so as to group themselves;
the passes from one valley to another, though not wanting
in altitude, are not close pressed together with overhanging
rocks, and are deficient in grandeur as well as loveliness.
And then, as a natural consequence of all this, the hotels—
are not quite as good as they should be.

But there is one mountain among them which can claim
to rank with the Píc du Midi or the Maledetta. No one can
pooh-pooh the stern old Canigou, standing high and solitary,
solemn and grand, between the two roads which run from
Perpignan into Spain, the one by Prades and the other
by Le Boulon. Under the Canigou, towards the west, lie
the hot baths of Vernet, in a close secluded valley, which,
as I have said before, is, as far as I know, the sweetest spot in
these Eastern Pyrenees.

The frequenters of these baths were a few years back
gathered almost entirely from towns not very far distant,
from Perpignan, Narbonne, Carcassonne, and Bézières, and
were not therefore famous, expensive, or luxurious; but those
who believed in them believed with great faith; and it was
certainly the fact that men and women who went thither
worn with toil, sick with excesses, and nervous through
over-care, came back fresh and strong, fit once more to
attack the world with all its woes. Their character in latter
days does not seem to have changed, though their circle of
admirers may perhaps be somewhat extended.

In those days, by far the most noted and illustrious person
in the village of Vernet was La Mère Bauche. That there
had once been a Père Bauche was known to the world, for

here was a Fils Bauche who lived with his mother; but not one seemed to remember more of him than that he had once existed. At Vernet he had never been known. La Mère Bauche was a native of the village, but her married life had been passed away from it, and she had returned in her early widowhood to become proprietress and manager, or, as one may say, the heart and soul of the Hôtel Bauche at Vernet.

This hotel was a large and somewhat rough establishment, intended for the accommodation of invalids who came to Vernet for their health. It was built immediately over one of the thermal springs, so that the water flowed from the bowels of the earth directly into the baths. There was accommodation for seventy people, and during the summer and autumn months the place was always full. Not a few also were to be found there during the winter and spring, for the charges of Madame Bauche were low, and the accommodation reasonably good.

And in this respect, as indeed in all others, Madame Bauche had the reputation of being an honest woman. She had a certain price, from which no earthly consideration would induce her to depart; and certain returns for this price in the shape of déjeuners and dinners, baths and beds, which she never failed to give in accordance with the dictates of a strict conscience. These were traits in the character of an hotel-keeper which cannot be praised too highly, and which had met their due reward in the custom of the public. But nevertheless there were those who thought that there was occasionally ground for complaint in the conduct even of Madame Bauche.

In the first place she was deficient in that pleasant smiling softness which should belong to any keeper of a house of public entertainment. In her general mode of life she was stern and silent with her guests, autocratic, authoritative, and sometimes contradictory in her house, and altogether irrational and unconciliatory when any change even for a day was proposed to her, or when any shadow of a complaint reached her ears.

Indeed of complaint, as made against the establishment, she was altogether intolerant. To such she had but one answer. He or she who complained might leave the place at a moment's notice if it so pleased them. There were always others ready to take their places. The power of making this answer came to her from the lowness of her prices; and it was a power which was very dear to her.

The baths were taken at different hours according to medical advice, but the usual time was from five to seven in the morning. The déjeuner or early meal was at nine o'clock, the dinner was at four. After that, no eating or drinking was allowed in the Hôtel Bauche. There was a café in the village, at which ladies and gentlemen could get a cup of coffee or a glass of eau sucré; but no such accommodation was to be had in the establishment. Not by any possible bribery or persuasion could any meal be procured at any other than the authorized hours. A visitor who should enter the salle à manger more than ten minutes after the last bell would be looked at very sourly by Madame Bauche, who on all occasions sat at the top of her own table. Should any one appear as much as half an hour late, he would receive only his share of what had not been handed round. But after the last dish had been so handed, it was utterly useless for any one to enter the room at all.

Her appearance at the period of our tale was perhaps not altogether in her favour. She was about sixty years of age and was very stout and short in the neck. She wore her own grey hair, which at dinner was always tidy enough; but during the whole day previous to that hour she might be seen with it escaping from under her cap in extreme disorder. Her eyebrows were large and bushy, but those alone would not have given to her face that look of indomitable sternness which it possessed. Her eyebrows were serious in their effect, but not so serious as the pair of green spectacles which she always wore under them. It was thought by those who had analyzed the subject that the great secret of Madame Bauche's power lay in her green spectacles.

Her custom was to move about and through the whole establishment every day from breakfast till the period came for her to dress for dinner. She would visit every chamber and every bath, walk once or twice round the salle à manger, and very repeatedly round the kitchen; she would go into every hole and corner, and peer into everything through her green spectacles: and in these walks it was not always thought pleasant to meet her. Her custom was to move very slowly, with her hands generally clasped behind her back: she rarely spoke to the guests unless she was spoken to, and on such occasions she would not often diverge into general conversation. If any one had aught to say connected with the business of the establishment, she would listen, and then she would make her answers—often not pleasant in the hearing.

And thus she walked her path through the world, a stern, hard, solemn old woman, not without gusts of passionate explosion; but honest withal, and not without some inward benevolence and true tenderness of heart. Children she had had many, some seven or eight. One or two had died, others had been married; she had sons settled far away from home, and at the time of which we are now speaking but one was left in any way subject to parental authority.

Adolphe Bauche was the only one of her children of whom much was remembered by the present denizens and hangers-on of the hotel. He was the youngest of the number, and having been born only very shortly before the return of Madame Bauche to Vernet, had been altogether reared there. It was thought by the world of those parts, and rightly thought, that he was his mother's darling—more so than had been any of his brothers and sisters—the very apple of her eye, and gem of her life. At this time he was about twenty-five years of age, and for the last two years had been absent from Vernet—for reasons which will shortly be made to appear. He had been sent to Paris to see something of the world, and learn to talk French instead of the patois of his valley; and having left Paris had come down south into Languedoc, and remained there picking up some agricultural lore which it was thought might prove useful in the valley farms of Vernet. He was now expected home again very speedily, much to his mother's delight.

That she was kind and gracious to her favourite child does not perhaps give much proof of her benevolence; but she had also been kind and gracious to the orphan child of a neighbour; nay, to the orphan child of a rival innkeeper. At Vernet there had been more than one water establishment, but the proprietor of the second had died some few years after Madame Bauche had settled herself at the place. His house had not thrived, and his only child, a little girl, was left altogether without provision.

This little girl, Marie Clavert, La Mère Bauche had taken into her own house immediately after the father's death, although she had most cordially hated that father. Marie was then an infant, and Madame Bauche had accepted the charge without much thought, perhaps, as to what might be the child's ultimate destiny. But since then she had thoroughly done the duty of a mother by the little girl, who had become the pet of the whole establishment, the favourite plaything of Adolphe Bauche—and at last of course his early sweetheart.

And then and therefore there had come troubles at Vernet. Of course all the world of the valley had seen what was taking place and what was likely to take place, long before Madame Bauche knew anything about it. But at last it broke upon her senses that her son, Adolphe Bauche, the heir to all her virtues and all her riches, the first young man in that or any neighbouring valley, was absolutely contemplating the idea of marrying that poor little orphan Marie Clavert!

That any one should ever fall in love with Marie Clavert had never occurred to Madame Bauche. She had always regarded the child as a child, as the object of her charity, and as a little thing to be looked on as poor Marie by all the world. She, looking through her green spectacles, had never seen that Marie Clavert was a beautiful creature, full of ripening charms, such as young men love to look on. Marie was of infinite daily use to Madame Bauche in a hundred little things about the house, and the old lady thoroughly recognized and appreciated her ability. But for this very reason she had never taught herself to regard Marie otherwise than as a useful drudge. She was very fond of her protégée—so much so that she would listen to her in affairs about the house when she would listen to no one else—but Marie's prettiness and grace and sweetness as a girl had all been thrown away upon Maman Bauche, as Marie used to call her.

But unluckily it had not been thrown away upon Adolphe. He had appreciated, as it was natural that he should do, all that had been so utterly indifferent to his mother; and consequently had fallen in love. Consequently also he had told his love; and consequently also, Marie had returned his love. Adolphe had been hitherto contradicted but in few things, and thought that all difficulty would be prevented by his informing his mother that he wished to marry Marie Clavert. But Marie, with a woman's instinct, had known better. She had trembled and almost crouched with fear when she confessed her love; and had absolutely hid herself from sight when Adolphe went forth, prepared to ask his mother's consent to his marriage.

The indignation and passionate wrath of Madame Bauche were past and gone two years before the date of this story, and I need not therefore much enlarge upon that subject. She was at first abusive and bitter, which was bad for Marie; and afterwards bitter and silent, which was worse. It was of course determined that poor Marie should be sent away to some asylum for orphans or penniless paupers—in short anywhere out of the way. What mattered her outlook into the world, her happiness, or indeed her very existence?

The outlook and happiness of Adolphe Bauche—was not that to be considered as everything at Vernet?

But this terrible sharp aspect of affairs did not last very long. In the first place La Mère Bauche had under those green spectacles a heart that in truth was tender and affectionate, and after the first two days of anger she admitted that something must be done for Marie Clavert; and after the fourth day she acknowledged that the world of the hotel, her world, would not go as well without Marie Clavert as it would with her. And in the next place Madame Bauche had a friend whose advice in grave matters she would sometimes take. This friend had told her that it would be much better to send away Adolphe, since it was so necessary that there should be a sending away of some one; that he would be much benefited by passing some months of his life away from his native valley; and that an absence of a year or two would teach him to forget Marie, even if it did not teach Marie to forget him.

And we must say a word or two about this friend. At Vernet he was usually called M. le Capitaine, though in fact he had never reached that rank. He had been in the army, and having been wounded in the leg while still a sous-lieutenant, had been pensioned, and had thus been interdicted from treading any further the thorny path that leads to glory. For the last fifteen years he had resided under the roof of Madame Bauche, at first as a casual visitor, going and coming, but now for many years as constant there as she was herself.

He was so constantly called Le Capitaine that his real name was seldom heard. It may however as well be known to us that this was Theodore Campan. He was a tall, well-looking man; always dressed in black garments, of a coarse description certainly, but scrupulously clean and well brushed; of perhaps fifty years of age, and conspicuous for the rigid uprightness of his back—and for a black wooden leg.

This wooden leg was perhaps the most remarkable trait in his character. It was always jet black, being painted, or polished, or japanned, as occasion might require, by the hands

of the capitaine himself. It was longer than ordinary wooden
legs, as indeed the capitaine was longer than ordinary men;
but nevertheless it never seemed in any way to impede the
rigid punctilious propriety of his movements. It was never in
his way as wooden legs usually are in the way of their wearers.
And then to render it more illustrious it had round its middle,
round the calf of the leg we may so say, a band of bright brass
which shone like burnished gold.

It had been the capitaine's custom, now for some years past,
to retire every evening at about seven o'clock into the sanctum
sanctorum of Madame Bauche's habitation, the dark little
private sitting-room in which she made out her bills and
calculated her profits, and there regale himself in her presence—
and indeed at her expense, for the items never appeared in
the bill—with coffee, and cognac. I have said that there was
neither eating nor drinking at the establishment after the
regular dinner-hours; but in so saying I spoke of the world
at large. Nothing further was allowed in the way of trade;
but in the way of friendship so much was nowadays always
allowed to the capitaine.

It was at these moments that Madame Bauche discussed
her private affairs, and asked for and received advice. For even
Madame Bauche was mortal; nor could her green spectacles
without other aid carry her through all the troubles of life.
It was now five years since the world of Vernet discovered
that La Mère Bauche was going to marry the capitaine; and
for eighteen months the world of Vernet had been full of this
matter: but any amount of patience is at last exhausted, and
as no further steps in that direction were ever taken beyond
the daily cup of coffee, that subject died away—very much
unheeded by La Mère Bauche.

But she, though she thought of no matrimony for herself,
thought much of matrimony for other people; and over most
of those cups of evening coffee and cognac a matrimonial
project was discussed in these latter days. It has been seen that
the capitaine pleaded in Marie's favour when the fury of

Madame Bauche's indignation broke forth; and that ultimately
Marie was kept at home, and Adolphe sent away by his advice.

"But Adolphe cannot always stay away", Madame Bauche
had pleaded in her difficulty. The truth of this the capitaine
had admitted; but Marie, he said, might be married to some
one else before two years were over. And so the matter had
commenced.

But to whom should she be married? To this question the
capitaine had answered in perfect innocence of heart, that
La Mère Bauche would be much better able to make such a
choice than himself. He did not know how Marie might stand
with regard to money. If madame would give some little
"dot", the affair, the capitaine thought, would be more easily
arranged.

All these things took months to say, during which period
Marie went on with her work in melancholy listlessness. One
comfort she had. Adolphe, before he went, had promised to
her, holding in his hand as he did so a little cross which she had
given him, that no earthly consideration should sever them—
that sooner or later he would certainly be her husband. Marie
felt that her limbs could not work nor her tongue speak were
it not for this one drop of water in her cup.

And then, deeply meditating, La Mère Bauche hit upon a
plan, and herself communicated it to the capitaine over a
second cup of coffee into which she poured a full teaspoonful
more than the usual allowance of cognac. Why should not he,
the capitaine himself, be the man to marry Marie Clavert?

It was a very startling proposal, the idea of matrimony for
himself never having as yet entered into the capitaine's head
at any period of his life; but La Mère Bauche did contrive
to make it not altogether unacceptable. As to that matter of
dowry she was prepared to be more than generous. She did
love Marie well, and could find it in her heart to give her
anything—anything except her son, her own Adolphe.
What she proposed was this. Adolphe, himself, would never
keep the baths. If the capitaine would take Marie for his wife,

Marie, Madame Bauche declared, should be the mistress after her death; subject of course to certain settlements as to Adolphe's pecuniary interests. The plan was discussed a thousand times, and at last so far brought to bear that Marie was made acquainted with it— having been called in to sit in presence with La Mère Bauche and her future proposed husband. The poor girl manifested no disgust to the stiff ungainly lover whom they assigned to her—who through his whole frame was in appearance almost as wooden as his own leg. On the whole, indeed, Marie liked the capitaine, and felt that he was her friend; and in her country such marriages were not uncommon. The capitaine was perhaps a little beyond the age at which a man might usually be thought justified in demanding the services of a young girl as his nurse and wife, but then Marie of herself had so little to give—except her youth, and beauty, and goodness.

But yet she could not absolutely consent; for was she not absolutely pledged to her own Adolphe? And therefore, when the great pecuniary advantages were, one by one, displayed before her, and when La Mère Bauche, as a last argument, informed her that as wife of the capitaine she would be regarded as a second mistress in the establishment and not as a servant— she could only burst out into tears, and say that she did not know.

"I will be very kind to you", said the capitaine; "as kind as a man can be."

Marie took his hard withered hand and kissed it; and then looked up into his face with beseeching eyes which were not without avail upon his heart.

"We will not press her now", said the capitaine. "There is time enough."

But let his heart be touched ever so much, one thing was certain. It could not be permitted that she should marry Adolphe. To that view of the matter he had given in his unrestricted adhesion; nor could he by any means withdraw it without losing altogether his position in the establishment

of Madame Bauche. Nor indeed did his conscience tell him
that such a marriage should be permitted. That would be too
much. If every pretty girl were allowed to marry the first
young man that might fall in love with her, what would the
world come to?

And it soon appeared that there was not time enough—
that the time was growing very scant. In three months
Adolphe would be back. And if everything was not arranged
by that time, matters might still go astray.

And then Madame Bauche asked her final question:
"You do not think, do you, that you can ever marry Adolphe?"
And as she asked it the accustomed terror of her green
spectacles magnified itself tenfold. Marie could only answer
by another burst of tears.

The affair was at last settled among them. Marie said that
she would consent to marry the capitaine when she should
hear from Adolphe's own mouth that he, Adolphe, loved her
no longer. She declared with many tears that her vows and
pledges prevented her from promising more than this. It was
not her fault, at any rate not now, that she loved her lover.
It was not her fault—not now at least—that she was bound
by these pledges. When she heard from his own mouth that
he had discarded her, then she would marry the capitaine—
or indeed sacrifice herself in any other way that La Mère Bauche
might desire. What would anything signify then?

Madame Bauche's spectacles remained unmoved; but not
her heart. Marie, she told the capitaine, should be equal to
herself in the establishment, when once she was entitled to be
called Madame Campan, and she should be to her quite as a
daughter. She should have her cup of coffee every evening,
and dine at the big table, and wear a silk gown at church, and
the servants should all call her Madame; a great career should
be open to her, if she would only give up her foolish girlish
childish love for Adolphe. And all these great promises were
repeated to Marie by the capitaine.

But nevertheless there was but one thing in the whole world

which in Marie's eyes was of any value; and that one thing was the heart of Adolphe Bauche. Without that she would be nothing; with that—with that assured, she could wait patiently till doomsday.

Letters were written to Adolphe during all these eventful doings; and a letter came from him saying that he greatly valued Marie's love, but that as it had been clearly proved to him that their marriage would be neither for her advantage, nor for his, he was willing to give it up. He consented to her marriage with the capitaine, and expressed his gratitude to his mother for the immediate pecuniary advantages which she had held out to him. Oh, Adolphe, Adolphe! But, alas, alas! Is not such the way of most men's hearts—and of the hearts of some women?

This letter was read to Marie, but it had no more effect upon her than would have had some dry legal document. In those days and in those places men and women did not depend much upon letters; nor when they were written, was there expressed in them much of heart or of feeling. Marie would understand, as she was well aware, the glance of Adolphe's eye and the tone of Adolphe's voice; she would perceive at once from them what her lover really meant, what he wished, what in the innermost corner of his heart he really desired that she should do. But from that stiff constrained written document she could understand nothing.

It was agreed therefore that Adolphe should return, and that she would accept her fate from his mouth. The capitaine, who knew more of human nature than did poor Marie, felt tolerably sure of his bride. Adolphe, who had seen something of the world, would not care very much for the girl of his own valley. Money and pleasure, and some little position in the world would soon wean him from his love; and then Marie would accept her destiny—as other girls in the same position had done since the French world began.

And now it was the evening before Adolphe's expected arrival. La Mère Bauche was discussing the matter with the capitaine over the usual cup of coffee. Madame Bauche had of late become rather nervous on the matter, thinking that they had been somewhat rash in acceding so much to Marie. It seemed to her that it was absolutely now left to the two young lovers to say whether or no they would have each other or not. Now nothing on earth could be further from Madame Bauche's intention than this. Her decree and resolve was to heap down blessings on all persons concerned— provided always that she could have her own way; but, provided she did not have her own way, to heap down— anything but blessings. She had her code of morality in this matter. She would do good if possible to everybody around her. But she would not on any score be induced to consent that Adolphe should marry Marie Clavert. Should that be in the wind she would rid the house of Marie, of the capitaine, and even of Adolphe himself.

She had become therefore somewhat querulous, and self-opinionated in her discussions with her friend.

"I don't know", she said on the evening in question; "I don't know. It may be all right; but if Adolphe turns against me, what are we to do then?"

"Mère Bauche", said the capitaine, sipping his coffee and puffing out the smoke of his cigar, "Adolphe will not turn against us." It had been somewhat remarked by many that the capitaine was more at home in the house, and somewhat freer in his manner of talking with Madame Bauche, since this matrimonial alliance had been on the tapis than he had ever been before. La Mère herself observed it, and did not quite like it; but how could she prevent it now? When the capitaine was once married she would make him know his place, in spite of all her promises to Marie.

"But if he says he likes the girl?" continued Madame Bauche.

"My friend, you may be sure that he will say nothing of the kind. He has not been away two years without seeing girls as pretty as Marie. And then you have his letter."

"That is nothing, capitaine; he would eat his letter as quick as you would eat an omelet *aux fines herbes*." Now the capitaine was especially quick over an omelet *aux fines herbes*.

"And, Mère Bauche, you also have the purse; he will know that he cannot eat that, except with your good will."

"Ah!" exclaimed Madame Bauche, "poor lad! He has not a *sous* in the world unless I give it to him." But it did not seem that this reflection was in itself displeasing to her.

"Adolphe will now be a man of the world", continued the capitaine. "He will know that it does not do to throw away everything for a pair of red lips. That is the folly of a boy, and Adolphe will be no longer a boy. Believe me, Mère Bauche, things will be right enough."

"And then we shall have Marie sick and ill and half dying on our hands", said Madame Bauche.

This was not flattering to the capitaine, and so he felt it. "Perhaps so, perhaps not", he said. "But at any rate she will get over it. It is a malady which rarely kills young women—especially when another alliance awaits them."

"Bah!" said Madame Bauche; and in saying that word she avenged herself for the too great liberty which the capitaine had lately taken. He shrugged his shoulders, took a pinch of snuff, and uninvited helped himself to a teaspoonful of cognac. Then the conference ended, and on the next morning before breakfast Adolphe Bauche arrived.

On that morning poor Marie hardly knew how to bear herself. A month or two back, and even up to the last day or two, she had felt a sort of confidence that Adolphe would be true to her; but the nearer came that fatal day the less strong was the confidence of the poor girl. She knew that those two long-headed, aged counsellors were plotting against her happiness, and she felt that she could hardly dare hope for success with such terrible foes opposed to her. On the evening before the day Madame Bauche had met her in the passages, and kissed her as she wished her good night. Marie knew little about sacrifices, but she felt that it was a sacrificial kiss.

In those days a sort of diligence with the mails for Olette passed through Prades early in the morning, and a conveyance was sent from Vernet to bring Adolphe to the baths. Never was prince or princess expected with more anxiety. Madame Bauche was up and dressed long before the hour, and was heard to say five several times that she was sure he would not come. The capitaine was out and on the high road, moving about with his wooden leg, as perpendicular as a lamp-post and almost as black. Marie also was up, but nobody had seen her. She was up and had been out about the place before any of them were stirring; but now that the world was on the move she lay hidden like a hare in its form.

And then the old char-à-banc clattered up to the door, and Adolphe jumped out of it into his mother's arms. He was fatter and fairer than she had last seen him, had a larger beard, was more fashionably clothed, and certainly looked more like a man. Marie also saw him out of her little window, and she thought that he looked like a god. Was it probable, she said to herself, that one so godlike would still care for her?

The mother was delighted with her son, who rattled away quite at his ease. He shook hands very cordially with the capitaine—of whose intended alliance with his own sweetheart he had been informed, and then as he entered the house with his hand under his mother's arm, he asked one question about her. "And where is Marie?" said he. "Marie! Oh, upstairs; you shall see her after breakfast", said La Mère Bauche. And so they entered the house, and went in to breakfast among the guests. Everybody had heard something of the story, and they were all on the alert to see the young man whose love or want of love was considered to be of so much importance.

"You will see that it will be all right", said the capitaine, carrying his head very high.

"I think so, I think so", said La Mère Bauche, who, now that the capitaine was right, no longer desired to contradict him.

"I know that it will be all right", said the capitaine. "I told you that Adolphe would return a man; and he is a man.

Look at him; he does not care this for Marie Clavert"; and
the capitaine, with much eloquence in his motion, pitched
over a neighbouring wall a small stone which he held in
his hand.

And then they all went to breakfast with many signs of
outward joy. And not without some inward joy; for Madame
Bauche thought she saw that her son was cured of his love.
In the meantime Marie sat upstairs still afraid to show herself.

"He has come", said a young girl, a servant in the house,
running up to the door of Marie's room.

"Yes", said Marie, "I could see that he has come."

"And, oh, how beautiful he is!" said the girl, putting her
hands together and looking up to the ceiling. Marie in her
heart of hearts wished that he was not half so beautiful, as
then her chance of having him might be greater.

"And the company are all talking to him as though he were
the préfet", said the girl.

"Never mind who is talking to him", said Marie, "go away,
and leave me—you are wanted for your work." Why before
this was he not talking to her? Why not, if he were really
true to her? Alas, it began to fall upon her mind that he would
be false! And what then? What should she do then? She
sat still gloomily, thinking of that other spouse that had been
promised to her.

As speedily after breakfast as was possible Adolphe was
invited to a conference in his mother's private room. She had
much debated in her own mind whether the capitaine should
be invited to this conference or no. For many reasons she
would have wished to exclude him. She did not like to teach
her son that she was unable to manage her own affairs, and she
would have been well pleased to make the capitaine understand that his assistance was not absolutely necessary to her.
But then she had an inward fear that her green spectacles
would not now be as efficacious on Adolphe as they had once
been, in old days, before he had seen the world and become a
man. It might be necessary that her son, being a man, should

be opposed by a man. So the capitaine was invited to the conference.

What took place there need not be described at length. The three were closeted for two hours, at the end of which time they came forth together. The countenance of Madame Bauche was serene and comfortable; her hopes of ultimate success ran higher than ever. The face of the capitaine was masked, as are always the faces of great diplomatists; he walked placid and upright, raising his wooden leg with an ease and skill that was absolutely marvellous. But poor Adolphe's brow was clouded. Yes, poor Adolphe! For he was poor in spirit. He had pledged himself to give up Marie, and to accept the liberal allowance which his mother tendered him; but it remained for him now to communicate these tidings to Marie herself.

"Could not you tell her?" he had said to his mother, with very little of that manliness in his face on which his mother now so prided herself. But La Mère Bauche explained to him that it was a part of the general agreement that Marie was to hear his decision from his own mouth.

"But you need not regard it", said the capitaine, with the most indifferent air in the world. "The girl expects it. Only she has some childish idea that she is bound till you yourself release her. I don't think she will be troublesome". Adolphe at that moment did feel that he should have liked to kick the capitaine out of his mother's house.

And where should the meeting take place? In the hall of the bath-house, suggested Madame Bauche; because, as she observed, they could walk round and round, and nobody ever went there at that time of day. But to this Adolphe objected; it would be so cold and dismal and melancholy.

The capitaine thought that Mère Bauche's little parlour was the place; but La Mère herself did not like this. They might be overheard, as she well knew; and she guessed that the meeting would not conclude without some sobs that would certainly be bitter and might perhaps be loud.

"Send her up to the grotto, and I will follow her", said Adolphe. On this therefore they agreed. Now the grotto was a natural excavation in a high rock which stood precipitously upright over the establishment of the baths. A steep zigzag path with almost never-ending steps had been made along the face of the rock from a little flower garden attached to the house which lay immediately under the mountain. Close along the front of the hotel ran a little brawling river, leaving barely room for a road between it and the door; over this there was a wooden bridge leading to the garden, and some two or three hundred yards from the bridge began the steps by which the ascent was made to the grotto.

When the season was full and the weather perfectly warm the place was much frequented. There was a green table in it, and four or five deal chairs; a green garden seat also was there, which however had been removed into the innermost back corner of the excavation, as its hinder legs were somewhat at fault. A wall about two feet high ran along the face of it, guarding its occupants from the precipice. In fact it was no grotto, but a little chasm in the rock, such as we often see up above our heads in rocky valleys, and which by means of these steep steps had been turned into a source of exercise and amusement for the visitors at the hotel.

Standing at the wall one could look down into the garden, and down also upon the shining slate roof of Madame Bauche's house; and to the left might be seen the sombre silent snow-capped top of stern old Canigou, king of mountains among those Eastern Pyrenees.

And so Madame Bauche undertook to send Marie up to the grotto, and Adolphe undertook to follow her thither. It was now spring; and though the winds had fallen and the snow was no longer lying on the lower peaks, still the air was fresh and cold, and there was no danger that any of the few guests at the establishment would visit the place.

"Make her put on her cloak, Mère Bauche", said the capitaine, who did not wish that his bride should have a cold in her head on their wedding-day. La Mère Bauche pished and pshawed, as though she were not minded to pay any attention to recommendations on such subjects from the capitaine. But nevertheless when Marie was seen slowly to creep across the little bridge about fifteen minutes after this time, she had a handkerchief on her head, and was closely wrapped in a dark brown cloak.

Poor Marie herself little heeded the cold fresh air, but she was glad to avail herself of any means by which she might hide her face. When Madame Bauche sought her out in her own little room, and with a smiling face and kind kiss bade her go to the grotto, she knew, or fancied that she knew that it was all over.

"He will tell you all the truth—how it all is", said La Mère. "We will do all we can, you know, to make you happy, Marie. But you must remember what Monsieur le Curé told us the other day. In this vale of tears we cannot have everything; as we shall have some day, when our poor wicked souls have been purged of all their wickedness. Now go, dear, and take your cloak."

"Yes, maman."

"And Adolphe will come to you. And try and behave well, like a sensible girl."

"Yes, maman"—and so she went, bearing on her brow another sacrificial kiss—and bearing in her heart such an unutterable load of woe!

Adolphe had gone out of the house before her; but standing in the stable yard, well within the gate so that she should not see him, he watched her slowly crossing the bridge and mounting the first flight of the steps. He had often seen her tripping up those stairs, and had, almost as often, followed her with his quicker feet. And she, when she would hear him, would run; and then he would catch her breathless at the top, and steal kisses from her when all power of refusing them had been robbed from her by her efforts at escape. There was no such running now, no such following, no thought of such kisses.

As for him, he would fain have skulked off and shirked the interview had he dared. But he did not dare; so he waited there, out of heart, for some ten minutes, speaking a word now and then to the bath-man, who was standing by, just to show that he was at his ease. But the bath-man knew that he was not at his ease. Such would-be lies as those rarely achieve deception —are rarely believed. And then, at the end of the ten minutes, with steps as slow as Marie's had been, he also ascended to the grotto.

Marie had watched him from the top, but so that she herself should not be seen. He however had not once lifted up his head to look for her; but, with eyes turned to the ground, had plodded his way up to the cave. When he entered she was standing in the middle, with her eyes downcast, and her hands clasped before her. She had retired some way from the wall, so that no eyes might possibly see her but those of her false lover. There she stood when he entered, striving to stand motionless, but trembling like a leaf in every limb.

It was only when he reached the top step that he made up his mind how he would behave. Perhaps after all, the capitaine was right; perhaps she would not mind it.

"Marie", said he, with a voice that attempted to be cheerful, "this is an odd place to meet in after such a long absence", and he held out his hand to her. But only his hand! He offered her no salute. He did not even kiss her cheek as a brother would have done! Of the rules of the outside world it must be remembered that poor Marie knew but little. He had been a brother to her, before he had become her lover.

But Marie took his hand saying, "Yes, it has been very long."

"And now that I have come back", he went on to say, "it seems that we are all in a confusion together. I never knew such a piece of work. However, it is all for the best, I suppose."

"Perhaps so", said Marie, still trembling violently, and still looking down upon the ground. And then there was silence between them for a minute or so.

"I tell you what it is, Marie", said Adolphe at last, dropping

her hand and making a great effort to get through the work
before him. "I am afraid we two have been very foolish.
Don't you think we have now? It seems quite clear that we
can never get ourselves married. Don't you see it in that
light?"

Marie's head turned round and round with her, but she was
not of the fainting order. She took three steps backwards and
leant against the wall of the cave. She also was trying to think
how she might best fight her battle. Was there no chance for
her? Could no eloquence, no love prevail? On her own beauty
she counted but little; but might not prayers do something,
and a reference to those old vows which had been so frequent,
so eager, so solemnly pledged between them?

"Never get ourselves married!" she said, repeating his words.
"Never, Adolphe? Can we never be married?"

"Upon my word, my dear girl, I fear not. You see my
mother is so dead against it."

"But we could wait; could we not?"

"Ah, but that's just it, Marie. We cannot wait. We must
decide now—to-day. You see I can do nothing without
money from her—and as for you, you see she won't even let
you stay in the house unless you marry old Campan at once.
He's a very good sort of fellow though, old as he is. And
if you do marry him, why you see you'll stay here, and have it
all your own way in everything. As for me, I shall come and
see you all from time to time, and shall be able to push my
way as I ought to do."

"Then, Adolphe, you wish me to marry the capitaine?"

"Upon my honour I think it is the best thing you can do;
I do indeed."

"Oh, Adolphe!"

"What can I do for you, you know? Suppose I was to go
down to my mother and tell her that I had decided to keep
you myself, what would come of it? Look at it in that light,
Marie."

"She could not turn you out—you her own son!"

"But she would turn you out; and deuced quick, too, I can assure you of that; I can, upon my honour."

"I should not care that", and she made a motion with her hand to show how indifferent she would be to such treatment as regarded herself. "Not that—; if I still had the promise of your love."

"But what would you do?"

"I would work. There are other houses besides that one", and she pointed to the slate roof of the Bauche establishment.

"And for me—I should not have a penny in the world", said the young man.

She came up to him and took his right hand between both of hers and pressed it warmly, oh, so warmly. "You would have my love", said she, "my deepest, warmest, best heart's love. I should want nothing more, nothing on earth, if I could still have yours." And she leaned against his shoulder and looked with all her eyes into his face.

"But, Marie; that's nonsense, you know."

"No, Adolphe; it is not nonsense. Do not let them teach you so. What does love mean, if it does not mean that? Oh, Adolphe, you do love me, you do love me; you do love me?"

"Yes—I love you", he said slowly—as though he would not have said it, if he could have helped it. And then his arm crept slowly round her waist, as though in that also he could not help himself.

"And do not I love you?" said the passionate girl. "Oh, I do, so dearly; with all my heart, with all my soul. Adolphe, I so love you, that I cannot give you up. Have I not sworn to be yours; sworn, sworn a thousand times? How can I marry that man! Oh, Adolphe, how can you wish that I should marry him?" And she clung to him, and looked at him, and besought him with her eyes.

"I shouldn't wish it—only—" and then he paused. It was hard to tell her that he was willing to sacrifice her to the old man because he wanted money from his mother.

"Only what! But, Adolphe, do not wish it at all! Have you

not sworn that I should be your wife? Look here, look at this"; and she brought out from her bosom a little charm that he had given her in return for that cross. "Did you not kiss that when you swore before the figure of the Virgin that I should be your wife? And do you not remember that I feared to swear too, because your mother was so angry; and then you made me? After that, Adolphe! Oh, Adolphe! Tell me that I may have some hope. I will wait; oh, I will wait so patiently."

He turned himself away from her and walked backwards and forwards uneasily through the grotto. He did love her— love her as such men do love sweet, pretty girls. The warmth of her hand, the affection of her touch, the pure bright passion of her tear-laden eye had re-awakened what power of love there was within him. But what was he to do? Even if he were willing to give up the immediate golden hopes which his mother held out to him, how was he to begin, and then how carry out this work of self-devotion? Marie would be turned away, and he would be left a victim in the hands of his mother, and of that stiff, wooden-legged militaire—a penniless victim, left to mope about the place without a grain of influence or a morsel of pleasure.

"But what can we do?" he exclaimed again, as he once more met Marie's searching eye.

"We can be true and honest, and we can wait", she said, coming close up to him and taking hold of his arm. "I do not fear it; and she is not my mother, Adolphe. You need not fear your own mother."

"Fear; no, of course I don't fear. But I don't see how the very devil we can manage it."

"Will you let me tell her that I will not marry the capitaine, that I will not give up your promises; and then I am ready to leave the house?"

"It would do no good."

"It would do every good, Adolphe, if I had your promised word once more; if I could hear from your own voice one more tone of love. Do you not remember this place? It was here that you forced me to say that I loved you. It is here also that you will tell me that I have been deceived."

"It is not I that would deceive you", he said. "I wonder that you should be so hard upon me. God knows that I have trouble enough."

"Well; if I am a trouble to you, be it so. Be it as you wish", and she leaned back against the wall of the rock, and crossing her arms upon her breast looked away from him and fixed her eyes upon the sharp granite peaks of Canigou.

He again betook himself to walk backwards and forwards through the cave. He had quite enough of love for her to make him wish to marry her; quite enough, now, at this moment, to make the idea of her marriage with the capitaine very distasteful to him; enough probably to make him become a decently good husband to her, should fate enable him to marry her; but not enough to enable him to support all the punishment which would be the sure effects of his mother's displeasure. Besides, he had promised his mother that he would give up Marie—had entirely given in his adhesion to that plan of the marriage with the capitaine. He had owned that the path of life as marked out for him by his mother was the one which it behoved him, as a man, to follow. It was this view of his duties as a man which had been specially urged on him with all the capitaine's eloquence. And old Campan had entirely succeeded. It is so easy to get the assent of such young men, so weak in mind and so weak in pocket, when the arguments are backed by a promise of two thousand francs a year.

"I'll tell you what I'll do", at last he said. "I'll get my mother by herself, and will ask her to let the matter remain as it is for the present."

"Not if it be a trouble, M. Adolphe"; and the proud girl still held her hands upon her bosom, and still looked towards the mountain.

"You know what I mean, Marie. You can understand how she and the capitaine are worrying me."

"But tell me, Adolphe, do you love me?"

"You know I love you, only——"

"And you will not give me up?"

"I will ask my mother. I will try and make her yield."

Marie could not feel that she received much confidence from her lover's promise; but still, even that, weak and unsteady as it was, even that was better than absolute fixed rejection. So she thanked him, promised him with tears in her eyes that she would always, always be faithful to him, and then bade him go down to the house. She would follow, she said, as soon as his passing had ceased to be observed.

Then she looked at him as though she expected some sign of renewed love. But no such sign was vouchsafed to her. Now that she thirsted for the touch of his lip upon her cheek, it was denied to her. He did as she bade him; he went down, slowly loitering, by himself; and in about half an hour she followed him and unobserved crept to her chamber.

Again we will pass over what took place between the mother and the son; but late in that evening, after the guests had gone to bed, Marie received a message, desiring her to wait on Madame Bauche in a small salon which looked out from one end of the house. It was intended as a private sitting-room should any special stranger arrive who required such accommodation, and therefore was but seldom used. Here she found La Mère Bauche sitting in an armchair behind a small table on which stood two candles; and on a sofa against the wall sat Adolphe. The capitaine was not in the room.

"Shut the door, Marie, and come in and sit down", said Madame Bauche. It was easy to understand from the tone of her voice that she was angry and stern, in an unbending mood, and resolved to carry out to the very letter all the threats conveyed by those terrible spectacles.

Marie did as she was bid. She closed the door and sat down on the chair that was nearest to her.

"Marie", said La Mère Bauche—and the voice sounded fierce in the poor girl's ears, and an angry fire glimmered through the green glasses—"what is all this about that I hear? Do you dare to say that you hold my son bound to marry you?" And then the august mother paused for an answer.

But Marie had no answer to give. She looked suppliantly towards her lover, as though beseeching him to carry on the fight for her. But if she could not do battle for herself, certainly he could not do it for her. What little amount of fighting he had had in him, had been thoroughly vanquished before her arrival.

"I will have an answer, and that immediately", said Madame Bauche. "I am not going to be betrayed into ignominy and disgrace by the object of my own charity. Who picked you out of the gutter, miss, and brought you up and fed you, when you would otherwise have gone to the foundling? And is this your gratitude for it all? You are not satisfied with being fed and clothed and cherished by me, but you must rob me of my son! Know this then, Adolphe shall never marry a child of charity such as you are."

Marie sat still, stunned by the harshness of these words. La Mère Bauche had often scolded her; indeed, she was given to much scolding; but she had scolded her as a mother may scold a child. And when this story of Marie's love first reached her ears, she had been very angry; but her anger had never brought her to such a pass as this. Indeed, Marie had not hitherto been taught to look at the matter in this light. No one had heretofore twitted her with eating the bread of charity. It had not occurred to her that on this account she was unfit to be Adolphe's wife. There, in that valley, they were all so nearly equal, that no idea of her own inferiority had ever pressed itself upon her mind. But now——!

When the voice ceased she again looked at him; but it was no longer with a beseeching look. Did he also altogether scorn her? That was now the inquiry which her eyes were called upon to make. No; she could not say that he did. It seemed to her that his energies were chiefly occupied in pulling to pieces the tassel of the sofa cushion.

"And now, miss, let me know at once whether this nonsense is to be over or not", continued La Mère Bauche, "and I will tell you at once, I am not going to maintain you here, in my house, to plot against our welfare and happiness. As Marie Clavert you shall not stay here. Capitaine Campan is willing to marry you; and as his wife I will keep my word to you, though you little deserve it. If you refuse to marry him, you must go. As to my son, he is there; and he will tell you now, in my presence, that he altogether declines the honour you propose for him."

And then she ceased, waiting for an answer, drumming the table with a wafer stamp which happened to be ready to her hand; but Marie said nothing. Adolphe had been appealed to; but Adolphe had not yet spoken.

"Well, miss?" said La Mère Bauche.

Then Marie rose from her seat, and walking round she touched Adolphe lightly on the shoulder. "Adolphe", she said, "it is for you to speak now. I will do as you bid me."

He gave a long sigh, looked first at Marie and then at his mother, shook himself slightly, and then spoke: "Upon my word, Marie, I think mother is right. It would never do for us to marry; it would not indeed."

"Then it is decided", said Marie, returning to her chair.

"And you will marry the capitaine?" said La Mère Bauche. Marie merely bowed her head in token of acquiescence.

"Then we are friends again. Come here, Marie, and kiss me. You must know that it is my duty to take care of my own son. But I don't want to be angry with you if I can help it; I don't indeed. When once you are Madame Campan, you shall be my own child; and you shall have any room in the house you like to choose—there!" And she once more imprinted a kiss on Marie's cold forehead.

How they all got out of the room, and off to their own chambers, I can hardly tell. But in five minutes from the time of this last kiss they were divided. La Mère Bauche had patted Marie, and smiled on her, and called her her dear good little

Madame Campan, her young little mistress of the Hôtel Bauche; and had then got herself into her own room, satisfied with her own victory.

Nor must my readers be too severe on Madame Bauche. She had already done much for Marie Clavert; and when she found herself once more by her own bedside, she prayed to be forgiven for the cruelty which she felt that she had shown to the orphan. But in making this prayer, with her favourite crucifix in her hand and the little image of the Virgin before her, she pleaded her duty to her son. Was it not right, she asked the Virgin, that she should save her son from a bad marriage? And then she promised ever so much of recompense, both to the Virgin and to Marie; a new trousseau for each, with candles to the Virgin, with a gold watch and chain for Marie, as soon as she should be Marie Campan. She had been cruel; she acknowledged it. But at such a crisis was it not defensible? And then the recompense should be so full!

But there was one other meeting that night, very short indeed, but not the less significant. Not long after they had all separated, just so long as to allow of the house being quiet, Adolphe, still sitting in his room, meditating on what the day had done for him, heard a low tap at his door. "Come in", he said, as men always do say; and Marie, opening the door, stood just within the verge of his chamber. She had on her countenance neither the soft look of entreating love which she had worn up there in the grotto, nor did she appear crushed and subdued as she had done before his mother. She carried her head somewhat more erect than usual, and looked boldly out at him from under her soft eyelashes. There might still be love there, but it was love proudly resolving to quell itself. Adolphe, as he looked at her, felt that he was afraid of her.

"It is all over then between us, M. Adolphe?" she said.

"Well, yes. Don't you think it had better be so, eh, Marie?"

"And this is the meaning of oaths and vows, sworn to each other so sacredly?"

"But, Marie, you heard what my mother said."

"Oh, sir! I have not come to ask you again to love me.
Oh, no! I am not thinking of that. But this, this would be a
lie if I kept it now; it would choke me if I wore it as that man's
wife. Take it back"; and she tendered to him the little charm
which she had always worn round her neck since he had given
it to her. He took it abstractedly, without thinking what he
did, and placed it on his dressing-table.

"And you", she continued, "can you still keep that cross?
Oh, no! You must give me back that. It would remind you
too often of vows that were untrue."

"Marie", he said, "do not be so harsh to me."

"Harsh!" said she. "No; there has been enough of harshness. I would not be harsh to you, Adolphe. But give me
the cross; it would prove a curse to you if you kept it."

He then opened a little box which stood upon the table,
and taking out the cross gave it to her.

"And now good-bye", she said. "We shall have but little
more to say to each other. I know this now, that I was wrong
ever to have loved you. I should have been to you as one of
the other poor girls in the house. But, oh! How was I to
help it?" To this he made no answer, and she, closing the door
softly, went back to her chamber. And thus ended the first
day of Adolphe Bauche's return to his own house.

On the next morning the capitaine and Marie were formally
betrothed. This was done with some little ceremony, in the
presence of all the guests who were staying at the establishment, and with all manner of gracious acknowledgments of
Marie's virtues. It seemed as though La Mère Bauche could
not be courteous enough to her. There was no more talk of
her being a child of charity; no more allusion now to the
gutter. La Mère Bauche with her own hand brought her cake
with a glass of wine after her betrothal was over, and patted
her on the cheek, and called her her dear little Marie Campan.
And then the capitaine was made up of infinite politeness,
and the guests all wished her joy, and the servants of the house
began to perceive that she was a person entitled to respect.

How different was all this from that harsh attack that was made on her the preceding evening! Only Adolphe—he alone kept aloof. Though he was present there he said nothing. He, and he only, offered no congratulations.

In the midst of all these gala doings Marie herself said little or nothing. La Mère Bauche perceived this, but she forgave it. Angrily as she had expressed herself at the idea of Marie's daring to love her son, she had still acknowledged within her own heart that such love had been natural. She could feel no pity for Marie as long as Adolphe was in danger; but now she knew how to pity her. So Marie was still petted and still encouraged, though she went through the day's work sullenly and in silence.

As to the capitaine it was all one to him. He was a man of the world. He did not expect that he should really be preferred, *con amore*, to a young fellow like Adolphe. But he did expect that Marie, like other girls, would do as she was bid; and that in a few days she would regain her temper and be reconciled to her life.

And then the marriage was fixed for a very early day; for as La Mère said, "What was the use of waiting? All their minds were made up now, and therefore the sooner the two were married the better. Did not the capitaine think so?"

The capitaine said that he did think so.

And then Marie was asked. It was all one to her, she said. Whatever Maman Bauche liked, that she would do; only she would not name a day herself. Indeed she would neither do nor say anything herself which tended in any way to a furtherance of these matrimonials. But then she acquiesced, quietly enough if not readily, in what other people did and said; and so the marriage was fixed for the day week after Adolphe's return.

The whole of that week passed much in the same way. The servants about the place spoke among themselves of Marie's perverseness, obstinacy, and ingratitude, because she would not look pleased, or answer Madame Bauche's courtesies

with gratitude; but La Mère herself showed no signs of anger.
Marie had yielded to her, and she required no more. And
she remembered also the harsh words she had used to gain
her purpose; and she reflected on all that Marie had lost.
On these accounts she was forbearing and exacted nothing—
nothing but that one sacrifice which was to be made in
accordance to her wishes.

And it was made. They were married in the great salon,
the dining-room, immediately after breakfast. Madame Bauche
was dressed in a new puce silk dress and looked very mag-
nificent on the occasion. She simpered and smiled, and looked
gay even in spite of her spectacles; and as the ceremony was
being performed, she held fast clutched in her hand the gold
watch and chain which were intended for Marie as soon as
ever the marriage should be completed.

The capitaine was dressed exactly as usual, only that all his
clothes were new. Madame Bauche had endeavoured to
persuade him to wear a blue coat; but he answered that such
a change would not, he was sure, be to Marie's taste. To tell
the truth, Marie would hardly have known the difference
had he presented himself in scarlet vestments.

Adolphe, however, was dressed very finely, but he did not
make himself prominent on the occasion. Marie watched him
closely, though none saw that she did so; and of his garments
she could have given an account with much accuracy—of his
garments, ay! and of every look. "Is he a man", she said at
last to herself, "that he can stand by and see all this?"

She too was dressed in silk. They had put on her what they
pleased, and she bore the burden of her wedding finery
without complaint and without pride. There was no blush
on her face as she walked up to the table at which the priest
stood, nor hesitation in her low voice as she made the necessary
answers. She put her hand into that of the capitaine when
required to do so; and when the ring was put on her finger she
shuddered, but ever so slight. No one observed it but La
Mère Bauche. "In one week she will be used to it, and then

we shall all be happy", said La Mère to herself. "And I—
I will be so kind to her!"

And so the marriage was completed, and the watch was at
once given to Marie. "Thank you, maman", said she, as the
trinket was fastened to her girdle. Had it been a pincushion
that had cost three *sous*, it would have affected her as much.
And then there was cake, and wine, and sweetmeats; and
after a few minutes Marie disappeared. For an hour or so the
capitaine was taken up with the congratulations of his
friends, and with the efforts necessary to the wearing of his
new honours with an air of ease; but after that time he began
to be uneasy because his wife did not come to him. At two
or three in the afternoon he went to La Mère Bauche to complain. "This lackadaisical nonsense is no good", he said.
"At any rate it is too late now. Marie had better come down
among us and show herself satisfied with her husband."

But Madame Bauche took Marie's part. "You must not be
too hard on Marie", she said. "She has gone through a good
deal this week past, and is very young; whereas, capitaine,
you are not very young."

The capitaine merely shrugged his shoulders. In the meantime Mère Bauche went up to visit her protégée in her own
room, and came down with a report that she was suffering
from a headache. She could not appear at dinner, Madame
Bauche said; but would make one at the little party which was
to be given in the evening. With this the capitaine was forced
to be content.

The dinner therefore went on quietly without her, much
as it did on other ordinary days. And then there was a little
time of vacancy, during which the gentlemen drank their
coffee and smoked their cigars at the café, talking over the
event that had taken place that morning, and the ladies brushed
their hair and added some ribbon or some brooch to their usual
apparel. Twice during this time did Madame Bauche go up
to Marie's room with offers to assist her. "Not yet, maman;
not quite yet", said Marie piteously through her tears, and

then twice did the green spectacles leave the room, covering eyes which also were not dry. Ah! What had she done? What had she dared to take upon herself to do? She could not undo it now.

And then it became quite dark in the passages and out of doors, and the guests assembled in the salon. La Mère came in and out three or four times, uneasy in her gait and unpleasant in her aspect, and everybody began to see that things were wrong. "She is ill, I am afraid", said one. "The excitement has been too much", said a second; "and he is so old", whispered a third. And the capitaine stalked about erect on his wooden leg, taking snuff, and striving to look indifferent; but he also was uneasy in his mind.

Presently La Mère came in again, with a quicker step than before, and whispered something, first to Adolphe and then to the capitaine, whereupon they both followed her out of the room. "Not in her chamber?" said Adolphe.

"Then she must be in yours", said the capitaine.

"She is in neither", said La Mère Bauche, with her sternest voice; "nor is she in the house."

And now there was no longer an affectation of indifference on the part of any of them. They were anything but indifferent. The capitaine was eager in his demands that the matter should still be kept secret from the guests. She had always been romantic, he said, and had now gone out to walk by the river-side. They three and the old bath-man would go out and look for her.

"But it is pitch dark", said La Mère Bauche.

"We will take lanterns", said the capitaine. And so they sallied forth with creeping steps over the gravel, so that they might not be heard by those within, and proceeded to search for the young wife. "Marie! Marie!" said La Mère Bauche, in piteous accents. "Do come to me; pray do!"

"Hush!" said the capitaine. "They'll hear you if you call." He could not endure that the world should learn that a marriage with him had been so distasteful to Marie Clavert.

"Marie, dear Marie!" called Madame Bauche, louder than before, quite regardless of the capitaine's feelings; but no Marie answered. In her innermost heart now did La Mère Bauche wish that this cruel marriage had been left undone.

Adolphe was foremost with his lamp, but he hardly dared to look in the spot where he felt that it was most likely that she should have taken refuge. How could he meet her again, alone, in that grotto? Yet he alone of the four was young. It was clearly for him to ascend. "Marie!" he shouted, "are you there?" as he slowly began the long ascent of the steps.

But he had hardly begun to mount when a whirring sound struck his ear, and he felt that the air near him was moved; and then there was a crash upon the lower platform of rock, and a moan, repeated twice but so faintly, and a rustle of silk, and a slight struggle somewhere as he knew within twenty paces of him; and then all was again quiet and still in the night air.

"What was that?" asked the capitaine in a harsh voice. He made his way half across the little garden, and he also was within forty or fifty yards of the flat rock. But Adolphe was unable to answer him. He had fainted and the lamp had fallen from his hands, and rolled to the bottom of the steps.

But the capitaine, though even his heart was all but quenched within him, had still strength enough to make his way up to the rock; and there, holding the lantern above his eyes, he saw all that was left for him to see of his bride.

As for La Mère Bauche, she never again sat at the head of that table—never again dictated to guests—never again laid down laws for the management of any one. A poor bedridden old woman, she lay there in her house at Vernet for some seven tedious years, and then was gathered to her fathers.

As for the capitaine—but what matters? He was made of sterner stuff. What matters either the fate of such a one as Adolphe Bauche?

FATHER GILES
OF BALLYMOY

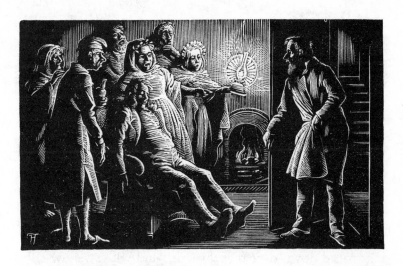

IT IS NEARLY THIRTY YEARS SINCE I, ARCHIBALD
Green, first entered the little town of Ballymoy, in the west
of Ireland, and became acquainted with one of the honestest
fellows and best Christians whom it has ever been my good
fortune to know. For twenty years he and I were fast friends,
though he was much my elder. As he has now been ten
years beneath the sod, I may tell the story of our first meeting.

Ballymoy is a so-called town—or was in the days of which I
am speaking—lying close to the shores of Lough Corrib, in
the county of Galway. It is on the road to no place, and, as the
end of a road, has in itself nothing to attract a traveller. The
scenery of Lough Corrib is grand; but the lake is very large,
and the fine scenery is on the side opposite to Ballymoy, and
hardly to be reached, or even seen, from that place. There is
fishing—but it is lake fishing. The salmon fishing of Lough
Corrib is far away from Ballymoy, where the little river runs
away from the lake down to the town of Galway. There was
then in Ballymoy one single street, of which the characteristic
at first sight most striking to a stranger was its general appearance of being thoroughly wet through. It was not simply
that the rain water was generally running down its unguttered

streets in muddy, random rivulets, hurrying towards the lake
with true Irish impetuosity, but that each separate house
looked as though the walls were reeking with wet; and the
alternated roofs of thatch and slate—the slated houses being
just double the height of those that were thatched—assisted
the eye and mind of the spectator in forming this opinion.
The lines were broken everywhere, and at every break it
seemed as though there was a free entrance for the waters of
heaven. The population of Ballymoy was its second wonder.
There had been no famine then; no rot among the potatoes;
and land round Ballymoy had been let for nine, ten, and even
eleven pounds an acre. At all hours of the day, and at nearly
all hours of the night, able-bodied men were to be seen standing in the streets, with knee-breeches unbuttoned, with stockings rolled down over their brogues, and with swallow-tailed
frieze coats. Nor, though thus idle, did they seem to suffer
any of the distress of poverty. There were plenty of beggars,
no doubt, in Ballymoy, but it never struck me that there was
much distress in those days. The earth gave forth its potatoes
freely, and neither man nor pig wanted more.

It was to be my destiny to stay a week at Ballymoy, on
business, as to the nature of which I need not trouble the present
reader. I was not, at that time, so well acquainted with the
manners of the people of Connaught as I became afterwards,
and I had certain misgivings as I was driven into the village
on a jaunting-car from Tuam. I had just come down from
Dublin, and had been informed there that there were two
"hotels" in Ballymoy, but that one of the "hotels"
might, perhaps, be found deficient in some of those comforts
which I, as an Englishman, might require. I was therefore to ask for the "hotel" kept by Pat Kirwan. The other
hotel was kept by Larry Kirwan; so that it behoved me to
be particular. I had made the journey down from Dublin
in a night and a day, travelling, as we then did travel in Ireland,
by canal boats and by Bianconi's long cars; and I had dined
at Tuam, and been driven over, after dinner on an April

evening; and when I reached Ballymoy I was tired to death and very cold.

"Pat Kirwan's hotel", I said to the driver, almost angrily. "Mind you don't go to the other."

"Shure, yer honour, and why not to Larry's? You'd be getting better enthertainment at Larry's, because of Father Giles."

I understood nothing about Father Giles, and wished to understand nothing. But I did understand that I was to go to Pat Kirwan's "hotel", and thither I insisted on being taken.

It was quite dusk at this time, and the wind was blowing down the street of Ballymoy, carrying before it wild gusts of rain. In the west of Ireland March weather comes in April, and it comes with a violence of its own, though not with the cruelty of the English east wind. At this moment my neck was ricked by my futile endeavours to keep my head straight on the side car, and the water had got under me upon the seat, and the horse had come to a standstill half-a-dozen times in the last two minutes, and my apron had been trailed in the mud, and I was very unhappy. For the last ten minutes I had been thinking evil of everything Irish, and especially of Connaught.

I was driven up to a queerly-shaped, three-cornered house, that stood at the bottom of the street, and which seemed to possess none of the outside appurtenances of an inn.

"Is this Pat Kirwan's hotel?" said I.

"Faix, and it is then, yer honour", said the driver. "And barring only that Father Giles——"

But I had rung the bell, and as the door was now opened by a barefooted girl, I entered the little passage without hearing anything further about Father Giles.

"Could I have a bedroom immediately, with a fire in it?"

Not answering me directly, the girl led me into a sitting-room, in which my nose was at once greeted by that peculiar perfume which is given out by the relics of hot whisky-punch mixed with a great deal of sugar, and there she left me.

"Where is Pat Kirwan himself?" said I, coming to the door, and blustering somewhat. For, let it be remembered, I was very tired; and it may be a fair question whether in the far west of Ireland a little bluster may not sometimes be of service. "If you have not a room ready, I will go to Larry Kirwan's", said I, showing that I understood the bearings of the place.

"It's right away at the furder end then, yer honour", said the driver, putting in his word, "and we comed by it ever so long since. But shure yer honour wouldn't think of leaving this house for that?"

This he said because Pat Kirwan's wife was close behind him.

Then Mrs. Kirwan assured me that I could and should be accommodated. The house, to be sure, was crowded, but she had already made arrangements, and had a bed ready. As for a fire in my bedroom, she could not recommend that, "becase the wind blew so mortial sthrong down the chimney since the pot had blown off—bad cess to it; and that loon, Mick Hackett, wouldn't lend a hand to put it up again, becase there were jobs going on at the big house—bad luck to every joint of his body, thin", said Mrs. Kirwan, with great energy. Nevertheless, she and Mick Hackett the mason were excellent friends.

I professed myself ready to go at once to the bedroom without the fire, and was led away upstairs. I asked where I was to eat my breakfast and dine on the next day, and was assured that I should have the room so strongly perfumed with whisky all to myself. I had been rather cross before, but on hearing this, I became decidedly sulky. It was not that I could not eat my breakfast in the chamber in question, but that I saw before me seven days of absolute misery, if I could have no other place of refuge for myself than a room in which, as was too plain, all Ballymoy came to drink and smoke. But there was no alternative, at any rate for that night and the following morning, and I therefore gulped down my anger without further spoken complaint, and followed the bare-footed maiden upstairs, seeing my portmanteau carried up before me. Ireland is not very well known now to all Englishmen, but it is much better known than it was in those days. On this my first visit into Connaught, I own that I was somewhat scared lest I should be made a victim to the wild lawlessness and general savagery of the people; and I fancied, as in the wet, windy gloom of the night, I could see the crowd of natives standing round the doors of the inn, and just discern their naked legs and old battered hats, that Ballymoy was probably one of those places so far removed from civilization and law, as to be an unsafe residence for an English Protestant. I had undertaken the service on which I was employed, with my eyes more or less open, and was determined to go through with it—but I confess that I was by this time alive to its dangers. It was an early resolution with me that I would not allow my portmanteau to be out of my sight. To that I would cling; with that ever close to me would I live; on that, if needful, would I die. I therefore required that it should be carried up the narrow stairs before me, and I saw it deposited safely in the bedroom.

The stairs were very narrow and very steep. Ascending them was like climbing into a loft. The whole house was built in a barbarous, uncivilized manner, and as fit to be an hotel as it was to be a church. It was triangular and all corners—the most uncomfortably arranged building I had ever seen. From the top of the stairs I was called upon to turn abruptly into the room destined for me; but there was a side step which I had not noticed under the glimmer of the small tallow candle, and I stumbled headlong into the chamber, uttering imprecations against Pat Kirwan, Ballymoy, and all Connaught.

I hope the reader will remember that I had travelled for thirty consecutive hours, had passed sixteen in a small comfortless canal boat without the power of stretching my legs, and that the wind had been at work upon me sideways for the last three hours. I was terribly tired, and I spoke very uncivilly to the young woman.

"Shure, yer honour, it's as clane as clane, and as dhry as dhry, and has been slept in every night since the big storm", said the girl, good-humouredly. Then she went on to tell me something more about Father Giles, of which, however, I could catch nothing, as she was bending over the bed, folding down the bedclothes. "Feel of 'em", said she, "they's dhry as dhry."

I did feel them, and the sheets were dry and clean, and the bed, though very small, looked as if it would be comfortable. So I somewhat softened my tone to her, and bade her call me the next morning at eight.

"Shure, yer honour, and Father Giles will call yer hisself", said the girl.

I begged that Father Giles might be instructed to do no such thing. The girl, however, insisted that he would, and then left me. Could it be that in this savage place, it was considered to be the duty of the parish priest to go round, with matins perhaps, or some other abominable papist ceremony, to the beds of all the strangers? My mother, who was a strict woman, had warned me vehemently against the machinations of the Irish priests, and I, in truth, had been disposed to ridicule her. Could it be that there were such machinations? Was it possible that my trousers might be refused me till I had taken mass? Or that force would be put upon me in some other shape, perhaps equally disagreeable?

Regardless of that and other horrors, or rather, I should perhaps say, determined to face manfully whatever horrors the night or morning might bring upon me, I began to prepare for bed. There was something pleasant in the romance of sleeping at Pat Kirwan's house in Ballymoy, instead of in my own room in Keppel Street, Russell Square. So I chuckled inwardly at Pat Kirwan's idea of an hotel, and unpacked my things.

There was a little table covered with a clean cloth, on which I espied a small comb. I moved the comb carefully without touching it, and brought the table up to my bedside. I put out my brushes and clean linen for the morning, said my prayers, defying Father Giles and his machinations, and jumped into bed. The bed certainly was good, and the sheets were very pleasant. In five minutes I was fast asleep.

How long I had slept when I was awakened, I never knew. But it was at some hour in the dead of night, when I was disturbed by footsteps in my room, and on jumping up, I saw a tall, stout, elderly man standing with his back towards me, in the middle of the room, brushing his clothes with the utmost care. His coat was still on his back, and his pantaloons on his legs; but he was most assiduous in his attention to every part of his body which he could reach.

I sat upright, gazing at him, as I thought then, for ten minutes—we will say that I did so perhaps for forty seconds—and of one thing I became perfectly certain—namely, that the clothes-brush was my own! Whether, according to Irish hotel law, a gentleman would be justified in entering a stranger's room at midnight for the sake of brushing his clothes, I could not say; but I felt quite sure that in such a case, he would be bound at least to use the hotel brush or his own. There was a manifest trespass in regard to my property.

"Sir", said I, speaking very sharply, with the idea of startling him, "what are you doing here in this chamber?"

"Deed, then, and I'm sorry I've waked ye, my boy", said the stout gentleman.

"Will you have the goodness, sir, to tell me what you are doing here?"

"Bedad, then, just at this moment it's brushing my clothes, I am. It was badly they wanted it."

"I daresay they did. And you were doing it with my clothes-brush."

"And that's thrue too. And if a man hasn't a clothes-brush of his own, what else can he do but use somebody else's?"

"I think it's a great liberty, sir", said I.

"And I think it's a little one. It's only in the size of it we

differ. But I beg your pardon. There is your brush. I hope
it will be none the worse."

Then he put down the brush, seated himself on one of the
two chairs which the room contained, and slowly proceeded
to pull off his shoes, looking me full in the face all the
while.

"What are you going to do, sir?" said I, getting a little
further out from under the clothes, and leaning over the table.

"I am going to bed", said the gentleman.

"Going to bed! where?"

"Here", said the gentleman; and he still went on untying
the knot of his shoe-string.

It had always been a theory with me, in regard not only
to my own country, but to all others, that civilization displays
itself never more clearly than when it ordains that every man
shall have a bed for himself. In older days Englishmen of
good position—men supposed to be gentlemen—would
sleep together and think nothing of it, as ladies, I am told,
will still do. And in outlandish regions, up to this time, the
same practice prevails. In parts of Spain you will be told that
one bed offers sufficient accommodation for two men, and in
Spanish America the traveller is considered to be fastidious
who thinks that one on each side of him is oppressive. Among
the poorer classes with ourselves this grand touchstone of
civilization has not yet made itself felt. For aught I know there
might be no such touchstone in Connaught at all. There clearly
seemed to be none such at Ballymoy.

"You can't go to bed here", said I, sitting bolt upright on
the couch.

"You'll find you are wrong there, my friend", said the
elderly gentleman. "But make yourself aisy, I won't do you
the least harm in life, and I sleep as quiet as a mouse."

It was quite clear to me that time had come for action. I certainly would not let this gentleman get into my bed. I had been
the first comer, and was for the night, at least, the proprietor
of this room. Whatever might be the custom of this country

in these wild regions, there could be no special law in the land
justifying the landlord in such treatment of me as this.

"You won't sleep here, sir", said I, jumping out of the bed,
over the table, on to the floor, and confronting the stranger
just as he had succeeded in divesting himself of his second
shoe. "You won't sleep here to-night, and so you may as well
go away."

With that I picked up his two shoes, took them to the door,
and chucked them out. I heard them go rattling down the
stairs, and I was glad that they made so much noise. He would
see that I was quite in earnest.

"You must follow your shoes", said I, "and the sooner the
better."

I had not even yet seen the man very plainly, and even now,
at this time, I hardly did so, though I went close up to him
and put my hand upon his shoulder. The light was very
imperfect, coming from one small farthing candle, which was
nearly burnt out in the socket. And I, myself, was confused,
ill at ease, and for the moment unobservant. I knew that the
man was older than myself, but I had not recognized him as
being old enough to demand or enjoy personal protection
by reason of his age. He was tall, and big, and burly—as he
appeared to me then. Hitherto, till his shoes had been chucked
away, he had maintained imperturbable good humour. When
he heard the shoes clattering downstairs, it seemed that he
did not like it, and he began to talk fast and in an angry voice.
I would not argue with him, and I did not understand him,
but still keeping my hand on the collar of his coat, I insisted
that he should not sleep there. Go away out of that chamber
he should.

"But it's my own", he said, shouting the words a dozen
times. "It's my own room. It's my own room."

So this was Pat Kirwan himself—drunk probably, or
mad.

"It may be your own", said I, "but you've let it to me for
to-night, and you sha'n't sleep here"; so saying I backed him

towards the door, and in so doing I trod upon his unguarded toe.

"Bother you, thin, for a pig-headed Englishman!" said he. "You've kilt me entirely now. So take your hands off my neck, will ye, before you have me throttled outright?"

I was sorry to have trod on his toe, but I stuck to him all the same. I had him near the door now, and I was determined to put him out into the passage. His face was very round and very red, and I thought that he must be drunk; and since I had found out that it was Pat Kirwan the landlord, I was more angry with the man than ever.

"You sha'n't sleep here, so you might as well go", I said, as I backed him away towards the door. This had not been closed since the shoes had been thrown out, and with something of a struggle between the doorposts, I got him out. I remembered nothing whatever as to the suddenness of the stairs. I had been fast asleep since I came up them, and hardly even as yet knew exactly where I was. So, when I got him through the aperture of the door, I gave him a push, as was most natural, I think, for me to do. Down he went backwards— down the stairs, all in a heap, and I could hear that in his fall he had stumbled against Mrs. Kirwan, who was coming up, doubtless to ascertain the cause of all the trouble above her head.

A hope crossed my mind that the wife might be of assistance to her husband in this time of his trouble. The man had fallen very heavily, I knew, and had fallen backwards. And I remembered then how steep the stairs were. Heaven and earth! Suppose that he were killed—or even seriously injured in his own house. What, in such case as that, would my life be worth in that wild country? Then I began to regret that I had been so hot. It might be that I had murdered a man on my first entrance into Connaught!

For a moment or two I could not make up my mind what I would first do. I was aware that both the landlady and the servant were occupied with the body of the ejected occupier

of my chamber, and I was aware also that I had nothing on
but my night-shirt. I returned, therefore, within the door,
but could not bring myself to shut myself in and return to bed
without making some inquiry as to the man's fate. I put my
head out, therefore, and did make inquiry.

"I hope he is not much hurt by his fall", I said.

"Ochone, ochone! murdher, murdher! Spake, Father Giles,
dear, for the love of God!" Such and many such exclamations
I heard from the women at the bottom of the stairs.

"I hope he is not much hurt", I said again, putting my head
out from the doorway; "but he shouldn't have forced himself
into my room."

"His room, the omadhaun!—the born idiot!" said the landlady.

"Faix, ma'am, and Father Giles is a dead man", said the girl,
who was kneeling over the prostrate body in the passage below.

I heard her say Father Giles as plain as possible, and then I
became aware that the man whom I had thrust out was not
the landlord, but the priest of the parish! My heart became
sick within me as I thought of the troubles around me. And I
was sick also with fear lest the man who had fallen should be
seriously hurt. But why—why—why had he forced his way
into my room? How was it to be expected that I should have
remembered that the stairs of the accursed house came flush
up to the door of the chamber?

"He shall be hanged if there's law in Ireland", said a voice
down below; and as far as I could see it might be that I should
be hung. When I heard that last voice I began to think that I
had in truth killed a man, and a cold sweat broke out all over
me, and I stood for a while shivering where I was. Then I
remembered that it behoved me as a man to go down among
my enemies below, and to see what had really happened, to
learn whom I had hurt—let the consequences to myself be what
they might. So I quickly put on some of my clothes—a pair
of trousers, a loose coat, and a pair of slippers, and I descended
the stairs. By this time they had taken the priest into the whisky-

perfumed chamber below, and although the hour was late, there were already six or seven persons with him. Among them was the real Pat Kirwan himself, who had not been so particular about his costume as I had.

Father Giles—for indeed it was Father Giles, the priest of the parish—had been placed in an old armchair, and his head was resting against Mrs. Kirwan's body. I could tell from the moans which he emitted that there was still, at any rate, hope of life.

Pat Kirwan, who did not quite understand what had happened, and who was still half asleep, and as I afterwards learned, half tipsy, was standing over him wagging his head. The girl was also standing by, with an old woman and two men who had made their way in through the kitchen.

"Have you sent for a doctor?" said I.

"Oh, you born blagghuard!" said the woman. "You thief of the world! That the like of you should ever have darkened my door!"

"You can't repent it more than I do, Mrs. Kirwan; but hadn't you better send for the doctor?"

"Faix, and for the police too, you may be shure of that, young man. To go and chuck him out of the room like that— his own room too, and he a priest and an ould man—he that had given up the half of it, though I axed him not to do so, for a sthranger as nobody knowed nothing about."

The truth was coming out by degrees. Not only was the man I had put out Father Giles, but he was also the proper occupier of the room. At any rate somebody ought to have told me all this before they put me to sleep in the same bed with the priest.

I made my way round to the injured man, and put my hand upon his shoulder, thinking that perhaps I might be able to ascertain the extent of the injury. But the angry woman, together with the girl, drove me away, heaping on me terms of reproach, and threatening me with the gallows at Galway.

I was very anxious that a doctor should be brought as soon

as possible; and as it seemed that nothing was being done, I offered to go and search for one. But I was given to understand that I should not be allowed to leave the house until the police had come. I had therefore to remain there for half-an-hour, or nearly so, till a sergeant, with two other policemen, really did come. During this time I was in a most wretched frame of mind. I knew no one at Ballymoy or in the neighbourhood. From the manner in which I was addressed, and also threatened by Mrs. Kirwan and by those who came in and out of the room, I was aware that I should encounter the most intense hostility. I had heard of Irish murders, and heard also of the love of the people for their priests, and I really began to doubt whether my life might not be in danger.

During this time, while I was thus waiting, Father Giles himself recovered his consciousness. He had been stunned by the fall, but his mind came back to him, though by no means all at once; and while I was left in the room with him he hardly seemed to remember all the events of the past hour.

I was able to discover from what was said that he had been for some days past, or, as it afterwards turned out for the last month, the tenant of the room, and that when I arrived he had been drinking tea with Mrs. Kirwan. The only other public bedroom in the hotel was occupied, and he had with great kindness given the landlady permission to put the Saxon stranger into his chamber. All this came out by degrees, and I could see how the idea of my base and cruel ingratitude rankled in the heart of Mrs. Kirwan. It was in vain that I expostulated and explained, and submitted myself humbly to everything that was said around me.

"But, ma'am", I said, "if I had only been told that it was the reverend gentleman's bed!"

"Bed, indeed! To hear the blagghuard talk you'd think it was axing Father Giles to sleep along with the likes of him we were. And there's two beds in the room as dacent as any Christian iver stretched in."

It was a new light to me. And yet I had known overnight,

before I undressed, that there were two bedsteads in the room!
I had seen them, and had quite forgotten the fact in my confusion when I was woken. I had been very stupid, certainly.
I felt that now. But I had truly believed that that big man was
going to get into my little bed. It was terrible as I thought of
it now. The good-natured priest, for the sake of accommodating a stranger, had consented to give up half of his room,
and had been repaid for his kindness by being—perhaps
murdered! And yet, though just then I hated myself cordially,
I could not quite bring myself to look at the matter as they
looked at it. There were excuses to be made, if only I could
get anyone to listen to them.

"He was using my brush—my clothes-brush—indeed he
was", I said. "Not but what he'd be welcome; but it made me
think he was an intruder."

"And wasn't it too much honour for the likes of ye?"
said one of the women, with infinite scorn in the tone of her
voice.

"I did use the gentleman's clothes-brush, certainly", said the
priest. They were the first collected words he had spoken,
and I felt very grateful to him for them. It seemed to me that
a man who could condescend to remember that he had used a
clothes-brush, could not really be hurt to death, even though
he had been pushed down such very steep stairs as those
belonging to Pat Kirwan's hotel.

"And I'm sure you were very welcome, sir", said I. "It
wasn't that I minded the clothes-brush. It wasn't, indeed;
only I thought—indeed, I did think that there was only one
bed. And they had put me into the room, and had not said
anything about anybody else. And what was I to think when
I woke up in the middle of the night?"

"Faix, and you'll have enough to think of in Galway gaol,
for that's where you're going to", said one of the bystanders.

I can hardly explain the bitterness that was displayed against
me. No violence was absolutely shown to me, but I could not
move without eliciting a manifest determination that I was

not to be allowed to stir out of the room. Red, angry eyes were glowering at me, and every word I spoke called down some expression of scorn and ill-will. I was beginning to feel glad that the police were coming, thinking that I needed protection. I was thoroughly ashamed of what I had done, and yet I could not discover that I had been very wrong at any particular moment. Let any man ask himself the question, what he would do, if he supposed that a stout old gentleman had entered his room at an inn and insisted on getting into his bed? It was not my fault that there had been no proper landing-place at the top of the stairs.

Two sub-constables had been in the room for some time before the sergeant came, and with the sergeant arrived also the doctor, and another priest—Father Columb he was called —who, as I afterwards learned, was curate or coadjutor to Father Giles. By this time there was quite a crowd in the house, although it was past one o'clock, and it seemed that all Ballymoy knew that its priest had been foully misused. It was manifest to me that there was something in the Roman Catholic religion which made the priests very dear to the people; for I doubt whether in any village in England, had such an accident happened to the rector, all the people would have roused themselves at midnight to wreak their vengeance on the assailant. For vengeance they were now beginning to clamour, and even before the sergeant of police had come, the two sub-constables were standing over me; and I felt that they were protecting me from the people in order that they might give me up—to the gallows!

I did not like the Ballymoy doctor at all—then, or even at a later period of my visit to that town. On his arrival he made his way up to the priest through the crowd, and would not satisfy their affection or my anxiety by declaring at once that there was no danger. Instead of doing so he insisted on the terrible nature of the outrage and the brutality shown by the assailant. And at every hard word he said, Mrs. Kirwan would urge him on.

"That's thrue for you, doctor!" "'Deed, and you may say that, doctor; two as good beds as ever Christian stretched in!" "'Deed, and it was just Father Giles's own room, as you may say, since the big storm fetched the roof off his riverence's house below there."

Thus gradually I was learning the whole history. The roof had been blown off Father Giles's own house, and therefore he had gone to lodge at the inn! He had been willing to share his lodging with a stranger, and this had been his reward!

"I hope, doctor, that the gentleman is not much hurt", said I, very meekly.

"Do you suppose a gentleman like that, sir, can be thrown down a long flight of stairs without being hurt?" said the doctor, in an angry voice. "It is no thanks to you, sir, that his neck has not been sacrificed."

Then there arose a hum of indignation, and the two policemen standing over me bustled about a little, coming very close to me, as though they thought they should have something to do to protect me from being torn to pieces.

I bethought me that it was my special duty in such a crisis to show a spirit, if it were only for the honour of my Saxon blood among the Celts. So I spoke up again, as loud as I could well speak.

"No one in this room is more distressed at what has occurred than I am. I am most anxious to know, for the gentleman's sake, whether he has been seriously hurt?"

"Very seriously hurt indeed", said the doctor, "very seriously hurt. The vertebrae may have been injured for aught I know at present."

"Arrah, blazes, man", said a voice, which I learned afterwards had belonged to an officer of the revenue corps of men which was then stationed at Ballymoy, a gentleman with whom I became afterwards familiarly acquainted; Tom Macdermot was his name, Captain Tom Macdermot, and he came from the county of Leitrim—"Arrah, blazes, man; do ye think a

gentleman's to fall sthrait headlong backwards down such a
ladder as that, and not find it inconvanient? Only that he's
the priest, and has had his own luck, sorrow a neck belonging
to him there would be this minute."

"Be aisy, Tom", said Father Giles himself; and I was
delighted to hear him speak. Then there was a pause for a
moment. "Tell the gentleman I ain't so bad at all", said the
priest; and from that moment I felt an affection to him which
never afterwards waned.

They got him upstairs back into the room from which he
had been evicted, and I was carried off to the police-station,
where I positively spent the night. What a night it was! I had
come direct from London, sleeping on my road but once in
Dublin, and now I found myself accommodated with a
stretcher in the police barracks at Ballymoy! And the worst
of it was that I had business to do at Ballymoy which required
that I should hold up my head and make much of myself.
The few words which had been spoken by the priest had
comforted me, and had enabled me to think again of my own
position. Why was I locked up? No magistrate had committed me. It was really a question whether I had done anything illegal. As that man whom Father Giles called Tom had
very properly explained, if people will have ladders instead
of staircases in their houses, how is anybody to put an intruder
out of the room without risk of breaking the intruder's neck?
And as to the fact—now an undoubted fact—that Father Giles
was no intruder, the fault in that lay with the Kirwans, who
had told me nothing of the truth. The boards of the stretcher
in the police station were very hard, in spite of the blankets
with which I had been furnished; and as I lay there I began
to remind myself that there certainly must be law in county
Galway. So I called to the attendant policeman and asked him
by whose authority I was locked up.

"Ah, thin, don't bother", said the policeman, "shure, and
you've given throuble enough this night!" The dawn was
at that moment breaking so I turned myself on the stretcher,

and resolved that I would put a bold face on it all when the day should come.

The first person I saw in the morning was Captain Tom, who came into the room where I was lying, followed by a little boy with my portmanteau. The sub-inspector of police who ruled over the men at Ballymoy lived, as I afterwards learned, at Oranmore, so that I had not, at this conjuncture, the honour of seeing him. Captain Tom assured me that he was an excellent fellow, and rode to hounds like a bird. As in those days I rode to hounds myself—as nearly like a bird as I was able—I was glad to have such an account of my head-gaoler. The sub-constables seemed to do just what Captain Tom told them, and there was, no doubt, a very good understanding between the police force and the revenue officer.

"Well, now, I'll tell you what you must do, Mr. Green", said the Captain.

"In the first place", said I, "I must protest that I'm now locked up here illegally."

"Oh, bother; now don't make yourself unaisy."

"That's all very well, Captain —— I beg your pardon, sir, but I didn't catch any name plainly except the Christian name."

"My name is Macdermot—Tom Macdermot. They call me Captain—but that's neither here nor there."

"I suppose, Captain Macdermot, the police here cannot lock up anybody they please, without a warrant?"

"And where would you have been if they hadn't locked you up? I'm blessed if they wouldn't have had you into the Lough before this time."

There might be something in that, and I therefore resolved to forgive the personal indignity which I had suffered, if I could secure something like just treatment for the future. Captain Tom had already told me that Father Giles was doing pretty well.

"He's as sthrong as a horse, you see, or, sorrow a doubt, he'd be a dead man this minute. The back of his neck is as black as your hat with the bruises, and it's the same way with him all down his loins. A man like that, you know, not just as young as he was once, falls mortial heavy. But he's as jolly as a four-year-old", said Captain Tom, "and you're to go and ate your breakfast with him, in his bedroom, so that you may see with your own eyes that there are two beds there."

"I remembered it afterwards quite well", said I.

"'Deed, and Father Giles got such a kick of laughter this morning, when he came to understand that you thought he was going to get into bed alongside of you, that he strained himself all over again, and I thought he'd have frightened the house, yelling with the pain. But anyway you've to go over and see him. So now you'd better get yourself dressed."

This announcement was certainly very pleasant. Against Father Giles, of course, I had no feeling of bitterness. He had behaved well throughout, and I was quite alive to the fact that the light of his countenance would afford me a better aegis against the ill-will of the people of Ballymoy, than anything the law would do for me. So I dressed myself in the barrack-room, while Captain Tom waited without; and then I sallied out under his guidance to make a second visit to Pat Kirwan's hotel. I was amused to see that the police, though by no means subject to Captain Tom's orders, let me go without the least difficulty, and that the boy was allowed to carry my portmanteau away with him.

"Oh, it's all right", said Captain Tom when I alluded to this. "You're not down in the sheet. You were only there for protection, you know."

Nevertheless, I had been taken there by force, and had been locked up by force. If, however, they were disposed to forget all that, so was I. I did not return to the barracks again; and when, after that, the policemen whom I had known met me in the street, they always accosted me as though I were an old friend; hoping my honour had found a better bed than when they last saw me. They had not looked at me with any friendship in their eyes when they had stood over me in Pat Kirwan's parlour.

This was my first view of Ballymoy, and of the "hotel" by daylight. I now saw that Mrs. Pat Kirwan kept a grocery establishment, and that the three-cornered house which had so astonished me was very small. Had I seen it before I entered it, I should hardly have dared to look there for a night's lodging. As it was, I stayed there for a fortnight, and was by no means uncomfortable. Knots of men and women were now standing in groups round the door, and, indeed, the lower end of the street was almost crowded.

"They're all here", whispered Captain Tom, "because they've heard how Father Giles has been murdered during the night by a terrible Saxon; and there isn't a man or woman among them who doesn't know that you are the man who did it."

"But they know also, I suppose", said I, "that Father Giles is alive."

"Bedad, yes, they know that, or I wouldn't be in your skin, my boy. But come along. We mustn't keep the priest waiting for his breakfast."

I could see that they all looked at me, and there were some of them, especially among the women, whose looks I did not even yet like. They spoke among each other in Gaelic, and I could perceive that they were talking of me.

"Can't you understand, then", said Captain Tom, speaking to them aloud, just as he entered the house, "that Father Giles, the Lord be praised, is as well as ever he was in his life? Shure it was only an accident."

"An accident done on purpose, Captain Tom", said one person.

"What is it to you how it was done, Mick Healy? If Father Giles is satisfied, isn't that enough for the likes of you? Get out of that, and let the gentleman pass." Then Captain Tom pushed Mick away roughly, and the others let us enter the house. "Only they wouldn't do it unless somebody gave them the wink, they'd pull you in pieces this moment for a dandy of punch—they would, indeed."

Perhaps Captain Tom exaggerated the prevailing feeling, thinking thereby to raise the value of his own service in protecting me; but I was quite alive to the fact that I had done a most dangerous deed, and had a most narrow escape.

I found Father Giles sitting up in his bed, while Mrs. Kirwan was rubbing his shoulder diligently with an embrocation of arnica. The girl was standing by with a basin half full of the same, and I could see that the priest's neck and shoulders were as red as a raw beefsteak. He winced grievously under the rubbing, but he bore it like a man.

"And here comes the hero", said Father Giles. "Now stop a minute or two, Mrs. Kirwan, while we have a mouthful of breakfast, for I'll go bail that Mr. Green is hungry after his night's rest. I hope you got a better bed, Mr. Green, than the one I found you in when I was unfortunate enough to waken you last night. There it is, all ready for you still", said he, "and if you accept of it to-night, take my advice and don't let a trifle stand in the way of your dhraims."

"I hope, thin, the gintleman will contrive to suit hisself elsewhere", said Mrs. Kirwan.

"He'll be very welcome to take up his quarters here if he likes", said the priest. "And why not? But, bedad, sir, you'd better be a little more careful the next time you see a stranger using your clothes-brush. They are not so strict here in their ideas of meum and tuum as they are perhaps in England; and if you had broken my neck for so small an offence, I don't know but what they'd have stretched your own."

We then had breakfast together, Father Giles, Captain Tom, and I; and a very good breakfast we had. By degrees even Mrs. Kirwan was induced to look favourably at me, and before the day was over I found myself to be regarded as a friend in the establishment. And as a friend I certainly was regarded by Father Giles—then, and for many a long day afterwards. And many times when he has, in years since that, but years nevertheless which are now long back, come over and visited me in my English home, he has told the story of the manner in which we first became acquainted. "When you find a gentleman asleep", he would say, "always ask his leave before you take a liberty with his clothes-brush."

THE SPOTTED DOG

Part I.—The Attempt

SOME FEW YEARS SINCE WE RECEIVED THE following letter:

"Dear Sir,

"I write to you for literary employment, and I implore you to provide me with it if it be within your power to do so. My capacity for such work is not small, and my acquirements are considerable. My need is very great, and my views in regard to remuneration are modest. I was educated at —, and was afterwards a scholar of — College, Cambridge. I left the university without a degree, in consequence of a quarrel with the college tutor. I was rusticated, and not allowed to return. After that I became for a while a student for the Chancery Bar. I then lived for some years in Paris, and I understand and speak French as though it were my own language. For all purposes of literature I am equally conversant with German. I read Italian. I am, of course, familiar with Latin. In regard to Greek I will only say that I am less ignorant of it than nineteen-twentieths of our national scholars. I am well read in modern and ancient history. I have especially studied political economy. I have not neglected other matters necessary to the education of an enlightened man—unless it be natural philosophy. I can write English, and can write it with rapidity. I am a poet—at least, I so esteem myself. I am not a believer. My character will not bear investigation—in saying which, I mean you to understand, not that I steal or cheat, but that I live in a dirty lodging, spend many of my hours in a public-house, and cannot pay trades-men's bills where tradesmen have been found to trust me. I have a wife and four children—which burden forbids me to free myself from all care by a bare bodkin. I am just past forty, and since I quarrelled with my family because I could not understand The Trinity, I have never been the owner of a ten-pound note. My wife was not a lady. I married her because I was determined to take refuge from the conventional thraldom of so-called 'gentlemen' amidst the liberty of the lower orders. My life, of course, has been a mistake. Indeed, to live at all—is it not a folly?

"I am at present employed on the staff of two or three of the 'Penny Dreadfuls'. Your august highness in literature has perhaps never heard of a 'Penny Dreadful'. I write for them matter, which we among ourselves call 'blood and nastiness', and which is copied from one to another. For this I am paid forty-five shillings a week. For thirty shillings a week I will do any work that you may impose upon me for the term of six months. I write this letter as a last effort to rescue myself from the filth of my present position, but I entertain no hope of any success. If you ask it I will come and see you; but do not send for me unless you mean to employ me, as I am ashamed of myself. I live at No. 3 Cucumber Court, Gray's Inn Lane—but if you write, address to the care of Mr. Grimes, the Spotted Dog, Liquorpond Street. Now I have told you my whole life, and you may help me if you will. I do not expect an answer.

                                                        Yours truly,
                                              "JULIUS MACKENZIE."

Indeed he had told us his whole life, and what a picture of a life he had drawn! There was something in the letter which compelled attention. It was impossible to throw it, half read, into the waste-paper basket, and to think of it not at all. We did read it, probably twice, and then put ourselves to work to consider how much of it might be true and how much false. Had the man been a boy at —, and then a scholar of his college? We concluded that, so far, the narrative was true. Had he abandoned his dependence on wealthy friends from conscientious scruples, as he pretended; or had other and less creditable reasons caused the severance? On that point we did not quite believe him. And then, as to those assertions made by himself in regard to his own capabilities—how far did they gain credence with us? We think that we believed them all, making some small discount—with the exception of that one in which he proclaimed himself to be a poet. A man may know whether he understands French, and be quite ignorant whether the rhymed lines which he produces are or are not poetry. When he told us that he was an infidel, and that his character would not bear investigation, we went with him altogether. His allusion to suicide we regarded as a foolish boast. We gave him credit for the four children, but were not certain about the wife. We quite believed the general assertion of his impecuniosity. That stuff about "conventional thraldom" we hope we took at its worth. When he told us that his life had been a mistake he spoke to us Gospel truth.

Of the "Penny Dreadfuls", and of "blood and nastiness", so called, we had never before heard, but we did not think it remarkable that a man so gifted as our correspondent should earn forty-five shillings a week by writing for the cheaper periodicals. It did not, however, appear to us probable that any one so remunerated would be willing to leave that engagement for another which should give him only thirty shillings. When he spoke of the "filth of his present position", our heart began to bleed for him. We know what it is so well, and can fathom so accurately the degradation of the educated man

who, having been ambitious in the career of literature, falls
into that slough of despond by which the profession of literature is almost surrounded. There we were with him, as brothers
together. When we came to Mr. Grimes and the Spotted
Dog, in Liquorpond Street, we thought that we had better
refrain from answering the letter—by which decision on our
part he would not, according to his own statement, be much
disappointed. Mr. Julius Mackenzie! Perhaps at this very
time rich uncles and aunts were buttoning up their pockets
against the sinner because of his devotion to the Spotted Dog.
There are well-to-do people among the Mackenzies. It might
be the case that that heterodox want of comprehension in
regard to The Trinity was the cause of it; but we have observed
that in most families, grievous as are doubts upon such sacred
subjects, they are not held to be cause of hostility so invincible
as is a thorough-going devotion to a Spotted Dog. If the
Spotted Dog had brought about these troubles, any inter-
position from ourselves would be useless.

For twenty-four hours we had given up all idea of answering
the letter; but it then occurred to us that men who have become
disreputable as drunkards do not put forth their own abomina-
tions when making appeals for aid. If this man were really
given to drink he would hardly have told us of his association
with the public-house. Probably he was much at the Spotted
Dog, and hated himself for being there. The more we thought
of it the more we fancied that the gist of his letter might be
true. It seemed that the man had desired to tell the truth as
he himself believed it.

It so happened that at that time we had been asked to provide
an index to a certain learned manuscript in three volumes.
The intended publisher of the work had already procured an
index from a professional compiler of such matters; but the
thing had been so badly done that it could not be used. Some
knowledge of the classics was required, though it was not
much more than a familiarity with the names of Latin and
Greek authors, to which perhaps should be added some

acquaintance, with the names also, of the better-known editors and commentators. The gentleman who had had the task in hand had failed conspicuously, and I had been told by my enterprising friend Mr. X, the publisher, that £25 would be freely paid on the proper accomplishment of the undertaking. The work, apparently so trifling in its nature, demanded a scholar's acquirements, and could hardly be completed in less than two months. We had snubbed the offer, saying that we should be ashamed to ask an educated man to give his time and labour for so small a remuneration— but to Mr. Julius Mackenzie £25 for two months' work would manifestly be a godsend. If Mr. Julius Mackenzie did in truth possess the knowledge for which he gave himself credit; if he was, as he said, "familiar with Latin", and was "less ignorant of Greek than nineteen-twentieths of our national scholars", he might perhaps be able to earn this £25. We certainly knew no one else who could and who would do the work properly for that money. We therefore wrote to Mr. Julius Mackenzie, and requested his presence. Our note was short, cautious, and also courteous. We regretted that a man so gifted should be driven by stress of circumstances to such need. We could undertake nothing, but if it would not put him to too much trouble to call upon us, we might perhaps be able to suggest something to him. Precisely at the hour named Mr. Julius Mackenzie came to us.

We well remember his appearance, which was one unutterably painful to behold. He was a tall man, very thin— thin we might say as a whipping-post, were it not that one's idea of a whipping-post conveys erectness and rigidity, whereas this man, as he stood before us, was full of bends, and curves, and crookedness. His big head seemed to lean forward over his miserably narrow chest. His back was bowed, and his legs were crooked and tottering. He had told us that he was over forty, but we doubted, and doubt now, whether he had not added something to his years, in order partially to excuse the wan, worn weariness of his countenance. He carried an infinity of thick, ragged, wild, dirty hair, dark in colour, though not black, which age had not yet begun to grizzle. He wore a miserable attempt at a beard, stubbly, uneven, and half shorn—as though it had been cut down within an inch of his chin with blunt scissors. He had two ugly projecting teeth, and his cheeks were hollow. His eyes were deep-set, but very bright, illuminating his whole face; so that it was impossible to look at him and to think him to be one wholly insignificant. His eyebrows were large and shaggy, but well formed, not meeting across the brow, with single, stiffly-projecting hairs—a pair of eyebrows which added much strength to his countenance. His nose was long and well shaped—but red as a huge carbuncle. The moment we saw him we connected that nose with the Spotted Dog. It was not a blotched nose, not a nose covered with many carbuncles, but a brightly red, smooth, well-formed nose, one glowing carbuncle in itself. He was dressed in a long brown greatcoat, which was buttoned up round his throat, and which came nearly to his feet. The binding of the coat was frayed, the buttons were half uncovered, the button-holes were tattered, the velvet collar had become parti-coloured with dirt and usage. It was in the month of December, and a greatcoat was needed; but this greatcoat looked as though it were worn because other garments were not at his command. Not an inch of linen or even of flannel shirt was visible. Below his coat we could only see his broken boots and the soiled legs of his trousers, which had reached that age which in trousers defies description. When we looked at him we could not but ask ourselves whether this man had been born a gentleman and was still a scholar. And yet there was that in his face which prompted us to believe the account he had given of himself. As we looked at him we felt sure that he possessed keen intellect, and that he was too much of a man to boast of acquirements which he did not believe himself to possess. We shook hands with him, asked him to sit down, and murmured something of our sorrow that he should be in distress.

"I am pretty well used to it", said he. There was nothing mean in his voice—there was indeed a touch of humour in it, and in his manner there was nothing of the abjectness of supplication. We had his letter in our hands, and we read a portion of it again as he sat opposite to us. We then remarked that we did not understand how he, having a wife and family dependent on him, could offer to give up a third of his income with the mere object of changing the nature of his work. "You don't know what it is", said he, "to write for the 'Penny Dreadfuls'. I'm at it seven hours a day, and hate the very words that I write. I cursed myself afterwards for sending that letter. I know that to hope is to be an ass. But I did send it, and here I am."

We looked at his nose and felt that we must be careful before we suggested to our learned friend Dr. — to put his manuscript into the hands of Mr. Julius Mackenzie. If it had been a printed book the attempt might have been made without much hazard, but our friend's work, which was elaborate, and very learned, had not yet reached the honours of the printing-house. We had had our own doubts whether it might ever assume the form of a real book; but our friend, who was a wealthy as well as a learned man, was, as yet, very determined. He desired, at any rate, that the thing should be perfected, and his publisher had therefore come to us offering £25 for the codification and index. Were anything other than good to befall his manuscript, his lamentations would be loud, not on his own score—but on behalf of learning in general. It behoved us therefore to be cautious. We pretended to read the letter again, in order that we might gain time for a decision, for we were greatly frightened by that gleaming nose.

Let the reader understand that the nose was by no means Bardolphian. If we have read Shakespeare aright Bardolph's nose was a thing of terror from its size as well as its hue. It was a mighty vat, into which had ascended all the divinest particles distilled from the cellars of the hostelry in Eastcheap.

Such at least is the idea which stage representations have left upon all our minds. But the nose now before us was a well-formed nose, would have been a commanding nose—for the power of command shows itself much in the nasal organ—had it not been for its colour. While we were thinking of this, and doubting much as to our friend's manuscript, Mr. Mackenzie interrupted us. "You think I am a drunkard", said he. The man's mother-wit had enabled him to read our inmost thoughts.

As we looked up the man had risen from his chair, and was standing over us. He loomed upon us very tall, although his legs were crooked, and his back bent. Those piercing eyes, and that nose which almost assumed an air of authority as he carried it, were a great way above us. There seemed to be an infinity of that old brown greatcoat. He had divined our thoughts, and we did not dare to contradict him. We felt that a weak, vapid, unmanly smile was creeping over our face. We were smiling as a man smiles who intends to imply some contemptuous assent with the self-depreciating comment of his companion. Such a mode of expression is in our estimation most cowardly, and most odious. We had not intended it, but we knew that the smile had pervaded us. "Of course you do", said he. "I was a drunkard, but I am not one now. It doesn't matter—only I wish you hadn't sent for me. I'll go away at once."

So saying, he was about to depart, but we stopped him. We assured him with much energy that we did not mean to offend him. He protested that there was no offence. He was too well used to that kind of thing to be made "more than wretched by it". Such was his heart-breaking phrase. "As for anger, I've lost all that long ago. Of course you take me for a drunkard, and I should still be a drunkard, only——"

"Only what?" I asked.

"It don't matter", said he. "I need not trouble you with more than I have said already. You haven't got anything for me to do, I suppose?" Then I explained to him that I had something he might do, if I could venture to entrust him with the work. With some trouble I got him to sit down again, and to listen while I explained to him the circumstances. I had been grievously afflicted when he alluded to his former habit of drinking—a former habit as he himself now stated—but I entertained no hesitation in raising questions as to his erudition. I felt almost assured that his answers would be satisfactory, and that no discomfiture would arise from such questioning. We were quickly able to perceive that we at any rate could not examine him in classical literature. As soon as we mentioned the name and nature of the work he went off at score, and satisfied us amply that he was familiar at least with the title-pages of editions. We began, indeed, to fear whether he might not be too caustic a critic on our own friend's performance. "Dr. — is only an amateur himself ", said we, deprecating in advance any such exercise of the red-nosed man's too severe erudition. "We never get much beyond dilettanteism here", said he, "as far as Greek and Latin are concerned." What a terrible man he would have been could he have got upon the staff of the *Saturday Review*, instead of going to the Spotted Dog!

We endeavoured to bring the interview to an end by telling him that we would consult the learned Doctor from whom the manuscript had emanated; and we hinted that a reference would be of course acceptable. His impudence—or perhaps we should rather call it his straightforward sincere audacity—was unbounded. "Mr. Grimes of the Spotted Dog knows me better than any one else", said he. We blew the breath out of our mouth with astonishment. "I'm not asking you to go to him to find out whether I know Latin and Greek", said Mr. Mackenzie. "You must find that out for yourself." We assured him that we thought we had found that out. "But he can tell you that I won't pawn your manu-script." The man was so grim and brave that he almost frightened us. We hinted, however, that literary reference should be given. The gentleman who paid him forty-five shillings a week—the manager, in short, of the "Penny Dreadful"—might tell us something of him. Then he wrote for us a name on a scrap of paper, and added to it an address in the close vicinity of Fleet Street, at which we remembered to have seen the title of a periodical which we now knew to be a "Penny Dreadful".

Before he took his leave he made us a speech, again standing up over us, though we also were on our legs. It was that bend in his neck, combined with his natural height, which gave him such an air of superiority in conversation. He seemed to overshadow us, and to have his own way with us, because he was enabled to look down upon us. There was a footstool on our hearth-rug, and we remember to have attempted to stand upon that, in order that we might escape this supervision; but we stumbled, and had to kick it from us, and something was added to our sense of inferiority by this little failure. "I don't expect much from this", he said. "I never do expect much. And I have misfortunes independent of my poverty which make it impossible that I should be other than a miserable wretch."

"Bad health?" we asked.

"No—nothing absolutely personal—but never mind. I must not trouble you with more of my history. But if you can do this thing for me, it may be the means of redeeming me from utter degradation." We then assured him that we would do our best, and he left us with a promise that he would call again on that day week.

The first step which we took on his behalf was one the very idea of which had at first almost moved us to ridicule. We made inquiry respecting Mr. Julius Mackenzie, of Mr. Grimes, the landlord of the Spotted Dog. Though Mr. Grimes did keep the Spotted Dog, he might be a man of sense and, possibly, of conscience. At any rate he would tell us something, or confirm our doubts by refusing to tell us anything. We found Mr. Grimes seated in a very neat little back parlour, and were peculiarly taken by the appearance of a lady in a

little cap and black silk gown, whom we soon found to be
Mrs. Grimes. Had we ventured to employ our intellect in
personifying for ourselves an imaginary Mrs. Grimes as the
landlady of a Spotted Dog public-house in Liquorpond Street,
the figure we should have built up for ourselves would have
been the very opposite of that which this lady presented to us.
She was slim, and young, and pretty, and had pleasant little
tricks of words, in spite of occasional slips in her grammar,
which made us almost think that it might be our duty to
come very often to the Spotted Dog to inquire about Mr.
Julius Mackenzie. Mr. Grimes was a man about forty—fully
ten years the senior of his wife—with a clear grey eye, and a
mouth and chin from which we surmised that he would be
competent to clear the Spotted Dog of unruly visitors after
twelve o'clock, whenever it might be his wish to do so. We
soon made known our request. Mr. Mackenzie had come to
us for literary employment. Could they tell us anything about
Mr. Mackenzie?

"He's as clever an author, in the way of writing and that
kind of thing, as there is in all London", said Mrs. Grimes
with energy. Perhaps her opinion ought not to have been
taken for much, but it had its weight. We explained, however,
that at the present moment we were specially anxious to know
something of the gentleman's character and mode of life.
Mr. Grimes, whose manner to us was quite courteous, sat
silent, thinking how to answer us. His more impulsive and
friendly wife was again ready with her assurance. "There
ain't an honester gentleman breathing—and I say he is a
gentleman, though he's that poor he hasn't sometimes a shirt
to his back."

"I don't think he's ever very well off for shirts", said Mr.
Grimes.

"I wouldn't be slow to give him one of yours, John, only
I know he wouldn't take it", said Mrs. Grimes. "Well now,
look here, sir—we've that feeling for him that our young
woman there would draw anything for him he'd ask—money

or no money. She'd never venture to name money to him if he wanted a glass of anything—hot or cold, beer or spirits. Isn't that so, John?"

"She's fool enough for anything as far as I know", said Mr. Grimes.

"She ain't no fool at all; and I'd do the same if I was there— and so'd you, John. There is nothing Mackenzie'd ask as he wouldn't give him", said Mrs. Grimes, pointing with her thumb over her shoulder to her husband, who was standing on the hearth-rug—"that is, in the way of drawing liquor, and refreshments, and such like. But he never raised a glass to his lips in this house as he didn't pay for, nor yet took a biscuit out of that basket. He's a gentleman all over, is Mackenzie."

It was strong testimony; but still we had not quite got at the bottom of the matter. "Doesn't he raise a great many glasses to his lips?" we asked.

"No he don't," said Mrs. Grimes—"only in reason."

"He's had misfortunes", said Mr. Grimes.

"Indeed he has", said the lady—"what I call the very trouble-somest of troubles. If you was troubled like him, John, where'd you be?"

"I know where you'd be", said John.

"He's got a bad wife, sir; the worst as ever was", continued Mrs. Grimes. "Talk of drink—there is nothing that woman wouldn't do for it. She'd pawn the very clothes off her child-ren's back in mid-winter to get it. She'd rob the food out of her husband's mouth for a drop of gin. As for herself—she ain't no woman's notions left of keeping herself any way. She'd as soon be picked out of the gutter as not—and as for words out of her mouth or clothes on her back, she hasn't got, sir, not an item of a female's feelings left about her."

Mrs. Grimes had been very eloquent, and had painted the "troublesomest of all troubles" with glowing words. This was what the wretched man had come to by marrying a woman who was not a lady in order that he might escape the "con-

ventional thraldom" of gentility! But still the drunken wife
was not all. There was the evidence of his own nose against
himself, and the additional fact that he had acknowledged
himself to have been formerly a drunkard. "I suppose he has
drunk, himself?" we said.

"He has drunk, in course", said Mrs. Grimes.

"The world has been pretty rough with him, sir", said
Mr. Grimes.

"But he don't drink now", continued the lady. "At least
if he do, we don't see it. As for her, she wouldn't show
herself inside our door."

"It ain't often that man and wife draws their milk from the
same cow", said Mr. Grimes.

"But Mackenzie is here every day of his life", said Mrs.
Grimes. "When he's got a sixpence to pay for it, he'll come
in here and have a glass of beer and a bit of something to eat.
We does make him a little extra welcome, and that's the truth
of it. We knows what he is, and we knows what he was.
As for book learning, sir—it don't matter what language it is,
it's all as one to him. He knows 'em all round just as I know
my catechism."

"Can't you say fairer than that for him, Polly?" asked
Mr. Grimes.

"Don't you talk of catechisms, John; nor yet of nothing
else as a man ought to set his mind to—unless it is keeping
the Spotted Dog. But as for Mackenzie—he knows off by
heart whole books full of learning. There was some furreners
here as come from—I don't know where it was they came
from, only it wasn't France, nor yet Germany, and he talked
to them just as though he hadn't been born in England at all.
I don't think there ever was such a man for knowing things.
He'll go on with poetry out of his own head till you think it
comes from him like web from a spider." We could not help
thinking of the wonderful companionship which there must
have been in that parlour while the reduced man was spinning
his web and Mrs. Grimes, with her needle-work lying idle in

her lap, was sitting by, listening with rapt admiration. In passing by the Spotted Dog one would not imagine such a scene to have its existence within. But then so many things do have existence of which we imagine nothing!

Mr. Grimes ended the interview. "The fact is, sir, if you can give him employment better than what he has now, you'll be helping a man who has seen better days, and who only wants help to see 'em again. He's got it all there", and Mr. Grimes put his finger up to his head.

"He's got it all here too", said Mrs. Grimes, laying her hand upon her heart. Hereupon we took our leave, suggesting to these excellent friends that if it should come to pass that we had further dealings with Mr. Mackenzie we might perhaps trouble them again. They assured us that we should always be welcome, and Mr. Grimes himself saw us to the door, having made profuse offers of such good cheer as the house afforded. We were upon the whole much taken with the Spotted Dog.

From thence we went to the office of the "Penny Dreadful", in the vicinity of Fleet Street. As we walked thither we could not but think of Mrs. Grimes' words. The troublesomest of troubles! We acknowledged to ourselves that they were true words. Can there be any trouble more troublesome than that of suffering from the shame inflicted by a degraded wife? We had just parted from Mr. Grimes—not, indeed, having seen very much of him in the course of our interview—but little as we had seen, we were sure that he was assisted in his position by a buoyant pride in that he called himself the master, and owner, and husband of Mrs. Grimes. In the very step with which he passed in and out of his own door you could see that there was nothing that he was ashamed of about his household. When abroad he could talk of his "missus" with a conviction that the picture which the word would convey to all who heard him would redound to his honour. But what must have been the reflections of Julius Mackenzie when his mind dwelt upon his wife? We remembered the words of his letter. "I have a wife and four children, which burden forbids me to free myself from all care with a bare bodkin." As we thought of them, and of the story which had been told to us at the Spotted Dog, they lost that tone of rhodomontade with which they had invested themselves when we first read them. A wife who is indifferent to being picked out of the gutter, and who will pawn her children's clothes for gin, must be a trouble than which none can be more troublesome.

We did not find that we ingratiated ourselves with the people at the office of the periodical for which Mr. Mackenzie worked; and yet we endeavoured to do so, assuming in our manner and tone something of the familiarity of a common pursuit. After much delay we came upon a gentleman sitting in a dark cupboard, who twisted round his stool to face us while he spoke to us. We believe that he was the editor of more than one "Penny Dreadful", and that as many as a dozen serial novels were being issued to the world at the same time under his supervision. "Oh!" said he, "so you're at that game, are you?" We assured him that we were at no game at all, but were simply influenced by a desire to assist a distressed scholar. "That be blowed", said our brother. "Mackenzie's doing as well here as he'll do anywhere. He's a drunken blackguard, when all's said and done. So you're going to buy him up, are you? You won't keep him long—and then he'll have to starve." We assured the gentleman that we had no desire to buy up Mr. Mackenzie; we explained our ideas as to the freedom of the literary profession, in accordance with which Mr. Mackenzie could not be wrong in applying to us for work; and we especially deprecated any severity on our brother's part towards the man, more especially begging that nothing might be decided, as we were far from thinking it certain that we could provide Mr. Mackenzie with any literary employment. "That's all right", said our brother, twisting back his stool. "He can't work for both of us—that's all. He has his bread here regular, week after week; and I

don't suppose you'll do as much as that for him." Then we
went away, shaking the dust off our feet, and wondering
much at the great development of literature which latter
years have produced. We had not even known of the existence
of these papers—and yet there they were, going forth into
the hands of hundreds of thousands of readers, all of whom
were being, more or less, instructed in their modes of life
and manner of thinking by the stories which were thus brought
before them.

But there might be truth in what our brother had said to
us. Should Mr. Mackenzie abandon his present engagement
for the sake of the job which we proposed to put in his hands,
might he not thereby injure rather than improve his prospects?
We were acquainted with only one learned doctor desirous
of having his manuscripts codified and indexed at his own
expense. As for writing for the periodical with which we were
connected, we knew enough of the business to be aware that
Mr. Mackenzie's gifts of erudition would very probably not
so much assist him in attempting such work as would his late
training act against him. A man might be able to read and
even talk a dozen languages—"just as though he hadn't been
born in England at all"—and yet not write the language with
which we dealt after the fashion which suited our readers.
It might be that he would fly much above our heads, and do
work infinitely too big for us. We did not regard our own
heads as being very high. But, for such altitude as they held,
a certain class of writing was adapted. The gentleman whom
we had just left would require, no doubt, altogether another
style. It was probable that Mr. Mackenzie had already fitted
himself to his present audience. And, even were it not so,
we could not promise him forty-five shillings a week, or even
that thirty shillings for which he asked. There is nothing more
dangerous than the attempt to befriend a man in middle life
by transplanting him from one soil to another.

When Mr. Mackenzie came to us again we endeavoured
to explain all this to him. We had in the meantime seen our

friend the Doctor, whose beneficence of spirit in regard to the
unfortunate man of letters was extreme. He was charmed with
our account of the man, and saw with his mind's eye the work,
for the performance of which he was pining, perfected in a
manner that would be a blessing to the scholars of all future
ages. He was at first anxious to ask Julius Mackenzie down to
his rectory, and, even after we had explained to him that this
would not at present be expedient, was full of a dream of
future friendship with a man who would be able to discuss
the digamma with him, who would have studied Greek
metres, and have an opinion of his own as to Porson's canon.
We were in possession of the manuscript, and had our friend's
authority for handing it over to Mr. Mackenzie.

He came to us according to appointment, and his nose
seemed to be redder than ever. We thought that we discovered
a discouraging flavour of spirits in his breath. Mrs. Grimes
had declared that he drank—only in reason; but the ideas
of the wife of a publican—even though that wife were Mrs.
Grimes—might be very different from our own as to what was
reasonable in that matter. And as we looked at him he seemed
to be more rough, more ragged, almost more wretched than
before. It might be that, in taking his part with my brother of
the "Penny Dreadful", with the Doctor, and even with
myself in thinking over his claims, I had endowed him with
higher qualities than I had been justified in giving to him. As
I considered him and his appearance I certainly could not
assure myself that he looked like a man worthy to be trusted.
A policeman, seeing him at a street corner, would have had
an eye upon him in a moment. He rubbed himself together
within his old coat, as men do when they come out of gin-
shops. His eye was as bright as before, but we thought that his
mouth was meaner, and his nose redder. We were almost
disenchanted with him. We said nothing to him at first about
the Spotted Dog, but suggested to him our fears that if he
undertook work at our hands he would lose the much more
permanent employment which he got from the gentleman

whom we had seen in the cupboard. We then explained to him that we could promise to him no continuation of employment.

The violence with which he cursed the gentleman who had sat in the cupboard appalled us, and had, we think, some effect in bringing back to us that feeling of respect for him which we had almost lost. It may be difficult to explain why we respected him because he cursed and swore horribly. We do not like cursing and swearing, and were any of our younger contributors to indulge themselves after that fashion in our presence we should, at the very least—frown upon them. We did not frown upon Julius Mackenzie, but stood up, gazing into his face above us, again feeling that the man was powerful. Perhaps we respected him because he was not in the least afraid of us. He went on to assert that he cared not —not a straw, we will say—for the gentleman in the cupboard. He knew the gentleman in the cupboard very well; and the gentleman in the cupboard knew him. As long as he took his work to the gentleman in the cupboard, the gentleman in the cupboard would be only too happy to purchase that work at the rate of sixpence for a page of manuscript containing two hundred and fifty words. That was his rate of payment for prose fiction, and at that rate he could earn forty-five shillings a week. He wasn't afraid of the gentleman in the cupboard. He had had some words with the gentleman in the cupboard before now, and they two understood each other very well. He hinted, moreover, that there were other gentlemen in other cupboards; but with none of them could he advance beyond forty-five shillings a week. For this he had to sit, with his pen in his hand, seven hours seven days a week, and the very paper, pens, and ink came to fifteen pence out of the money. He had struck for wages once, and for a halcyon month or two had carried his point of sevenpence-halfpenny a page; but the gentlemen in the cupboards had told him that it could not be. They, too, must live. His matter was no doubt attractive; but any price above sixpence a page unfitted it for

their market. All this Mr. Julius Mackenzie explained to us
with much violence of expression. When I named Mrs.
Grimes to him the tone of his voice was altered. "Yes", said
he—"I thought they'd say a word for me. They're the best
friends I've got now. I don't know that you ought quite to
believe her, for I think she'd perhaps tell a lie to do me a
service." We assured him that we did believe every word
Mrs. Grimes had said to us.

After much pausing over the matter we told him that we
were empowered to trust him with our friend's work, and
the manuscript was produced upon the table. If he would
undertake the work and perform it, he should be paid
£8 6s. 8d. for each of the three volumes as they were completed. And we undertook, moreover, on our own responsibility, to advance him money in small amounts through the
hands of Mrs. Grimes, if he really settled himself to the task.
At first he was in ecstasies, and as we explained to him the way
in which the index should be brought out and the codification
performed, he turned over the pages rapidly, and showed us
that he understood at any rate the nature of the work to be
done. But when we came to details he was less happy. In
what workshop was this new work to be performed? There
was a moment in which we almost thought of telling him to
do the work in our own room; but we hesitated, luckily,
remembering that his continual presence with us for two
or three months would probably destroy us altogether. It
appeared that his present work was done sometimes at the
Spotted Dog, and sometimes at home in his lodgings. He said
not a word to us about his wife, but we could understand that
there would be periods in which to work at home would be
impossible to him. He did not pretend to deny that there might
be danger on that score, nor did he ask permission to take the
entire manuscript at once away to his abode. We knew that
if he took part he must take the whole, as the work could not
be done in parts. Counter references would be needed.
"My circumstances are bad—very bad indeed", he said. We

expressed the great trouble to which we should be subjected if any evil should happen to the manuscript. "I will give it up", he said, towering over us again, and shaking his head. "I cannot expect that I should be trusted." But we were determined that it should not be given up. Sooner than give the matter up we would make some arrangement by hiring a place in which he might work. Even though we were to pay ten shillings a week for a room for him out of the money, the bargain would be a good one for him. At last we determined that we would pay a second visit to the Spotted Dog, and consult Mrs. Grimes. We felt that we should have a pleasure in arranging together with Mrs. Grimes any scheme of benevolence on behalf of this unfortunate and remarkable man. So we told him that we would think over the matter, and send a letter to his address at the Spotted Dog, which he should receive on the following morning. He then gathered himself up, rubbed himself together again inside his coat, and took his departure.

As soon as he was gone we sat looking at the learned Doctor's manuscript, and thinking of what we had done. There lay the work of years, by which our dear and venerable old friend expected that he would take rank among the great commentators of modern times. We, in truth, did not anticipate for him all the glory to which he looked forward. We feared that there might be disappointment. Hot discussion on verbal accuracies or on rules of metre are perhaps not so much in vogue now as they were a hundred years ago. There might be disappointment and great sorrow; but we could not with equanimity anticipate the prevention of this sorrow by the possible loss or destruction of the manuscript which had been entrusted to us. The Doctor himself had seemed to anticipate no such danger. When we told him of Mackenzie's learning and misfortunes, he was eager at once that the thing should be done, merely stipulating that he should have an interview with Mr. Mackenzie before he returned to his rectory.

That same day we went to the Spotted Dog, and found Mrs. Grimes alone. Mackenzie had been there immediately after leaving our room, and had told her what had taken place. She was full of the subject and anxious to give every possible assistance. She confessed at once that the papers would not be safe in the rooms inhabited by Mackenzie and his wife. "He pays five shillings a week", she said, "for a wretched place round in Cucumber Court. They are all huddled together, anyway; and how he manages to do a thing at all there—in the way of author-work—is a wonder to everybody. Sometimes he can't, and then he'll sit for hours together at the little table in our tap-room." We went into the tap-room and saw the little table. It was a wonder indeed that any one should be able to compose and write tales of imagination in a place so dreary, dark, and ill-omened. The little table was hardly more than a long slab or plank, perhaps eighteen inches wide. When we visited the place there were two brewers' draymen seated there, and three draggled, wretched-looking women. The carters were eating enormous hunches of bread and bacon, which they cut and put into their mouths slowly, solemnly, and in silence. The three women were seated on a bench, and when I saw them had no signs of festivity before them. It must be presumed that they had paid for something, or they would hardly have been allowed to sit there. "It's empty now", said Mrs. Grimes, taking no immediate notice of the men or of the women; "but sometimes he'll sit writing in that corner, when there's such a jabber of voices as you wouldn't hear a cannon go off over at Reid's, and that thick with smoke you'd a'most cut it with a knife. Don't he, Peter?" The man whom she addressed endeavoured to prepare himself for answer by swallowing at the moment three square inches of bread and bacon, which he had just put into his mouth. He made an awful effort, but failed; and, failing, nodded his head three times. "They all know him here, sir", continued Mrs. Grimes. "He'll go on writing, writing, writing, for hours together; and nobody'll say nothing to him. Will they, Peter?" Peter, who was now half-way through the work he had laid out for himself, muttered some inarticulate grunt of assent.

We then went back to the snug little room inside the bar. It was quite clear to me that the man could not manipulate the Doctor's manuscript, of which he would have to spread a dozen sheets before him at the same time, in the place I had just visited. Even could he have occupied the chamber alone, the accommodation would not have been sufficient for the purpose. It was equally clear that he could not be allowed to use Mrs. Grimes' snuggery. "How are we to get a place for him?" said I, appealing to the lady. "He shall have a place", she said, "I'll go bail; he shan't lose the job for want of a workshop." Then she sat down and began to think it over. I was just about to propose the hiring of some decent room in the neighbourhood, when she made a suggestion, which I acknowledge startled me. "I'll have a big table put into my own bedroom", said she, "and he shall do it there. There ain't another hole or corner about the place as'd suit; and he can lay the gentleman's papers all about on the bed, square and clean and orderly. Can't he now? And I can see after 'em, as he don't lose 'em. Can't I now?"

By this time there had sprung up an intimacy between ourselves and Mrs. Grimes which seemed to justify an expression of the doubt which I then threw on the propriety of such a disarrangement of her most private domestic affairs. "Mr. Grimes will hardly approve of that", we said.

"Oh, John won't mind. What'll it matter to John as long as Mackenzie is out in time for him to go to bed? We ain't early birds, morning or night—that's true. In our line folks can't be early. But from ten to six there's the room, and he shall have it. Come up and see, sir." So we followed Mrs. Grimes up the narrow staircase to the marital bower. "It ain't large, but there'll be room for the table, and for him to sit at it—won't there now?"

It was a dark little room, with one small window looking

out under the low roof, and facing the heavy high dead wall of the brewery opposite. But it was clean and sweet, and the furniture in it was all solid and good, old-fashioned, and made of mahogany. Two or three of Mrs. Grimes' gowns were laid upon the bed, and other portions of her dress were hung on pegs behind the doors. The only untidy article in the room was a pair of "John's" trousers, which he had failed to put out of right. She was not a bit abashed, but took them up and folded them and patted them, and laid them in the capacious wardrobe. "We'll have all these things away", she said, "and then he can have all his papers out upon the bed just as he pleases."

We own that there was something in the proposed arrangement which dismayed us. We also were married, and what would our wife have said had we proposed that a contributor —even a contributor not red-nosed and seething with gin— that any best-disciplined contributor should be invited to write an article within the precincts of our sanctum? We could not bring ourselves to believe that Mr. Grimes would authorize the proposition. There is something holy about the bedroom of a married couple; and there would be a special desecration in the continued presence of Mr. Julius Mackenzie. We thought it better that we should explain something of all this to her. "Do you know", we said, "this seems to be hardly prudent?"

"Why not prudent?" she asked.

"Up in your bedroom, you know! Mr. Grimes will be sure to dislike it."

"What—John! Not he. I know what you're a-thinking of, Mr. —," she said. "But we're different in our ways than what you are. Things to us are only just what they are. We haven't time, nor yet money, nor perhaps edication, for seemings and thinkings as you have. If you was travelling out amongst the wild Injeans, you'd ask any one to have a bit in your bedroom as soon as look at 'em, if you'd got a bit for 'em to eat. We're travelling among wild Injeans all our

lives, and a bedroom ain't no more to us than any other room.
Mackenzie shall come up here, and I'll have the table fixed
for him, just there by the window." I hadn't another word to
say to her, and I could not keep myself from thinking for
many an hour afterwards, whether it may not be a good thing
for men, and for women also, to believe that they are always
travelling among wild Indians.

When we went down Mr. Grimes himself was in the
little parlour. He did not seem at all surprised at seeing his
wife enter the room from above accompanied by a stranger.
She at once began her story, and told the arrangement which
she proposed—which she did, as I observed, without any
actual request for his sanction. Looking at Mr. Grimes'
face, I thought that he did not quite like it; but he accepted it,
almost without a word, scratching his head and raising his
eyebrows. "You know, John, he could no more do it at home
than he could fly", said Mrs. Grimes.

"Who said he could do it at home?"

"And he couldn't do it in the tap-room—could he? If so,
there ain't no other place, and so that's settled." John Grimes
again scratched his head, and the matter was settled. Before
we left the house Mackenzie himself came in, and was told
in our presence of the accommodation which was to be
prepared for him. "It's just like you, Mrs. Grimes", was all
he said in the way of thanks. Then Mrs. Grimes made her
bargain with him somewhat sternly. He should have the room
for five hours a day—ten till three, or twelve till five; but he
must settle which, and then stick to his hours. "And I won't
have nothing up there in the way of drink", said John
Grimes.

"Who's asking to have drink there?" said Mackenzie.

"You're not asking now, but maybe you will. I won't
have it, that's all."

"That shall be all right, John", said Mrs. Grimes, nodding
her head.

"Women are that soft—in the way of judgment—that

they'll go and do a'most anything, good or bad when they've got their feelings up." Such was the only rebuke which in our hearing Mr. Grimes administered to his pretty wife. Mackenzie whispered something to the publican, but Grimes only shook his head. We understood it all thoroughly. He did not like the scheme, but he would not contradict his wife in an act of real kindness. We then made an appointment with the scholar for meeting our friend and his future patron at our rooms, and took our leave of the Spotted Dog. Before we went, however, Mrs. Grimes insisted on producing some cherry-bounce, as she called it, which after sundry refusals on our part, was brought in on a small round shining tray, in a little bottle covered all over with gold sprigs, with four tiny glasses similarly ornamented. Mrs. Grimes poured out the liquor, using a very sparing hand when she came to the glass which was intended for herself. We find it, as a rule, easier to talk with the Grimeses of the world than to eat with them or to drink with them. When the glass was handed to us we did not know whether or no we were expected to say something. We waited, however, till Mr. Grimes and Mackenzie had been provided with their glasses. "Proud to see you at the Spotted Dog, Mr. —," said Grimes. "That we are", said Mrs. Grimes, smiling at us over her almost imperceptible drop of drink. Julius Mackenzie just bobbed his head, and swallowed the cordial at a gulp—as a dog does a lump of meat, leaving the impression on his friends around him that he has not got from it half the enjoyment which it might have given him had he been a little more patient in the process. I could not but think that had Mackenzie allowed the cherry-bounce to trickle a little in his palate, as I did, myself, it would have gratified him more than it did in being chucked down his throat with all the impetus which his elbow could give to the glass. "That's tidy tipple", said Mr. Grimes, winking his eye. We acknowledged that it was tidy. "My mother made it, as used to keep the Pig and Magpie, at Colchester", said Mrs. Grimes. In this way we learned a good deal of Mrs. Grimes' history. Her very earliest years had been passed among wild Indians.

Then came the interview between the Doctor and Mr. Mackenzie. We must confess that we greatly feared the impression which our younger friend might make on the elder. We had of course told the Doctor of the red nose, and he had accepted the information with a smile. But he was a man who would feel the contamination of contact with a drunkard, and who would shrink from an unpleasant association. There are vices of which we habitually take altogether different views in accordance with the manner in which they are brought under our notice. This vice of drunkenness is often a joke in the mouths of those to whom the thing itself is a horror. Even before our boys we talk of it as being rather funny, though to see one of them funny himself would almost break our hearts. The learned commentator had accepted our account of the red nose as though it were simply a part of the undeserved misery of the wretched man; but should he find the wretched man to be actually redolent of gin his feelings might be changed. The Doctor was with us first, and the volumes of the MS. were displayed upon the table. The compiler of them, as he lifted here a page and there a page, handled them with the gentleness of a lover. They had been exquisitely arranged, and were very fair. The pagings, and the margins, and the chapterings, and all the complementary paraphernalia of authorship, were perfect. "A lifetime, my friend; just a lifetime!" the Doctor had said to us, speaking of his own work while we were waiting for the man to whose hands was to be entrusted the result of so much labour and scholarship. We wished at that moment that we had never been called on to interfere in the matter.

Mackenzie came, and the introduction was made. The Doctor was a gentleman of the old school, very neat in his attire—dressed in perfect black, with knee-breeches and black gaiters, with a closely-shorn chin, and an exquisitely white cravat. Though he was in truth simply the rector of his parish, his parish was one which entitled him to call himself a dean, and he wore a clerical rosette on his hat. He was a well-made, tall, portly gentleman, with whom to take the slightest liberty would have been impossible. His well-formed full face was singularly expressive of benevolence, but there was in it too an air of command which created an involuntary respect. He was a man whose means were ample, and who could afford to keep two curates, so that the appanages of a Church dignitary did in some sort belong to him. We doubt whether he really understood what work meant—even when he spoke with so much pathos of the labour of his life; but he was a man not at all exacting in regard to the work of others, and who was anxious to make the world as smooth and rosy to those around him as it had been to himself. He came forward, paused a moment, and then shook hands with Mackenzie. Our work had been done, and we remained in the background during the interview. It was now for the Doctor to satisfy himself with the scholarship—and, if he chose to take cognizance of the matter, with the morals of his proposed assistant.

Mackenzie himself was more subdued in his manner than he had been when talking with ourselves. The Doctor made a little speech, standing at the table with one hand on one volume and the other on another. He told of all his work, with a mixture of modesty as to the thing done, and self-assertion as to his interest in doing it, which was charming. He acknowledged that the sum proposed for the aid which he required was inconsiderable—but it had been fixed by the proposed publisher. Should Mr. Mackenzie find that the labour was long he would willingly increase it. Then he commenced a conversation respecting the Greek dramatists, which had none of the air or tone of an examination, but which still served the purpose of enabling Mackenzie to show his scholarship. In that respect there was no doubt that the ragged, red-nosed, disreputable man, who stood there longing for his job, was the greater proficient of the two. We never discovered that he had had access to books in later years;

but his memory of the old things seemed to be perfect. When it was suggested that references would be required, it seemed that he did know his way into the library of the British Museum. "When I wasn't quite so shabby", he said boldly, "I used to be there." The Doctor instantly produced a ten-pound note, and insisted that it should be taken in advance. Mackenzie hesitated, and we suggested that it was premature; but the Doctor was firm. "If an old scholar mayn't assist one younger than himself", he said, "I don't know when one man may aid another. And this is no alms. It is simply a pledge for work to be done." Mackenzie took the money, muttering something of an assurance that as far as his ability went, the work should be done well. "It should certainly", he said, "be done diligently."

When money had passed, of course the thing was settled; but in truth the bank-note had been given, not from judgment in settling the matter, but from the generous impulse of the moment. There was, however, no receding. The Doctor expressed by no hint a doubt as to the safety of his manuscript. He was by far too fine a gentleman to give the man whom he employed pain in that direction. If there were risk, he would now run the risk. And so the thing was settled.

We did not, however, give the manuscript on that occasion into Mackenzie's hands, but took it down afterwards, locked in an old despatch box of our own, to the Spotted Dog, and left the box with the key of it in the hands of Mrs. Grimes. Again we went up into that lady's bedroom, and saw that the big table had been placed by the window for Mackenzie's accommodation. It so nearly filled the room, that, as we observed, John Grimes could not get round at all to his side of the bed. It was arranged that Mackenzie was to begin on the morrow.

PART II.—

THE RESULT

DURING THE NEXT MONTH WE SAW A GOOD deal of Mr. Julius Mackenzie, and made ourselves quite at home in Mrs. Grimes' bedroom. We went in and out of the Spotted Dog as if we had known that establishment all our lives, and spent many a quarter of an hour with the hostess in her little parlour, discussing the prospects of Mr. Mackenzie and his family. He had procured for himself decent, if not exactly new, garments out of the money so liberally provided by my learned friend the Doctor, and spent much of his time in the library of the British Museum. He certainly worked very hard, for he did not altogether abandon his old engagement. Before the end of the first month the index of the first volume, nearly completed, had been sent down for the inspection of the Doctor, and had been returned with ample eulogium and some little criticism. The criticisms Mackenzie answered by letter, with true scholarly spirit, and the Doctor was delighted. Nothing could be more pleasant to him than a correspondence, prolonged almost indefinitely, as to the respective merits of a τό or a τὸυ, or on the demand for a spondee or an iamb. When he found that the work was really in industrious hands, he ceased to be clamorous for early publication, and gave us to understand privately that Mr. Mackenzie was not to be limited to the sum named. The matter of remuneration was, indeed, left very much to ourselves, and Mackenzie had certainly found a most efficient friend in the author whose works had been confided to his hands.

All this was very pleasant, and Mackenzie throughout that month worked very hard. According to the statements made to me by Mrs. Grimes he took no more gin than what was necessary for a hard-working man. As to the exact quantity of that cordial which she imagined to be beneficial and needful, we made no close inquiry. He certainly kept himself in a condition for work, and so far all went on happily. Nevertheless

there was a terrible skeleton in the cupboard—or rather out
of the cupboard, for the skeleton could not be got to hide
itself. A certain portion of his prosperity reached the hands of
his wife, and she was behaving herself worse than ever.
The four children had been covered with decent garments
under Mrs. Grimes' care, and then Mrs. Mackenzie had
appeared at the Spotted Dog, loudly demanding a new outfit
for herself. She came not only once, but often, and Mr.
Grimes was beginning to protest that he saw too much of the
family. We had become very intimate with Mrs. Grimes,
and she did not hesitate to confide to us her fears lest "John
should cut up rough" before the thing was completed. "You
see", she said, "it is against the house, no doubt, that woman
coming nigh it." But still she was firm, and Mackenzie was
not disturbed in the possession of the bedroom. At last Mrs.
Mackenzie was provided with some articles of female attire—
and then, on the very next day, she and the four children were
again stripped almost naked. The wretched creature must have
steeped herself in gin to the shoulders, for in one day she
made a sweep of everything. She then came in a state of
furious intoxication to the Spotted Dog, and was removed
by the police under the express order of the landlord.

We can hardly say which was the most surprising to us,
the loyalty of Mrs. Grimes or the patience of John. During
that night, as we were told two days afterwards by his wife,
he stormed with passion. The papers she had locked up in
order that he should not get at them and destroy them.
He swore that everything should be cleared out on the following morning. But when the morning came he did not even
say a word to Mackenzie, as the wretched, downcast, broken-
hearted creature passed upstairs to his work. "You see I
knows him, and how to deal with him", said Mrs. Grimes,
speaking of her husband. "There ain't another like himself
nowheres—he's that good. A softer-hearteder man there ain't
in the public line. He can speak dreadful when his dander is
up, and can look—; oh, laws, he just can look at you! But

he could no more put his hands upon a woman, in the way of hurting—no more than be an archbishop." Where could be the man, thought we to ourselves as this was said to us, who could have put a hand—in the way of hurting—upon Mrs. Grimes?

On that occasion, to the best of our belief, the policeman contented himself with depositing Mrs. Mackenzie at her own lodgings. On the next day she was picked up drunk in the street, and carried away to the lock-up house. At the very moment in which the story was being told to us by Mrs. Grimes, Mackenzie had gone to the police office to pay the fine, and to bring his wife home. We asked with dismay and surprise why he should interfere to rescue her—why he did not leave her in custody as long as the police would keep her? "Who'd there be to look after the children?" asked Mrs. Grimes, as though she were offended at our suggestion. Then she went on to explain that in such a household as that of poor Mackenzie the wife is absolutely a necessity, even though she be an habitual drunkard. Intolerable as she was, her services were necessary to him. "A husband as drinks is bad", said Mrs. Grimes—with something, we thought, of an apologetic tone for the vice upon which her own prosperity was partly built—"but when a woman takes to it, it's the —— devil." We thought that she was right, as we pictured to ourselves that man of letters satisfying the magistrate's demand for his wife's misconduct, and taking the degraded, half-naked creature once more home to his children.

We saw him about twelve o'clock on that day, and he had then, too evidently, been endeavouring to support his misery by the free use of alcohol. We did not speak of it down in the parlour; but even Mrs. Grimes, we think, would have admitted that he had taken more than was good for him. He was sitting up in the bedroom with his head hanging upon his hand, with a swarm of our learned friend's papers spread on the table before him. Mrs. Grimes, when he entered the house, had gone upstairs to give them out to him; but he had made no attempt to settle himself to his work. "This kind of thing must come to an end", he said to us with a thick, husky voice. We muttered something to him as to the need there was that he should exert a manly courage in his troubles. "Manly!" he said. "Well, yes; manly. A man should be a man, of course. There are some things which a man can't bear. I've borne more than enough, and I'll have an end of it."

We shall never forget that scene. After a while he got up, and became almost violent. Talk of bearing! Who had borne half as much as he? There were things a man should not bear. As for manliness, he believed that the truly manly thing would be to put an end to the lives of his wife, his children, and himself at one swoop. Of course the judgment of a mealy-mouthed world would be against him, but what would that matter to him when he and they had vanished out of this miserable place into the infinite realms of nothingness? Was he fit to live, or were they? Was there any chance for his children but that of becoming thieves and prostitutes? And for that poor wretch of a woman, from out of whose bosom even her human instincts had been washed by gin—would not death to her be, indeed, a charity? There was but one drawback to all this. When he should have destroyed them, how would it be with him if he should afterwards fail to make sure work with his own life? In such case it was not hanging that he would fear, but the self-reproach that would come upon him in that he had succeeded in sending others out of their misery, but had flinched when his own turn had come. Though he was drunk when he said these horrid things, or so nearly drunk that he could not perfect the articulation of his words, still there was a marvellous eloquence with him.

When we attempted to answer, and told him of that canon which had been set against self-slaughter, he laughed us to scorn. There was something terrible to us in the audacity of the arguments which he used, when he asserted for himself the right to shuffle off from his shoulders a burden which they had not been made broad enough to bear. There was an intensity and a thorough hopelessness of suffering in his case, an openness of acknowledged degradation, which robbed us for the time of all that power which the respectable ones of the earth have over the disreputable. When we came upon him with our wise saws, our wisdom was shattered instantly, and flung back upon us in fragments. What promise could we dare to hold out to him that further patience would produce any result that could be beneficial? What further harm could any such doing on his part bring upon him? Did we think that were he brought out to stand at the gallows' foot with the knowledge that ten minutes would usher him into what folks called eternity, his sense of suffering would be as great as it had been when he conducted that woman out of court and along the streets to his home, amidst the jeering congratulations of his neighbours? "When you have fallen so low", said he, "that you can fall no lower, the ordinary trammels of the world cease to bind you." Though his words were knocked against each other with the dulled utterances of intoxication, his intellect was terribly clear, and his scorn for himself, and for the world that had so treated him, was irrepressible.

We must have been over an hour with him up there in the bedroom, and even then we did not leave him. As it was manifest that he could do no work on that day, we collected the papers together, and proposed that he should take a walk with us. He was patient as we shovelled together the Doctor's pages, and did not object to our suggestion. We found it necessary to call up Mrs. Grimes to assist us in putting away the *Opus magnum*, and were astonished to find how much she had come to know about the work. Added to the Doctor's manuscript there were now the pages of Mackenzie's indexes —and there were other pages of reference, for use in making future indexes—as to all of which Mrs. Grimes seemed to be quite at home. We have no doubt that she was familiar with the names of Greek tragedians, and could have pointed out to us in print the performances of the chorus. "A little fresh air'll

do you a deal of good, Mr. Mackenzie", she said to the unfortunate man—"only take a biscuit in your pocket." We
got him out into the street, but he angrily refused to take the
biscuit which she endeavoured to force into his hands.

That was a memorable walk. Turning from the end of
Liquorpond Street up Gray's Inn Lane towards Holborn,
we at once came upon the entrance into a miserable court.
"There", said he; "it is down there that I live. She is sleeping
it off now, and the children are hanging about her, wondering
whether mother has got money to have another go at it when
she rises. I'd take you down to see it all, only it'd sicken you."
We did not offer to go down the court, abstaining rather for
his sake than for our own. The look of the place was as of a
spot squalid, fever-stricken, and utterly degraded. And this
man who was our companion had been born and bred a
gentleman—had been nourished with that soft and gentle
care which comes of wealth and love combined—had received
the education which the country gives to her most favoured
sons, and had taken such advantage of that education as is
seldom taken by any of those favoured ones—and Cucumber
Court, with a drunken wife and four half-clothed, half-starved
children, was the condition to which he had brought himself!
The world knows nothing higher nor brighter than had been
his outset in life—nothing lower nor more debased than the
result. And yet he was one whose time and intellect had been
employed upon the pursuit of knowledge—who even up
to this day had high ideas of what should be a man's career—
who worked very hard and had always worked—who as far
as we knew had struck upon no rocks in the pursuit of mere
pleasure. It had all come to him from that idea of his youth
that it would be good for him "to take refuge from the
conventional thraldom of so-called gentlemen amidst the
liberty of the lower orders." His life, as he had himself owned,
had indeed been a mistake.

We passed on from the court, and crossing the road went
through the squares of Gray's Inn, down Chancery Lane,

through the little iron gate into Lincoln's Inn, round through
the old square—than which we know no place in London
more conducive to suicide; and the new square—which has
a gloom of its own, not so potent, and savouring only of
madness, till at last we found ourselves in the Temple Gardens.
I do not know why we had thus clung to the purlieus of the
Law, except it was that he was telling us how in his early days,
when he had been sent away from Cambridge—as on this
occasion he acknowledged to us, for an attempt to pull the
tutor's nose, in revenge for a supposed insult—he had intended
to push his fortunes as a barrister. He pointed up to a certain
window in a dark corner of that suicidal old court, and told
us that for one year he had there sat at the feet of a great
Gamaliel in Chancery, and had worked with all his energies.
Of course we asked him why he had left a prospect so alluring.
Though his answers to us were not quite explicit, we think
that he did not attempt to conceal the truth. He learned to
drink, and that Gamaliel took upon himself to rebuke the
failing, and by the end of that year he had quarrelled
irreconcilably with his family. There had been great wrath
at home when he was sent from Cambridge, greater wrath
when he expressed his opinion upon certain questions of
religious faith, and wrath to the final severance of all family
relations when he told the chosen Gamaliel that he should
get drunk as often as he pleased. After that he had "taken
refuge among the lower orders", and his life, such as it was,
had come of it.

In Fleet Street, as we came out of the Temple, we turned
into an eating-house and had some food. By this time the
exercise and the air had carried off the fumes of the liquor
which he had taken, and I knew that it would be well that he
should eat. We had a mutton chop and a hot potato and a
pint of beer each, and sat down to table for the first and last
time as mutual friends. It was odd to see how in his
converse with us on that day he seemed to possess a double
identity. Though the hopeless misery of his condition was

always present to him, was constantly on his tongue, yet he could talk about his own career and his own character as though they belonged to a third person. He could even laugh at the wretched mistake he had made in life, and speculate as to its consequences. For himself he was well aware that death was the only release that he could expect. We did not dare to tell him that if his wife should die, then things might be better with him. We could only suggest to him that work itself, if he would do honest work, would console him for many sufferings. "You don't know the filth of it", he said to us. Ah, dear; how well we remember the terrible word, and the gesture with which he pronounced it, and the gleam of his eyes as he said it! His manner to us on this occasion was completely changed, and we had a gratification in feeling that a sense had come back upon him of his old associations. "I remember this room so well", he said—"when I used to have friends and money." And, indeed, the room was one which has been made memorable by Genius. "I did not think ever to have found myself here again." We observed, however, that he could not eat the food that was placed before him. A morsel or two of the meat he swallowed, and struggled to eat the crust of his bread, but he could not make a clean plate of it, as we did—regretting that the nature of chops did not allow of ampler dimensions. His beer was quickly finished, and we suggested to him a second tankard. With a queer, half-abashed twinkle of the eye, he accepted our offer, and then the second pint disappeared also. We had our doubts on the subject, but at last decided against any further offer. Had he chosen to call for it he must have had a third; but he did not call for it. We left him at the door of the tavern, and he then promised that in spite of all that he had suffered and all that he had said he would make another effort to complete the Doctor's work. "Whether I go or stay", he said, "I'd like to earn the money that I've spent." There was something terrible in that idea of his going! Whither was he to go?

The Doctor heard nothing of the misfortune of these three

or four inauspicious days; and the work was again going on prosperously when he came up again to London at the end of the second month. He told us something of his banker, and something of his lawyer, and murmured a word or two as to a new curate whom he needed; but we knew that he had come up to London because he could not bear a longer absence from the great object of his affections. He could not endure to be thus parted from his manuscript, and was again childishly anxious that a portion of it should be in the printer's hands. "At sixty-five, sir", he said to us, "a man has no time to dally with his work." He had been dallying with his work all his life, and we sincerely believed that it would be well with him if he could be contented to dally with it to the end. If all that Mackenzie said of it was true, the Doctor's erudition was not equalled by his originality, or by his judgment. Of that question, however, we could take no cognizance. He was bent upon publishing, and as he was willing and able to pay for his whim and was his own master, nothing that we could do would keep him out of the printer's hands.

He was desirous of seeing Mackenzie, and was anxious even to see him once at his work. Of course he could meet his assistant in our editorial room, and all the papers could easily be brought backwards and forwards in the old despatch-box. But in the interest of all parties we hesitated as to taking our revered and reverend friend to the Spotted Dog. Though we had told him that his work was being done at a public-house, we thought that his mind had conceived the idea of some modest inn, and that he would be shocked at being introduced to a place which he would regard simply as a gin-shop. Mrs. Grimes, or if not Mrs. Grimes, then Mr. Grimes, might object to another visitor to their bedroom; and Mackenzie himself would be thrown out of gear by the appearance of those clerical gaiters upon the humble scene of his labours. We, therefore, gave him such reasons as were available for submitting, at any rate for the present, to having the papers brought up to him at our room. And we ourselves went down to the Spotted Dog to make an appointment with Mackenzie for the following day. We had last seen him about a week before, and then the task was progressing well. He had told us that another fortnight would finish it. We had inquired also of Mrs. Grimes about the man's wife. All she could tell us was that the woman had not again troubled them at the Spotted Dog. She expressed her belief, however, that the drunkard had been more than once in the hands of the police since the day on which Mackenzie had walked with us through the squares of the Inns of Court.

It was late when we reached the public-house on the occasion to which we now allude, and the evening was dark and rainy. It was then the end of January, and it might have been about six o'clock. We knew that we should not find Mackenzie at the public-house; but it was probable that Mrs. Grimes could send for him, or, at least, could make the appointment for us. We went into the little parlour, where she was seated with her husband, and we could immediately see, from the countenance of both of them, that something was amiss. We began by telling Mrs. Grimes that the Doctor had come to town. "Mackenzie ain't here, sir", said Mrs. Grimes, and we almost thought that the very tone of her voice was altered. We explained that we had not expected to find him at that hour, and asked if she could send for him. She only shook her head. Grimes was standing with his back to the fire and his hands in his trousers pockets. Up to this moment he had not spoken a word. We asked if the man was drunk. She again shook her head. Could she bid him to come to us to-morrow, and bring the box and the papers with him? Again she shook her head.

"I've told her that I won't have no more of it", said Grimes; "nor yet I won't. He was drunk this morning—as drunk as an owl."

"He was sober, John, as you are, when he came for the papers this afternoon at two o'clock." So the box and the papers had all been taken away!

"And she was here yesterday rampaging about the place, without as much clothes on as would cover her nakedness", said Mr. Grimes. "I won't have no more of it. I've done for that man what his own flesh and blood wouldn't do. I know that; and I won't have no more of it. Mary Anne, you'll have that table cleared out after breakfast to-morrow." When a man, to whom his wife is usually Polly, addresses her as Mary Anne, then it may be surmised that that man is in earnest. We knew that he was in earnest, and she knew it also.

"He wasn't drunk, John—no, nor yet in liquor, when he come and took away that box this afternoon." We understood this reiterated assertion. It was in some sort excusing to us her own breach of trust in having allowed the manuscript to be withdrawn from her own charge, or was assuring us that, at the worst, she had not been guilty of the impropriety of allowing the man to take it away when he was unfit to have it in his charge. As for blaming her, who could have thought of it? Had Mackenzie at any time chosen to pass downstairs with the box in his hands, it was not to be expected that she should stop him violently. And now that he had done so we could not blame her; but we felt that a great weight had fallen upon our own hearts. If evil should come to the manuscript would not the Doctor's wrath fall upon us with a crushing weight? Something must be done at once. And we suggested that it would be well that somebody should go round to Cucumber Court. "I'd go as soon as look", said Mrs. Grimes, "but he won't let me."

"You don't stir a foot out of this to-night—not that way", said Mr. Grimes.

"Who wants to stir?" said Mrs. Grimes.

We felt that there was something more to be told than we had yet heard, and a great fear fell upon us. The woman's manner to us was altered, and we were sure that this had come not from altered feelings on her part, but from circumstances which had frightened her. It was not her husband that she feared, but the truth of something that her husband had said to her. "If there is anything more to tell, for God's sake tell it", we said, addressing ourselves rather to the man than to the woman. Then Grimes did tell us his story. On the previous evening Mackenzie had received three or four sovereigns from Mrs. Grimes, being, of course, a portion of the Doctor's payments; and early on that morning all Liquorpond Street had been in a state of excitement with the drunken fury of Mackenzie's wife. She had found her way into the Spotted Dog, and was being actually extruded by the strength of Grimes himself—of Grimes, who had been brought down, half dressed, from his bedroom by the row— when Mackenzie himself, equally drunk, appeared upon the scene. "No, John—not equally drunk", said Mrs. Grimes. "Bother!" exclaimed her husband, going on with his story. The man had struggled to take the woman by the arm, and the two had fallen and rolled in the street together. "I was looking out of the window, and it was awful to see", said Mrs. Grimes. We felt that it was "awful to hear". A man— and such a man, rolling in the gutter with a drunken woman— himself drunk—and that woman his wife! "There ain't to be no more of it at the Spotted Dog; that's all", said John Grimes, as he finished his part of the story.

Then, at last, Mrs. Grimes became voluble. All this had occurred before nine in the morning. "The woman must have been at it all night", she said. "So must the man", said John. "Anyways he came back about dinner, and he was sober then. I asked him not to go up, and offered to make him a cup of tea. It was just as you'd gone out after dinner, John."

"He won't have no more tea here", said John.

"And he didn't have any then. He wouldn't, he said, have any tea, but went upstairs. What was I to do? I couldn't tell him as he shouldn't. Well—during the row in the morning John had said something as to Mackenzie not coming about the premises any more."

"Of course I did", said Grimes.

"He was a little cut, then, no doubt", continued the lady;

"and I didn't think as he would have noticed what John had said."

"I mean it to be noticed now."

"He had noticed it then, sir, though he wasn't just as he should be at that hour of the morning. Well—what does he do? He goes upstairs and packs up all the papers at once. Leastways, that's as I suppose. They ain't there now. You can go and look if you please, sir. Well; when he came down, whether I was in the kitchen—though it isn't often as my eyes is off the bar, or in the tap-room, or busy drawing, which I do do sometimes, sir, when there are a many calling for liquor, I can't say—but if I ain't never to stand upright again, I didn't see him pass out with the box. But Miss Wilcox did. You can ask her." Miss Wilcox was the young lady in the bar, whom we did not think ourselves called upon to examine, feeling no doubt whatever as to the fact of the box having been taken away by Mackenzie. In all this Mrs. Grimes seemed to defend herself, as though some serious charge was to be brought against her; whereas all that she had done had been done out of pure charity; and in exercising her charity towards Mackenzie she had shown an almost exaggerated kindness towards ourselves.

"If there's anything wrong, it isn't your fault", we said.

"Nor yet mine", said John Grimes.

"No, indeed", we replied.

"It ain't none of our faults", continued he, "only this— you can't wash a blackamoor white, nor it ain't no use trying. He don't come here any more, that's all. A man in drink we don't mind. We has to put up with it. And they ain't that tarnation desperate as is a woman. As long as a man can keep his legs he'll try to steady hisself; but there is women who, when they've liquor, gets a fury for rampaging. There ain't a many as can beat this one, sir. She's that strong, it took four of us to hold her; though she can't hardly do a stroke of work, she's that weak when she's sober."

We had now heard the whole story, and, while hearing it,

had determined that it was our duty to go round into Cucumber Court and seek the manuscript and the box. We were unwilling to pry into the wretchedness of the man's home; but something was due to the Doctor; and we had to make that appointment for the morrow, if it were still possible that such an appointment should be kept. We asked for the number of the house, remembering well the entrance into the court. Then there was a whisper between John and his wife, and the husband offered to accompany us. "It's a roughish place", he said, "but they know me." "He'd better go along with you", said Mrs. Grimes. We, of course, were glad of such companionship, and glad also to find that the landlord, upon whom we had inflicted so much trouble, was still sufficiently our friend to take this trouble on our behalf.

"It's a dreary place enough", said Grimes, as he led us up the narrow archway. Indeed it was a dreary place. The court spread itself a little in breadth, but very little, when the passage was passed, and there were houses on each side of it. There was neither gutter nor, as far as we saw, drain, but the broken flags were slippery with moist mud, and here and there, strewed about between the houses, there were the remains of cabbages and turnip-tops. The place swarmed with children, over whom one ghastly gas-lamp at the end of the court threw a flickering and uncertain light. There was a clamour of scolding voices, to which it seemed that no heed was paid; and there was a smell of damp, rotting nastiness, amidst which it seemed to us to be almost impossible that life should be continued. Grimes led the way, without further speech, to the middle house on the left hand of the court, and asked a man who was sitting on the low threshold of the door whether Mackenzie was within. "So that be you, Muster Grimes; be it?" said the man, without stirring. "Yes; he's there I guess, but they've been and took her." Then we passed on into the house. "No matter about that", said the man, as we apologized for kicking him in our passage. He had not moved, and it had been impossible to enter without kicking him.

It seemed that Mackenzie held the two rooms on the ground floor, and we entered them at once. There was no light, but we could see the glimmer of a fire in the grate; and presently we became aware of the presence of children. Grimes asked after Mackenzie, and a girl's voice told us that he was in the inner room. The publican then demanded a light, and the girl, with some hesitation, lit the end of a farthing candle, which was fixed in a small bottle. We endeavoured to look round the room by the glimmer which this afforded, but could see nothing but the presence of four children, three of whom seemed to be seated in apathy on the floor. Grimes, taking the candle in his hand, passed at once into the other room, and we followed him. Holding the bottle something over his head, he contrived to throw a gleam of light upon one of the two beds with which the room was fitted, and there we saw the body of Julius Mackenzie stretched in the torpor of dead intoxication. His head lay against the wall, his body was across the bed, and his feet dangled on to the floor. He still wore his dirty boots, and his clothes as he had worn them in the morning. No sight so piteous, so wretched, and at the same time so eloquent had we ever seen before. His eyes were closed, and the light of his face was therefore quenched. His mouth was open, and the slaver had fallen upon his beard. His dark, clotted hair had been pulled over his face by the unconscious movement of his hands. There came from him a stertorous sound of breathing, as though he were being choked by the attitude in which he lay; and even in his drunkenness there was an uneasy twitching as of pain about his face. And there sat, and had been sitting for hours past, the four children in the other room, knowing the condition of the parent whom they most respected, but not even endeavouring to do anything for his comfort. What could they do? They knew, by long training and thorough experience, that a fit of drunkenness had to be got out of by sleep. To them there was nothing shocking in it. It was but a periodical misfortune. "She'll have to own he's been and done it now", said Grimes, looking down upon the man, and alluding to his wife's good-natured obstinacy. He handed the candle to us, and, with a mixture of tenderness and roughness, of which the roughness was only in the manner and the tenderness was real, he raised Mackenzie's head and placed it on the bolster, and lifted the man's legs on to the bed. Then he took off the man's boots and the old silk handkerchief from the neck, and pulled the trousers straight, and arranged the folds of the coat. It was almost as though he were laying out one that was dead. The eldest girl was now standing by us, and Grimes asked her how long her father had been in that condition. "Jack Hoggart brought him in just afore it was dark", said the girl. Then it was explained to us that Jack Hoggart was the man whom we had seen sitting on the door-step.

"And your mother?" asked Grimes.

"The perlice took her afore dinner."

"And you children—what have you had to eat?" In answer to this the girl only shook her head. Grimes took no immediate notice of this, but called the drunken man by his name, and shook his shoulder, and looked round to a broken ewer which stood on the little table, for water to dash upon him—but there was no water in the jug. He called again, and repeated the shaking, and at last Mackenzie opened his eyes, and in a dull, half-conscious manner looked up at us. "Come, my man", said Grimes, "shake this off and have done with it."

"Hadn't you better try to get up?" we asked.

There was a faint attempt at rising, then a smile—a smile which was terrible to witness, so sad was all which it said; then a look of utter, abject misery, coming, as we thought, from a momentary remembrance of his degradation; and after that he sank back in the dull, brutal, painless, death-like apathy of absolute unconsciousness.

"It'll be morning afore he'll move", said the girl.

"She's about right", said Grimes. "He's got it too heavy for us to do anything but just leave him. We'll take a look for the box and the papers."

And the man upon whom we were looking down had been born a gentleman, and was a finished scholar—one so well educated, so ripe in literary acquirement, that we knew few whom we could call his equal. Judging of the matter by the light of our reason, we cannot say that the horror of the scene should have been enhanced to us by these recollections. Had the man been a shoemaker or a coalheaver there would have been enough of tragedy in it to make an angel weep— that sight of the child standing by the bedside of her drunken father, while the other parent was away in custody—and in no degree shocked at what she saw, because the thing was so common to her! But the thought of what the man had been, of what he was, of what he might have been, and the steps by which he had brought himself to the foul degradation which we witnessed, filled us with a dismay which we should hardly have felt had the gifts which he had polluted and the intellect which he had wasted been less capable of noble uses.

Our purpose in coming to the court was to rescue the Doctor's papers from danger, and we turned to accompany Grimes into the other room. As we did so the publican asked the girl if she knew anything of a black box which her father had taken away from the Spotted Dog. "The box is here", said the girl.

"And the papers?" asked Grimes. Thereupon the girl shook her head, and we both hurried into the outer room. I hardly know who first discovered the sight which we encountered, or whether it was shown to us by the child. The whole fire-place was strewn with half-burnt sheets of manuscript. There were scraps of pages of which almost the whole had been destroyed, others which were hardly more than scorched, and heaps of paper-ashes all lying tumbled together about the fender. We went down on our knees to examine them, thinking at the moment that the poor creature might in his despair have burned his own work and have spared that of the Doctor. But it was not so. We found scores of charred pages of the Doctor's elaborate handwriting.

By this time Grimes had found the open box, and we perceived that the sheets remaining in it were tumbled and huddled together in absolute confusion. There were pages of the various volumes mixed with those which Mackenzie himself had written, and they were all crushed, and rolled, and twisted, as though they had been thrust thither as waste-paper—out of the way. "'Twas mother as done it", said the girl, "and we put 'em back again when the perlice took her."

There was nothing more to learn—nothing more by the hearing which any useful clue could be obtained. What had been the exact course of the scenes which had been enacted there that morning it little booted us to inquire. It was enough and more than enough that we knew that the mischief had been done. We went down on our knees before the fire, and rescued from the ashes with our hands every fragment of manuscript that we could find. Then we put the mass all together into the box, and gazed upon the wretched remnants almost in tears. "You'd better go and get a bit of some'at to eat", said Grimes, handing a coin to the elder girl. "It's hard on them to starve 'cause their father's drunk, sir." Then he took the closed box in his hand, and we followed him out into the street. "I'll send or step up and look after him to-morrow", said Grimes, as he put us and the box into a cab. We little thought, when we made to the drunkard that foolish request to arise, that we should never speak to him again.

As we returned to our office in the cab that we might deposit the box there ready for the following day, our mind was chiefly occupied in thinking over the undeserved grievances which had fallen upon ourselves. We had been moved by the charitable desire to do services to two different persons—to the learned Doctor and to the red-nosed drunkard, and this had come of it! There had been nothing for us to gain by assisting either the one or the other. We had taken infinite trouble, attempting to bring together two men who wanted each other's services—working hard in sheer benevolence—and what had been the result? We had spent half an hour on

our knees in the undignified and almost disreputable work of
raking among Mrs. Mackenzie's cinders, and now we had to
face the anger, the dismay, the reproach, and—worse than all—
the agony of the Doctor. As to Mackenzie—we asserted to
ourselves again and again that nothing further could be done
for him. He had made his bed, and he must lie upon it;
but, oh! why—why had we attempted to meddle with a being
so degraded? We got out of the cab at our office door, thinking of the Doctor's countenance as we should see it on the
morrow. Our heart sank within us, and we asked ourselves,
if it was so bad with us now, how it would be with us when
we returned to the place on the following morning.

But on the following morning we did return. No doubt
each individual reader to whom we address ourselves has at
some period felt that indescribable load of personal, short-lived
care, which causes the heart to sink down into the boots. It
is not great grief that does it—nor is it excessive fear; but the
unpleasant operation comes from the mixture of the two. It
is the anticipation of some imperfectly-understood evil that
does it—some evil out of which there might perhaps be an
escape if we could only see the way. In this case we saw no
way out of it. The Doctor was to be with us at one o'clock,
and he would come with smiles, expecting to meet his learned
colleague. How should we break it to the Doctor? We might
indeed send to him, putting off the meeting, but the advantage
coming from that would be slight, if any. We must see the
injured Grecian sooner or later; and we had resolved, much
as we feared, that the evil hour should not be postponed.
We spent an hour that morning in arranging the fragments.
Of the first volume about a third had been destroyed. Of
the second nearly every page had been either burned or
mutilated. Of the third but little had been injured. Mackenzie's
own work had fared better than the Doctor's; but there was
no comfort in that. After what had passed I thought it quite
improbable that the Doctor would make any use of Mackenzie's
work. So much of the manuscript as could still be placed in

continuous pages, we laid out upon the table, volume by volume—that in the middle sinking down from its original goodly bulk almost to the dimensions of a poor sermon—and the half-burned bits we left in the box. Then we sat ourselves down at our accustomed table, and pretended to try to work. Our ears were very sharp, and we heard the Doctor's step upon our stairs within a minute or two of the appointed time. Our heart went to the very toes of our boots. We shuffled in our chair, rose from it, and sat down again—and were conscious that we were not equal to the occasion. Hitherto we had, after some mild literary form, patronized the Doctor —as a man of letters in town will patronize his literary friend from the country—but we now feared him as a truant school-boy fears his master. And yet it was so necessary that we should wear some air of self-assurance!

In a moment he was with us, wearing that bland smile which we knew so well, and which at the present moment almost overpowered us. We had been sure that he would wear that smile, and had especially feared it. "Ah", said he, grasping us by the hand, "I thought I should have been late. I see that our friend is not here yet."

"Doctor", we replied, "a great misfortune has happened."

"A great misfortune! Mr. Mackenzie is not dead?"

"No—he is not dead. Perhaps it would have been better that he had died long since. He has destroyed your manuscript." The Doctor's face fell, and his hands at the same time, and he stood looking at us. "I need not tell you, Doctor, what my feelings are, and how great my remorse."

"Destroyed it!" Then we took him by the hand and led him to the table. He turned first upon the appetizing and comparatively uninjured third volume, and seemed to think that we had hoaxed him. "This is not destroyed", he said, with a smile. But before I could explain anything, his hands were among the fragments in the box. "As I am a living man, they have burned it!" he exclaimed. "I—I—I—" Then he turned from us, and walked twice the length of the room, backwards and forwards, while we stood still, patiently waiting the explosion of his wrath. "My friend", he said, when his walk was over, " a great man underwent the same sorrow. Newton's manuscript was burned. I will take it home with me, and we will say no more about it." I never thought very much of the Doctor as a divine, but I hold him to have been as good a Christian as I ever met.

But that plan of his of saying no more about it could not quite be carried out. I was endeavouring to explain to him, as I thought it necessary to do, the circumstances of the case, and he was protesting his indifference to any such details, when there came a knock at the door, and the boy who waited on us below ushered Mrs. Grimes into the room. As the reader is aware, we had, during the last two months, become very intimate with the landlady of the Spotted Dog, but we had never hitherto had the pleasure of seeing her outside her own house. "Oh, Mr.——" she began, and then she paused, seeing the Doctor.

We thought it expedient that there should be some introduction. "Mrs. Grimes", we said, "this is the gentleman whose invaluable manuscript has been destroyed by that unfortunate drunkard."

"Oh, then—you're the Doctor, sir?" The Doctor bowed and smiled. His heart must have been very heavy, but he bowed politely and smiled sweetly. "Oh, dear", said she, "I don't know how to tell you!"

"To tell us what?" asked the Doctor.

"What has happened since?" we demanded. The woman stood shaking before us, and then sank into a chair. Then arose to us at the moment some idea that the drunken woman, in her mad rage, had done some great damage to the Spotted Dog —had set fire to the house, or injured Mr. Grimes personally, or perhaps run amuck amidst the jugs and pitchers, window glass, and gas lights. Something had been done which would give the Grimeses a pecuniary claim on me or on the Doctor, and the woman had been sent hither to make the first protest.

Oh—when should I see the last of the results of my imprudence
in having attempted to befriend such a one as Julius Mackenzie!
"If you have anything to tell you had better tell it", we said,
gravely.

"He's been, and——"

"Not destroyed himself?" asked the Doctor.

"Oh yes, sir. He have indeed—from ear to ear—and is now
a lying at the Spotted Dog!"

And so, after all, that was the end of Julius Mackenzie!
We need hardly say that our feelings, which up to that moment
had been very hostile to the man, underwent a sudden revul-
sion. Poor, overburdened, struggling, ill-used, abandoned
creature! The world had been hard upon him, with a severity
which almost induced one to make complaint against Omni-
potence. The poor wretch had been willing to work, had been
industrious in his calling, had had capacity for work; and he
had also struggled gallantly against his evil fate, had recognized
and endeavoured to perform his duty to his children and to
the miserable woman who had brought him to his ruin! And
that sin of drunkenness had seemed to us to be in him rather
the reflex of her vice than the result of his own vicious
tendencies. Still it might be doubtful whether she had not
learned the vice from him. They had both in truth been
drunkards as long as they had been known in the neighbourhood of the Spotted Dog; but it was stated by all who had
known them there that he was never seen to be drunk unless
when she had disgraced him by the public exposure of her
own abomination. Such as he was he had now come to his end!
This was the upshot of his loud claims for liberty from his
youth upwards—liberty as against his father and family;
liberty as against his college tutor; liberty as against all pastors,
masters, and instructors; liberty as against the conventional
thraldom of the world! He was now lying a wretched corpse
at the Spotted Dog, with his throat cut from ear to ear, till

the coroner's jury should have decided whether or not they
would call him a suicide!

Mrs. Grimes had come to tell us that the coroner was to be
at the Spotted Dog at four o'clock, and to say that her husband
hoped that we would be present. We had seen Mackenzie so
lately, and had so much to do with the employment of the
last days of his life, that we could not refuse this request,
though it came accompanied by no legal summons. Then
Mrs. Grimes again became voluble, and poured out to us her
biography of Mackenzie as far as she knew it. He had been
married to the woman ten years, and certainly had been a
drunkard before he married her. "As for her, she'd been well-
nigh suckled on gin", said Mrs. Grimes, "though he didn't
know it, poor fellow". Whether this was true or not, she
had certainly taken to drink soon after her marriage, and
then his life had been passed in alternate fits of despondency
and desperate efforts to improve his own condition and that
of his children. Mrs. Grimes declared to us that when the
fit came on them—when the woman had begun and the man
had followed—they would expend upon drink in two days
what would have kept the family for a fortnight. "They say
as how it was nothing for them to swallow forty shillings'
worth of gin in forty-eight hours." The Doctor held up his
hands in horror. "And it didn't, none of it, come our way",
said Mrs. Grimes. "Indeed, John wouldn't let us serve it
for 'em."

She sat there for half an hour, and during the whole time
she was telling us of the man's life; but the reader will already
have heard more than enough of it. By what immediate demon
the woman had been instigated to burn the husband's work
almost immediately on its production within her own home,
we never heard. Doubtless there had been some terrible scene
in which the man's sufferings must have been carried almost
beyond endurance. "And he had feelings, sir, he had", said
Mrs. Grimes, "he knew as a woman should be decent, and a
man's wife especial; I'm sure we pitied him so, John and I,

that we could have cried over him. John would say a hard
word to him at times, but he'd have walked round London
to do him a good turn. John ain't to say edicated hisself, but
he do respect learning."

When she had told us all, Mrs. Grimes went, and we were
left alone with the Doctor. He at once consented to accompany us to the Spotted Dog, and we spent the hour that still
remained to us in discussing the fate of the unfortunate man.
We doubt whether an allusion was made during the time to
the burned manuscript. If so, it was certainly not made by
the Doctor himself. The tragedy which had occurred in
connection with it had made him feel it to be unfitting even
to mention his own loss. That such a one should have gone
to his account in such a manner, without hope, without belief,
and without fear—as Burley said to Bothwell, and Bothwell
boasted to Burley—that was the theme of the Doctor's
discourse. "The mercy of God is infinite", he said, bowing his
head, with closed eyes and folded hands. To threaten while
the life is in the man is human. To believe in the execution
of those threats when the life has passed away is almost beyond
the power of humanity.

At the hour fixed we were at the Spotted Dog, and found
there a crowd assembled. The coroner was already seated in
Mrs. Grimes' little parlour, and the body as we were told had
been laid out in the tap-room. The inquest was soon over.
The fact that he had destroyed himself in the low state of
physical suffering and mental despondency which followed his
intoxication was not doubted. At the very time that he was
doing it, his wife was being taken from the lock-up house
to the police office in the police van. He was not penniless,
for he had sent the children out with money for their break-
fasts, giving special caution as to the youngest, a little toddling
thing of three years old—and then he had done it. The eldest
girl, returning to the house, had found him lying dead upon
the floor. We were called upon for our evidence, and went
into the tap-room accompanied by the Doctor. Alas! the

very table which had been dragged upstairs into the landlady's bedroom with the charitable object of assisting Mackenzie in his work—the table at which we had sat with him conning the Doctor's pages—had now been dragged down again and was used for another purpose. We had little to say as to the matter, except that we had known the man to be industrious and capable, and that we had, alas! seen him utterly prostrated by drink on the evening before his death.

The saddest sight of all on this occasion was the appearance of Mackenzie's wife—whom we had never before seen. She had been brought there by a policeman, but whether she was still in custody we did not know. She had been dressed, either by the decency of the police or by the care of her neighbours, in an old black gown, which was a world too large and too long for her. And on her head there was a black bonnet which nearly enveloped her. She was a small woman, and, as far as we could judge from the glance we got of her face, pale, and worn, and wan. She had not such outward marks of a drunkard's career as those which poor Mackenzie always carried with him. She was taken up to the coroner, and what answers she gave to him were spoken in so low a voice that they did not reach us. The policeman, with whom we spoke, told us that she did not feel it much—that she was callous now and beyond the power of mental suffering. "She's frightened just this minute, sir; but it isn't more than that", said the policeman. We gave one glance along the table at the burden which it bore, but we saw nothing beyond the outward lines of that which had so lately been the figure of a man. We should have liked to see the countenance once more. The morbid curiosity to see such horrid sights is strong with most of us. But we did not wish to be thought to wish to see it— especially by our friend the Doctor—and we abstained from pushing our way to the head of the table. The Doctor himself remained quiescent in the corner of the room the farthest from the spectacle. When the matter was submitted to them, the jury lost not a moment in declaring their verdict. They said that the man had destroyed himself while suffering under temporary insanity produced by intoxication. And that was the end of Julius Mackenzie, the scholar.

On the following day the Doctor returned to the country, taking with him our black box, to the continued use of which, as a sarcophagus, he had been made very welcome. For our share in bringing upon him the great catastrophe of his life, he never uttered to us, either by spoken or written word, a single reproach. That idea of suffering as the great philosopher had suffered seemed to comfort him. "If Newton bore it, surely I can", he said to us with his bland smile, when we renewed the expression of our regret. Something passed between us, coming more from us than from him, as to the expediency of finding out some youthful scholar who could go down to the rectory, and reconstruct from its ruins the edifice of our friend's learning. The Doctor had given us some encouragement, and we had begun to make inquiry, when we received the following letter:

" —— Rectory, —— ——, 18—.

"DEAR MR. ——,—You were so kind as to say that you would endeavour to find for me an assistant in arranging and reconstructing the fragments of my work on The Metres of the Greek Dramatists. Your promise has been an additional kindness." Dear, courteous, kind old gentleman! For we knew well that no slightest sting of sarcasm was intended to be conveyed in these words. "Your promise has been an additional kindness; but looking upon the matter carefully, and giving to it the best consideration in my power, I have determined to relinquish the design. That which has been destroyed cannot be replaced; and it may well be that it was not worth replacing. I am old now, and never could do again that which perhaps I was never fitted to do with any fair prospect of success. I will never turn again to the ashes of my unborn child; but will console myself with the memory of my grievance, knowing well, as I do so, that consolation from the severity of harsh but just criticism might have been more difficult to find. When I think of the end of my efforts as a scholar, my mind reverts to the terrible and fatal catastrophe of one whose scholarship was infinitely more finished and more ripe than mine.

"When ever it may suit you to come into this part of the country, pray remember that it will give very great pleasure to myself and to my daughter to welcome you at our parsonage.

"Believe me to be,
"My dear Mr. ——,
"Yours very sincerely,
"—— ——."

We never have found the time to accept the Doctor's invitation, and our eyes have never again rested on the black box containing the ashes of the unborn child to which the Doctor will never turn again. We can picture him to ourselves standing, full of thought, with his hand upon the lid, but never venturing to turn the lock. Indeed, we do not doubt but that the key of the box is put away among other secret treasures, a lock of his wife's hair, perhaps, and the little shoe of the boy who did not live long enough to stand at his father's knee. For a tender, soft-hearted man was the Doctor, and one who fed much on the memories of the past.

We often called upon Mr. and Mrs. Grimes at the Spotted Dog, and would sit there talking of Mackenzie and his family. Mackenzie's widow soon vanished out of the neighbourhood, and no one there knew what was the fate of her or of her children. And then also Mr. Grimes went and took his wife with him. But they could not be said to vanish. Scratching his head one day, he told me with a dolorous voice that he had—made his fortune. "We've got as snug a little place as ever you see, just two miles out of Colchester", said Mrs. Grimes triumphantly—"with thirty acres of land just to amuse John. And as for the Spotted Dog, I'm that sick of it, another

year'd wear me to a dry bone." We looked at her, and saw
no tendency that way. And we looked at John, and thought
that he was not triumphant.

Who followed Mr. and Mrs. Grimes at the Spotted Dog
we have never visited Liquorpond Street to see.

ALICE DUGDALE

ALICE DUGDALE

Chapter I.—The Doctor's Family

IT USED TO BE SAID IN THE VILLAGE OF BEETHAM that nothing ever went wrong with Alice Dugdale—the meaning of which, perhaps, lay in the fact that she was determined that things should be made to go right. Things as they came were received by her with a gracious welcome, and "things", whatever they were, seemed to be so well pleased with the treatment afforded to them, that they too for the most part made themselves gracious in return.

Nevertheless she had had sorrows, as who has not? But she had kept her tears for herself, and had shown her smiles for the comfort of those around her. In this little story it shall be told how in a certain period of her life she had suffered much—how she still smiled, and how at last she got the better of her sorrow.

Her father was the country doctor in the populous and straggling parish of Beetham. Beetham is one of those places so often found in the south of England, half village, half town, for the existence of which there seems to be no special reason.

It had no mayor, no municipality, no market, no pavements, and no gas. It was therefore no more than a village—but it had a doctor, and Alice's father, Dr. Dugdale, was the man. He had been established at Beetham for more than thirty years, and knew every pulse and every tongue for ten miles round. I do not know that he was very great as a doctor—but he was a kind-hearted, liberal man, and he enjoyed the confidence of the Beethamites, which is everything. For thirty years he had worked hard and had brought up a large family without want. He was still working hard, though turned sixty, at the time of which we are speaking. He had even in his old age many children dependent on him, and though he had fairly prospered, he had not become a rich man.

He had been married twice, and Alice was the only child left at home by his first wife. Two elder sisters were married, and an elder brother was away in the world. Alice had been much younger than they, and had been the only child living with him when he had brought to his house a second mother for her. She was then fifteen. Eight or nine years had since gone, and almost every year had brought an increase to the doctor's family. There were now seven little Dugdales in and about the nursery; and what the seven would do when Alice should go away the folk of Beetham always declared that they were quite at a loss even to guess. For Mrs. Dugdale was one of those women who succumb to difficulties—who seem originally to have been made of soft material and to have become warped, out of joint, tattered, and almost useless under the wear of the world. But Alice had been constructed of thoroughly seasoned timber, so that, let her be knocked about as she might, she was never out of repair. Now the doctor, excellent as he was at doctoring, was not very good at household matters—so that the folk at Beetham had reason to be at a loss when they bethought themselves as to what would happen when Alice should "go away".

Of course there is always that prospect of a girl's "going away". Girls not unfrequently intend to go away. Sometimes they "go away" very suddenly, without any previous intention. At any rate such a girl as Alice cannot be regarded as a fixture in a house. Binding as may be her duties at home, it is quite understood that should any adequate provocation to "go away" be brought within her reach, she will go, let the duties be what they may. Alice was a thoroughly good girl—good to her father, good to her little brothers and sisters, unutterably good to that poor foolish stepmother—but, no doubt, she would "go away" if duly asked.

When that vista of future discomfort in the doctor's house first made itself clearly apparent to the Beethamites, an idea that Alice might perhaps go very soon had begun to prevail in the village. The eldest son of the vicar, Parson Rossiter, had come back from India as Major Rossiter, with an appointment, as some said, of £2,000 a year—let us put it down as £1,500 —and had renewed his acquaintance with his old playfellow. Others, more than one or two, had endeavoured before this to entice Alice to "go away", but it was said that the dark-visaged warrior, with his swarthy face and black beard, and bright eyes—probably, too, something in him nobler than those outward bearings—had whispered words which had prevailed. It was supposed that Alice now had a fitting lover, and that therefore she would "go away".

There was no doubt in the mind of any single inhabitant of Beetham as to the quality of the lover. It was considered on all sides that he was fitting—so fitting that Alice would of course go when asked. John Rossiter was such a man that every Beethamite looked upon him as a hero—so that Beetham was proud to have produced him. In small communities a man will come up now and then as to whom it is surmised that any young lady would of course accept him. This man, who was now about ten years older than Alice, had everything to recommend him. He was made up of all good gifts of beauty, conduct, dignity, good heart—and fifteen hundred a year at the very least. His official duties required him to live in London, from which Beetham was seventy miles distant; but those duties allowed him ample time for visiting the parsonage. So very fitting he was to take any girl away upon whom he might fix an eye of approbation, that there were others, higher than Alice in the world's standing, who were said to grudge the young lady of the village so great a prize. For Alice Dugdale was a young lady of the village and no more; whereas there were county families around, with daughters, among whom the Rossiters had been in the habit of mixing. Now that such a Rossiter had come to the fore, the parsonage family was held to be almost equal to county people.

To whatever extent Alice's love affairs had gone, she herself had been very silent about them; nor had her lover as yet taken the final step of being closeted for ten minutes with her father. Nevertheless everybody had been convinced in Beetham that it would be so—unless it might be Mrs. Rossiter. Mrs. Rossiter was ambitious for her son, and in this matter sympathized with the county people. The county people certainly were of opinion that John Rossiter might do better, and did not altogether see what there was in Alice Dugdale to make such a fuss about. Of course she had a sweet countenance, rather brown, with good eyes. She had not, they said, another feature in her face which could be called handsome. Her nose was broad. Her mouth was large. They did not like that perpetual dimpling of the cheek which, if natural, looked as if it were practised. She was stout, almost stumpy, they thought. No doubt she danced well, having a good ear and being active and healthy; but with such a waist no girl could really be graceful. They acknowledged her to be the best nursemaid that ever a mother had in her family; but they thought it a pity that she should be taken away from duties for which her presence was so much desired, at any rate by such a one as John Rossiter. I, who knew Beetham well, and who though turned the hill of middle life had still an eye for female charms, used to declare to myself that Alice, though she was decidedly village and not county, was far, far away the prettiest girl in that part of the world.

The old parson loved her, and so did Miss Rossiter—Miss Janet Rossiter—who was four or five years older than her brother, and therefore quite an old maid. But John was so great a man that neither of them dared to say much to encourage him—as neither did Mrs. Rossiter to use her eloquence on the other side. It was felt by all of them that any persuasion might have on John anything but the intended effect. When a man at the age of thirty-three is Deputy Assistant Inspector-General of Cavalry, it is not easy to talk him this way or that in a matter of love. And John Rossiter, though the best fellow in the world, was apt to be taciturn on such a subject. Men frequently marry almost without thinking about it at all. "Well; perhaps I might as well. At any rate I cannot very well help it." That too often is the frame of mind. Rossiter's discussion to himself was of a higher nature than that, but perhaps not quite what it should have been. "This is a thing of such moment that it requires to be pondered again and again. A man has to think of himself, and of her, and of the children which have to come after him—of the total good or total bad which may come of such a decision." As in the one manner there is too much of negligence, so in the other three there may be too much of care. The "perhaps I might as wells"—so good is Providence—are sometimes more successful than those careful, long-pondering heroes. The old parson was very sweet to Alice, believing that she would be his daughter-in-law, and so was Miss Rossiter, thoroughly approving of such a sister. But Mrs. Rossiter was a little cold—all of which Alice could read plainly and digest, without saying a word. If it was to be, she would welcome her happy lot with heartfelt acknowledgment of the happiness provided for her; but if it was not to be, no human being should know that she had sorrowed. There should be nothing lackadaisical in her life or conduct. She had her work to do, and she knew that as long as she did that, grief would not overpower her.

In her own house it was taken for granted that she was to "go", in a manner that distressed her. "You'll never be here to lengthen 'em", said her stepmother to her, almost whining, when there was a question as to flounces in certain juvenile petticoats which might require to be longer than they were first made before they should be finally abandoned.

"That I certainly shall if Tiny grows as she does now."

"I suppose he'll pop regularly when he next comes down", said Mrs. Dugdale.

There was ever so much in this which annoyed Alice. In the first place, the word "pop" was to her abominable. Then she was almost called upon to deny that he would "pop", when in her heart she thought it very probable that he might. And the word, she knew, had become intelligible to the eldest of her little sisters who was present. Moreover, she was most unwilling to discuss the subject at all, and could hardly leave it undiscussed when such direct questions were asked. "Mamma", she said, "don't let us think about anything of the kind." This did not at all satisfy herself. She ought to have repudiated the lover altogether; and yet she could not bring herself to tell the necessary lie.

"I suppose he will come—some day", said Minnie, the child old enough to understand the meaning of such coming.

> "For men may come and men may go,
> But I go on for ever—for ever",

said or sang Alice, with a pretence of drollery, as she turned herself to her little sister. But even in her little song there was a purpose. Let any man come or let any man go, she would go on, at any rate apparently untroubled, in her walk of life.

"Of course he'll take you away, and then what am I to do?" said Mrs. Dugdale moaning. It is sad enough for a girl thus to have her lover thrown in her face when she is by no means sure of her lover.

A day or two afterwards another word, much more painful, was said to her up at the parsonage. Into the parsonage she went frequently to show that there was nothing in her heart to prevent her visiting her old friends as had been her wont.

"John will be down here next week", said the parson, whom she met on the gravel drive just at the hall door.

"How often he comes! What do they do at the Horse Guards, or wherever it is that he goes to?"

"He'll be more steady when he has taken a wife", said the old man.

"In the meantime what becomes of the cavalry?"

"I dare say you'll know all about that before long", said the parson laughing.

"Now, my dear, how can you be so foolish as to fill the girl's head with nonsense of that kind?" said Mrs. Rossiter, who at that moment came out from the front door. "And you're doing John an injustice. You are making people believe that he has said that which he has not said."

Alice at the moment was very angry—as angry as she well could be. It was certain that Mrs. Rossiter did not know what her son had said or had not said. But it was cruel that she who had put forward no claim, who had never been forward in seeking her lover, should be thus almost publicly rebuked. Quiet as she wished to be, it was necessary that she should say one word in her own defence. "I don't think Mr. Rossiter's little joke will do John any injustice or me any harm", she said. "But, as it may be taken seriously, I hope he will not repeat it."

"He could not do better for himself. That's my opinion", said the old man, turning back into the house. There had been words before on the subject between him and his wife, and he was not well pleased with her at this moment.

"My dear Alice, I am sure you know that I mean everything the best for you", said Mrs. Rossiter.

"If nobody would mean anything, but just let me alone, that would be best. And as for nonsense, Mrs. Rossiter, don't you know of me that I'm not likely to be carried away by foolish ideas of that kind?"

"I do know that you are very good."

"Then why should you talk at me as though I were very bad?" Mrs. Rossiter felt that she had been reprimanded, and was less inclined than ever to accept Alice as a daughter-in-law.

Alice, as she walked home, was low in spirits, and angry with herself because it was so. People would be fools. Of course that was to be expected. She had known all along that Mrs. Rossiter wanted a grander wife for her son, whereas the parson was anxious to have her for his daughter-in-law. Of course she loved the parson better than his wife. But why was it that she felt at this moment that Mrs. Rossiter would prevail?

"Of course it will be so", she said to herself. "I see it now. And I suppose he is right. But then certainly he ought not to have come here. But perhaps he comes because he wishes to— see Miss Wanless." She went a little out of her road home, not only to dry a tear, but to rid herself of the effect of it, and then spent the remainder of the afternoon swinging her brothers and sisters in the garden.

CHAPTER II

MAJOR ROSSITER

"PERHAPS HE IS COMING HERE TO SEE MISS Wanless", Alice had said to herself. And in the course of that week she found that her surmise was correct. John Rossiter stayed only one night at the parsonage, and then went over to Brook Park where lived Sir Walter Wanless and all the Wanlesses. The parson had not so declared when he told Alice that his son was coming, but John himself said on his arrival that this was a special visit made to Brook Park, and not to Beetham. It had been promised for the last three months, though only fixed lately. He took the trouble to come across to the doctor's house with the express purpose of explaining the fact. "I suppose you have always been intimate with them", said Mrs. Dugdale, who was sitting with Alice and a little crowd of the children round them. There was a tone of sarcasm in the words not at all hidden. "We all know that you are a great deal finer than we mere village folk. We don't know the Wanlesses, but of course you do. You'll find yourself much more at home at Brook Park than you can in such a place as this." All that, though not spoken, was contained in the tone of the lady's speech.

"We have always been neighbours", said John Rossiter.

"Neighbours ten miles off!" said Mrs. Dugdale.

"I dare say the Good Samaritan lived thirty miles off", said Alice.

"I don't think distance has much to do with it", said the Major.

"I like my neighbours to be neighbourly. I like Beetham neighbours", said Mrs. Dugdale. There was a reproach in every word of it. Mrs. Dugdale had heard of Miss Georgiana Wanless, and Major Rossiter knew that she had done so. After her fashion the lady was accusing him for deserting Alice.

Alice understood it also, and yet it behoved her to hold herself well up and be cheerful. "I like Beetham people best myself", she said, "but then it is because I don't know any other. I remember going to Brook Park once, when there was a party of children, a hundred years ago, and I thought it quite a paradise. There was a profusion of strawberries by which my imagination has been troubled ever since. You'll just be in time for the strawberries, Major Rossiter." He had always been John till quite lately—John with the memories of childhood; but now he had become Major Rossiter.

She went out into the garden with him for a moment as he took his leave—not quite alone, as a little boy of two years old was clinging to her hand. "If I had my way", she said, "I'd have my neighbours everywhere—at any distance. I envy a man chiefly for that."

"Those one loves best should be very near, I think."

"Those one loves best of all? Oh, yes, so that one may do something. It wouldn't do not to have you every day, would it, Bobby?" Then she allowed the willing little urchin to struggle up into her arms and to kiss her, all smeared as was his face with bread and butter.

"Your mother meant to say that I was running away from my old friends."

"Of course she did. You see, you loom so very large to us here. You are—such a swell, as Dick says, that we are a little sore when you pass us by. Everybody likes to be bowed to by royalty. Don't you know that? Brook Park is, of course, the proper place for you; but you don't expect but what we are going to express our little disgusts and little prides when we find ourselves left behind!" No words could have less declared her own feelings on the matter than those she was uttering; but she found herself compelled to laugh at him, lest, in the other direction, something of tenderness might escape her, whereby he might be injured worse than by her raillery. In nothing that she might say could there be less of real reproach to him than in this.

"I hate that word 'swell'," he said.

"So do I."

"Then why do you use it?"

"To show you how much better Brook Park is than Beetham. I am sure they don't talk about swells at Brook Park."

"Why do you throw Brook Park in my teeth?"

"I feel an inclination to make myself disagreeable to-day. Are you never like that?"

"I hope not."

"And then I am bound to follow up what poor dear mamma began. But I won't throw Brook Park in your teeth. The ladies I know are very nice. Sir Walter Wanless is a little grand—isn't he?"

"You know", said he, "that I should be much happier here than there."

"Because Sir Walter is so grand?"

"Because my friends here are dearer friends. But still it is right that I should go. One cannot always be where one would be happiest."

"I am happiest with Bobby", said she; "and I can always have Bobby." Then she gave him her hand at the gate, and he went down to the parsonage.

That night Mrs. Rossiter was closeted for a while with her son before they both went to bed. She was supposed, in Beetham, to be of a higher order of intellect—of a higher stamp generally—than her husband or daughter, and to be in that respect nearly on a par with her son. She had not travelled as he had done, but she was of an ambitious mind and had thoughts beyond Beetham. The poor dear parson cared for little outside the bounds of his parish. "I am so glad you are going to stay for a while over at Brook Park", she said.

"Only for three days."

"In the intimacy of a house three days is a lifetime. Of course I do not like to interfere." When this was said the Major frowned, knowing well that his mother was going to interfere. "But I cannot help thinking how much a connection with the Wanlesses would do for you."

"I don't want anything from any connection."

"That is all very well, John, for a man to say; but in truth we all depend on connections one with another. You are beginning the world."

"I don't know about that, mother."

"To my eyes you are. Of course, you look upwards."

"I take all that as it comes."

"No doubt; but still you must have it in your mind to rise. A man is assisted very much by the kind of wife he marries. Much would be done for a son-in-law of Sir Walter Wanless."

"Nothing, I hope, ever for me on that score. To succeed by favour is odious."

"But even to rise by merit, so much outside assistance is often necessary! Though you will assuredly deserve all that you will

ever get, yet you may be more likely to get it as a son-in-law
to Sir Walter Wanless than if you were married to some
obscure girl. Men who make the most of themselves in the
world do think of these things. I am the last woman in the
world to recommend my boy to look after money in marriage."

"The Miss Wanlesses will have none."

"And therefore I can speak the more freely. They will have
very little—as coming from such a family. But he has great
influence. He has contested the county five times. And then—
where is there a handsomer girl than Georgiana Wanless?"
The Major thought that he knew one, but did not answer the
question. "And she is all that such a girl ought to be. Her
manners are perfect—and her conduct. A constant performance of domestic duties is of course admirable. If it çomes
to one to have to wash linen, she who washes her linen well is
a good woman. But among mean things high spirits are not
to be found."

"I am not so sure of that."

"It must be so. How can the employment of every hour in
the day on menial work leave time for the mind to fill itself?
Making children's frocks may be a duty, but it must also be an
impediment."

"You are speaking of Alice."

"Of course I am speaking of Alice."

"I would wager my head that she has read twice more in the
last two years than Georgiana Wanless. But, mother, I am
not disposed to discuss either the one young lady or the other.
I am not going to Brook Park to look for a wife; and if ever
I take one, it will be simply because I like her best, and not
because I wish to use her as a rung of a ladder by which to
climb upwards into the world." That all this and just this
would be said to her Mrs. Rossiter had been aware; but still
she had thought that a word in season might have its effect.

And it did have its effect. John Rossiter, as he was driven
over to Brook Park on the following morning, was uncon-
sciously mindful of that allusion to the washerwoman. He had

seen that Alice's cheek had been smirched by the greasy crumbs from her little brother's mouth, he had seen that the tips of her fingers showed the mark of the needle; he had seen fragments of thread about her dress, and the mud even from the children's boots on her skirts. He had seen this, and had been aware that Georgiana Wanless was free from all such soil on her outward raiment. He liked the perfect grace of unspotted feminine apparel, and he had, too, thought of the hours in which Alice might probably be employed amidst the multifarious needs of a nursery, and had argued to himself much as his mother had argued. It was good and homely—worthy of a thousand praises; but was it exactly that which he wanted in a wife? He had repudiated with scorn his mother's cold, worldly doctrine; but yet he had felt that it would be a pleasant thing to have it known in London that his wife was the daughter of Sir Walter Wanless. It was true that she was wonderfully handsome—a complexion perfectly clear, a nose cut as out of marble, a mouth delicate as of a goddess, with a waist quite to match it. Her shoulders were white as alabaster. Her dress was at all times perfect. Her fingers were without mark or stain. There might perhaps be a want of expression; but faces so symmetrical are seldom expressive. And then, to crown all this, he was justified in believing that she was attached to himself. Almost as much had been said to him by Lady Wanless herself—a word which would amount to as much, coupled as it was with an immediate invitation to Brook Park. Of this he had given no hint to any human being; but he had been at Brook Park once before, and some rumour of something between him and Miss Georgiana Wanless had reached the people at Beetham—had reached, as we have seen, not only Mrs. Rossiter, but also Alice Dugdale.

There had been moments up in London when his mind had veered round towards Miss Wanless. But there was one little trifle which opposed the action of his mind, and that was his heart. He had begun to think that it might be his duty to marry Georgiana—but the more he thought so the more

clearly would the figure of Alice stand before him, so that no
veil could be thrown over it. When he tried to summon to his
imagination the statuesque beauty of the one girl, the bright
eyes of the other would look at him, and the words from her
speaking mouth would be in his ears. He had once kissed
Alice, immediately on his return, in the presence of her father,
and the memory of the halcyon moment was always present
to him. When he thought most of Miss Wanless he did not
think much of her kisses. How grand she would be at his
dining-table, how glorious in his drawing-room! But with
Alice how sweet would it be to sit by some brook-side and
listen to the waters!

And now since he had been at Beetham, from the nature of
things which sometimes make events to come from exactly
contrary causes, a new charm had been added to Alice, simply
by the little effort she had made to annoy him. She had talked
to him of "swells", and had pretended to be jealous of the
Wanlesses, just because she had known that he would hate to
hear such a word from her lips, and that he would be vexed
by exhibition of such a feeling on her part! He was quite sure
that she had not committed these sins because they belonged
to her as a matter of course. Nothing could be more simple
than her natural language or her natural feelings. But she had
chosen to show him that she was ready to run into little faults
which might offend him. The reverse of her ideas came upon
him. She had said, as it were—"See how little anxious I
must be to dress myself in your mirror when I put myself in
the same category with my poor stepmother." Then he said to
himself that he could see her as he was fain to see her, in her
own mirror, and he loved her the better because she had dared
to run the risk of offending him.

As he was driven up to the house at Brook Park he knew
that it was his destiny to marry either the one girl or the other;
and he was afraid of himself—that before he left the house he
might be engaged to the one he did not love. There was a
moment in which he thought he would turn round and go

back. "Major Rossiter", Lady Wanless had said, "you know how glad we are to see you here. There is no young man of the day of whom Sir Walter thinks so much." Then he had thanked her. "But—may I say a word in warning?"

"Certainly."

"And I may trust to your honour?"

"I think so, Lady Wanless."

"Do not be much with that sweet darling of mine—unless indeed—" And then she had stopped. Major Rossiter, though he was a major and had served some years in India, blushed up to his eyebrows and was unable to answer a word. But he knew that Georgiana Wanless had been offered to him, and was entitled to believe that the young lady was prone to fall in love with him. Lady Wanless, had she been asked for an excuse for such conduct, would have said that the young men of the present day were slow in managing their own affairs, unless a little help were given to them.

When the Major was almost immediately invited to return to Brook Park, he could not but feel that, if he were so to make his choice, he would be received there as a son-in-law. It may be that unless he intended so to be received, he should not have gone. This he felt as he was driven across the park, and was almost minded to return to Beetham.

CHAPTER III

LADY WANLESS

SIR WALTER WANLESS WAS ONE OF THOSE GREAT men who never do anything great, but achieve their greatness partly by their tailors, partly by a breadth of eyebrow and carriage of the body—what we may call deportment—and partly by the outside gifts of fortune. Taking his career

altogether we must say that he had been unfortunate. He was
a baronet with a fine house and park—and with an income
hardly sufficient for the place. He had contested the county
four times on old Whig principles, and had once been in
Parliament for two years. There he had never opened his
mouth; but in his struggle to get there had greatly embarrassed
his finances. His tailor had been well chosen, and had always
turned him out as the best-dressed old baronet in England. His
eyebrow was all his own, and certainly commanded respect
from those with whom eyebrows are efficacious. He never
read; he eschewed farming, by which he had lost money in
early life; and had, so to say, no visible occupation at all. But
he was Sir Walter Wanless, and what with his tailor and what
with his eyebrow he did command a great deal of respect in
the country round Beetham. He had, too, certain good gifts
for which people were thankful as coming from so great a man.
He paid his bills, he went to church, he was well behaved, and
still maintained certain old-fashioned family charities, though
money was not plentiful with him.

He had two sons and five daughters. The sons were in the
army, and were beyond his control. The daughters were all at
home, and were altogether under the control of their mother.
Indeed everything at Brook Park was under the control of
Lady Wanless—though no man alive gave himself airs more
autocratic than Sir Walter. It was on her shoulders that fell
the burden of the five daughters, and of maintaining with
straitened means the hospitality of Brook Park on their behoof.
A hard-worked woman was Lady Wanless, in doing her duty
—with imperfect lights no doubt, but to the best of her abilities
with such lights as she possessed. She was somewhat fine in
her dress, not for any comfort that might accrue to herself, but
from a feeling that an alliance with the Wanlesses would not be
valued by the proper sort of young men unless she were grand
herself. The girls were beautifully dressed; but oh, with such
care and economy and daily labour among them, herself, and
the two ladies'-maids upstairs! The father, what with his

election and his farming, and a period of costly living early in
his life, had not done well for the family. That she knew, and
never rebuked him. But it was for her to set matters right,
which she could only do by getting husbands for the daughters.
That this might be achieved the Wanless prestige must be
maintained; and with crippled means it is so hard to maintain
a family prestige! A poor duke may do it, or perhaps an earl;
but a baronet is not high enough to give bad wines to his
guests without serious detriment to his unmarried daughters.

A beginning to what might be hoped to be a long line of
successes had already been made. The eldest girl, Sophia, was
engaged. Lady Wanless did not look very high, knowing that
failure in such operations will bring with it such unutterable
misfortune. Sophia was engaged to the eldest son of a neighbouring squire—whose property indeed was not large, nor
was the squire likely to die very soon; but there were the means
of present living and a future rental of £4,000 a year. Young
Mr. Cobble was now staying at the house, and had been duly
accepted by Sir Walter himself. The youngest girl, who was
only nineteen, had fallen in love with a young clergyman in
the neighbourhood. That would not do at all, and the young
clergyman was not allowed within the Park. Georgiana was
the beauty; and for her, if for any, some great destiny might
have been hoped. But it was her turn, a matter of which
Lady Wanless thought a great deal, and the Major was too
good to be allowed to escape. Georgiana, in her cold, im-
passive way, seemed to like the Major, and therefore Lady
Wanless paired them off instantly with that decision which was
necessary amidst the labours of her life. She had no scruples in
what she did, feeling sure that her daughters would make honest,
good wives, and that the blood of the Wanlesses was a dowry
in itself.

The Major had been told to come early, because a party
was made to visit certain ruins about eight miles off—Castle
Owless, as it was called—to which Lady Wanless was accustomed to take her guests, because the family history declared

that the Wanlesses had lived there at some very remote period. It still belonged to Sir Walter, though unfortunately the intervening lands had for the most part fallen into other hands. Owless and Wanless were supposed to be the same, and thus there was room for a good deal of family tattle.

"I am delighted to see you at Brook Park", said Sir Walter as they met at the luncheon table. "When I was at Christchurch your father was at Wadham, and I remember him well." Exactly the same words had been spoken when the Major, on a former occasion, had been made welcome at the house, and clearly implied a feeling that Christchurch, though much superior, may condescend to know Wadham—under certain circumstances. Of the Baronet nothing further was heard or seen till dinner.

Lady Wanless went in the open carriage with three daughters, Sophia being one of them. As her affair was settled it was not necessary that one of the two side-saddles should be allotted to her use. Young Cobble, who had been asked to send two horses over from Cobble Hall so that Rossiter might ride one, felt this very hard. But there was no appeal from Lady Wanless. "You'll have plenty enough of her all the evening", said the mother, patting him affectionately, "and it is so necessary just at present that Georgiana and Edith should have horse exercise." In this way it was arranged that Georgiana should ride with the Major, and Edith, the third daughter, with young Burmeston, the son of Cox and Burmeston, brewers at the neighbouring town of Slowbridge. A country brewer is not quite what Lady Wanless would have liked; but with difficulties such as hers a rich young brewer might be worth having. All this was hard upon Mr. Cobble, who would not have sent his horses over had he known it.

Our Major saw at a glance that Georgiana rode well. He liked ladies to ride, and doubted whether Alice had ever been on horseback in her life. After all, how many advantages does a girl lose by having to pass her days in a nursery! For a moment some such idea crossed his mind. Then he asked Georgiana some question as to the scenery through which they were passing. "Very fine, indeed", said Georgiana. She looked square before her, and sat with her back square to the horse's tail. There was no hanging in the saddle, no shifting about in uneasiness. She could rise and fall easily, even gracefully, when the horse trotted. "You are fond of riding I can see", said the Major. "I do like riding", answered Georgiana. The tone in which she spoke of her present occupation was much more lively than that in which she had expressed her approbation of scenery.

At the ruin they all got down, and Lady Wanless told them the entire story of the Owlesses and the Wanlesses, and filled the brewer's mind with wonder as to the antiquity and dignity of the family. But the Major was the fish just at this moment in hand. "The Rossiters are very old, too", she said smiling; "but perhaps that is a kind of thing you don't care for."

"Very much indeed", said he. Which was true—for he was proud of knowing that he had come from the Rossiters who had been over four hundred years in Herefordshire. "A remembrance of old merit will always be an incitement to new."

"It is just that, Major Rossiter. It is strange how very nearly in the same words Georgiana said the same thing to me yesterday." Georgiana happened to overhear this, but did not contradict her mother, though she made a grimace to her sister which was seen by no one else. Then Lady Wanless slipped aside to assist the brewer and Edith, leaving the Major and her second daughter together. The two younger girls, of whom the youngest was the wicked one with the penchant for the curate, were wandering among the ruins by themselves.

"I wonder whether there ever were any people called Owless", said Rossiter, not quite knowing what subject of conversation to choose.

"Of course there were. Mamma always says so."

"That settles the question—does it not?"

"I don't see why there shouldn't be Owlesses. No; I won't
sit on the wall, thank you, because I should stain my habit."

"But you'll be tired."

"Not particularly tired. It is not so very far. I'd go back in
the carriage, only of course we can't because of the habits. Oh,
yes; I'm very fond of dancing—very fond indeed. We always
have two balls every year at Slowbridge. And there are some
others about the county. I don't think you ever have balls at
Beetham."

"There is no one to give them."

"Does Miss Dugdale ever dance?"

The Major had to think for a moment before he could answer
the question. Why should Miss Wanless ask as to Alice's
dancing? "I am sure she does. Now I think of it I have heard
her talk of dancing. You don't know Alice Dugdale?" Miss
Wanless shook her head. "She is worth knowing."

"I am quite sure she is. I have always heard that you thought
so. She is very good to all those children; isn't she?"

"Very good indeed."

"She would be almost pretty if she wasn't so—so, so dumpy
I should say." Then they got on their horses again and rode
back to Brook Park. Let Georgiana be ever so tired she did not
show it, but rode in under the portico with perfect equestrian
grace.

"I'm afraid you took too much out of her", said Lady
Wanless to the Major that evening. Georgiana had gone to
bed a little earlier than the others.

This was in some degree hard upon him, as he had not
proposed the ride—and he excused himself. "It was you
arranged it all, Lady Wanless."

"Yes indeed", said she, smiling. "I did arrange the little
excursion, but it was not I who kept her talking the whole day."
Now this again was felt to be unfair, as nearly every word of
conversation between the young people has been given in this
little chronicle.

On the following day the young people were again thrust

together, and before they parted for the night another little
word was spoken by Lady Wanless which indicated very
clearly that there was some special bond of friendship between
the Major and her second daughter. "You are quite right",
she had said in answer to some extracted compliment; "she
does ride very well. When I was up in town in May I thought
I saw no one with such a seat in the Row. Miss Green, who
taught the Duchess of Ditchwater's daughters, declared that she
knew nothing like it."

On the third morning he returned to Beetham early, as he
intended to go up to town the same afternoon. Then there
was prepared for him a little valedictory opportunity in which
he could not but press the young lady's fingers for a moment.
As he did so no one was looking at him, but then he knew that
it was so much the more dangerous because no one was looking.
Nothing could be more knowing than the conduct of the young
lady, who was not in any way too forward. If she admitted
that slight pressure, it was done with a retiring rather than
obtrusive favour. It was not by her own doing that she was
alone with him for a moment. There was no casting down
or casting up of her eyes. And yet it seemed to him as he left
her and went out into the hall that there had been so much
between them that he was almost bound to propose to her. In
the hall there was the Baronet to bid him farewell—an
honour which he did to his guests only when he was minded
to treat them with great distinction. "Lady Wanless and I are
delighted to have had you here", he said. "Remember me to
your father, and tell him that I remember him very well when
I was at Christchurch and he was at Wadham." It was something to have had one's hand taken in so paternal a manner by
a baronet with such an eyebrow, and such a coat.

And yet when he returned to Beetham he was not in a good
humour with himself. It seemed to him that he had been almost
absorbed among the Wanlesses without any action or will of
his own. He tried to comfort himself by declaring that
Georgiana was, without doubt, a remarkably handsome young

woman, and that she was a perfect horsewoman—as though
all that were a matter to him of any moment! Then he went
across to the doctor's house to say a word of farewell to Alice.

"Have you had a pleasant visit?" she asked.

"Oh, yes; all very well."

"That second Miss Wanless is quite beautiful; is she not?"

"She is handsome certainly."

"I call her lovely", said Alice. "You rode with her the other
day over to that old castle."

Who could have told this of him already? "Yes; there was
a party of us went over."

"When are you going there again?" Now something had
been said of a further visit, and Rossiter had almost promised
that he would return. It is impossible not to promise when
undefined invitations are given. A man cannot declare that he
is engaged for ever and ever. But how was it that Alice knew
all that had been said and done? "I cannot say that I have fixed
any exact day", he replied almost angrily.

"I've heard all about you, you know. That young Mr.
Burmeston was at Mrs. Tweed's and told them what a
favourite you are. If it be true I will congratulate you,
because I do really think that the young lady is the most
beautiful that I ever saw in my life." This she said with a smile
and a good-humoured little shake of the head. If it was to be
that her heart must be broken he at least should not know it.
And she still hoped, she still thought, that by being very
constant at her work she might get over it.

CHAPTER IV

THE BEETHAMITES

IT WAS TOLD ALL THROUGH BEETHAM BEFORE
a week was over that Major Rossiter was to marry the second
Miss Wanless, and Beetham liked the news. Beetham was

proud that one of her sons should be introduced into the great neighbouring family, and especially that he should be honoured by the hand of the acknowledged beauty. Beetham, a month ago, had declared that Alice Dugdale, a Beethamite herself from her babyhood—who had been born and bred at Beetham and had ever lived there—was to be honoured by the hand of the young hero. But it may be doubted whether Beetham had been altogether satisfied with the arrangement. We are apt to envy the good luck of those who have always been familiar with us. Why should it have been Alice Dugdale any more than one of the Tweed girls, or Miss Simkins, the daughter of the attorney, who would certainly have a snug little fortune of her own—which unfortunately would not be the case with Alice Dugdale? It had been felt that Alice was hardly good enough for their hero—Alice who had been seen about with all the Dugdale children, pushing them in perambulators almost every day since the eldest was born! We prefer the authority of a stranger to that of one chosen from among ourselves. As the two Miss Tweeds, and Miss Simkins, with Alice and three or four others, could not divide the hero among them, it was better then that the hero should go from among them, and choose a fitting mate in a higher realm. They all felt the greatness of the Wanlesses, and argued with Mrs. Rossiter that the rising star of the village should obtain such assistance in rising as would come to him from an almost noble marriage.

There had been certainly a decided opinion that Alice was to be the happy woman. Mrs. Dugdale, the stepmother, had boasted of the promotion; and old Mr. Rossiter had whispered his secret conviction into the ear of every favoured parishioner. The doctor himself had allowed his patients to ask questions about it. This had become so common that Alice herself had been inwardly indignant—would have been outwardly indignant but that she could not allow herself to discuss the matter. That having been so, Beetham ought to have been scandalized by the fickleness of her hero. Beetham ought to have felt that her hero was most unheroic. But, at any rate among the ladies, there was no shadow of such a feeling. Of course such a man as the Major was bound to do the best for himself. The giving away of his hand in marriage was a very serious thing, and was not to be obligatory on a young hero because he had been carried away by the fervour of old friendship to kiss a young lady immediately on his return home. The history of the kiss was known all over Beetham, and was declared by competent authorities to have amounted to nothing. It was a last lingering touch of childhood's happy embracings, and if Alice was such a fool as to take it for more, she must pay the penalty of her folly. "It was in her father's presence", said Mrs. Rossiter, defending her son to Mrs. Tweed, and Mrs. Tweed had expressed her opinion that the kiss ought to go for nothing. The Major was to be acquitted—and the fact of the acquittal made its way even to the doctor's nursery; so that Alice knew that the man might marry that girl at Brook Park with clean hands. That, as she declared to herself, did not increase her sorrow. If the man were minded to marry the girl he was welcome for her. And she apologized for him to her own heart. What a man generally wants, she said, is a beautiful wife; and of the beauty of Miss Georgiana Wanless there could be no doubt. Only—only—only, there had been a dozen words which he should have left unspoken!

That which riveted the news on the minds of the Beetham-ites was the stopping of the Brook Park carriage at the door of the parsonage one day about a week after the Major's visit. It was not altogether an unprecedented occurrence. Had there been no precedent it could hardly have been justified on the present occasion. Perhaps once in two years Lady Wanless would call at the parsonage, and then there would be a return visit during which a reference would always be made to Wadham and Christchurch. The visit was now out of its order, only nine months having elapsed—of which irregu-larity Beetham took due notice. On this occasion Miss Wanless and the third young lady accompanied their mother,

leaving Georgiana at home. What was whispered between
the two old ladies Beetham did not quite know—but made its
surmises. It was in this wise. "We were so glad to have the
Major over with us", said her ladyship.

"It was so good of you", said Mrs. Rossiter.

"He is a great favourite with Sir Walter."

"That is so good of Sir Walter."

"And we are quite pleased to have him among our young
people." That was all, but it was quite sufficient to tell Mrs.
Rossiter that John might have Georgiana Wanless for the
asking, and that Lady Wanless expected him to ask. Then the
parting was much more affectionate than it had ever been
before, and there was a squeezing of the hand and a nodding of
the head which meant a great deal.

Alice held her tongue, and did her work, and attempted to
be cheery through it all. Again and again she asked herself—
what did it matter? Even though she were unhappy, even
though she felt a keen, palpable, perpetual aching at her heart,
what would it matter so long as she could go about and do her
business? Some people in this world had to be unhappy—
perhaps most people. And this was a sorrow which, though it
might not wear off, would by wearing become dull enough to
be bearable. She distressed herself in that there was any sorrow.
Providence had given to her a certain condition of life to which
many charms were attached. She thoroughly loved the people
about her—her father, her little brothers and sisters, even her
overworn and somewhat idle stepmother. She was a queen
in the house, a queen among her busy toils; and she liked being
a queen, and liked being busy. No one ever scolded her or
crossed her or contradicted her. She had the essential satisfaction of the consciousness of usefulness. Why should not
that suffice to her? She despised herself because there was a
hole in her heart—because she felt herself to shrink all over
when the name of Georgiana Wanless was mentioned in her
hearing. Yet she would mention the name herself, and speak
with something akin to admiration of the Wanless family.

And she would say how well it was that men should strive to rise in the world, and how that the world progressed through such individual efforts. But she would not mention the name of John Rossiter, nor would she endure that it should be mentioned in her hearing with any special reference to herself.

Mrs. Dugdale, though she was overworn and idle—a warped and almost useless piece of furniture, made, as was said before, of bad timber—yet saw more of this than anyone else, and was indignant. To lose Alice, to have no one to let down those tucks and take up those stitches, would be to her the loss of all her comforts. But, though she was feckless, she was true-hearted, and she knew that Alice was being wronged. It was Alice that had a right to the hero, and not that stuck-up young woman at Brook Park. It was thus she spoke of the affair to the doctor, and after a while found herself unable to be silent upon the subject to Alice herself. "If what they say does take place I shall think worse of John Rossiter than I ever did of any man I ever knew." This she said in the presence both of her husband and her stepdaughter.

"John Rossiter will not be very much the worse for that", said Alice without relaxing a moment from her work. There was a sound of drolling in her voice, as though she were quizzing her stepmother for her folly.

"It seems to me that men may do anything now", continued Mrs. Dugdale.

"I suppose they are the same now as they always were", said the doctor. "If a man chose to be false he could always be false."

"I call it unmanly", said Mrs. Dugdale. "If I were a man I would beat him."

"What would you beat him for?" said Alice, getting up, and as she did so throwing down on the table before her the little frock she was making. "If you had the power of beating him, why would you beat him?"

"Because he is ill-using you."

"How do you know that? Did I ever tell you so? Have you ever heard a word that he has said to me, either direct from himself, or second-hand, that justifies you in saying that he has ill-used me? You ill-use me when you speak like that."

"Alice, do not be so violent", said the doctor.

"Father, I will speak of this once, and once for all—and then pray, pray, let there be no further mention of it. I have no right to complain of anything in Major Rossiter. He has done me no wrong. Those who love me should not mention his name in reference to me."

"He is a villain", said Mrs. Dugdale.

"He is no villain. He is a gentleman, as far as I know, from the crown of his head to the sole of his foot. Does it ever occur to you how little you make of me when you talk of him in this way? Dismiss it all from your mind, father, and let things be as they were. Do you think that I am pining for any man's love? I say that Major Rossiter is a true man and a gentleman—but I would not give my Bobby's little finger for all his whole body." Then there was silence, and afterwards the doctor told his wife that the Major's name had better not be mentioned again among them. Alice on this occasion was, or appeared to be, very angry with Mrs. Dugdale; but on that evening and the next morning there was an accession of tenderness in her usually sweet manner to her stepmother. The expression of her mother's anger against the Major had been wrong—but the feeling of anger was not the less endearing.

Some time after that, one evening, the parson came upon Alice as she was picking flowers in one of the Beetham lanes. She had all the children with her, and was filling Minnie's apron with roses from the hedge. Old Mr. Rossiter stopped and talked to them, and after a while succeeded in getting Alice to walk on with him. "You haven't heard from John?" he said.

"Oh, no", replied Alice, almost with a start. And then she added quickly, "There is no one at our house likely to hear from him. He does not write to anyone there."

"I did not know whether any message might have reached you."

"I think not."

"He is to be here again before long", said the parson.

"Oh, indeed." She had but a moment to think of it all; but, after thinking, she continued, "I suppose he will be going over to Brook Park."

"I fear he will."

"Fear—why should you fear, Mr. Rossiter? If that is true, it is the place where he ought to be."

"But I doubt its truth, my dear."

"Ah! I know nothing about that. If so he had better stay up in London, I suppose."

"I don't think John can care much for Miss Wanless."

"Why not? She is the most thoroughly beautiful young woman I ever saw."

"I don't think he does, because I believe his heart is elsewhere. Alice, you have his heart."

"No."

"I think so, Alice."

"No, Mr. Rossiter. I have not. It is not so. I know nothing of Miss Wanless, but I can speak of myself."

"It seems to me that you are speaking of him now."

"Then why does he go there?"

"That is just what I cannot answer. Why does he go there? Why do we do the worst thing so often, when we see the better?"

"But we don't leave undone the thing which we wish to do, Mr. Rossiter."

"That is just what we do do—under constraint. Alice, I hope, I hope that you may become his wife." She endeavoured to deny that it could ever be so—she strove to declare that she herself was much too heart-free for that; but the words would not come to her lips, and she could only sob while she struggled to retain her tears. "If he does come to you give him a chance again, even though he may have been untrue to you for a moment."

Then she was left alone among the children. She could dry her tears and suppress her sobs, because Minnie was old enough to know the meaning of them if she saw them; but she could not for a while go back into the house. She left them in the paassge and then went out again, and walked up and down a little pathway that ran through the shrubs at the bottom of the garden. "I believe his heart is elsewhere." Could it be that it was so? And if so, of what nature can be a man's love, if when it be given in one direction, he can go in another with his hand? She could understand that there had not been much heart in it— that he, being a man and not a woman, could have made this turning point of his life an affair of calculation, and had taken himself here or there without much love at all; that as he would seek a commodious house, so would he also a convenient wife. Resting on that suggestion to herself, she had dared to declare to her father and mother that Major Rossiter was, not a villain, but a perfect gentleman. But all that was not compatible with his father's story. "Alice, you have his heart", the old man had said. How had it come to pass that the old man had known it? And yet the assurance was so sweet, so heavenly, so laden to her ears with divine music, that at this moment she would not even ask herself to disbelieve it. "If he does come to you, give him a chance again." Why—yes! Though she never spoke a word of Miss Wanless without praise, though she had tutored herself to swear that Miss Wanless was the very wife for him, yet she knew herself too well not to know that she was better than Miss Wanless. For his sake, she could with a clear con- science—give him a chance again. The dear old parson! He had seen it all. He had known. He had appreciated. If it should ever come to pass that she was to be his daughter-in- law, he should have his reward. She would not tell herself that she expected him to come again; but, if he did come, she would give the parson his chance. Such was her idea at that moment. But she was forced to change it before long.

CHAPTER V

THE INVITATION

WHEN MAJOR ROSSITER DISCUSSED HIS OWN
conduct with himself as men are so often compelled to do by
their own conscience, in opposition to their own wishes, he
was not well pleased with himself. On his return home from
India he had found himself possessed of a liberal income, and
had begun to enjoy himself without thinking much about
marrying. It is not often that a man looks for a wife because
he has made up his mind that he wants the article. He roams
about unshackled, till something, which at the time seems to be
altogether desirable, presents itself to him; and then he medi-
tates marriage. So it had been with our Major. Alice had
presented herself to him as something altogether desirable—a
something which, when it was touched and looked at, seemed
to be so full of sweetnesses, that to him it was for the moment
of all things the most charming. He was not a forward man—
one of those who can see a girl for the first time on a Monday,
and propose to her on the Tuesday. When the idea first
suggested itself to him of making Alice his wife he became
reticent and undemonstrative. The kiss had in truth meant no
more than Mrs. Tweed had said. When he began to feel that
he loved her, then he hardly dared to dream of kissing her.

But though he felt that he loved her—liked perhaps it would
be fairer to say in that early stage of his feelings—better than
any other woman, yet when he came to think of marriage,
the importance of it all made him hesitate; and he was reminded,
by little hints from others, and by words plain enough from
one person, that Alice Dugdale was after all a common thing.
There is a fitness in such matters—so said Mrs. Rossiter—and
a propriety in like being married to like. Had it been his lot
to be a village doctor, Alice would have suited him well.
Destiny, however, had carried him—the Major—higher up,

and would require him to live in London, among ornate people, with polished habits, and peculiar manners of their own. Would not Alice be out of her element in London? See the things among which she passed her life! Not a morsel of soap or a pound of sugar was used in the house, but what she gave it out. Her hours were passed in washing, teaching, and sewing for the children. In her very walks she was always pushing a perambulator. She was, no doubt, the doctor's daughter; but, in fact, she was the second Mrs. Dugdale's nursemaid. Nothing could be more praiseworthy. But there is a fitness in things; and he, the hero of Beetham, the Assistant Deputy Inspector-General of the British Cavalry, might surely do better than marry a praiseworthy nursery girl. It was thus that Mrs. Rossiter argued with her son, and her arguments were not without avail.

Then Georgiana Wanless had been, as it were, thrown at his head. When one is pelted with sugar-plums one can hardly resent the attack. He was clever enough to feel that he was pelted, but at first he liked the sweetmeats. A girl riding on horseback, with her back square to the horse's tail, with her reins well held, and a chimney-pot hat on her head, is an object, unfortunately, more attractive to the eyes of ordinary men, than a young woman pushing a perambulator with two babies. Unfortunately, I say, because in either case the young woman should be judged by her personal merits and not by externals. But the Major declared to himself that the personal merits would be affected by the externals. A girl who had pushed a perambulator for many years, would hardly have a soul above perambulators. There would be wanting the flavour of the aroma of romance, that something of poetic vagueness without which a girl can hardly be altogether charming to the senses of an appreciative lover. Then, a little later on, he asked himself whether Georgiana Wanless was romantic and poetic—whether there was much of true aroma there.

But yet he thought that fate would require him to marry

Georgiana Wanless, whom he certainly did not love, and to
leave Alice to her perambulator—Alice, whom he certainly
did love. And as he thought of this, he was ill at ease with
himself. It might be well that he should give up his Assistant
Deputy Inspector-Generalship, go back to India, and so get
rid of his two troubles together. Fate, as he personified fate
to himself in this matter—took the form of Lady Wanless. It
made him sad to think that he was but a weak creature in the
hands of an old woman, who wanted to use him for a certain
purpose—but he did not see his way of escaping. When he
began to console himself by reflecting that he would have one
of the handsomest women in London at his dinner-table he
knew that he would be unable to escape.

About the middle of July he received the following letter
from Lady Wanless:

"DEAR MAJOR ROSSITER—The girls have been at their father
for the last ten days to have an archery meeting on the lawn,
and have at last prevailed, though Sir Walter has all a father's
abhorrence to have the lawn knocked about. Now it is settled.
'I'll see about it', Sir Walter said at last, and when so much as
that had been obtained, they all knew that the archery meeting
was to be. Sir Walter likes his own way, and is not always to
be persuaded. But when he has made the slightest show of
concession, he never goes back from it. Then comes the question
as to the day, which is now in course of discussion in full
committee. In that matter Sir Walter is supposed to be
excluded from any voice. 'It cannot matter to him what day
of the week or what day of the month', said Georgiana very
irreverently. It will not, however, much matter to him so long
as it is all over before St. Partridge comes round.

"The girls one and all declared that you must be here—as
one of the guests in the house. Our rooms will be mostly full
of young ladies, but there will be one at any rate for you.
Now, what day will suit you—or rather what day will suit the
Cavalry generally? Everything must of course depend on the

Cavalry. The girls say that the Cavalry is sure to go out of town after the tenth of August. But they would put it off for a week longer rather than not have the Inspector-General. Would Wednesday 14th suit the Cavalry? They are all reading every word of my letter as it is written, and bid me say that if Thursday or Friday in that week, or Wednesday or Thursday in the next, will do better, the accommodation of the Cavalry shall be consulted. It cannot be on a Monday or Saturday because there would be some Sunday encroachment. On Tuesday we cannot get the band from Slowbridge.

"Now you know our great purpose and our little difficulties. One thing you cannot know—how determined we are to accommodate ourselves to the Cavalry. *The meeting is not to take place without the Inspector-General.* So let us have an early answer from that august functionary. The girls think that the Inspector had better come down before the day, so as to make himself useful in preparing.

"Pray believe me, with Sir Walter's kind regards, yours most sincerely,

"MARGARET WANLESS."

The Major felt that the letter was very flattering, but that it was false and written for a certain purpose. He could read between the lines at every sentence of it. The festival was to be got up, not at the instance of the girls but of Lady Wanless herself, as a final trap for the catching of himself—and perhaps for Mr. Burmeston. Those irreverent words had never come from Georgiana, who was too placid to have said them. He did not believe a word of the girls looking over the writing of the letter. In all such matters Lady Wanless had more life, more energy than her daughters. All that little fun about the Cavalry came from Lady Wanless herself. The girls were too like their father for such ebullitions. The little sparks of joke with which the names of the girls were connected—with which in his hearing the name of Georgiana had been specially connected—had, he was aware, their origin always with Lady

Wanless. Georgiana had said this funny thing and that—but Georgiana never spoke after that fashion in his hearing. The traps were plain to his eyes, and yet he knew that he would sooner or later be caught in the traps.

He took a day to think of it before he answered the letter, and meditated a military tour to Berlin just about the time. If so, he must be absent during the whole of August, so as to make his presence at the toxopholite meeting an impossibility. And yet at last he wrote and said that he would be there. There would be something mean in flight. After all, he need not ask the girl to be his wife unless he chose to do so. He wrote a very pretty note to Lady Wanless saying that he would be at Brook Park on the 14th, as she had suggested.

Then he made a great resolution and swore an oath to himself—that he would not be caught on that occasion, and that after this meeting he would go no more either to Brook Park or to Beetham for a while. He would not marry the girl to whom he was quite indifferent, nor her who from her position was hardly qualified to be his wife. Then he went about his duties with a quieted conscience, and wedded himself for once and for always to the Cavalry.

Some tidings of the doings proposed by the Wanlesses had reached the parson's ears when he told Alice in the lane that his son was soon coming down to Beetham again, and that he was again going to Brook Park. Before July was over the tidings of the coming festivity had been spread over all that side of the county. Such a thing had not been done for many years—not since Lady Wanless had been herself a young wife, with two sisters for whom husbands had to be—and were—provided. There were those who could still remember how well Lady Wanless had behaved on that occasion. Since those days hospitality on a large scale had not been rife at Brook Park— and the reason why it was so was well known. Sir Walter was determined not to embarrass himself further, and would do nothing that was expensive. It could not be but that there was great cause for such a deviation as this. Then the ladies of the neighbourhood put their heads together—and some of the gentlemen—and declared that a double stroke of business was to be done in regard to Major Rossiter and Mr. Burmeston. How great a relief that would be to the mother's anxiety if the three eldest girls could be married and got rid of all on the same day!

Beetham, which was ten miles from Brook Park, had a station of its own, whereas Slowbridge with its own station was only six miles from the house. The Major would fain have reached his destination by Slowbridge, so as to have avoided the chance of seeing Alice, were it not that his father and mother would have felt themselves aggrieved by such desertion. On this occasion his mother begged him to give them one night. She had much that she wished to say to him, and then of course he could have the parsonage horse and the parsonage phaeton to take him over to Brook Park free of expense. He did go down to Beetham, did spend an evening there, and did go on to the Park without having spoken to Alice Dugdale.

"Everybody says you are to marry Georgiana Wanless", said Mrs. Rossiter.

"If there were no other reason why I should not, the saying of everybody would be sufficient against it."

"That is unreasonable, John. The thing should be looked at itself, whether it is good or bad. It may be the case that Lady Wanless talks more than she ought to do. It may be the case that, as people say, she is looking out for husbands for her daughters. I don't know but that I should do the same if I had five of them on my hands and very little means for them. And if I did, how could I get a better husband for one of them than—such a one as Major John Rossiter?" Then she kissed his forehead.

"I hate the kind of thing altogether", said he. He pretended to be stern, but yet he showed that he was flattered by his mother's softness.

"It may well be, John, that such a match shall be desirable to them and to you too. If so, why should there not be a fair bargain between the two of you? You know that you admire the girl." He would not deny this, lest it should come to pass hereafter that she should become his wife. "And everybody knows that as far as birth goes there is not a family in the county stands higher. I am so proud of my boy that I wish to see him mated with the best."

He reached the parsonage that evening only just before dinner, and on the next morning he did not go out of the house till the phaeton came round to take him to Brook Park. "Are you not going up to see the old doctor?" said the parson after breakfast.

"No—I think not. He is never at home, and the ladies are always surrounded by the children."

"She will take it amiss", said the father almost in a whisper.

"I will go as I come back", said he, blushing as he spoke at his own falsehood. For, if he held to his present purpose, he would return by Slowbridge. If Fate intended that there should be nothing further between him and Alice, it would certainly be much better that they should not be brought together any more. He knew too what his father meant, and was more unwilling to take counsel from his father even than his mother. Yet he blushed because he knew that he was false.

"Do not seem to slight her", said the old man. "She is too good for that."

Then he drove himself over to Brook Park, and, as he made his way by one of the innumerable turnings out of Beetham, he saw at one of the corners Alice, still with the children and still with the perambulator. He merely lifted his hat as he passed, but did not stop to speak to her.

CHAPTER VI

THE ARCHERY MEETING

THE ASSISTANT DEPUTY INSPECTOR-GENERAL, when he reached Brook Park, found that things were to be done on a great scale. The two drawing-rooms were filled with flowers, and the big dining-room was laid out for to-morrow's lunch, in preparation for those who would prefer the dining-room to the tent. Rossiter was first taken into the Baronet's own room, where Sir Walter kept his guns and administered justice. "This is a terrible bore, Rossiter", he said.

"It must disturb you a great deal, Sir Walter."

"Oh, dear—dreadfully! What would my old friend, your father, think of having to do this kind of thing? Though, when I was at Christchurch and he at Wadham, we used to be gay enough. I'm not quite sure that I don't owe it to you."

"To me, Sir Walter!"

"I rather think you put the girls up to it." Then he laughed as though it were a very good joke and told the Major where he would find the ladies. He had been expressly desired by his wife to be genial to the Major, and had been as genial as he knew how.

Rossiter, as he went out on to the lawn, saw Mr. Burmeston, the brewer, walking with Edith, the third daughter. He could not but admire the strategy of Lady Wanless when he acknowledged to himself how well she managed all these things. The brewer would not have been allowed to walk with Gertrude, the fourth daughter, nor even with Maria, the naughty girl who liked the curate—because it was Edith's turn. Edith was certainly the plainest of the family, and yet she had her turn. Lady Wanless was by far too good a mother to have favourites among her own children.

He then found the mother, the eldest daughter, and

Gertrude overseeing the decoration of a tent, which had been put up as an addition to the dining-room. He expected to find Mr. Cobble, to whom he had taken a liking, a nice, pleasant, frank young country gentleman; but Mr. Cobble was not wanted for any express purpose, and might have been in the way. Mr. Cobble was landed and safe. Before long he found himself walking round the garden with Lady Wanless herself. The other girls, though they were to be his sisters, were never thrown into any special intimacy with him. "She will be down before long now that she knows you are here", said Lady Wanless. "She was fatigued a little, and I thought it better that she should lie down. She is so impressionable, you know." "She" was Georgiana. He knew that very well. But why should Georgiana be called "She" to him, by her mother? Had "She" been in truth engaged to him it would have been intelligible enough. But there had been nothing of the kind. As "She" was thus dinned into his ears, he thought of the very small amount of conversation which had ever taken place between himself and the young lady.

Then there occurred to him an idea that he would tell Lady Wanless in so many words that there was a mistake. The doing so would require some courage, but he thought that he could summon up manliness for the purpose—if only he could find the words and occasion. But though "She" were so frequently spoken of, still nothing was said which seemed to give him the opportunity required. It is hard for a man to have to reject a girl when she has been offered—but harder to do so before the offer has in truth been made. "I am afraid there is a little mistake in your ideas as to me and your daughter." It was thus that he would have had to speak, and then to have endured the outpouring of her wrath, when she would have declared that the ideas were only in his own arrogant brain. He let it pass by and said nothing, and before long he was playing lawn-tennis with Georgiana, who did not seem to have been in the least fatigued.

"My dear, I will not have it", said Lady Wanless about an

hour afterwards, coming up and disturbing the game. "Major Rossiter, you ought to know better." Whereupon she playfully took the racket out of the Major's hand. "Mamma is such an old bother", said Georgiana as she walked back to the house with her Major. The Major had on a previous occasion perceived that the second Miss Wanless rode very well, and now he saw that she was very stout at lawn-tennis; but he observed none of that peculiarity of mental or physical development which her mother had described as "impressionable". Nevertheless she was a handsome girl, and if to play at lawn-tennis would help to make a husband happy, so much at any rate she could do.

This took place on the day before the meeting—before the great day. When the morning came the girls did not come down early to breakfast, and our hero found himself left alone with Mr. Burmeston. "You have known the family a long time", said the Major as they were sauntering about the gravel paths together, smoking their cigars.

"No, indeed", said Mr. Burmeston. "They only took me up about three months ago—just before we went over to Owless. Very nice people—don't you think so?"

"Very nice", said the Major.

"They stand so high in the county, and all that sort of thing. Birth does go a long way, you know."

"So it ought", said the Major.

"And though the Baronet does not do much in the world, he has been in the House, you know. All those things help." Then the Major understood that Mr. Burmeston had looked the thing in the face, and had determined that for certain considerations it was worth his while to lead one of the Miss Wanlesses to the hymeneal altar. In this Mr. Burmeston was behaving with more manliness than he—who had almost made up his mind half-a-dozen times, and had never been satisfied with the way he had done it.

About twelve the visitors had begun to come, and Sophia with Mr. Cobble were very soon trying their arrows together.

Sophia had not been allowed to have her lover on the previous day, but was now making up for it. That was all very well, but Lady Wanless was a little angry with her eldest daughter. Her success was insured for her. Her business was done. Seeing how many sacrifices had been made to her during the last twelve months, surely now she might have been active in aiding her sisters, instead of merely amusing herself.

The Major was not good at archery. He was no doubt an excellent Deputy Inspector-General of Cavalry; but if bows and arrows had still been the weapons used in any part of the British army, he would not, without further instruction, have been qualified to inspect that branch. Georgiana Wanless, on the other hand, was a proficient. Such shooting as she made was marvellous to look at. And she was a very image of Diana, as with her beautiful figure and regular features, dressed up to the work, she stood with her bow raised in her hand and let twang the arrows. The circle immediately outside the bull's-eye was the farthest from the mark she ever touched. But good as she was and bad as was the Major, nevertheless they were appointed always to shoot together. After a world of failures the Major would shoot no more—but not the less did he go backwards and forwards with Georgiana when she changed from one end to the other, and found himself absolutely appointed to that task. It grew upon him during the whole day that this second Miss Wanless was supposed to be his own— almost as was the elder the property of Mr. Cobble. Other young men would do no more than speak to her. And when once, after the great lunch in the tent, Lady Wanless came and put her hand affectionately upon his arm, and whispered some word into his ear in the presence of all the assembled guests, he knew that the entire county had recognized him as caught.

There was old Lady Deepbell there. How it was that towards the end of the day's delights Lady Deepbell got hold of him he never knew. Lady Deepbell had not been intro- duced to him, and yet she got hold of him. "Major Rossiter, you are the luckiest man of the day", she said to him.

"Pretty well", said he, affecting to laugh; "but why so?"

"She is the handsomest young woman out. There hasn't been one in London this season with such a figure."

"You are altogether wrong in your surmise, Lady Deepbell."

"No, no; I am right enough. I see it all. Of course the poor girl won't have any money; but then how nice it is when a gentleman like you is able to dispense with that. Perhaps they do take after their father a little, and he certainly is not bright; but upon my word, I think a girl is all the better for that. What's the good of having such a lot of talkee-talkee?"

"Lady Deepbell, you are alluding to a young lady without the slightest warrant", said the Major.

"Warrant enough—warrant enough", said the old woman, toddling off.

Then young Cobble came to him, and talked to him as though he were a brother of the house. Young Cobble was an honest fellow, and quite in earnest in his matrimonial intentions. "We shall be delighted if you'll come to us on the first", said Cobble. The first of course meant the first of September. "We ain't so badly off just for a week's shooting. Sophia is to be there, and we'll get Georgiana too."

The Major was fond of shooting, and would have been glad to accept the offer; but it was out of the question that he should allow himself to be taken in at Cobble Hall under a false pretext. And was it not incumbent on him to make this young man understand that he had no pretensions whatever to the hand of the second Miss Wanless? "You are very good", said he.

"We should be delighted", said young Cobble.

"But I fear there is a mistake. I can't say anything more about it now because it doesn't do to name people—but there is a mistake. Only for that I should have been delighted. Good-bye." Then he took his departure, leaving young Cobble in a state of mystified suspense.

The day lingered on to a great length. The archery and the lawn-tennis were continued till late after the so-called lunch,

and towards the evening a few couples stood up to dance. It
was evident to the Major that Burmeston and Edith were
thoroughly comfortable together. Gertrude amused herself
well, and even Maria was contented, though the curate as a
matter of course was not there. Sophia with her legitimate
lover was as happy as the day and evening were long. But
there came a frown upon Georgiana's brow, and when at last
the Major, as though forced by destiny, asked her to dance,
she refused. It had seemed to her a matter of course that he
should ask her, and at last he did—but she refused. The
evening with him was very long, and just as he thought that
he would escape to bed, and was meditating how early he
would be off on the morrow, Lady Wanless took possession
of him and carried him off alone into one of the desolate
chambers. "Is she very tired?" asked the anxious mother.

"Is who tired?" The Major at that moment would have
given twenty guineas to have been in his lodgings near
St. James's Street.

"My poor girl", said Lady Wanless, assuming a look of great
solicitude.

It was vain for him to pretend not to know who was the
"she" intended. "Oh, ah, yes; Miss Wanless."

"Georgiana."

"I think she is tired. She was shooting a great deal. Then
there was a quadrille—but she didn't dance. There has been a
great deal to tire young ladies."

"You shouldn't have let her do so much."

How was he to get out of it? What was he to say? If a man
is clearly asked his intentions he can say that he has not got any.
That used to be the old fashion when a gentleman was supposed
to be dilatory in declaring his purpose. But it gave the oscil-
lating lover so easy an escape! It was like the sudden jerk of
the hand of the unpractised fisherman: if the fish does not
succumb at once it goes away down the stream and is no more
heard of. But from this new process there is no mode of
immediate escape. "I couldn't prevent her because she is

nothing to me." That would have been the straightforward answer—but one most difficult to make. "I hope she will be none the worse to-morrow morning", said the Major.

"I hope not, indeed. Oh, Major Rossiter!" The mother's position was also difficult, as it is of no use to play with a fish too long without making an attempt to stick the hook into his gills.

"Lady Wanless!"

"What am I to say to you? I am sure you know my feelings. You know how sincere is Sir Walter's regard."

"I am very much flattered, Lady Wanless."

"That means nothing." This was true, but the Major did not mean to intend anything. "Of all my flock she is the fairest." That was true also. The Major would have been delighted to accede to the assertion of the young lady's beauty, if this might have been the end of it. "I had thought——"

"Had thought what, Lady Wanless?"

"If I am deceived in you, Major Rossiter, I never will believe in a man again. I have looked upon you as the very soul of honour."

"I trust that I have done nothing to lessen your good opinion."

"I do not know. I cannot say. Why do you answer me in this way about my child?" Then she held her hands together and looked up into his face imploringly. He owned to himself that she was a good actress. He was almost inclined to submit and to declare his passion for Georgiana. For the present that way out of the difficulty would have been so easy!

"You shall hear from me to-morrow morning", he said, almost solemnly.

"Shall I?" she asked, grasping his hand. "Oh, my friend, let it be as I desire. My whole life shall be devoted to making you happy—you and her." Then he was allowed to escape.

Lady Wanless, before she went to bed, was closeted for awhile with the eldest daughter. As Sophia was now almost as good as a married woman, she was received into closer counsel than the others. "Burmeston will do", she said; "but, as for that Cavalry man, he means it no more than the chair." The pity was that Burmeston might have been secured without the archery meeting, and that all the money, spent on behalf of the Major, should have been thrown away.

CHAPTER VII

AFTER THE PARTY

WHEN THE MAJOR LEFT BROOK PARK ON THE morning after the archery amusements he was quite sure of this—that under no circumstances whatever would he be induced to ask Miss Georgiana Wanless to be his wife. He had promised to write a letter—and he would write one instantly. He did not conceive it possible but that Lady Wanless should understand what would be the purport of that letter, although as she left him on the previous night she had pretended to hope otherwise. That her hopes had not been very high we know from the words which she spoke to Sophia in the privacy of her own room.

He had intended to return by Slowbridge, but when the morning came he changed his mind and went to Beetham. His reason for doing so was hardly plain, even to himself. He tried to make himself believe that the letter had better be written from Beetham—hot, as it were, from the immediate neighbourhood—than from London; but, as he thought of this, his mind was crowded with ideas of Alice Dugdale. He would not propose to Alice. At this moment, indeed, he was averse to matrimony, having been altogether disgusted with female society at Brook Park; but he had to acknowledge a sterling worth about Alice, and the existence of a genuine friendship between her and himself, which made it painful to him to leave the country without other recognition than that raising of his hat when he saw her at the corner of the lane. He had behaved badly in this Brook Park affair—in having been tempted thither in opposition to those better instincts which had made Alice so pleasant a companion to him—and was ashamed of himself. He did not think that he could go back to his former ideas. He was aware that Alice must think ill of him—would not believe him to be now such as she had once thought him. England and London were distasteful to him. He would go abroad on that foreign service which he had proposed to himself. There was an opening for him to do so if he liked, and he could return to his present duties after a year or two. But he would see Alice again before he went. Thinking of all this, he drove himself back to Beetham.

On that morning tidings of the successful festivities at Brook Park reached the doctor's house. Tidings of the coming festivities, then of the preparations, and at last of the festal day itself, had reached Alice, so that it seemed to her that all Beetham talked of nothing else. Old Lady Deepbell had caught a cold, walking about on the lawn with hardly anything on her old shoulders—stupid old woman—and had sent for the doctor the first thing in the morning. "Positively settled", she had said to the doctor, "absolutely arranged, Dr. Dugdale. Lady Wanless told me so herself, and I congratulated the gentleman." She did not go on to say that the gentleman had denied the accusation—but then she had not believed the denial. The doctor, coming home, had thought it his duty to tell Alice, and Alice had received the news with a smile. "I knew it would be so, father."

"And you?" This he said, holding her hand and looking tenderly into her eyes.

"Me! It will not hurt me. Not that I mean to tell a lie to you, father", she added after a moment. "A woman isn't hurt because she doesn't get a prize in the lottery. Had it ever come about, I dare say I should have liked him well enough."

"No more than that?"

"And why should it have come about?" she went on saying,
avoiding her father's last question, determined not to lie if she
could help it, but determined, also, to show no wound. "I
think my position in life very happy, but it isn't one from which
he would choose a wife."

"Why not, my dear?"

"A thousand reasons; I am always busy, and he would
naturally like a young lady who had nothing to do." She
understood the effect of the perambulator and the constant
needle and thread. "Besides, though he might be all very well,
he could never, I think, be as dear to me as the bairns. I should
feel that I lost more than I got by going." This she knew to
be a lie, but it was so important that her father should believe
her to be contented with her home duties! And she was
contented, though very unhappy. When her father kissed her,
she smiled into his face—oh, so sweetly, so pleasantly! And the
old man thought that she could not have loved very deeply.
Then she took herself to her own room, and sat a while alone
with a countenance much changed. The lines of sorrow about
her brow were terrible. There was not a tear; but her mouth
was close pressed, and her hand was working constantly by
her side. She gazed at nothing, but sat with her eyes wide open,
staring straight before her. Then she jumped up quickly, and
striking her hand upon her heart, she spoke aloud to herself.
"I will cure it", she said. "He is not worthy, and it should
therefore be easier. Though he were worthy, I would cure it.
Yes, Bobby, I am coming." Then she went about her work.

That might have been about noon. It was after their early
dinner with the children that the Major came up to the doctor's
house. He had reached the parsonage in time for a late breakfast,
and had then written his letter. After that he had sat idling
about on the lawn—not on the best terms with his mother,
to whom he had sworn that, under no circumstances, would he
make Georgiana Wanless his wife. "I would sooner marry a
girl from a troop of tight-rope dancers", he had said in his
anger. Mrs. Rossiter knew that he intended to go up to the

doctor's house, and therefore the immediate feeling between the mother and son was not pleasant. My readers, if they please, shall see the letter to Lady Wanless.

"MY DEAR LADY WANLESS—It is a great grief to me to say that there has been, I fear, a misconception between you and me on a certain matter. This is the more a trouble to me because you and Sir Walter have been so very kind to me. From a word or two which fell from you last night I was led to fear that you suspected feelings on my part which I have never entertained, and aspirations to which I have never pretended. No man can be more alive than I am to the honour which has been suggested, but I feel bound to say that I am not in a condition to accept it.

"Pray believe me to be,
"Dear Lady Wanless,
"Yours always very faithfully,
"JOHN ROSSITER."

The letter, when it was written, was, to himself, very un-satisfactory. It was full of ambiguous words and namby-pamby phraseology which disgusted him. But he did not know how to alter it for the better. It is hard to say an uncivil thing civilly without ambiguous namby-pamby language. He could not bring it out in straightforward stout English: "You want me to marry your daughter, but I won't do anything of the kind." So the letter was sent. The conduct of which he was really ashamed did not regard Miss Wanless, but Alice Dugdale.

At last, very slowly, he took himself up to the doctor's house. He hardly knew what it was that he meant to say when he found himself there, but he was sure that he did not mean to make an offer. Even had other things suited, there would have been something distasteful to him in doing this so quickly after the affair of Miss Wanless. He was in no frame now for making love; but yet it would be ungracious in him, he thought,

to leave Beetham without seeing his old friend. He found the
two ladies together, with the children still around them, sitting
near a window which opened down to the ground. Mrs.
Dugdale had a novel in hand, and, as usual, was leaning back in
a rocking-chair. Alice had also a book open on the table before
her, but she was bending over a sewing-machine. They had
latterly divided the cares of the family between them. Mrs.
Dugdale had brought the children into the world, and Alice
had washed, clothed, and fed them when they were there.
When the Major entered the room, Alice's mind was, of course,
full of the tidings she had heard from her father—which
tidings, however, had not been communicated to Mrs.
Dugdale.

Alice at first was very silent while Mrs. Dugdale asked as to
the festivities. "It has been the grandest thing anywhere about
here for a long time."

"And, like other grand things, a great bore", said the Major.

"I don't suppose you found it so, Major Rossiter", said the
lady.

Then the conversation ran away into a description of what
had been done during the day. He wished to make it understood that there was no permanent link binding him to Brook
Park, but he hardly knew how to say it without going beyond
the lines of ordinary conversation. At last there seemed to be
an opening—not exactly what he wished, but still an opening.
"Brook Park is not exactly the place", said he, "at which I
should ever feel myself quite at home." This was in answer
to some chance word which had fallen from Mrs. Dugdale.

"I am sorry for that", said Alice. She would have given a
guinea to bring the word back after it had been spoken. But
spoken words cannot be brought back.

"Why sorry?" he asked, smiling.

"Because—— Oh, because it is so likely that you may be
there often."

"I don't know that at all."

"You have become so intimate with them!" said Alice,

"We are told in Beetham that the party was got up all for your honour."

So Sir Walter had told him, and so Maria, the naughty girl, had said also—"Only for your beaux yeux, Major Rossiter, we shouldn't have had any party at all." This had been said by Maria when she was laughing at him about her sister Georgiana. "I don't know how that may be", said the Major; "but all the same I shall never be at home at Brook Park."

"Don't you like the young ladies?" asked Mrs. Dugdale.

"Oh, yes; very much; and Lady Wanless; and Sir Walter. I like them all, in a way. But yet I shall never find myself at home at Brook Park."

Alice was very angry with him. He ought not to have gone there at all. He must have known that he could not be there without paining her. She thoroughly believed that he was engaged to marry the girl of whose family he spoke in this way. He had thought—so it seemed to her—that he might lessen the blow to her by making little of the great folk among whom his future lot was to be cast. But what could be more mean? He was not the John Rossiter to whom she had given her heart. There had been no such man. She had been mistaken. "I am afraid you are one of those", she said, "who, wherever they find themselves, at once begin to wish for something better."

"That is meant to be severe."

"My severity won't go for much."

"I am sure you have deserved it", said Mrs. Dugdale, most indiscreetly.

"Is this intended for an attack?" he asked, looking from one to the other.

"Not at all", said Alice, affecting to laugh. "I should have said nothing if I thought mamma would take it up so seriously. I was only sorry to hear you speak of your new friends so slightingly."

After that the conversation between them was very difficult, and he soon got up to go away. As he did so, he asked Alice

to say a word to him out in the garden, having already
explained to them both that it might be some time before he
would be again down at Beetham. Alice rose slowly from her
sewing-machine, and, putting on her hat, led the way with a
composed and almost dignified step out through the window.
Her heart was beating within her, but she looked as though
she were mistress of every pulse. "Why did you say that to
me?" he asked.

"Say what?"

"That I always wished for better things and better people
than I found."

"Because I think you ambitious—and discontented. There
is nothing disgraceful in that, though it is not the character
which I myself like the best."

"You meant to allude specially to the Wanlesses?"

"Because you have just come from there, and were speaking
of them."

"And to one of that family specially?"

"No, Major Rossiter. There you are wrong. I alluded to
no one in particular. They are nothing to me. I do not know
them; but I hear that they are kind and friendly people, with
good manners and very handsome. Of course I know, as we
all know everything of each other in this little place, that you
have of late become very intimate with them. Then when I
hear you aver that you are already discontented with them, I
cannot help thinking that you are hard to please. I am sorry
that mamma spoke of deserving. I did not intend to say
anything so seriously."

"Alice!"

"Well, Major Rossiter."

"I wish I could make you understand me."

"I do not know that that would do any good. We have
been old friends, and of course I hope that you may be happy.
I must say good-bye now. I cannot go beyond the gate,
because I am wanted to take the children out."

"Good-bye then. I hope you will not think ill of me."

"Why should I think ill of you? I think very well—only that you are ambitious." As she said this, she laughed again, and then she left him.

He had been most anxious to tell her that he was not going to marry that girl, but he had not known how to do it. He could not bring himself to declare that he would not marry a girl when by such declaration he would have been forced to assume that he might marry her if he pleased. So he left Alice at the gate, and she went back to the house still convinced that he was betrothed to Georgiana Wanless.

CHAPTER VIII

SIR WALTER UP IN LONDON

THE MAJOR, WHEN HE LEFT THE DOCTOR'S house, was more thoroughly in love with Alice than ever. There had been something in her gait as she led the way out through the window, and again, as with determined purpose she bade him speedily farewell at the gate, which forced him to acknowledge that the dragging of perambulators and the making of petticoats had not detracted from her feminine charm or from her feminine dignity. She had been dressed in her ordinary morning frock—the very frock on which he had more than once seen the marks of Bobby's dirty heels; but she had pleased his eye better than Georgiana, clad in all the glory of her toxophilite array. The toxophilite feather had been very knowing, the tight leathern belt round her waist had been bright in colour and pretty in design. The looped-up dress, fit for the work in hand, had been gratifying. But with it all there had been the show of a thing got up for ornament and not for use. She was like a box of painted sugar-plums, very pretty to the eye, but of which no one wants to extract any for the

purpose of eating them. Alice was like a housewife's store,
kept beautifully in order, but intended chiefly for comfortable
use. As he went up to London he began to doubt whether he
would go abroad. Were he to let a few months pass by would
not Alice be still there, and willing perhaps to receive him with
more kindness when she should have heard that his follies at
Brook Park were at an end?

Three days after his return, when he was sitting in his offices
thinking perhaps more of Alice Dugdale than of the whole
British Cavalry, a soldier who was in waiting brought a card
to him. Sir Walter Wanless had come to call upon him. If he
were disengaged Sir Walter would be glad to see him. He
was not at all anxious to see Sir Walter; but there was no
alternative, and Sir Walter was shown into the room.

In explaining the purport of Sir Walter's visit we must go
back for a few minutes to Brook Park. When Sir Walter came
down to breakfast on the morning after the festivities he was
surprised to hear that Major Rossiter had taken his departure.
There sat young Burmeston. He at any rate was safe. And there
sat young Cobble, who by Sophia's aid had managed to get
himself accommodated for the night, and all the other young
people, including the five Wanless girls. The father, though
not observant, could see that Georgiana was very glum. Lady
Wanless herself affected a good-humour which hardly
deceived him, and certainly did not deceive any one else. "He
was obliged to be off this morning, because of his duties", said
Lady Wanless. "He told me that it was to be so, but I did not
like to say anything about it yesterday." Georgiana turned
up her nose, as much as to say that the going and coming of
Major Rossiter was not a matter of much importance to any
one there, and, least of all, to her. Except the father, there was
not a person in the room who was not aware that Lady
Wanless had missed her fish.

But she herself was not quite sure even yet that she had failed
altogether. She was a woman who hated failure, and who
seldom failed. She was brave of heart too, and able to fight a

losing battle to the last. She was very angry with the Major, who she well knew was endeavouring to escape from her toils. But he would not on that account be the less useful as a son-in-law—nor on that account was she the more willing to allow him to escape. With five daughters without fortunes it behoved her as a mother to be persistent. She would not give it up, but must turn the matter well in her mind before she took further steps. She feared that a simple invitation could hardly bring the Major back to Brook Park. Then there came the letter from the Major which did not make the matter easier.

"My dear", she said to her husband, sitting down opposite to him in his room, "that Major Rossiter isn't behaving quite as he ought to do."

"I'm not a bit surprised", said the Baronet angrily. "I never knew anybody from Wadham behave well."

"He's quite a gentleman, if you mean that", said Lady Wanless; "and he's sure to do very well in the world; and poor Georgiana is really fond of him—which doesn't surprise me in the least."

"Has he said anything to make her fond of him? I suppose she has gone and made a fool of herself—like Maria."

"Not at all. He has said a great deal to her—much more than he ought to have done, if he meant nothing. But the truth is, young men nowadays never know their own minds unless there is somebody to keep them up to the mark. You must go and see him."

"I!" said the afflicted father.

"Of course, my dear. A few judicious words in such a case may do so much. I would not ask Walter to go"—Walter was the eldest son, who was with his regiment—"because it might lead to quarrelling. I would not have anything of that kind, if only for the dear girl's sake. But what you would say would be known to nobody; and it might have the desired effect. Of course you will be very quiet—and very serious also. Nobody could do it better than you will. There can be no doubt that he has trifled with the dear girl's affections. Why else has he

been with her whenever he has been here? It was so visible on
Wednesday that everybody was congratulating me. Old Lady
Deepbell asked whether the day was fixed. I treated him quite
as though it were settled. Young men do so often get these
sudden starts of doubt. Then sometimes just a word afterwards
will put it all right." In this way the Baronet was made to
understand that he must go and see the Major.

He postponed the unwelcome task till his wife at last drove
him out of the house. "My dear", she said, "will you let your
child die broken-hearted for want of a word?" When it was
put to him in that way he found himself obliged to go, though,
to tell the truth, he could not find any sign of heart-breaking
sorrow about his child. He was not allowed to speak to
Georgiana herself, his wife telling him that the poor child would
be unable to bear it.

Sir Walter, when he was shown into the Major's room, felt
himself to be very ill able to conduct the business in hand, and
to the Major himself the moment was one of considerable
trouble. He had thought it possible that he might receive an
answer to his letter, a reply that might be indignant, or piteous,
admonitory, or simply abusive, as the case might be—one which
might too probably require a further correspondence; but it had
never occurred to him that Sir Walter would come in person.
But here he was—in the room—by no means with that pretended air of geniality with which he had last received the
Major down at Brook Park. The greeting, however, between
the gentlemen was courteous if not cordial, and then Sir
Walter began his task. "We were quite surprised you should
have left us so early that morning."

"I had told Lady Wanless."

"Yes; I know. Nevertheless we were surprised. Now,
Major Rossiter, what do you mean to do about—about—
about this young lady?" The Major sat silent. He could not
pretend to be ignorant what young lady was intended after
the letter which he had himself written to Lady Wanless. "This,
you know, is a very painful kind of thing, Major Rossiter."

"Very painful indeed, Sir Walter."

"When I remembered that I had been at Christchurch and your excellent father at Wadham both at the same time, I thought that I might trust you in my house without the slightest fear."

"I make bold to say, Sir Walter, that you were quite justified in that expectation, whether it was founded on your having been at Christchurch or on my position and character in the world." He knew that the scene would be easier to him if he could work himself up to a little indignation on his own part.

"And yet I am told—I am told——"

"What are you told, Sir Walter?"

"There can, I think, be no doubt that you have—in point of fact, paid attention to my daughter." Sir Walter was a gentleman, and felt that the task imposed upon him grated against his better feelings.

"If you mean that I have taken steps to win her affections, you have been wrongly informed."

"That's what I do mean. Were you not received just now at Brook Park as—as paying attention to her?"

"I hope not."

"You hope not, Major Rossiter?"

"I hope no such mistake was made. It certainly was not made by me. I felt myself much flattered by being received at your house. I wrote the other day a line or two to Lady Wanless and thought I had explained all this."

Sir Walter opened his eyes when he heard, for the first time, of the letter, but was sharp enough not to exhibit his ignorance at the moment. "I don't know about explaining", he said. "There are some things which can't be so very well explained. My wife assures me that that poor girl has been deceived— cruelly deceived. Now I put it to you, Major Rossiter, what ought you as a gentleman to do?"

"Really, Sir Walter, you are not entitled to ask me any such question."

"Not on behalf of my own child?"

"I cannot go into the matter from that view of the case. I can only declare that I have said nothing and done nothing for which I can blame myself. I cannot understand how there should have been such a mistake; but it did not, at any rate, arise with me."

Then the Baronet sat dumb. He had been specially instructed not to give up the interview till he had obtained some sign of weakness from the enemy. If he could only induce the enemy to promise another visit to Brook Park that would be much. If he could obtain some expression of liking or admiration for the young lady that would be something. If he could induce the Major to allude to delay as being necessary, further operations would be founded on that base. But nothing had been obtained. "It's the most—the most—the most astonishing thing I ever heard", he said at last.

"I do not know that I can say anything further."

"I'll tell you what", said the Baronet. "Come down and see Lady Wanless. The women understand these things much better than we do. Come down and talk it over with Lady Wanless. She won't propose anything that isn't proper." In answer to this the Major shook his head. "You won't?"

"It would do no good, Sir Walter. It would be painful to me, and must, I should say, be distressing to the young lady."

"Then you won't do anything!"

"There is nothing to be done."

"Upon my word, I have never heard such a thing in all my life, Major Rossiter. You come down to my house; and then—then—then you won't—you won't come again! To be sure he was at Wadham; but I did think your father's son would have behaved better." Then he picked up his hat from the floor and shuffled out of the room without another word.

Tidings that Sir Walter had been up to London and had called upon Major Rossiter made their way into Beetham and reached the ears of the Dugdales—but not correct tidings as to the nature of the conversation. "I wonder when it will be", said Mrs.

Dugdale to Alice. "As he has been up to town I suppose it'll be settled soon."

"The sooner the better for all parties", said Alice cheerily. "When a man and a woman have agreed together, I can't see why they shouldn't at once walk off to the church arm in arm."

"The lawyers have so much to do."

"Bother the lawyers! The parson ought to do all that is necessary, and the sooner the better. Then there would not be such paraphernalia of presents and gowns and eatings and drinkings, all of which is got up for the good of the tradesmen. If I were to be married, I should like to slip out round the corner, just as though I were going to get an extra loaf of bread from Mrs. Bakewell."

"That wouldn't do for my lady at Brook Park."

"I suppose not."

"Nor yet for the Major."

Then Alice shook her head and sighed, and took herself out to walk alone for a few minutes among the lanes. How could it be that he should be so different from that which she had taken him to be! It was now September, and she could remember an early evening in May, when the leaves were beginning to be full, and they were walking together with the spring air fresh around them, just where she was now creeping alone with the more perfect and less fresh beauty of the autumn around her. How different a person he seemed to her to be now from that which he had seemed to be then—not different because he did not love her, but different because he was not fit to be loved! "Alice", he had then said, "you and I are alike in this, that simple, serviceable things are dear to both of us." The words had meant so much to her that she had never forgotten them. Was she simple and serviceable, so that she might be dear to him? She had been sure then that he was simple, and that he was serviceable, so that she could love him. It was thus that she had spoken of him to herself, thinking herself to be sure of his character. And now, before the summer was over, he was engaged to marry such a one as

Georgiana Wanless and to become the hero of a fashionable
wedding!

But she took pride to herself as she walked alone that she
had already overcome the bitterness of the malady which,
for a day or two, had been so heavy that she had feared for
herself that it would oppress her. For a day or two after that
farewell at the gate she had with a rigid purpose tied herself
to every duty—even to the duty of looking pleasant in her
father's eyes, of joining in the children's games, of sharing the
gossip of her stepmother. But this she had done with an
agony that nearly crushed her. Now she had won her way
through it, and could see her path before her. She had not
cured altogether that wound in her heart; but she had assured
herself that she could live on without further interference
from the wound.

CHAPTER IX

LADY DEEPBELL

THEN BY DEGREES IT BEGAN TO BE RUMOURED
about the country, and at last through the lanes of Beetham
itself, that the alliance between Major Rossiter and Miss
Georgiana Wanless was not quite a settled thing. Mr.
Burmeston had whispered in Slowbridge that there was a
screw loose, perhaps thinking that if another could escape,
why not he also? Cobble, who had no idea of escaping,
declared his conviction that Major Rossiter ought to be
horsewhipped; but Lady Deepbell was the real town-crier
who carried the news far and wide. But all of them heard it
before Alice, and when others believed it Alice did not believe
it—or, indeed, care to believe or not to believe.

Lady Deepbell filled a middle situation, half-way between
the established superiority of Brook Park and the recognized

humility of Beetham. Her title went for something; but her husband had been only a Civil Service Knight, who had deserved well of his country by a meritorious longevity. She lived in a pretty little cottage half-way between Brook Park and Beetham, which was just large enough to enable her to talk of her grounds. She loved Brook Park dearly, and all the county people; but in her love for social intercourse generally she was unable to eschew the more frequent gatherings of the village. She was intimate not only with Mrs. Rossiter, but with the Tweeds and Dugdales and Simkinses, and, while she could enjoy greatly the grandeur of the Wanless aristocracy, so could she accommodate herself comfortably to the cosy gossip of the Beethamites. It was she who first spread the report in Beetham that Major Rossiter was—as she called it—"off."

She first mentioned the matter to Mrs. Rossiter herself; but this she did in a manner more subdued than usual. The "alliance" had been high, and she was inclined to think that Mrs. Rossiter would be disappointed. "We did think, Mrs. Rossiter, that these young people at Brook Park had meant something the other day."

Mrs. Rossiter did not stand in awe of Lady Deepbell, and was not pleased at the allusion. "It would be much better if young people could be allowed to arrange their own affairs without so much tattling about it," she said angrily.

"That's all very well, but tongues will talk, you know, Mrs. Rossiter. I am sorry for both their sakes, because I thought that it would do very well."

"Very well indeed, if the young people, as you call them, liked each other."

"But I suppose it's over now, Mrs. Rossiter?"

"I really know nothing about it, Lady Deepbell." Then the old woman, quite satisfied after this that the "alliance" had fallen to the ground, went on to the Tweeds.

"I never thought it would come to much", said Mrs. Tweed.

"I don't see why it shouldn't", said Matilda Tweed.

"Georgiana Wanless is good-looking in a certain way; but they none of them have a penny, and Major Rossiter is quite a fashionable man." The Tweeds were quite outside the Wanless pale; and it was the feeling of this that made Matilda love to talk about the second Miss Wanless by her Christian name.

"I suppose he will go back to Alice now", said Clara, the younger Tweed girl.

"I don't see that at all", said Mrs. Tweed.

"I never believed much in that story", said Lady Deepbell.

"Nor I either", said Matilda. "He used to walk about with her, but what does that come to? The children were always with them. I never would believe that he was going to make so little of himself."

"But is it quite sure that all the affair at Brook Park will come to nothing, after the party and everything?" asked Mrs. Tweed.

"Quite positive", said Lady Deepbell authoritatively. "I am able to say certainly that that is all over." Then she toddled off and went to the Simkinses.

The rumour did not reach the doctor's house on that day. The conviction that Major Rossiter had behaved badly to Alice—that Alice had been utterly thrown over by the Wanless "alliance"—had been so strong, that even Lady Deepbell had not dared to go and probe wilfully that wound. The feeling in this respect had been so general that no one in Beetham had been hard-hearted enough to speak to Alice either of the triumph of Miss Wanless, or of the misconduct of the Major; and now Lady Deepbell was afraid to carry her story thither.

It was the doctor himself who first brought the tidings to the house, and did not do this till some days after Lady Deepbell had been in the village. "You had better not say anything to Alice about it." Such at first had been the doctor's injunction to his wife. "One way or the other, it will only be a trouble to her." Mrs. Dugdale, full of her secret, anxious to be obedient, thinking that the gentleman, relieved from his second love, would be ready at once to be on again with his first, was so fluttered and fussy that Alice knew that there was something to be told. "You have got some great secret, mamma", she said. "What secret, Alice?" "I know you have. Don't wait for me to ask you to tell it. If it is to come, let it come." "I'm not going to say anything." "Very well, mamma. Then nothing shall be said." "Alice, you are the most provoking young woman I ever had to deal with in my life. If I had twenty secrets I would not tell you one of them."

On the next morning Alice heard it all from her father. "I knew there was something by mamma's manner", she said. "I told her not to say anything." "So I suppose. But what does it matter to me, papa, whether Major Rossiter does or does not marry Miss Wanless? If he has given her his word, I am sure I hope that he will keep it." "I don't suppose he ever did." "Even then it doesn't matter. Papa, do not trouble yourself about him." "But you?" "I have gone through the fire, and have come out without being much scorched. Dear papa, I do so wish that you should understand it all. It is so nice to have someone to whom everything can be told. I did like him." "And he?" "I have nothing to say about that—not a word. Girls, I suppose, are often foolish, and take things for more than they are intended to mean. I have no accusation to make against him. But I did—I did allow myself to be weak. Then came this about Miss Wanless, and I was unhappy. I woke from a dream, and the waking was painful. But I have got over it. I do not think that you will ever know from your girl's manner that anything has been the matter with her." "My brave girl!" "But don't let mamma talk to me as though he could come

back because the other girl has not suited him. He is welcome
to the other girl—welcome to do without her—welcome
to do with himself as it may best please him; but he shall not
trouble me again." There was a stern strength in her voice as
she said this, which forced her father to look at her almost with
amazement. "Do not think that I am fierce, papa."

"Fierce, my darling!"

"But that I am in earnest. Of course, if he comes to Beetham
we shall see him. But let him be like anybody else. Don't
let it be supposed that because he flitted here once, and was
made welcome, like a bird that comes in at the window, and
then flitted away again, that he can be received in at the window
just as before, should he fly this way any more. That's all,
all, papa." Then, as before, she went off by herself—to give
herself renewed strength by her solitary thinkings. She had so
healed the flesh round that wound that there was no longer
danger of mortification. She must now take care that there
should be no further wound. The people around her would
be sure to tell her of this breach between her late lover and
the Wanless young lady. The Tweeds and the Simkinses,
and old Lady Deepbell would be full of it. She must take care
so to answer them at the first word that they should not dare
to talk to her of Major Rossiter. She had cured herself so that
she no longer staggered under the effects of the blow. Having
done that, she would not allow herself to be subject to the
little stings of the little creatures around her. She had had
enough of love—of a man's love, and would make herself
happy now with Bobby and the other bairns.

"He'll be sure to come back", said Mrs. Dugdale to her
husband.

"We shall do no good by talking about it", said the doctor.
"If you will take my advice, you will not mention his name to
her. I fear that he is worthless and unworthy of mention."
That might be very well, thought Mrs. Dugdale; but no one
in the village doubted that he had at the very least £1,500 a
year, and that he was a handsome man, and such a one as is

not to be picked up under every hedge. The very men who go about the world most like butterflies before marriage "steady down the best" afterwards. These were her words as she discussed the matter with Mrs. Tweed, and they both agreed that if the hero showed himself again at the doctor's house "bygones ought to be bygones."

Lady Wanless, even after her husband's return from London, declared to herself that even yet the game had not been altogether played out. Sir Walter, who had been her only possible direct messenger to the man himself, had been, she was aware, as bad a messenger as could have been selected. He could be neither authoritative nor persuasive. Therefore when he told her, on coming home, that it was easy to perceive that Major Rossiter's father could not have been educated at Christchurch, she did not feel very much disappointed. As her next step she determined to call on Mrs. Rossiter. If that should fail she must beard the lion in his den, and go herself to Major Rossiter at the Horse Guards. She did not doubt but that she would at least be able to say more than Sir Walter. Mrs. Rossiter, she was aware, was herself favourable to the match.

"My dear Mrs. Rossiter", she said in her most confidential manner, "there is a little something wrong among these young people, which I think you and I can put right if we put our heads together."

"If I know one of the young people", said Mrs. Rossiter, "it will be very hard to make him change his mind."

"He has been very attentive to the young lady."

"Of course I know nothing about it, Lady Wanless. I never saw them together."

"Dear Georgiana is so very quiet that she said nothing even to me, but I really thought that he had proposed to her. She won't say a word against him, but I believe he did. Now, Mrs. Rossiter, what has been the meaning of it?"

"How is a mother to answer for her son, Lady Wanless?"

"No—of course not. I know that. Girls, of course, are

different. But I thought that perhaps you might know something about it, for I did imagine you would like the connection."

"So I should. Why not? Nobody thinks more of birth than I do, and nothing in my opinion could have been nicer for John. But he does not see with my eyes. If I were to talk to him for a week it would have no effect."

"Is it that girl of the doctor's, Mrs. Rossiter?"

"I think not. My idea is that when he has turned it all over in his mind he has come to the conclusion that he will be better without a wife than with one."

"We might cure him of that, Mrs. Rossiter. If I could only have him down there at Brook Park for another week, I am sure he would come to." Mrs. Rossiter, however, could not say that she thought it probable that her son would be induced soon to pay another visit to Brook Park.

A week after this Lady Wanless absolutely did find her way into the Major's presence at the Horse Guards—but without much success. The last words at that interview only shall be given to the reader—the last words as they were spoken both by the lady and by the gentleman. "Then I am to see my girl die of a broken heart?" said Lady Wanless, with her handkerchief up to her eyes.

"I hope not, Lady Wanless; but in whatever way she might die, the fault would not be mine." There was a frown on the gentleman's brow as he said this which cowed even the lady.

As she went back to Slowbridge that afternoon, and then home to Brook Park, she determined at last that the game must be looked upon as played out. There was no longer any ground on which to stand and fight. Before she went to bed that night she sent for Georgiana. "My darling child", she said, "that man is unworthy of you."

"I always thought he was", said Georgiana. And so there was an end to that little episode in the family of the Wanlesses.

CHAPTER X

THE BIRD THAT PECKED AT THE WINDOW

THE BIRD THAT HAD FLOWN IN AT THE WINDOW and had been made welcome, had flown away ungratefully. Let him come again pecking as he might at the window, no more crumbs of love should be thrown to him. Alice, with a steady purpose, had resolved on that. With all her humble ways, her continual darning of stockings, her cutting of bread and butter for the children, her pushing of the perambulator in the lanes, there was a pride about her, a knowledge of her own dignity as a woman, which could have been stronger in the bosom of no woman of title, of wealth, or of fashion. She claimed nothing. She had expected no admiration. She had been contented to take the world as it came to her, without thinking much of love or romance. When John Rossiter had first shown himself at Beetham, after his return from India, and when he had welcomed her so warmly—too warmly—as his old playfellow, no idea had occurred to her that he would ever be more to her than her old playfellow. Her own heart was too precious to herself to be given away idly to the first comer. Then the bird had flown in at the window, and it had been that the coming of the stranger had been very sweet to her. But, even for the stranger, she would not change her ways—unless, perchance, some day she might appertain to the stranger. Then it would be her duty to fit herself entirely to him. In the meantime, when he gave her little hints that something of her domestic slavery might be discontinued, she would not abate a jot from her duties. If he liked to come with her when she pushed the children, let him come. If he cared to see her when she was darning a stocking or cutting bread and butter, let him pay his visits. If he thought those things derogatory, certainly let him stay away. So the thing had grown till she had found

herself surprised, and taken, as it were, into a net—caught in a
pitfall of love. But she held her peace, stuck manfully to the
perambulator, and was a little colder in her demeanour than
heretofore. Whereupon Major Rossiter, as the reader is aware,
made two visits to Brook Park. The bird might peck at the
window, but he should never again be taken into the room.

But the bird, from the moment in which he had packed up
his portmanteau at Brook Park, had determined that he would
be taken in at the window again—that he would at any rate
return to the window, and peck at the glass with constancy,
soliciting that it might be opened. As he now thought of the
two girls, the womanliness of the one, as compared with the
worldliness of the other, conquered him completely. There
had never been a moment in which his heart had in truth
inclined itself towards the young athlete of Brook Park—
never a moment, hardly a moment, in which his heart had
been untrue to Alice. But glitter had for a while prevailed
with him, and he had, just for a moment, allowed himself
to be discontented with the homely colour of unalloyed gold.
He was thoroughly ashamed of himself, knowing well that
he had given pain. He had learned, clearly enough, from
what his father, mother, and others had said to him, that there
were those who expected him to marry Alice Dugdale, and
others who hoped that he would marry Georgiana Wanless.
Now, at last, he could declare that no other love than that
which was warm within his heart at present could ever have
been possible to him. But he was aware that he had much
to do to recover his footing. Alice's face and her manner as
she bade him good-bye at the gate were very clear before his
eyes.

Two months passed by before he was again seen at Beetham.
It had happened that he was, in truth, required elsewhere, on
duty, during the period, and he took care to let it be known
at Beetham that such was the case. Information to this effect
was in some shape sent to Alice. Openly, she took no notice
of it; but, inwardly, she said to herself that they who troubled

themselves by sending her such tidings, troubled themselves in vain. "Men may come and men may go", she sang to herself, in a low voice. How little they knew her, to come to her with news as to Major Rossiter's coming and going!

Then one day he came. One morning early in December the absolute fact was told at the dinner table. "The Major is at the parsonage", said the maid-servant. Mrs. Dugdale looked at Alice, who continued, however, to distribute hashed mutton with an equanimity which betrayed no flaw.

After that not a word was said about him. The doctor had warned his wife to be silent; and though she would fain have spoken, she restrained herself. After dinner the usual work went on, and then the usual playing in the garden. The weather was dry and mild for the time of year, so that Alice was swinging two of the children when Major Rossiter came up through the gate. Minnie, who had been a favourite, ran to him, and he came slowly across the lawn to the tree on which the swing was hung. For a moment Alice stopped her work that she might shake hands with him, and then at once went back to her place. "If I were to stop a moment before Bobby has had his turn", she said, "he would feel the injustice."

"No, I isn't", said Bobby. "Oo may go 'is time."

"But I don't want to go, Bobby, and Major Rossiter will find mamma in the drawing-room;" and Alice for a moment thought of getting her hat and going off from the place. Then she reflected that to run away would be cowardly. She did not mean to run away always because the man came. Had she not settled it with herself that the man should be nothing to her? Then she went on swinging the children—very deliberately, in order that she might be sure of herself, that the man's coming had not even flurried her.

In ten minutes the Major was there again. It had been natural to suppose that he should not be detained long in conversation by Mrs. Dugdale. "May I swing one of them for a time?" he asked.

"Well, no; I think not. It is my allotted exercise, and I

never give it up." But Minnie, who knew what a strong arm could do, was imperious, and the Major got possession of the swing.

Then of a sudden he stopped. "Alice", he said, "I want you to take a turn with me up the road."

"I am not going out at all to-day", she said. Her voice was steady and well preserved; but there was a slight rising of colour on her cheeks.

"But I wish it expressly. You must come to-day."

She could consider only for a moment—but for a moment she did think the matter over. If the man chose to speak to her seriously, she must listen to him—once, and once only. So much he had a right to demand. When a bird of that kind pecks in that manner some attention must be paid to him. So she got her hat, and leading the way down the road, opened the gate and turned up the lane away from the street of the village. For some yards he did not speak. She, indeed, was the first to do so. "I cannot stay out very long, Major Rossiter; so, if there is anything——?"

"There is a something, Alice." Of course she knew, but she was quite resolved. Resolved! Had not every moment of her life since last she had parted with him been given up to the strengthening of this resolution? Not a stitch had gone through the calico which had not been pulled the tighter by the tightening of her purpose! And now he was there. Oh, how more than earthly sweet it had been to have him there, when her resolutions had been of another kind! But she had been punished for that, and was strong against such future ills. "Alice, it had better come out simply. I love you, and have ever loved you with all my heart." Then there was a frown and a little trampling of the ground beneath her feet, but she said not a word. Oh, if it only could have come sooner —a few weeks sooner! "I know what you would say to me, but I would have you listen to me, if possible, before you say it. I have given you cause to be angry with me."

"Oh no!" she cried, interrupting him.

"But I have never been untrue to you for a moment. You seemed to slight me."

"And if I did?"

"That may pass. If you should slight me now, I must bear it. Even though you should deliberately tell me that you cannot love me, I must bear that. But with such a load of love as I have at my heart, it must be told to you. Day and night it covers me from head to foot. I can think of nothing else. I dream that I have your hand in mine, but when I wake I think it can never be so."

There was an instinct with her at the moment to let her fingers glide into his; but it was shown only by the gathering together of her two hands, so that no rebellious fingers straying from her in that direction might betray her. "If you have never loved me, never can love me, say so, and I will go away." She should have spoken now, upon the instant; but she simply moved her foot upon the gravel and was silent. "That I should be punished might be right. If it could be possible that the punishment should extend to two, that could not be right."

She did not want to punish him—only to be brave herself. If to be obdurate would in truth make him unhappy, then would it be right that she should still be firm? It would be bad enough, after so many self-assurances, to succumb at the first word; but for his sake—for his sake—would it not be possible to bear even that? "If you never have loved me, and never can love me, say so, and I will go." Even to herself, she had not pledged herself to lie. If he asked her to be his wife in the plain way, she could say that she would not. Then the way would be plain before her. But what reply was she to make in answer to such a question as this? Could she say that she had not loved him—or did not love him? "Alice", he said, putting his hand up to her arm.

"No!"

"Alice, can you not forgive me?"

"I have forgiven."

"And will you not love me?"

She turned her face upon him with a purpose to frown, but the fulness of his eyes upon her was too much, and the frown gave way, and a tear came into her eye, and her lips trembled; and then she acknowledged to herself that her resolution had not been worth a straw to her.

It should be added that considerably before Alice's wedding, both Sophia and Georgiana Wanless were married—Sophia, in due order, as of course, to young Cobble, and Georgiana to Mr. Burmeston, the brewer. This, as the reader will remember, was altogether unexpected; but it was a great and guiding principle with Lady Wanless that the girls should not be taken out of their turns.

The End

MARY GRESLEY

AND OTHER STORIES

NOTE

Anthony Trollope was born on April 24th, 1815, at 6 Keppel Street, Russell Square, London, the fourth son of a clever, unsuccessful barrister and of Frances Trollope, who was a popular writer from 1832 onwards. He was educated, and was profoundly miserable, at Harrow and Winchester. He served in the General Post Office from 1834 until 1867, in London, Ireland, and many parts of England, inventing the pillar-box, making substantial improvements in postal services at home and overseas, going on official missions to the Middle East, the West Indies, and North America, and travelling extensively in Europe, Australia, New Zealand, South Africa and Iceland. His first novel was published in 1847 and his last, posthumously, in 1884. His total output was prodigious,—well over a hundred and thirty volumes of novels, tales, travel, essays, biographies, and one of the best of English autobiographies. He died at 34 Welbeck Street, London, on December 6th, 1882.

The O'Conors of Castle Conor was first published in "Harper's New Monthly Magazine," May, 1860, and "Tales of All Countries," 1861; The Journey to Panama in an anthology, "The Victoria Regia," edited by A. A. Procter and dedicated to Queen Victoria, 1861, and "Lotta Schmidt and other Stories," 1867; Katchen's Caprices in "Harper's Weekly," December, 1866—January, 1867; The Turkish Bath and Mary Gresley in "St. Paul's Magazine," under Trollope's editorship, in October and November, 1869, and "An Editor's Tales," 1870. For these data I am once again gratefully indebted to Trollope: A Bibliography *by Michael Sadleir.*

Katchen's Caprices is here reprinted, apparently for the first time, from photostats of the copies in the British Museum Newspaper Room of "Harper's Weekly: A Journal of Civilisation," Nos. 521-524, New York, December 22nd and 29th, 1866, and January 5th and 12th, 1867. Two sentences in this make nonsense. They appear on page 311 of the present edition, lines 14 to 18, beginning with 'Caspar Ebner was in love ....' The American compositor may have dropped a word or a phrase (Trollope's handwriting was not very clear) or may have substituted 'not' for 'now', Trollope having written 'At all events he did now perceive ...' But as I am unable to amend the passage except by guess-work I have let it stand.

J. H.

INTRODUCTION

ANTHONY TROLLOPE the man was born in London, in the year of Waterloo, but Anthony Trollope the writer might well have claimed Ireland as his birthplace twenty-eight years later. It is true that all through his wretched boyhood and his miserable seven years as a junior clerk at St. Martin's-le-Grand he told himself stories in the manner of a novelist-to-be: 'I learned in this way', he says in his famous *Autobiography*, 'to maintain an interest in a fictitious story, to dwell on a work created by my own imagination, and to live in a world altogether outside my own material life'. Yet when he landed in Dublin in 1841 he had made no known attempt at writing and had nothing behind him, in his own view, except 'twenty-six years of suffering, disgrace and inward remorse'. It was in Ireland that he first earned enough to keep himself out of debt, became an efficient civil servant, found health and happiness and his Yorkshire wife, and began to write.

So it is appropriate enough that the first short story he published, which is the first in this book, should be completely Irish (like his first novel and his last) in setting and character. 'It was altogether a very jolly life that I led in Ireland', he says. 'Some adventures I had;—two of which I told in the *Tales of All Countries* under the names of "The O'Conors of Castle Conor" and "Father Giles of Ballymoy". I will not swear to every detail in these stories, but the main purport of each is true'. *The O'Conors* has none of that ebullient high spirits which Trollope admired so much in the Irish novels and the conversation of his 'dear old friend Charles Lever', and it has very few of the qualities, except perhaps a certain plain honesty in character-drawing, which have made Trollope's work so much loved; it is an ingenious piece of mild comedy, and its main interest now is its social setting.

In *The Journey to Panama*, however, the novelist of character is deeply engaged and although personal experience has no doubt contributed a good deal it has been imaginatively recreated. This story was written soon after an official visit to the West Indies in 1858-59 which not only enabled Trollope to improve their postal services but produced the first and perhaps the best of his travel books: *The West Indies and the Spanish Main*. Hence the graphic touches of detail still fresh in his memory which add so much verisimilitude: 'The sun became very powerful, and the passengers in the lower part of the ship complained loudly of having their portholes closed. The Spaniards sat gambling in the cabin all day....' In his lesser tales 'local colour' is used merely to decorate a threadbare theme. Here it is integral to the story, for the circumstances in which they find themselves not only bring Emily Viner and Ralph Forrest together, but determine the development of their friendship. Trollope never shows greater imaginative sympathy and insight than when dealing with a woman in such a position as Emily's, and there is much of his own personality in Ralph. Moreover he was writing in the first maturity of his powers and the first glow of success, for the serialisation of *Framley Parsonage* in the 'Cornhill Magazine' during 1860 had made him famous. The generalisations of the opening paragraphs go on too long, but from the real beginning to the abortive ending, in which truth triumphs over Victorian wedding bells, the story is managed with a subtlety and skill unsurpassed in Trollope's tales. In both feeling and technique it is more akin to the short story of to-day than to that of the eighteen-sixties.

The only *nouvelle* in this volume, *Katchen's Caprices*, is a reminder that this literary form, now almost extinct in England, was used with distinction by many nineteenth-century writers, from Scott and Stevenson to Conrad and Henry James. It is a reminder also of the many European holidays from which Trollope drew numerous short stories and some of his most interesting minor novels, such as *Nina Balatka* and *The Golden Lion of Granpère*. It displays, indeed, 'local colour' and a threadbare theme—the young girl kept from her lover by family or social pressures and sometimes compelled to accept an older, more prosperous suitor; a theme which Trollope uses far too often, for he regarded the plot as 'the most insignificant of a tale'. Sometimes the result is banal; sometimes it is splendidly redeemed, as in *Dr. Thorne* and *Framley Parsonage*, by strength of characterization and delicate insight into the hearts of the young lovers. *Katchen's Caprices* cannot rank with these, yet it deserves a better fate than burial in the files of *Harper's Weekly*, where it has lain, apparently unreprinted, since 1867, for the characters are shrewdly and sincerely drawn, the narrative is skilfully unfolded, and the setting has a pleasant charm.

Eight months after the publication of *Katchen's Caprices* Trollope resigned regretfully from the civil service, partly from weariness, partly in pique that he had been refused the post of Under-Secretary, and he had already accepted the editorship of *St. Paul's Magazine*, which began publication on October 1st, 1867. It had little success, but before Trollope left it in 1870 he had contributed to its pages some of the best of his short stories, including *The Turkish Bath* and *Mary Gresley*. 'I do not think', he says in his *Autobiography*, 'that there is a single incident in [*An Editor's Tales*] which could bring back to anyone concerned the memory of a past event. And yet there is not an incident in it which was not presented to my mind by the remembrance of some fact.' It is, on the whole, his best volume of stories, and none of them shows a more shrewd and tolerant eye for the idiosyncrasies of human nature than *The Turkish Bath*, while none is more characteristic and self-revealing than *Mary Gresley*.

The latter—which is, incidentally, named after his maternal grandmother—brings to mind his innocent encounter, ten years before, with a pretty, coloured girl in Jamaica, when he wrote half humorously, 'I am not a very young man, and my friends have told me that I show strongly that steady married appearance of a paterfamilias which is so apt to lend assurance to maiden timidity.' Happily and faithfully married as he was, he had indeed, as Henry James put it, 'fallen in love with the English miss', or with any other miss who was attractive enough, and *Mary Gresley* is not only one of the best of his short stories, it does more perhaps than anything else he wrote to explain why his women characters are in general more convincing than those of any other Victorian novelist. His love for Mary Gresley is of the kind which is the beginning of understanding. Yet his compassion is still more significant, for it is evoked as fully by the troublesome, lunatic Irishmen as by his irresistible Mary, and clear-sighted compassion is the beginning of wisdom.

1951   J. H.

THE O'CONORS
OF CASTLE CONOR

I SHALL never forget my first introduction to country life in Ireland, my first day's hunting there, or the manner in which I passed the evening afterwards. Nor shall I ever cease to be grateful for the hospitality which I received from the O'Conors of Castle Conor. My acquaintance with the family was first made in the following manner. But before I begin my story, let me inform my reader that my name is Archibald Green.

I had been for a fortnight in Dublin, and was about to proceed into county Mayo on business which would occupy me there for some weeks. My headquarters would, I found, be at the town of Ballyglass; and I soon learned that Ballyglass was not a place in which I should find hotel accommodation of a luxurious kind, or much congenial society indigenous to the place itself.

'But you are a hunting man, you say', said old Sir P—— C——; 'and in that case you will soon know Tom O'Conor. Tom won't let you be dull. I'd write you a letter to Tom, only he'll certainly make you out without my taking the trouble.'

I did think at the time that the old baronet might have written the letter for me, as he had been a friend of my father's in former days; but he did not, and I started for Ballyglass with no other introduction to any one in the county than that contained in Sir P——'s promise that I should soon know Mr. Thomas O'Conor.

I had already provided myself with a horse, groom, saddle and bridle, and these I sent down, en avant, that the Ballyglassians might know that I was somebody. Perhaps, before I arrived, Tom O'Conor might learn that a hunting man was coming into the neighbourhood, and I might find at the inn a polite note intimating that a bed was at my service at Castle Conor. I had heard so much of the free hospitality of the Irish gentry as to imagine that such a thing might be possible.

But I found nothing of the kind. Hunting gentlemen in those days were very common in county Mayo, and one horse was no great evidence of a man's standing in the world. Men there, as I learnt afterwards, are sought for themselves quite as much as they are elsewhere; and though my groom's top-boots were neat, and my horse a very tidy animal, my entry into Ballyglass created no sensation whatever.

In about four days after my arrival, when I was already infinitely disgusted with the little pot-house in which I was forced to stay, and had made up my mind that the people in county Mayo were a churlish set, I sent my horse on to a meet of the fox-hounds, and followed after myself on an open car.

No one but an erratic fox-hunter such as I am—a fox-hunter, I mean, whose lot it has been to wander about from one pack of hounds to another—can understand the melancholy feeling which a man has when he first intrudes himself, unknown by any one, among an entirely new set of sportsmen. When a stranger falls thus, as it were out of the moon into a hunt, it is impossible that men should not stare at him and ask who he is. And it is so disagreeable to be stared at, and to have such questions asked! This feeling does not come upon a man in Leicestershire or Gloucestershire, where the numbers are large, and a stranger or two will always be overlooked, but in small hunting fields it is so painful that a man has to pluck up much courage before he encounters it.

We met on the morning in question at Bingham's Grove. There were not above twelve or fifteen men out, all of whom, or nearly all, were cousins to each other. They seemed to be all Toms, and Pats, and Larrys, and Micks. I was done up very knowingly in pink, and thought that I looked quite the thing; but for two or three hours nobody noticed me.

I had my eyes about me, however, and soon found out which of them was Tom O'Conor. He was a fine-looking fellow, thin and tall, but not largely made, with a piercing gray eye, and a beautiful voice for speaking to a hound. He had two sons there also, short, slight fellows, but exquisite horsemen. I already felt that I had a kind of acquaintance with the father, but I hardly knew on what ground to put in my claim.

We had no sport early in the morning. It was a cold bleak February day, with occasional storms of sleet. We rode from cover to cover, but all in vain. 'I am sorry, sir, that we are to have such a bad day, as you are a stranger here', said one gentleman to me. This was Jack O'Conor, Tom's eldest son, my bosom friend for many a year after. Poor Jack! I fear that the Encumbered Estates Court sent him altogether adrift upon the world.

'We may still have a run from Poulnaroe, if the gentleman chooses to come on', said a voice coming from behind with a sharp trot. It was Tom O'Conor.

'Wherever the hounds go, I'll follow', said I.

'Then come on to Poulnaroe', said Mr. O'Conor. I trotted on quickly by his side, and before we reached the cover, had managed to slip in something about Sir P. C.

'What the deuce!' said he. 'What! a friend of Sir P——'s? Why the deuce didn't you tell me so? What are you doing down here? Where are you staying', &c., &c., &c.

At Poulnaroe we found a fox, but before we did so Mr. O'Conor had asked me over to Castle Conor. And this he did in such a way that there was no possibility of refusing him—or, I should rather say, of disobeying him. For his invitation came quite in the tone of a command.

'You'll come to us of course when the day is over—and let me see; we're near Ballyglass now, but the run will be right away in our direction. Just send word for them to send your things to Castle Conor.'

'But they're all about, and unpacked', said I.

'Never mind. Write a note and say what you want now, and go and get the rest to-morrow yourself. Here, Patsey!—Patsey! run into Ballyglass for this gentleman at once. Now don't be long, for the chances are we shall find here.' And then, after giving some further hurried instructions he left me to write a line in pencil to the innkeeper's wife on the bank of a ditch.

This I accordingly did. 'Send my small portmanteau', I said, 'and all my black dress clothes, and shirts, and socks, and all that, and above all my dressing things which are on the little table, and the satin neck-handkerchief, and whatever you do, mind you send my *pumps*'; and I underscored the latter word; for Jack O'Conor, when his father left me, went on pressing the invitation. 'My sisters are going to get up a dance', said he; 'and if you are fond of that kind of thing perhaps we can amuse you.' Now in those days I was very fond of dancing—and very fond of young ladies too, and therefore glad enough to learn that Tom O'Conor had daughters as well as sons. On this account I was very particular in underscoring the word pumps.

'And hurry, you young divil', he said to Patsey.

'I have told him to take the portmanteau over on a car', said I.

'All right; then you'll find it there on our arrival.'

We had an excellent run in which I may make bold to say that I did not acquit myself badly. I stuck very close to the hounds, as did the whole of the O'Conor brood; and when the fellow contrived to earth himself, as he did, I received those compliments on my horse, which is the most approved praise which one fox-hunter ever gives to another.

'We'll buy that fellow of you before we let you go', said Peter, the youngest son.

'I advise you to look sharp after your money if you sell him to my brother', said Jack.

And then we trotted slowly off to Castle Conor, which, however, was by no means near to us. 'We have ten miles to go—good Irish miles', said the father. 'I don't know that I ever remember a fox from Poulnaroe taking that line before.'

'He wasn't a Poulnaroe fox', said Peter.

'I don't know that', said Jack; and then they debated that question hotly.

Our horses were very tired, and it was late before we reached Mr. O'Conor's house. That getting home from hunting with a thoroughly weary animal, who has no longer sympathy or example to carry him on, is very tedious work. In the present instance I had company with me; but when a man is alone, when his horse toes at every ten steps, when the night is dark and the rain pouring, and there are yet eight miles of road to be conquered—at such times a man is almost apt to swear that he will give up hunting.

At last we were in the Castle Conor stable yard—for we had approached the house by some back way; and as we entered the house by a door leading through a wilderness of back passages, Mr. O'Conor said out loud, 'Now, boys, remember I sit down to dinner in twenty minutes.' And then turning expressly to me, he laid his hand kindly upon my shoulder and said, 'I hope you will make yourself quite at home at Castle Conor—and whatever you do, don't keep us waiting for dinner. You can dress in twenty minutes, I suppose?'

'In ten!' said I, glibly.

'That's well. Jack and Peter will show you your room', and so he turned away and left us.

My two young friends made their way into the great hall, and thence into the drawing-room, and I followed them. We were all dressed in pink, and had waded deep through bog and mud. I did not exactly know whither I was being led in this guise, but I soon found myself in the presence of two young ladies, and of a girl about thirteen years of age.

'My sisters', said Jack, introducing me very laconically; 'Miss O'Conor, Miss Kate O'Conor, Miss Tizzy O'Conor'.

'My name is not Tizzy', said the younger; 'it's Eliza. How do you do, sir? I hope you had a fine hunt! Was papa well up, Jack?'

Jack did not condescend to answer this question, but asked one of the elder girls whether anything had come, and whether a room had been made ready for me.

'Oh yes!' said Miss O'Conor; 'they came, I know, for I saw them brought into the house; and I hope Mr. Green will find everything comfortable.' As she said this I thought I saw a slight smile steal across her remarkably pretty mouth.

They were both exceedingly pretty girls. Fanny the elder wore long glossy curls—for I write, oh reader, of bygone days, as long ago as that, when ladies wore curls if it pleased them so to do, and gentlemen danced in pumps, with black handkerchiefs round their necks—yes, long black, or nearly black silken curls; and then she had such eyes—I never knew whether they were most wicked or most bright; and her face was all dimples, and each dimple was laden with laughter and laden with love. Kate was probably the prettier girl of the two, but on the whole not so attractive. She was fairer than her sister, and wore her hair in braids; and was also somewhat more demure in her manner.

In spite of the special injunctions of Mr. O'Conor senior, it was impossible not to loiter for five minutes over the drawing-room fire talking to these houris—more especially as I seemed to know them intimately by intuition before half of the five minutes was over. They were so easy, so pretty, so graceful, so kind, they seemed to take it so much as a matter of course that I should stand there talking in my red coat and muddy boots.

'Well; do go and dress yourselves', at last said Fanny, pretending to speak to her brothers but looking more especially at me. 'You know how mad papa will be. And remember,

Mr. Green, we expect great things from your dancing to-night. Your coming just at this time is such a Godsend.' And again that soupcon of a smile passed over her face.

I hurried up to my room, Peter and Jack coming with me to the door. 'Is everything right?' said Peter, looking among the towels and water-jugs. 'They've given you a decent fire for a wonder', said Jack stirring up the red-hot turf which blazed in the grate. 'All right as a trivet', said I. 'And look alive like a good fellow', said Jack. We had scowled at each other in the morning as very young men do when they are strangers; and now, after a few hours, we were intimate friends.

I immediately turned to my work, and was gratified to find that all my things were laid out ready for dressing; my portmanteau had of course come open, as my keys were in my pocket, and therefore some of the excellent servants of the house had been able to save me all the trouble of unpacking. There was my shirt hanging before the fire; my black clothes were spread upon the bed, my socks and collar and hand-kerchief beside them; my brushes were on the toilet table, and everything prepared exactly as though my own man had been there. How nice!

I immediately went to work at getting off my spurs and boots, and then proceeded to loosen the buttons at my knees. In doing this I sat down in the arm-chair which had been drawn up for me, opposite the fire. But what was the object on which my eyes then fell—the objects I should rather say!

Immediately in front of my chair was placed, just ready for my feet, an enormous pair of shooting-boots—half-boots, made to lace up round the ankles, with thick double leather soles, and each bearing half a stone of iron in the shape of nails and heel-pieces. I had superintended the making of these shoes in Burlington Arcade with the greatest diligence. I was never a good shot; and, like some other sportsmen, intended to make up for my deficiency in performance by the excellence of my shooting apparel. 'Those nails are not large enough', I had said; 'not nearly large enough.' But when the boots came home they struck even me as being too heavy, too metalsome.

'He, he, he', laughed the boot-boy as he turned them up for me to look at. It may therefore be imagined of what nature were the articles which were thus set out for the evening's dancing.

And then the way in which they were placed! When I saw this the conviction flew across my mind like a flash of lightning that the preparation had been made under other eyes than those of the servant. The heavy big boots were placed so prettily before the chair, and the strings of each were made to dangle down at the sides, as though just ready for tying! They seemed to say, the boots did, 'Now, make haste. We at any rate are ready—you cannot say that you were kept waiting for us.' No mere servant's hand had ever enabled a pair of boots to laugh at one so completely.

But what was I to do? I rushed at the small portmanteau, thinking that my pumps also might be there. The woman surely could not have been such a fool as to send me those tons of iron for my evening wear! But alas, alas! no pumps were there. There was nothing else in the way of covering for my feet; not even a pair of slippers.

And now what was I to do? The absolute magnitude of my misfortune only loomed upon me by degrees. The twenty minutes allowed by that stern old paterfamilias were already gone and I had done nothing towards dressing. And indeed it was impossible that I should do anything that would be of avail. I could not go down to dinner in my stocking feet, nor could I put on my black dress trousers over a pair of mud painted top-boots. As for those iron-soled horrors—and then I gave one of them a kick with the side of my bare foot which sent it half-way under the bed.

But what was I to do? I began washing myself and brushing my hair with this horrid weight upon my mind. My first plan was to go to bed, and send down word that I had been taken suddenly ill in the stomach; then to rise early in the morning and get away unobserved. But by such a course of action I should lose all chance of any further acquaintance with those pretty girls! That they were already aware of the extent of my predicament, and were now enjoying it—of that I was quite sure.

What if I boldly put on the shooting-boots, and clattered down to dinner in them? What if I took the bull by the horns, and made myself the most of the joke? This might be very well for the dinner, but it would be a bad joke for me when the hour for dancing came. And, alas! I felt that I lacked the courage. It is not every man that can walk down to dinner, in a strange house full of ladies, wearing such boots as those I have described.

Should I not attempt to borrow a pair? This, all the world will say, should have been my first idea. But I have not yet mentioned that I am myself a large-boned man, and that my feet are especially well developed. I had never for a moment entertained a hope that I should find any one in that house whose boot I could wear. But at last I rang the bell. I would send for Jack, and if everything failed, I would communicate my grief to him.

I had to ring twice before anybody came. The servants, I well knew, were putting the dinner on the table. At last a man entered the room, dressed in rather shabby black, whom I afterwards learned to be the butler.

'What is your name, my friend', said I, determined to make an ally of the man.

'My name? Why Larry sure, yer honer. And the masther is out of his sinses in a hurry, becase yer honer don't come down.'

'Is he though? Well now, Larry, tell me this: which of all the gentlemen in the house has got the largest foot?'

'Is it the largest foot, yer honer?' said Larry, altogether surprised by my question.

'Yes; the largest foot', and then I proceeded to explain to him my misfortune. He took up first my top-boot, and then the shooting-boot—in looking at which he gazed with wonder at the nails—and then he glanced at my feet, measuring them with his eye; and after this he pronounced his opinion.

'Yer honer couldn't wear a morsel of leather belonging to ere a one of 'em, young or ould. There niver was a foot like that among the O'Conors.'

'But are there no strangers staying here?'

'There's three or four on 'em come in to dinner; but they'll be wanting their own boots I'm thinking. And there's young Misther Dillon; he's come to stay. But Lord love you——' and he again looked at the enormous extent which lay between the heel and the toe of the shooting apparatus which he still held in his hand. 'I niver see such a foot as that in the whole barony', he said, 'barring my own.'

Now Larry was a large man, much larger altogether than myself, and as he said this I looked down involuntarily at his feet; or rather at his foot, for as he stood I could only see one. And then a sudden hope filled my heart. On that foot there glittered a shoe—not indeed such as were my own which were now resting ingloriously at Ballyglass while they were so sorely needed as Castle Conor; but one which I could wear before ladies, without shame—and in my present frame of mind with infinite contentment.

'Let me look at that one of your own', said I to the man, as though it were merely a subject for experimental inquiry. Larry, accustomed to obedience, took off the shoe and handed it to me. My own foot was immediately in it, and I found that it fitted me like a glove.

'And now the other', said I—not smiling, for a smile would have put him on his guard; but somewhat sternly, so that habit of obedience should not desert him at this perilous moment. And then I stretched out my hand.

'But yer honer can't keep 'em, you know', said he. 'I haven't the ghost of another shoe to my feet.' But I only looked more sternly than before, and still held out my hand. Custom prevailed. Larry stooped down slowly, looking at me the while, and pulling off the other slipper handed it to me with much hesitation. Alas! as I put it to my foot I found that it was old, and worn, and irredeemably down at heel— that it was in fact no counterpart at all to that other one which was to do duty as its fellow. But nevertheless I put my foot into it, and felt that a descent to the drawing-room was now possible.

'But yer honer will give 'em back to a poor man?' said Larry almost crying. 'The masther's mad this minute becase the dinner's not up. Glory to God, only listhen to that.' And as he spoke a tremendous peal rang out from some bell downstairs that had evidently been shaken by an angry hand.

'Larry', said I—and I endeavoured to assume a look of very grave importance as I spoke—'I look to you to assist me in this matter.'

'Och—wirra sthrue then, and will you let me go? just listhen to that', and another angry peal rang out, loud and repeated.

'If you do as I ask you', I continued, 'you shall be well rewarded. Look here; look at these boots', and I help up the shooting-boots new from Burlington Arcade. 'They cost thirty shillings—thirty shillings! and I will give them to you for the loan of this pair of slippers.'

'They'd be no use at all to me, yer honer; not the laist use in life.'

'You could do with them very well for to-night, and then you could sell them. And here are ten shillings besides', and I held out half a sovereign which the poor fellow took into his hand.

I waited no further parley but immediately walked out of the room. With one foot I was sufficiently pleased. As regarded that I felt that I had overcome my difficulty. But the other was not so satisfactory. Whenever I attempted to lift it from the ground the horrid slipper would fall off, or only just hang by the toe. As for dancing, that would be out of the question.

'Och, murther, murther', sang out Larry, as he heard me going downstairs. 'What will I do at all? 'Tare and 'ounds; there, he's at it agin, as mad as blazes.' This last exclamation had reference to another peal which was evidently the work of the master's hand.

I confess I was not quite comfortable as I walked downstairs. In the first place I was nearly half an hour late, and I knew from the vigour of the peals that had sounded that my slowness had already been made the subject of strong remarks. And then my left shoe went flop, flop on every alternate step of the stairs; by no exertion of my foot in the drawing up of my toe could I induce it to remain permanently fixed upon my foot. But over and above and worse than all this was the conviction strong upon my mind that I should become a subject of merriment to the girls as soon as I entered the room. They would understand the cause of my distress, and probably at this moment were expecting to hear me clatter through the stone hall with those odious metal boots.

However, I hurried down and entered the drawing-room, determined to keep my position near the door, so that I might have as little as possible to do on entering and as little as possible in going out. But I had other difficulties in store for me. I had not as yet been introduced to Mrs. O'Conor; nor to Miss O'Conor, the squire's unmarried sister.

'Upon my word I thought you were never coming', said Mr. O'Conor as soon as he saw me. 'It is just one hour since we entered the house. Jack, I wish you would find out what has come to that fellow Larry', and again he rang the bell. He was too angry, or it might be too impatient, to go through the ceremony of introducing me to anybody.

I saw that the two girls looked at me very sharply, but I stood at the back of an arm-chair so that no one could see my feet. But that little imp Tizzy walked round deliberately, looked at my heels, and then walked back again. It was clear that she was in the secret.

There were eight or ten people in the room, but I was too much fluttered to notice well who they were.

'Mamma', said Miss O'Conor, 'let me introduce Mr. Green to you.'

It luckily happened that Mrs. O'Conor was on the same side of the fire as myself, and I was able to take the hand which she offered me without coming round into the middle of the circle. Mrs. O'Conor was a little woman, apparently not of much importance in the world, but, if one might judge from first appearance, very good-natured.

'And my aunt Die, Mr. Green', said Kate, pointing to a very straight-backed, grim-looking lady, who occupied a corner of a sofa, on the opposite side of the hearth. I knew that politeness required that I should walk across the room and make acquaintance with her. But under the existing circumstances how was I to obey the dictates of politeness? I was determined therefore to stand my ground, and merely bowed across the room at Miss O'Conor. In so doing I made an enemy who never deserted me during the whole of my intercourse with the family. But for her, who knows who might have been sitting opposite to me as I now write?

'Upon my word, Mr. Green, the ladies will expect much from an Adonis who takes so long over his toilet', said Tom O'Conor in that cruel tone of banter which he knew so well how to use.

'You forget, father, that men in London can't jump in and out of their clothes as quick as we wild Irishmen', said Jack.

'Mr. Green knows that we expect a great deal from him this evening. I hope you polk well, Mr. Green', said Kate.

I muttered something about never dancing, but I knew that that which I said was inaudible.

'I don't think Mr. Green will dance', said Tizzy; 'at least not much.' The impudence of that child was, I think, unparalleled by any that I have ever witnessed.

'But in the name of all that's holy, why don't we have dinner?' And Mr. O'Conor thundered at the door. 'Larry, Larry, Larry!' he screamed.

'Yes, yer honer, it'll be all right in two seconds', answered Larry, from some bottomless abyss. 'Tare an' ages; what'll I do at all', I heard him continuing, as he made his way into the hall. Oh what a clatter he made upon the pavement— for it was all stone! And how the drops of perspiration stood upon my brow as I listened to him!

And then there was a pause, for the man had gone into the dining-room. I could see now that Mr. O'Conor was becoming very angry, and Jack the eldest son—oh, how often he and I have laughed over all this since—left the drawing-room for the second time. Immediately afterwards, Larry's footsteps were again heard, hurrying across the hall, and then there was a great slither, and an exclamation, and the noise of a fall— and I could plainly hear poor Larry's head strike against the stone floor.

'Ochone, ochone!' he cried at the top of his voice—'I'm murthered with'em now intirely; and d—— 'em for boots— St. Peter be good to me.'

There was a general rush into the hall, and I was carried with the stream. The poor fellow who had broken his head would be sure to tell how I had robbed him of his shoes. The coachman was already helping him up, and Peter good-naturedly lent a hand.

'What on earth is the matter?' said Mr. O'Conor.

'He must be tipsy', whispered Miss O'Conor, the maiden sister.

'I ain't tipsy at all thin', said Larry, getting up and rubbing the back of his head, and sundry other parts of his body. 'Tipsy indeed!' And then he added when he was quite upright, 'The dinner is sarved—at last.'

And he bore it all without telling. 'I'll give that fellow a guinea to-morrow morning', said I to myself—'if it's the last that I have in the world.'

I shall never forget the countenance of the Miss O'Conors as Larry scrambled up cursing the unfortunate boots—'What on earth has he got on?' said Mr. O'Conor.

'Sorrow take 'em for shoes', ejaculated Larry. But his spirit was good and he said not a word to betray me.

We all then went in to dinner how we best could. It was useless for us to go back into the drawing-room, that each might seek his own partner. Mr. O'Conor 'the masther', not caring much for the girls who were around him, and being already half beside himself with the confusion and delay, led the way by himself. I as a stranger should have given my arm to Mrs. O'Conor; but as it was I took her eldest daughter instead, and contrived to shuffle along into the dining-room without exciting much attention, and when there I found myself happily placed between Kate and Fanny.

'I never knew anything so awkward', said Fanny; 'I declare I can't conceive what has come to our old servant Larry. He's generally the most precise person in the world, and now he is nearly an hour late—and then he tumbles down in the hall.'

'I am afraid I am responsible for the delay', said I.

'But not for the tumble I suppose', said Kate from the other side. I felt that I blushed up to the eyes, but I did not dare to enter into explanations.

'Tom', said Tizzy, addressing her father across the table, 'I hope you had a good run to-day.' It did seem odd to me that a young lady should call her father Tom, but such was the fact.

'Well; pretty well', said Mr. O'Conor.

'And I hope you were up with the hounds.'

'You may ask Mr. Green that. He at any rate was with them, and therefore he can tell you.'

'Oh, he wasn't before you, I know. No Englishman could get before you—I am quite sure of that.'

'Don't you be impertinent, miss', said Kate. 'You can easily see, Mr. Green, that papa spoils my sister Eliza.'

'Do you hunt in top-boots, Mr. Green?' said Tizzy.

To this I made no answer. She would have drawn me into a conversation about my feet in half a minute, and the slightest allusion to the subject threw me into a fit of perspiration.

'Are you fond of hunting, Miss O'Conor?' asked I, blindly hurrying into any other subject of conversation.

Miss O'Conor owned that she was fond of hunting—just a little; only papa would not allow it. When the hounds met anywhere within reach of Castle Conor, she and Kate would ride out to look at them; and if papa was not there that day—an omission of rare occurrence—they would ride a few fields with the hounds.

'But he lets Tizzy keep with them the whole day', said she, whispering.

'And has Tizzy a pony of her own?'

'Oh yes, Tizzy has everything. She papa's pet, you know.'

'And whose pet are you?' I asked.

'Oh—I am nobody's pet, unless sometimes Jack makes a pet of me when he's in a good humour. Do you make pets of your sisters, Mr. Green?'

'I have none. But if I had I should not make pets of them.'

'Not of your own sisters?'

'No. As for myself I'd sooner make a pet of my friend's sister; a great deal.'

'How very unnatural', said Miss O'Conor with the prettiest look of surprise imaginable.

'Not at all unnatural I think', said I, looking tenderly and lovingly into her face. Where does one find girls so pretty, so easy, so sweet, so talkative as the Irish girls? And then with all their talking and all their ease, who ever hears of their misbehaving? They certainly love flirting as they also love dancing. But they flirt without mischief and without malice.

I had now quite forgotten my misfortune, and was beginning to think how well I should like to have Fanny O'Conor for my wife. In this frame of mind I was bending over towards her as a servant took away a plate from the other side when a sepulchral note sounded in my ear. It was like the memento mori of the old Roman—as though some one pointed in the midst of my bliss to the sword hung over my head by a thread. It was the voice of Larry, whispering in his agony just above my head——

'They's disthroying my poor feet intirely, intirely; so they is! I can't bear it much longer, yer honer.' I had committed murder like Macbeth; and now my Banquo had come to disturb me at my feast.

'What is it he says to you?' asked Fanny.

'Oh nothing', I answered, once more in my misery.

'There seems to be some point of confidence between you and our Larry', she remarked.

'Oh no', said I, quite confused; 'not at all.'

'You need not be ashamed of it. Half the gentlemen in the county have their confidences with Larry—and some of the ladies too, I can tell you. He was born in this house, and never lived anywhere else; and I am sure he has a larger circle of acquaintance than anyone else in it.'

I could not recover my self-possession for the next ten minutes. Whenever Larry was on our side of the table I was afraid he was coming to me with another agonized whisper. When he was opposite I could not but watch him as he hobbled in his misery. It was evident that the boots were too tight for him, and had they been made throughout of iron they could not have been less capable of yielding to the feet. I pitied him from the bottom of my heart. And I pitied myself also, wishing that I was well in bed upstairs with some feigned malady, so that Larry might have had his own again.

And then for a moment I missed him from the room. He had doubtless gone to relieve his tortured feet in the servants' hall, and as he did so was cursing my cruelty. But what mattered it? Let him curse. If he would only stay away and do that I would appease his wrath when we were alone together with pecuniary satisfaction.

But there was no such rest in store for me. 'Larry, Larry', shouted Mr. O'Conor, 'where on earth has the fellow gone to?' They were all cousins at the table except myself, and Mr. O'Conor was not therefore restrained by any feeling of ceremony. 'There is something wrong with that fellow to-day; what is it, Jack?'

'Upon my word, sir, I don't know', said Jack.

'I think he must be tipsy', whispered Miss O'Conor, the maiden sister, who always sat at her brother's left hand. But a whisper though it was, it was audible all down the table.

'No, ma'am; it aint dhrink at all', said the coachman. 'It is his feet as does it.'

'His feet!' shouted Tom O'Conor.

'Yes; I know it's his feet', said that horrid Tizzy. 'He's got on great thick nailed shoes. It was that that made him tumble down in the hall.'

I glanced at each side of me and could see that there was a certain consciousness expressed in the face of each of my two neighbours—on Kate's mouth there was decidedly a smile, or rather perhaps the slightest possible inclination that way; whereas on Fanny's part I thought I saw something like a rising sorrow at my distress. So at least I flattered myself.

'Send him back into the room immediately', said Tom, who looked at me as though he had some consciousness that I had introduced all this confusion into his household. What should I do? Would it not be best for me to make a clean breast of it before them all? But alas! I lacked the courage.

The coachman went out, and we were left for five minutes without any servant, and Mr. O'Conor the while became more and more savage. I attempted to say a word to Fanny, but failed—*Vox faucibus hæsit*.

'I don't think he has got any others', said Tizzy—'at least none others left.'

On the whole I am glad I did not marry into the family, as I could not have endured that girl to stay in my house as a sister-in-law.

'Where the d—— has that other fellow gone to?' said Tom. 'Jack, do go out and see what is the matter. If anybody is drunk send for me.'

'Oh, there is nobody drunk', said Tizzy.

Jack went out, and the coachman returned; but what was done and said I hardly remember. The whole room seemed to swim round and round, and as far as I can recollect the company sat mute, neither eating nor drinking. Presently Jack returned.

'It's all right', said he. I always liked Jack. At the present moment he just looked towards me and laughed slightly.

'All right?' said Tom. 'But is the fellow coming?'

'We can do with Richard, I suppose', said Jack.

'No—I can't do with Richard', said the father. 'And I will know what it all means. Where is that fellow Larry?'

Larry had been standing just outside the door, and now he entered gently as a mouse. No sound came from his footfall, nor was there in his face that look of pain which it had worn for the last fifteen minutes. But he was not the less abashed, frightened, and unhappy.

'What is all this about, Larry?' said his master, turning to him. 'I insist upon knowing.'

'Och thin, Mr. Green, yer honer, I wouldn't be afther telling agin yer honer; indeed I wouldn't thin, av' the masther would only let me hould my tongue.' And he looked across at me, deprecating my anger.

'Mr. Green!' said Mr. O'Conor.

'Yes, yer honer. It's all along of his honer's thick shoes', and Larry, stepping backwards towards the door, lifted them up from some corner, and coming well forward, exposed them with the soles uppermost to the whole table.

'And that's not all, yer honer; but they've squoze the very toes of me into a jelly.'

There was now a loud laugh, in which Jack and Peter and Fanny and Kate and Tizzy all joined; as too did Mr. O'Conor —and I also myself after a while.

'Whose boots are they?' demanded Miss O'Conor senior, with her severest tone and grimmest accent.

''Deed then and the divil may have them for me, Miss', answered Larry. 'They war Mr. Green's, but the likes of him won't wear them agin afther the likes of me—barring he wanted them very particular', added he, remembering his own pumps.

I began muttering something, feeling that the time had come when I must tell the tale. But Jack with great good nature, took up the story and told it so well, that I hardly suffered in the telling.

'And that's it', said Tom O'Conor, laughing till I thought he would have fallen from his chair. 'So you've got Larry's shoes on——'

'And very well he fills them', said Jack.

'And it's his honer that's welcome to 'em', said Larry, grinning from ear to ear now that he saw that 'the masther' was once more in a good humour.

'I hope they'll be nice shoes for dancing', said Kate.

'Only there's one down at the heel I know', said Tizzy.

'The servant's shoes!' This was an exclamation made by the maiden lady, and intended apparently only for her brother's ear. But it was clearly audible by all the party.

'Better that than no dinner', said Peter.

'But what are you to do about the dancing?' said Fanny, with an air of dismay on her face which flattered me with an idea that she did care whether I danced or no.

In the meantime, Larry, now as happy as an emperor, was tripping round the room without any shoes to encumber him as he withdrew the plates from the table.

'And it's his honer that's welcome to 'em', said he again, as he pulled off the table-cloth with a flourish. 'And why wouldn't he, and he able to folly the hounds better nor any Englishman that iver war in these parts before—anyways so Mick says!'

Now Mick was the huntsman, and this little tale of eulogy from Larry went far towards easing my grief. I had ridden well to the hounds that day, and I knew it.

There was nothing more said about the shoes, and I was soon again at my ease, although Miss O'Conor did say something about the impropriety of Larry walking about in his stocking feet. The ladies however soon withdrew—to my sorrow, for I was getting on swimmingly with Fanny; and then we gentlemen gathered round the fire and filled our glasses.

In about ten minutes a very light tap was heard, the door was opened to the extent of three inches, and a female voice which I readily recognized called to Jack.

Jack went out, and in a second or two put his head back into the room and called to me—'Green', he said, 'just step here a moment, there's a good fellow.' I went out, and there I found Fanny standing with her brother.

'Here are the girls at their wits' ends', said he, 'about your dancing. So Fanny has put a boy upon one of the horses, and proposes that you should send another line to Mrs. Meehan at Ballyglass. It's only ten miles, and he'll be back in two hours.'

I need hardly say that I acted in conformity with this advice. I went into Mr. O'Conor's book room, with Jack and his sister, and there scribbled a note. It was delightful to feel how intimate I was with them, and how anxious they were to make me happy.

'And we won't begin till they come', said Fanny.

'Oh, Miss O'Conor, pray don't wait', said I.

'Oh, but we will', she answered. 'You have your wine to drink, and then there's the tea; and then we'll have a song or two. I'll spin it out; see if I don't.' And so we went to the front door where the boy was already on his horse—her own nag as I afterwards found.

'And, Patsey', said she, 'ride for your life now; and Patsey, whatever you do, don't come back without Mr. Green's pumps —his dancing-shoes you know.'

And in about two hours the pumps did arrive; and I don't think I ever spent a pleasanter evening or got more satisfaction out of a pair of shoes. They had not been two minutes on my feet before Larry was carrying a tray of negus across the room in those which I had worn at dinner.

'The Dillon girls are going to stay here', said Fanny as I wished her good night at two o'clock. 'And we'll have dancing every evening as long as you remain.'

'But I shall leave to-morrow', said I.

'Indeed you won't. Papa will take care of that.'

And so he did. 'You had better go over to Ballyglass yourself to-morrow', said he, 'and collect your own things. There's no knowing else what you may have to borrow of Larry.'

I stayed there three weeks, and in the middle of the third I thought that everything would be arranged between me and Fanny. But the aunt interfered; and in about a twelvemonth after my adventures she consented to make a more fortunate man happy for his life.

THE JOURNEY
TO PANAMA

THERE is perhaps no form of life in which men and
women of the present day frequently find themselves
for a time existing, so unlike their customary conventional life, as that experienced on board the large ocean
steamers. On the voyages so made, separate friendships are
formed and separate enmities are endured. Certain lines of
temporary politics are originated by the energetic, and
intrigues, generally innocent in their conclusions, are carried
on with the keenest spirit by those to whom excitement is
necessary; whereas the idle and torpid sink into insignificance
and general contempt—as it is their lot to do on board ship
as in other places. But the enjoyments and activity of such a
life do not display themselves till the third or fourth day of the
voyage. The men and women at first regard each with distrust
and ill-concealed dislike. They by no means anticipate the
strong feelings which are to arise, and look forward to ten,
fifteen, or twenty days of gloom or sea-sickness. Sea-sickness
disappears, as a general condition, on the evening of the second
day, and the gloom about noon on the fourth. Then the men
begin to think that the women are not so ugly, vulgar, and
insipid; and the women drop their monosyllables, discontinue the close adherence to their own niches, which they

first observed, and become affable, perhaps even beyond their wont on shore. And alliances spring up among the men themselves. On their first entrance to this new world, they generally regard each other with marked aversion, each thinking that those nearest to him are low fellows, or perhaps worse; but by the fourth day, if not sooner, every man has his two or three intimate friends with whom he talks and smokes, and to whom he communicates those peculiar politics, and perhaps intrigues, of his own voyage. The female friendships are slower in their growth, for the suspicion of women is perhaps stronger than that of men; but when grown they also are stronger, and exhibit themselves sometimes in instances of feminine affection.

But the most remarkable alliances are those made between gentlemen and ladies. This is a matter of course on board ship quite as much as on shore, and it is of such an alliance that the present tale purports to tell the story. Such friendships, though they may be very dear, can seldom be very lasting. Though they may be full of sweet romance—for people become very romantic among the discomforts of a sea voyage —such romance is generally short-lived and delusive, and occasionally is dangerous.

There are several of these great ocean routes, of which, by the common consent, as it seems, of the world, England is the centre. There is the Great Eastern line, running from Southampton across the Bay of Biscay and up the Mediterranean. It crosses the Isthmus of Suez, and branches away to Australia, to India, to Ceylon, and to China. There is the great American line, traversing the Atlantic to New York and Boston with the regularity of clockwork. The voyage here is so much a matter of every-day routine, that romance has become scarce upon the route. There are one or two other North American lines, perhaps open to the same objection. Then there is the line of packets to the African coast —very romantic, as I am given to understand; and there is the great West-Indian route, to which the present little history is attached—great, not on account of our poor West Indian

Islands, which cannot at the present moment make anything great, but because it spreads itself out from thence to Mexico and Cuba, to Guiana and the republics of Grenada and Venezuela, to Central America, the Isthmus of Panama, and from thence to California, Vancouver's Island, Peru and Chili.

It may be imagined how various are the tribes which leave the shores of Great Britain by this route. There are Frenchmen for the French sugar islands, as a rule not very romantic; there are old Spaniards, Spaniards of Spain, seeking to renew their fortunes amidst the ruins of their former empire; and new Spaniards—Spaniards, that is, of the American republics, who speak Spanish, but are unlike the Don both in manners and physiognomy—men and women with a touch perhaps of Indian blood, very keen after dollars, and not much given to the graces of life. There are Dutchmen too, and Danes, going out to their own islands. There are citizens of the stars and stripes, who find their way everywhere—and, alas! perhaps, now also citizens of the new Southern flag, with the palmetto leaf. And there are Englishmen of every shade and class, and Englishwomen also.

It is constantly the case that women are doomed to make the long voyage alone. Some are going out to join their husbands, some to find a husband, some few peradventure to leave a husband. Girls who have been educated at home in England, return to their distant homes across the Atlantic, and others follow their relatives who have gone before them as pioneers into a strange land. It must not be supposed that these females absolutely embark in solitude, putting their feet upon the deck without the aid of any friendly arm. They are generally consigned to some prudent elder, and appear as they first show themselves on the ship to belong to a party. But as often as not their real loneliness shows itself after a while. The prudent elder is not, perhaps, congenial; and by the evening of the fourth day a new friendship is created.

Not a long time since such a friendship was formed under

the circumstances which I am now about to tell. A young
man—not very young, for he had turned his thirtieth year,
but still a young man—left Southampton by one of the large
West Indian steam-boats, purposing to pass over the Isthmus
of Panama, and thence up to California and Vancouver's
Island. It would be too long to tell the cause which led to
these distant voyagings. Suffice to say, it was not the accursed
hunger after gold—*auri sacra fames*—which so took him; nor
had he any purpose of permanently settling himself in those
distant colonies of Great Britain. He was at the time a widower,
and perhaps his home was bitter to him without the young wife
whom he had early lost. As he stepped on board he was
accompanied by a gentleman some fifteen years his senior,
who was to be the companion of his sleeping apartment as
far as St. Thomas. The two had been introduced to each other,
and therefore appeared as friends on board the *Serrapiqui*;
but their acquaintance had commenced in Southampton, and
my hero, Ralph Forrest by name, was alone in the world as he
stood looking over the side of the ship at the retreating shores
of Hampshire.

'I say, old fellow, we'd better see about our places', said his
new friend, slapping him on his back. Mr. Matthew Morris
was an old traveller, and knew how to become intimate with
his temporary allies at a very short notice. A long course of
travelling had knocked all bashfulness out of him, and when
he had a mind to do so he could make any man his brother
in half-an-hour, and any woman his sister in ten minutes.

'Places? What places?' said Forrest.

'A pretty fellow you are to go to California. If you don't
look sharper than that you'll get little to drink and nothing
to eat till you come back again. Don't you know the ship's
as full as ever she can hold?'

Forrest acknowledged that she was full.

'There are places at table for about a hundred, and we have
a hundred and thirty on board. As a matter of course those who
don't look sharp will have to scramble. However I've put
cards on the plates and taken the seats. We had better go

down and see that none of these Spanish fellows oust us.' So
Forrest descended after his friend, and found that the long
tables were already nearly full of expectant dinner-eaters.
When he took his place a future neighbour informed him,
not in the most gracious voice, that he was encroaching on a
lady's seat; and when he immediately attempted to leave that
which he held, Mr. Matthew Morris forbade him to do so.
Thus a little contest arose, which, however, happily was
brought to a close without bloodshed. The lady was not
present at the moment, and the grumpy gentleman agreed to
secure for himself a vacant seat on the other side.

For the first three days the lady did not show herself. The
grumpy gentleman, who, as Forrest afterwards understood,
was the owner of stores in Bridgetown, Barbadoes, had other
ladies with him also. First came forth his daughter, creeping
down to dinner on the second day, declaring that she would be
unable to eat a morsel, and prophesying that she would be
forced to retire in five minutes. On this occasion, however, she
agreeably surprised herself and her friends. Then came the
grumpy gentleman's wife, and the grumpy gentleman's wife's
brother—on whose constitution the sea seemed to have an
effect quite as violent as on that of the ladies; and lastly, at
breakfast on the fourth day, appeared Miss Viner, and took
her place as Mr. Forrest's neighbour at his right hand.

He had seen her before on deck, as she lay on one of the
benches, vainly endeavouring to make herself comfortable,
and had remarked to his companion that she was very
unattractive and almost ugly. Dear young ladies, it is thus that
men always speak of you when they first see you on board
ship! She was disconsolate, sick at heart, and ill at ease in body
also. She did not like the sea. She did not in the least like the
grumpy gentleman, in whose hands she was placed. She did
not especially like the grumpy gentleman's wife; and she
altogether hated the grumpy gentleman's daughter, who was
the partner of her berth. That young lady had been very sick
and very selfish; and Miss Viner had been very sick also, and
perhaps equally selfish. They might have been angels, and yet

have hated each other under such circumstances. It was no wonder that Mr. Forrest thought her ugly as she twisted herself about on the broad bench, vainly striving to be comfortable.

'She'll brighten up wonderfully before we're in the tropics', said Mr. Morris. 'And you won't find her so bad then. It's she that is to sit next you.'

'Heaven forbid!' said Forrest. But, nevertheless, he was very civil to her when she did come down on the fourth morning. On board the West Indian Packets, the world goes down to its meals. In crossing between Liverpool and the States, the world goes up to them.

Miss Viner was by no means a very young lady. She also was nearly thirty. In guessing her age on board the ship the ladies said that she was thirty-six, but the ladies were wrong. She was an Irish woman, and when seen on shore, in her natural state, and with all her wits about her, was by no means without attraction. She was bright-eyed, with a clear dark skin, and good teeth; her hair was of a dark brown and glossy, and there was a touch of feeling and also of humour about her mouth, which would have saved her from Mr. Forrest's ill-considered criticism, had he first met her under more favourable circumstances.

'You'll see a good deal of her', Mr. Morris said to him, as they began to prepare themselves for luncheon, by a cigar immediately after breakfast. 'She's going across the Isthmus and down to Peru.'

'How on earth do you know?'

'I pretty well know where they're all going by this time. Old Grumpy told me so. He has her in tow as far as St. Thomas, but knows nothing about her. He gives her up there to the captain. You'll have a chance of making yourself very agreeable as you run across with her to the Spanish main.'

Mr. Forrest replied that he did not suppose he should know her much better than he did now; but he made no further remark as to her ugliness. She had spoken a word or two to him at table, and he had seen that her eyes were bright, and had found that her tone was sweet.

'I also am going to Panama', he said to her, on the morning of the fifth day. The weather at that time was very fine, and the October sun as it shone on them, while hour by hour they made more towards the south, was pleasant and genial. The big ship lay almost without motion on the bosom of the Atlantic, as she was driven through the waters at the rate of twelve miles per hour. All was as pleasant now as things can be on board a ship, and Forrest had forgotten that Miss Viner had seemed so ugly to him when he first saw her. At this moment, as he spoke to her, they were running through the Azores, and he had been assisting her with his field-glass to look for orange-groves on their sloping shores, orange-groves they had not succeeded in seeing, but their failure had not disturbed their peace.

'I also am going to Panama.'

'Are you, indeed?' said she. 'Then I shall not feel so terribly alone and disconsolate. I have been looking forward with such fear to that journey on from St. Thomas.'

'You shall not be disconsolate, if I can help it', he said. 'I am not much of a traveller myself, but what I can do I will.'

'Oh, thank you!'

'It is a pity Mr. Morris is not going on with you. He's at home everywhere, and knows the way across the Isthmus as well as he does down Regent Street.'

'Your friend, you mean?'

'My friend, if you call him so; and indeed I hope he is, for I like him. But I don't know more of him than I do of you. I also am as much alone as you are. Perhaps more so.'

'But', she said, 'a man never suffers in being alone.'

'Oh! does he not? Don't think me uncivil, Miss Viner, if I say that you may be mistaken in that. You feel your own shoe when it pinches, but do not realize the tight boot of your neighbour.'

'Perhaps not', said she. And then there was a pause, during which she pretended to look again for the orange-groves. 'But there are worse things, Mr. Forrest, than being alone in the world. It is often a woman's lot to wish that she were let alone.' Then she left him and retreated to the side of the grumpy gentleman's wife, feeling perhaps that it might be prudent to discontinue a conversation, which, seeing that Mr. Forrest was quite a stranger to her, was becoming particular.

'You're getting on famously, my dear', said the lady from Barbadoes.

'Pretty well, thank you, ma'am', said Miss Viner.

'Mr. Forrest seems to be making himself quite agreeable. I tell Amelia'—Amelia was the young lady to whom in their joint cabin Miss Viner could not reconcile herself—'I tell Amelia that she is wrong not to receive attentions from gentlemen on board ship. If it is not carried too far'—and she put great emphasis on the 'too far'—'I see no harm in it.'

'Nor I, either', said Miss Viner.

'But then Amelia is so particular.'

'The best way is to take such things as they come', said Miss Viner—perhaps meaning that such things never did come in the way of Amelia. 'If a lady knows what she is about she need not fear a gentleman's attentions.'

'That's just what I tell Amelia; but then, my dear, she has not had so much experience as you and I.'

Such being the amenities which passed between Miss Viner and the prudent lady who had her in charge, it was not wonderful that the former should feel ill at ease with her own 'party', as the family of the Grumpy Barbadian was generally considered to be by those on board.

'You're getting along like a house on fire with Miss Viner', said Matthew Morris, to his young friend.

'Not much fire I can assure you', said Forrest.

'She ain't so ugly as you thought her?'

'Ugly!—no; she's not ugly. I don't think I ever said she was. But she is nothing particular as regards beauty.'

'No; she won't be lovely for the next three days to come, I dare say. By the time you reach Panama, she'll be all that is perfect in woman. I know how these things go.'

'Those sort of things don't go at all quickly with me',

said Forrest, gravely. 'Miss Viner is a very interesting young woman, and as it seems that her route and mine will be together for some time, it is well that we should be civil to each other. And the more so, seeing that the people she is with are not congenial to her.'

'No; they are not. There is no young man with them. I generally observe that on board ship no one is congenial to unmarried ladies except unmarried men. It is a recognized nautical rule. Uncommon hot, isn't it? We are beginning to feel the tropical air. I shall go and cool myself with a cigar in the fiddle.' The 'fiddle' is a certain part of the ship devoted to smoking, and thither Mr. Morris betook himself. Forrest, however, did not accompany him, but going forward into the bow of the vessel, threw himself along upon the sail, and meditated on the loneliness of his life.

On board the *Serrapiqui*, the upper tier of cabins opened on to a long gallery, which ran round that part of the ship, immediately over the saloon, so that from thence a pleasant inspection could be made of the viands as they were being placed on the tables. The custom on board these ships is for two bells to ring preparatory to dinner, at an interval of half an hour. At the sound of the first, ladies would go to their cabins to adjust their toilets; but as dressing for dinner is not carried to an extreme at sea, these operations are generally over before the second bell, and the lady passengers would generally assemble in the balcony for some fifteen minutes before dinner. At first they would stand here alone, but by degrees they were joined by some of the more enterprising of the men, and so at last a kind of little drawing-room was formed. The cabins of Miss Viner's party opened to one side of this gallery, and that of Mr. Morris and Forrest on the other. Hitherto Forrest had been contented to remain on his own side, occasionally throwing a word across to the ladies on the other; but on this day he boldly went over as soon as he had washed his hands and took his place between Amelia and Miss Viner.

'We are dreadfully crowded here, ma'am', said Amelia.

'Yes, my dear, we are', said her mother. 'But what can one do?'

'There's plenty of room in the ladies' cabin', said Miss Viner. Now if there be one place on board a ship more distasteful to ladies than another, it is the ladies' cabin. Mr. Forrest stood his ground, but it may be doubted whether he would have done so had he fully understood all that Amelia had intended.

Then the last bell rang. Mr. Grumpy gave his arm to Mrs. Grumpy. The brother-in-law gave his arm to Amelia, and Forrest did the same to Miss Viner. She hesitated for a moment, and then took it, and by so doing transferred herself mentally and bodily from the charge of the prudent and married Mr. Grumpy to that of the perhaps imprudent, and certainly unmarried Mr. Forrest. She was wrong. A kind-hearted, motherly old lady from Jamaica, who had seen it all, knew that she was wrong, and wished that she could tell her so.

But there are things of this sort which kind-hearted old ladies cannot find it in their hearts to say. After all, it was only for the voyage. Perhaps Miss Viner was imprudent, but who in Peru would be the wiser? Perhaps, indeed, it was the world that was wrong, and not Miss Viner. *Honi soit qui mal y pense*, she said to herself, as she took his arm, and leaning on it, felt that she was no longer so lonely as she had been. On that day she allowed him to give her a glass of wine out of his decanter. "Hadn't you better take mine, Miss Viner?' asked Mr. Grumpy, in a loud voice, but before he could be answered, the deed had been done.

'Don't go too fast, old fellow', Morris said to our hero that night, as they were walking the deck together before they turned in. 'One gets into a hobble in such matters before one knows where one is.'

'I don't think I have anything particular to fear', said Forrest.

'I dare say not, only keep your eyes open. Such haridans as Mrs. Grumpy allow any latitude to their tongues out in these diggings. You'll find that unpleasant tidings will be put on board the ship going down to Panama, and everybody's eye will be upon you.' So warned, Mr. Forrest did put himself on his guard, and the next day and a half his intimacy with Miss Viner progressed but little. These were, probably, the dullest hours that he had on the whole voyage.

Miss Viner saw this and drew back. On the afternoon of that second day she walked a turn or two on deck with the weak brother-in-law, and when Mr. Forrest came near her, she applied herself to her book. She meant no harm; but if she were not afraid of what people might say, why should he be so? So she turned her shoulder towards him at dinner, and would not drink of his cup.

'Have some of mine, Miss Viner', said Mr. Grumpy, very loudly. But on that day Miss Viner drank no wine.

The sun sets quickly as one draws near to the tropics, and the day was already gone, and the dusk had come on, when Mr. Forrest walked out upon the deck that evening a little after six. But the night was beautiful and mild, and there was a hum of many voices from the benches. He was already uncomfortable, and sore with a sense of being deserted. There was but one person on board the ship that he liked, and why should he avoid her and be avoided? He soon perceived where she was standing. The Grumpy family had a bench to themselves, and she was opposite to it, on her feet, leaning against the side of the vessel. 'Will you walk this evening, Miss Viner?' he asked.

'I think not', she answered.

'Then I shall persevere in asking till you are sure. It will do you good, for I have not seen you walking all day.'

'Have you not? Then I will take a turn. Oh, Mr. Forrest, if you knew what it was to have to live with such people as those.' And then, out of that, on that evening, there grew up between them something like the confidence of real friendship. Things were told such as none but friends do tell to one another, and warm answering words were spoken such as the sympathy of friendship produces. Alas, they were both foolish; for friendship and sympathy should have deeper roots.

She told him all her story. She was going out to Peru to

be married to a man who was nearly twenty years her senior.
It was a long engagement, of ten years' standing. When
first made, it was made as being contingent on certain circumstances. An option of escaping from it had then been given
to her, but now there was no longer an option. He was rich,
and she was penniless. He had even paid her passage-money
and her outfit. She had not at last given way and taken these
irrevocable steps till her only means of support in England
had been taken from her. She had lived the last two years with
a relative who was now dead. 'And he also is my cousin—
a distant cousin—you understand that.'

'And do you love him?'

'Love him! What; as you loved her whom you have lost?—
as she loved you when she clung to you before she went? No;
certainly not. I shall never know anything of that love.'

'And is he good?'

'He is a hard man. Men become hard when they deal in
money as he has done. He was home five years since, and then
I swore to myself that I would not marry him. But his letters
to me are kind.'

Forrest sat silent for a minute or two, for they were up in
the bow again, seated on the sail that was bound round the
bowsprit, and then he answered her, 'A woman should never
marry a man unless she loves him.'

'Ah', says she, 'of course you will condemn me. That is the
way in which women are always treated. They have no choice
given them, and are then scolded for choosing wrongly.'

'But you might have refused him.'

'No; I could not. I cannot make you understand the whole—
how it first came about that the marriage was proposed, and
agreed to by me under certain conditions. Those conditions
have come about, and I am now bound to him. I have taken
his money and have no escape. It is easy to say that a woman
should not marry without love, as easy as it is to say that a
man should not starve. But there are men who starve—starve
although they work hard.'

'I did not mean to judge you, Miss Viner.'

'But I judge myself, and condemn myself so often. Where should I be in half an hour from this if I were to throw myself forward into the sea? I often long to do it. Don't you feel tempted sometimes to put an end to it all?'

'The waters look cool and sweet, but I own I am afraid of the bourne beyond.'

'So am I, and that fear will keep me from it.'

'We are bound to bear our burden of sorrow. Mine, I know, is heavy enough.'

'Yours, Mr. Forrest! Have you not all the pleasures of memory to fall back on, and every hope for the future? What can I remember, or what can I hope? But, however, it is near eight o'clock, and they have all been at tea this hour past. What will my Cerberus say to me? I do not mind the male mouth, if only the two feminine mouths could be stopped.' Then she rose and went back to the stern of the vessel; but as she slid into a seat, she saw that Mrs. Grumpy was standing over her.

From thence to St. Thomas the voyage went on in the customary manner. The sun became very powerful, and the passengers in the lower part of the ship complained loudly of having their portholes closed. The Spaniards sat gambling in the cabin all day, and the ladies prepared for the general move which was to be made at St. Thomas. The alliance between Forrest and Miss Viner went on much the same as ever, and Mrs. Grumpy said very ill-natured things. On one occasion she ventured to lecture Miss Viner; but that lady knew how to take her own part, and Mrs. Grumpy did not get the best of it. The dangerous alliance, I have said, went on the same as ever; but it must not be supposed that either person in any way committed aught that was wrong. They sat together and talked together, each now knowing the other's circumstances; but had it not been for the prudish caution of some of the ladies there would have been nothing amiss. As it was there was not much amiss. Few of the passengers really cared whether or no Miss Viner had found an admirer. Those who were going down to Panama were mostly Spaniards, and as the great separation became nearer, people had somewhat else of which to think.

And then the separation came. They rode into that pretty harbour of St. Thomas early in the morning, and were ignorant, the most of them, that they were lying in the very worst centre of yellow fever among all those plague-spotted islands. St. Thomas is very pretty as seen from the ships; and when that has been said, all has been said that can be said in its favour. There was a busy, bustling time of it then. One vessel after another was brought up alongside of the big ship that had come from England, and each took its separate freight of passengers and luggage. First started the boat that ran down the Leeward Islands to Demerara, taking with her Mr. Grumpy and all his family.

'Good-bye, Miss Viner', said Mrs. Grumpy. 'I hope you'll get quite safely to the end of your voyage; but do take care.'

'I'm sure I hope everything will be right', said Amelia, as she absolutely kissed her enemy. It is astonishing how well young women can hate each other, and yet kiss at parting.

'As to everything being right', said Miss Viner, 'that is too much to hope. But I do not know that anything is going especially wrong. Good-bye, Sir', and then she put out her hand to Mr. Grumpy. He was at the moment leaving the ship laden with umbrellas, sticks, and coats, and was forced to put them down in order to free his hand.

'Well, good-bye', he said. 'I hope you'll do, till you meet your friends at the Isthmus.'

'I hope I shall, sir', she replied; and so they parted.

Then the Jamaica packet started.

'I dare say we shall never see each other again', said Morris, as he shook his friend's hand heartily. 'One never does. Don't interfere with the rights of that gentleman in Peru, or he might run a knife into you.'

'I feel no inclination to injure him on that point.'

'That's well; and now good-bye.' And thus they also were parted. On the following morning the branch ship was dispatched to Mexico; and then, on the afternoon of the third day that for Colon—as we Englishmen call the town on this side of the Isthmus of Panama. Into that vessel Miss Viner and Mr. Forrest moved themselves and their effects; and now that the three-headed Cerberus was gone, she had no longer hesitated in allowing him to do for her all those little things which it is well that men should do for women when they are travelling. A woman without assistance under such circumstances is very forlorn, very apt to go to the wall, very ill able to assert her rights as to accommodation; and I think that few can blame Miss Viner for putting herself and her belongings under the care of the only person who was disposed to be kind to her.

Late in the evening the vessel steamed out of St. Thomas' harbour, and as she went Ralph Forrest and Emily Viner were standing together at the stern of the boat looking at the retreating lights of the Danish town, If there be a place on the earth's surface odious to me, it is that little Danish isle to which so many of our young seamen are sent to die—there being no good cause whatever for such sending. But the question is one which cannot well be argued here.

'I have five more days of self and liberty left me', said Miss Viner. 'That is my life's allowance.'

'For heaven's sake do not say words that are so horrible.'

'But am I to lie for heaven's sake, and say words that are false; or shall I be silent for heaven's sake, and say nothing during these last hours that are allowed to me for speaking? It is so. To you I can say that it is so, and why should you begrudge me the speech?'

'I would begrudge you nothing that I could do for you.'

'No, you should not. Now that my incubus has gone to Barbadoes, let me be free for a day or two. What chance is there, I wonder, that the ship's machinery should all go wrong, and that we should be tossed about in the seas here for the next six months? I suppose it would be very wicked to wish it?'

'We should all be starved; that's all.'

'What, with a cow on board, and a dozen live sheep, and thousands of cocks and hens! But we are to touch at Santa Martha and Cartagena. What would happen to me if I were to run away at Santa Martha?'

'I suppose I should be bound to run with you.'

'Oh, of course. And therefore, as I would not wish to destroy you, I won't do it. But it would not hurt you much to be shipwrecked, and wait for the next packet.'

'Miss Viner', he said after a pause—and in the meantime he had drawn nearer to her, too near to her, considering all things—'in the name of all that is good, and true, and womanly, go back to England. With your feelings, if I may judge of them by words which are spoken half in jest—'

'Mr. Forrest, there is no jest'.

'With your feelings a poorhouse in England would be better than a palace in Peru'.

'An English workhouse would be better, but an English poorhouse is not open to me. You do not know what it is to have friends—no, not friends, but people belonging to you—just so near as to make your respectability a matter of interest to them, but not so near that they should care for your happiness. Emily Viner married to Mr. Gorloch in Peru is put out of the way respectably. She will cause no further trouble, but her name may be mentioned in family circles without annoyance. The fact is, Mr. Forrest, that there are people who have no business to live at all'.

'I would go back to England', he added, after another pause. 'When you talk to me with such bitterness of five more days of living liberty you scare my very soul. Return, Miss Viner, and brave the worst. He is to meet you at Panama. Remain on this side of the Isthmus, and send him word that you must return. I will be the bearer of the message'.

'And shall I walk back to England?' said Miss Viner.

'I had not quite forgotten all that', he replied, very gently. 'There are moments when a man may venture to propose that which under ordinary circumstances would be a liberty. Money, in a small moderate way, is not greatly an object to me. As a return for my valiant defence of you against your West Indian Cerberus, you shall allow me to arrange that with the agent at Colon'.

'I do so love plain English, Mr. Forrest. You are proposing, I think, to give me something about fifty guineas'.

'Well, call it so if you will', said he, 'if you will have plain English that is what I mean'.

'So that by my journey out here, I should rob and deceive the man I do know, and also rob the man I don't know. I am afraid of that bourne beyond the waters of which we spoke; but I would rather face that than act as you suggest'.

'Of the feelings between him and you, I can of course be no judge'.

'No, no; you cannot. But what a beast I am not to thank you! I do thank you. That which it would be mean in me to take, it is noble, very noble, in you to offer. It is a pleasure to me—I cannot tell why—but it is a pleasure to me to have had the offer. But think of me as a sister, and you will feel that it would not be accepted;—could not be accepted, I mean, even if I could bring myself to betray that other man'.

Thus they ran across the Caribbean Sea, renewing very often such conversations as that just given. They touched at Santa Martha and Cartagena on the coast of the Spanish main, and at both places he went with her on shore. He found that she was fairly well educated, and anxious to see and to learn all that might be seen and learned in the course of her travels. On the last day, as they neared the Isthmus, she became more tranquil and quiet in the expression of her feelings than before, and spoke with less of gloom than she had done.

'After all ought I not to love him?' she said. 'He is coming all the way up from Callao merely to meet me. What man would go from London to Moscow to pick up a wife?'

'I would—and thence round the world to Moscow again—if she were the wife I wanted'.

'Yes; but a wife who has never said that she loved you! It is purely a matter of convenience. Well; I have locked my big box, and I shall give the key to him before it is ever again unlocked. He has a right to it, for he has paid for nearly all that it holds'.

'You look at things from such a mundane point of view',

'A woman should, or she will always be getting into difficulty. Mind, I shall introduce you to him, and tell him all that you have done for me. How you braved Cerberus and the rest of it'.

'I shall certainly be glad to meet him'.

'But I shall not tell him of your offer; —not yet at least. If he be good and gentle with me, I shall tell him that too after a time. I am very bad at keeping secrets, —as no doubt you have perceived. We go across the Isthmus at once; do we not?'

'So the Captain says'.

'Look!'—and she handed him back his own field-glass. 'I can see the men on the wooden platform. Yes; and I can see the smoke of an engine'. And then, in little more than an hour from that time the ship had swung round on her anchor.

Colon, or Aspinwall as it should be called, is a place in itself as detestable as St. Thomas. It is not so odious to an Englishman, for it is not used by Englishmen more than is necessary. We have no great depot of traffic there, which we might with advantage move elsewhere. Taken, however, on its own merits, Aspinwall is not a detestable place. Luckily, however, travellers across the Isthmus to the Pacific are never doomed to remain there long. If they arrive early in the day, the railway thence to Panama takes them on at once. If it be not so, they remain on board ship till the next morning. Of course it will be understood that the transit line chiefly affects Americans, as it is the highroad from New York to California.

In less than an hour from their landing, their baggage had been examined by the Custom House officers of New Grenada, and they were on the railway cars, crossing the Isthmus. The officials in those out-of-the-way places always seem like apes imitating the doings of men. The officers at Aspinwall open and look at the trunks just as monkeys might do, having clearly no idea of any duty to be performed, nor any conception that goods of this or that class should not be allowed to pass. It is the thing in Europe to examine luggage going into a new country; and why should not they be as good as Europeans?

'I wonder whether he will be at the station?' she said, when the three hours of the journey had nearly passed. Forrest could perceive that her voice trembled as she spoke, and that she was becoming nervous.

'If he has already reached Panama, he will be there. As far as I could learn the arrival up from Peru had not been telegraphed'.

'Then I have another day—perhaps two.   Nothing is so intolerable as suspense'.

'And the box must be opened again'.

When they reached the station at Panama they found that the vessel from the South American coast was in the roads, but that the passengers were not yet on shore.   Forrest, therefore, took Miss Viner down to the hotel, and there remained with her, sitting next to her in the common drawing-room of the house, when she had come back from her own bedroom.   It would be necessary that they should remain there four or five days, and Forrest had been quick in securing a room for her. He had assisted in taking up her luggage, had helped her in placing her big box, and had thus been recognized by the crowd in the hotel as her friend.   Then came the tidings that the passengers were landing, and he became nervous as she was.   'I will go down and meet him', said he, 'and tell him that you are here.   I shall soon find him by his name'.   And so he went out.

Everybody knows the scrambling manner in which passengers arrive at an hotel out of a big ship.   First came two or three energetic, heated men, who, by dint of screeching and bullying, have gotten themselves first disposed.   They always get the worst rooms at the inns, the housekeepers having a notion that the richest people, those with the most luggage, must be more tardy in their movements.   Four or five of this nature passed by Forrest in the hall, but he was not tempted to ask questions of them.   One, from his age, might have been Mr. Gorloch, but he instantly declared himself to be Count Sapparello. Then came an elderly man alone, with a small bag in his hand.   He was one of those who pride themselves on going from pole to pole without encumbrance, and who will be behoved to no one for the carriage of their luggage.   To him, as he was alone in the street, Forrest addressed himself. 'Gorloch', said he. 'Gorloch: are you a friend of his?'

'A friend of mine is so', said Forrest.

'Ah, indeed; yes', said the other. And then he hesitated. 'Sir', he then said, 'Mr. Gorloch died at Callao, just seven days before the ship sailed. You had better see Mr. Cox'. And then the elderly man passed in with his little bag.

Mr. Gorloch was dead. 'Dead!' said Forrest, to himself, as he leaned back against the wall of the hotel still standing on the street pavement. 'She has come out here; and now he is gone!' And then a thousand thoughts crowded on him. Who should tell her? And how would she bear it? Would it in truth be a relief to her to find that that liberty for which she had sighed had come to her? Or now that the testing of her feelings had come to her, would she regret the loss of home and wealth, and such position as life in Peru would give her? And above all would this sudden death of one who was to have been so near to her, strike her to the heart?

But what was he to do? How was he now to show his friendship? He was returning slowly in at the hotel door, where crowds of men and women were now thronging, when he was addressed by a middle-aged, good-looking gentleman, who asked him whether his name was Forrest. 'I am told,' said the gentleman, when Forrest had answered him, 'that you are a friend of Miss Viner's. Have you heard the sad tidings from Callao?' It then appeared that this gentleman had been a stranger to Mr. Gorloch, but had undertaken to bring a letter up to Miss Viner. This letter was handed to Mr. Forrest, and he found himself burdened with the task of breaking the news to his poor friend. Whatever he did do, he must do at once, for all those who had come up by the Pacific steamer knew the story, and it was incumbent on him that Miss Viner should not hear the tidings in a sudden manner and from a stranger's mouth.

He went up into the drawing-room, and found Miss Viner seated there in the midst of a crew of women. He went up to her, and taking her hand, asked her in a whisper whether she would come out with him for a moment.

'Where is he?' said she. 'I know that something is the matter. What is it?'

'There is such a crowd here. Step out for a moment'. And he led her away to her own room.

'Where is he?' said she. 'What is the matter? He has sent to say that he no longer wants me. Tell me; am I free from him?'

'Miss Viner, you are free'.

Though she had asked the question herself, she was astounded by the answer; but, nevertheless, no idea of the truth had yet come upon her. 'It is so', she said. 'Well, what else? Has he written? He has bought me, as he would a beast of burden, and has, I suppose, a right to treat me as he pleases'.

'I have a letter; but, dear Miss Viner—'

'Well, tell me all,—out at once. Tell me everything'.

'You are free, Miss Viner; but you will be cut to the heart when you learn the meaning of your freedom'.

'He has lost everything in trade. He is ruined'.

'Miss Viner, he is dead!'

She stood staring at him for a moment or two, as though she could not realize the information which he gave her. Then gradually she retreated to the bed, and sat upon it. 'Dead, Mr. Forrest!' she said. He did not answer her, but handed her the letter, which she took and read as though it were mechanically. The letter was from Mr. Gorloch's partner, and told her everything which it was necessary that she should know.

'Shall I leave you now?' he said, when he saw that she had finished reading it.

'Leave me; yes,—no. But you had better leave me, and let me think about it. Alas me, that I should have so spoken of him!'

'But you have said nothing unkind'.

'Yes; much that was unkind. But spoken words cannot be recalled. Let me be alone now, but come to me soon. There is no one else here that I can speak to'.

He went out, and finding that the hotel dinner was ready, he went in and dined. Then he strolled into the town, among the

hot, narrow, dilapidated streets; and then, after two hours'
absence, returned to Miss Viner's room, When he knocked,
she came and opened the door, and he found that the floor was
strewed with clothes. 'I am preparing, you see, for my return.
The vessel starts back for St. Thomas the day after to-morrow'.

'You are quite right to go,—to go at once. Oh, Miss Viner!
Emily, now at least you must let me help you'.

He had been thinking of her most during those last two hours,
and her voice had become pleasant to his ears, and her eyes very
bright to his sight.

'You shall help me', she said. 'Are you not helping me when
at such a time you come to speak to me?'

'And you will let me think that I have a right to act as your
protector?'

'My protector! I do know that I want such aid as that.
During the days that we are here together you shall be my
friend'.

'You shall not return alone. My journeys are nothing to
me. Emily, I will return with you to England'.

Then she rose up from her seat and spoke to him.

'Not for the world', she said. 'Putting out of question the
folly of your forgetting your own objects, do you think it
possible that I should go with you, now that he is dead? To
you I have spoken of him harshly; and now that it is my duty
to mourn for him, could I do so heartily if you were with me?
While he lived, it seemed to me that in those last days I had a
right to speak my thoughts plainly. You and I were to part
and meet no more, and I regarded us both as people apart, who
for a while might drop the common usages of the world. It
is so no longer. Instead of going with you farther, I must ask
you to forget that we were ever together'.

'Emily, I shall never forget you'.

'Let your tongue forget me. I have given you no cause to
speak good of me, and you will be too kind to speak evil'.

After that she explained to him all that the letter had contained. The arrangements for her journey had all been made;
money also had been sent to her; and Mr. Gorloch in his will

had provided for her, not liberally, seeing that he was rich, but still sufficiently.

And so they parted at Panama. She would not allow him even to cross the Isthmus with her, but pressed his hand warmly as he left her at the station. 'God bless you!' he said. 'And may God bless you, my friend!' she answered.

Thus alone she took her departure for England, and he went on his way to California.

KATCHEN'S
CAPRICES

KATCHEN'S CAPRICES

CHAPTER ONE

IT WAS a pretty picture, prettily set, that fair young face crowned with a lavish abundance of plaited tresses, looking forth from the quaintly-carved window-frame! The owner of the face was Katerina Kester: and if you had lived in the village of Gossan, or within twenty English miles of it, I should not have needed to say more. You would have known her by reputation, if not by sight. But, as it is, I had better explain who she was. Katerina's father, Josef Kester, kept an inn at the village of Gossan, in Upper Austria, close to the beautiful lake of Hallstadt. Not *the* inn where travellers stopped to dine and bait their horses, and whence they took boats for excursions on the lake: that was the Black Eagle. Josef's hostelry bore the sign of the Golden Lamb, and was of much humbler pretensions, being frequented only by the country people, or occasionally receiving a foot-sore 'Bursch', or German travelling workman, tramping through his probationary year of apprenticeship. The Black Eagle was flourishing, the Golden Lamb was decaying. The epithets black and golden might, indeed, have been reversed in their case: for the eagle had a glaring gilt beak and gilt talons, and a bright gilt crown on each of his two cruel-looking heads; while to believe that the poor lamb had ever been golden was a strain on one's faith, so begrimed and dingy had he grown with the blackening effects of time and weather. But the lamb, whether black or golden, possessed something of more beauty—ay, and some people thought of more value—than any article within the well-furnished rooms guarded by the fierce, spruce, double-headed eagle.

Katerina Kester, the landlord's daughter, was famed among the Gossaners, and for many a mile around Gossan, as being the prettiest girl in those parts. That might not be saying that she was really beautiful; for gloriously bountiful as Nature has been in making the surrounding scenery delightful to the eyes, she has not scattered female loveliness among its inhabitants with so lavish a hand. The women are in general tall and strong, but meagre, bony, brown-skinned, and betraying the effects of hard work and hard fare by a premature appearance of age. Katerina, however, was as fresh and fair and rounded as a Hebe. Her mother had been a Saxon woman, from Tirna on the Elbe; and from her Katerina inherited a blonde, peach-like skin, large, limpid, light-blue eyes, and an enormous wealth of fair hair. This hair was splendid from its silky quality and great quantity; but it had not the warm richness of colour which painters love. It was not golden, but resembled rather the pale brightness of moonlight than the dazzling glow of sunshine; and when uncoiled it fell down straight on her knees in a silky mass, unbroken by one ripple. So much for the picture; now for its frame. The Golden Lamb was an old house built chiefly of timber, and it had a great balcony running along two sides of it, whence a fine view up and down the lake was to be had. The window of Katerina's room was surrounded by carved wood-work, and garnished by a creeping plant, which thrust its delicate tresses even into the chamber when the frame filled with small glass panes was hooked back to admit the fresh air. On this particular Sunday morning the summer breeze came softly in at the window, heightening the rose on Katchen's cheek, ruffling the bright, smooth lake into dimples, and displaying the grace and lightness of the woodbine that waved backward and forward with a rocking movement.

'Ah, what a fine day!' thought Katerina. 'Dry and bright, but not too hot. Last night's shower will have laid the dust on the highway. How nice!' Katerina did not appreciate the full beauty of the grand scene that lay stretched out before her bedroom window. Lake and mountain were familiar to her sight, and, if I must tell the truth, our village belle was fonder of receiving than of giving admiration. It seemed to her very natural that people who had known her from a child should take unwearying pleasure in gazing on her pretty face, and extolling the length and softness of her hair. But if you had made any great demand on Katerina's powers of admiration on behalf of the lake and the mountains, she would have turned away with a pettish look, and would have told you that she had seen them every day—every day since she was born. The Kesters were Protestants, and attended service at the evangelical church in Hallstadt. Now to go from Gossan to Hallstadt there is but one really practicable way, and that is to row thither in a boat on the lake; therefore it seems odd that Katchen should have cared about the dust on the high-road. But Katchen had a lover who was the owner of a stout travelling-carriage and good team of horses, and who being, moreover, a steady driver, and a smart, honest young fellow, was often employed to convey travellers along the more unfrequented routes in the beautiful lake district—routes where railways were not, and diligences even few and far between.

This lover, Fritz Rosenheim, was expected to-day at Gossan. He had passed through the village the week before on his way to Ischl, and was to return toward Salzburg on this bright Sunday morning. For this reason the state of the road was interesting to Katchen. There was no regular engagement between her and Fritz Rosenheim. Old Josef Kester set himself very much against the idea of such a thing. He liked Fritz heartily, and was glad to see him, but—Fritz was poor. That was a misfortune from which the landlord of the Golden Lamb had suffered severely; and he was wont to say that he would never willingly expose his child to the cold, nipping airs of poverty. But Gossan folks maintained that Josef Kester had started in life with as good prospects as most men, and that it was mainly his own fault if things had gone ill with him, and the poor 'Lamb' had gradually been shorn of its golden fleece. Gossan folks were not less hard in their judgment of the unsuccessful man than London folks or Paris folks. But there was a grain of truth in what they said for all that. Josef had too much of the inert passive good-humour which distinguishes many of his countrymen to push his way energetically through the world. Perhaps he could reckon as many pleasant hours in his past life as the richest of his neighbours. But the pleasant hours were over and gone, and had left him with empty pockets to look old age in the face. The hard-working, well-to-do neighbours *might* sometimes—but this they never acknowledged —envy the clear, smooth forehead and placid smile which made old Josef look younger than his years; but they had only to put their hands in their pockets and feel a soft bundle of very dirty and tattered bank-notes to recover their self-esteem and good spirits immediately.

Katchen drew in her head from the window and went to take one more look at herself in the green mirror, which distorted her pretty face in a heart-breaking manner. But Katchen knew the original by heart, and was not distressed by the bad translation she beheld in her glass. She proceeded to perch a tall sugar-loaf black hat on the top of her thick plaits of hair, and to stick a long silver arrow into the coil at the back.

'Katchen! Katchen!' called her father from the lake below. He was sitting in a little boat just beneath her window, dressed in his best clothes, and ready to row to Hallstadt to church. 'Make haste, my child, service will have begun!'

'Coming, father, coming!' said Katchen, as she ran swiftly down the stairs, through the open house door, and stepped into the little boat that lay rocking gently within a stone's-throw of the inn. Katchen stood up in the boat and took an oar, which she managed with strength and skill. All the young women about Hallstadt and Gossan were used to propel themselves about the lake, and to handle an oar was as ordinary an accomplishment as to wield a knitting-needle. Katchen rowed standing, and at every dip of her paddle into the water she bent well forward, displaying in the action a plump, well-turned leg and neat ankle, encased in the Sunday gear of white stockings and stout black boots.

'Fine bright day, Herr Kester!' shouted a neighbour, whose boat, propelled by four stout damsels, shot past Katchen's.

'Ay, very fine, very fine. Bright, as you say, but not sultry. Any news up your way?'

'Nothing very interesting', bawled back the neighbour, whose boat was rapidly shooting ahead of the Kester's little craft. 'Only one thing your Katchen may care to hear. Fritz Rosenheim got a return fare at Ischl. Some foreigners wanted to go back to Salzburg the very day he was coming away. Lucky for him, isn't it?'

'My Katchen doesn't care a button about it,' roared Josef, angrily; but it is to be feared his words did not reach the ears for which they were intended. Katchen's pink cheeks grew scarlet, and she knit her flaxen eyebrows.

'Why should you say that, father?' she asked, pettishly. 'I *do* care a button, more than a button, for Fritz's good luck.'

'You don't care in the way neighbour Nelbeck meant. And I don't choose to allow folks to talk to me as if you did, Katchen.'

'But, father, I do care——'

'Nonsense! You think you do when you're contradicted, but it's all moonshine. You know you wouldn't marry Fritz if I gave my consent to-morrow.'

'Will you try me, father?'

'No, I won't. I disapprove of the whole thing. The prettiest girl in the district to throw herself away on a poor devil of a kutscher—a fellow who knows nothing in the world but how to guide his horses up and down the mountain roads, rain or hail, shade or shine—it's monstrous! And you, that might do so much better too! Better, dowerless as you are, than many a well-portioned lass I could mention.'

The boat grazed the pebbly landing-place at Hallstadt while Josef Kester was still in the midst of his grumblings against Katchen, against his poverty, against his neighbours, and especially against the guilty Fritz—guilty, by his own confession, of being in love with a pretty girl whose father did not want him as a son-in-law. The crime is heinous, though, alas! too common. But old Josef's discontent dispersed itself in words, and left him placid and smiling as usual when he walked into the little evangelical place of worship, followed by his pretty daughter.

CHAPTER TWO

KATCHEN sat very still during the long controversial discourse that flew high over the heads of the simple congregation. Very still and seemingly attentive sat little Katchen, but her thoughts were busily occupied, and *not* with the sermon. 'Was she really, really so fond of Fritz after all? or was her father right in saying it was only moonshine?' She acknowledged to herself that she never did feel so kindly disposed toward her lover as when some sage adviser set before her the folly and unsuitableness of marrying him. Next to *this* spur to her affections came the idea of any other girl winning Fritz Rosenheim. The young man was very popular, and in his roving life he had opportunities of making many acquaintances. Smart chamber-maids at the big hotels in Salzburg and Ischl knew and smiled upon him. Even land-ladies' daughters at the mountain inns condescended to a little flirtation with the good-looking kutscher. And his unflagging good-humour and gallant bearing toward the fair made the jingle of his horses' bells a very welcome sound to many feminine ears along his line of route. But then— To be sure it was very nice to have Fritz so admiring and so devoted, and to hear him protest that there was not in all Austria, nay, in all Germany, a girl fit to wipe the little shoes of Katerina

Kester. Yes, that was pleasant, without doubt. But it wouldn't last so! Fritz couldn't be content to let that agreeable state of things continue comfortably. It was very unreasonable of him, but he actually wanted to have a formal promise of marriage from his idol, and to be publicly betrothed to her. Katchen gave such an impatient little shiver at the idea of being irrevocably bound to marry Fritz, and tossed up her head so like a wild colt that has never known bit or bridle, that I, for my part, believe her father to have been right about the moonshine, and that she wasn't so very much in love after all.

The cessation of the pastor's sonorous German polysyllables startled her from a reverie. Katchen was not much given to reverie in general, but there was still a wide-eyed look of abstraction on her countenance as she walked forth with her father from the little church. At the entrance they came on quite a crowd of country-folks, some of whom had just been hearing mass in the Catholic chapel. A rosy, well-fed couple of Sisters of Mercy passed through the knot of people, receiving pleasant and respectful salutations alike from the orthodox and the heretics. Josef Kester was known to everybody, and stood for some time exchanging gossip with his neighbours, and taking long, luxurious pulls at the gaudy china pipe suspended by a green cord round his neck. Katchen, still in an unusually thoughtful mood, walked slowly down to the brink of the lake, whence a narrow wooden plank ran out a short distance into the water, for the convenience of boatmen and their passengers. Katchen seated herself on a pile of wood cut and stacked for fuel, and stared absently at the lake, and the opposite hills rich in colour, and steeped in a great glory of sunlight.

'Good-day, Mam'sell Katerina', said a high, thin voice close at her ear. She started and looked round. The address was unusually formal and respectful. Her own acquaintance never bestowed on her the title of 'Mam'sell', and usually abbreviated the utterance of her Christian name. The polite speaker was a tall, spare man of about five-and-forty, with a very high, bald forehead, a sallow face, and thick, hay-coloured moustaches.

He wore spectacles, and blinked very much with his light-grey eyes. "Good-day, Mam'sell Katerina', said he again, seeing that Katchen stared at him without speaking. 'I fear you do not recognize me. I am Caspar Ebner, the landlord of the Black Eagle in Gossan, at your service.' And he drew himself up a little, and twisted his fingers in a heavy silver watch-chain that crossed his black satin waistcoat. Herr Ebner wore a suit of dark-blue cloth, with gilt buttons, a tall, shiny French hat, and the black satin waistcoat aforesaid.

'Thou dear Heaven!' cried Katchen, jumping up from her seat and making a little curtsy. 'I beg your pardon, Herr Ebner, but I couldn't for the moment think who it was.' She might have added that her surprise was not much diminished when she did know who it was; for the rich landlord of the Black Eagle had never accosted her in her life before, though she knew him by sight well enough, and had sometimes fancied he looked at her with a certain amount of admiration.

'The Herr Pastor was somewhat lengthy to-day', said Ebner, half seating himself on the log of wood on which Katchen had resumed her place.

'Was he?' asked she, without thinking of what she was saying, for her brain was busily trying to puzzle out why Herr Ebner should speak to her.

'Yes; somewhat lengthy. At least I fancied so. You were a more devout and attentive listener, mam'sell. I observed your absorption.'

Katchen coloured, partly from a prick of conscience, partly at at the idea of having been watched. Then the thought that was in her mind came to her tongue, although she had not wished to betray it. 'I never saw you in church before, Herr Ebner', said she.

It was now the landlord's turn to colour; that is to say, the lemon hue of his face deepened to orange. 'Most likely not, Mam'sell Katerina. I—in fact, I don't go to church in a usual way. I read though, and think a good deal on these subjects, and I have formed, I confess, certain theories, which——' Here he stopped abruptly, catching Katchen's point-blank stare of bewilderment. 'I—I beg pardon. These grave and speculative topics are hardly suited to one so young, and—and—ahem—so lovely as yourself.'

'Here's father!' cried Katchen, with an unmistakable look of relief; and she even made a little step toward her father and away from Ebner.

'Good-day, Herr Ebner', said Kester, pulling off his soft felt hat—a courtesy which the other instantly requited by lifting his own stiff, shiny head-covering high in the air. 'I've been staying behind to have a little chat with some old neighbours, and kept this young woman of mine waiting, you see.'

Old Kester glanced sharply at his daughter as he spoke, and Katchen noticed that her father did not seem nearly so much surprised as she had been to see the host of the Black Eagle speaking so affably to her.

'I am—I mean—are you', stammered Ebner, with an awkward hesitation.

'Are we going to row back to Gossan now? Yes, we are', said Kester, promptly.

'My boat is here, with three of the boatmen from St. Emmerau. Would you—that is, if Mam'sell Katerina—It's hot, rowing in the middle of the day——'

'Thank you, Herr Ebner', responded the rival landlord, with —to Katchen—astonishing alacrity; and then, before she understood the arrangement clearly, she was handed into Ebner's boat and seated in state on a cushioned bench under an awning, instead of standing up with a heavy paddle in her sunburnt hand. One of the boatmen made Kester's deserted little craft fast to the stern of the larger boat, and away they went, swiftly cutting a bright furrow through the glassy water, and breaking into fragments the peaceful shadows of the great hills that lay deep in the lake with their peaks pointing downward into a second and still bluer heaven than that which stretched overhead. Katchen was bewildered. That she should be in a boat at all, without aiding to propel that boat, was wonderful; but that the Black Eagle should have doffed his usual imperial fierceness, and—instead of sticking his long

talons into the fleece of the Golden Lamb—should coo with
dove-like softness, and invite his rival even into his own nest—
this was more wonderful by far. Not that Caspar Ebner was
really very fierce in himself. But Katchen was used to think
of him as a very high and mighty personage—one to whose
successful rapacity was partly owing the decay and ill fortune
that hung about the meeker Lamb. Josef Kester's ill success
was, on his own showing, always 'somebody else's' fault. In
this respect, perhaps, Josef Kester was not entirely singular.
And so the indefinite 'somebody else', who wrought all the
mischief to the Golden Lamb, had gradually taken shape in
Katchen's mind, and Herr Caspar Ebner was its living
embodiment.

Many an evening in the old raftered kitchen of the inn had
Katchen listened to her father's long speeches, uttered oracu-
larly from behind dense clouds of coarse tobacco-smoke, when
the old man would descant on the Lamb's ill-treatment and the
undeserved prosperity of the Eagle, and lament the strange
perversity of travellers who *would* frequent Herr Ebner's house,
to the neglect and detriment of his own establishment. And
now behold, here was her father sitting placidly under the
enemy's awning, rowed luxuriously by the enemy's boatmen,
and chatting cheerfully. with the enemy himself! The boat
scudded along lightly, bounding to the strong strokes of the
rowers, and soon reached the landing-place at Gossan, where
Katchen was handed out by Herr Ebner, with much politeness,
though a little awkwardly. She and her father bade him farewell, and thanked him, and were about to draw their own
little boat up high and dry on the beach, but Ebner desired his
own boatmen to do that, and asked Kester and Katchen to do
him the honour of dining with him, as the mid-day meal was
just ready. Josef made some little objection, but only by way
of what he considered good manners; for he finally accepted
the invitation for his daughter and himself, and they followed
their host into his private sitting-room at the Black Eagle. It
was a pleasant apartment on the ground-floor, with windows
looking on to the lake. Here the cloth was laid for dinner, and

a tall chamber-maid came forward to take Katchen's hat from her, and to offer her any assistance she might need in the arrangement of her dress. She had, of course, taken the cue from her master's behaviour, for Katchen knew well enough that at most times Therese would consider herself quite above waiting on the daughter of old Josef Kester, of the Golden Lamb. The dinner was very good and the wine excellent, but somehow the little party did not seem to be quite at ease. Josef, it is true, ate and drank unrestrained by shyness; but Katchen was too full of wonder at the unexpected honour to feel much appetite, and Herr Ebner blinked nervously through his spectacles, and hesitated and stammered in his speech in a very disconcerting manner.

When the dinner was over, the guests rose to take their leave, Josef protesting that he must go, as he had 'so many things to attend to.' Ebner accompanied them to the entrance-hall, and there bashfully offered a bunch of roses to Katchen. He had them gathered in his little garden during dinner-time, and now they were lying ready to be presented in a tasteful little straw basket. Katchen took the fragrant June roses with a smile and a bright blush of pleasure. It was certainly very nice to be treated like a real lady, and she was quite enough of a coquette to enjoy the consciousness of being admired. But all of a sudden she gave a start, and the colour left her round cheeks for a moment, to rush back deeper than before; for there stood Fritz Rosenheim right in the doorway, looking at her in blank astonishment. He had a long driving-whip in his hand and wore his smartest suit—a bright blue postilion's jacket, studded with silver buttons, leathern breeches, and high boots coming above the knee; and in his low-crowned hat, stuck on one side of his head, was fastened a bunch of rich red carnations, the gift, probably, of some coquettish chamber-maid or landlady along his line of route.

'Good-day, Fritz', said Katchen, desperately, speaking first; for poor Fritz's presence of mind seemed clean gone. He muttered some salutation in reply, and then turned to grasp the hand which Josef Kester heartily held out to him. 'Welcome,

Fritz, my boy', said he; 'I expected you to-day, for I heard
news of you from old Nelbeck.' Then Fritz dropped his hat
respectfully to the landlord of the Black Eagle, who gravely
nodded in return.

'I've brought some travellers from Ischl, Sir', said Fritz;
'a foreign lady and gentleman and their courier. I told them
they couldn't be anywhere better treated or more comfortable than at the Black Eagle in Gossan.'

'They will be taken care of, kutscher. I hope you have seen
to your horses. Yes—eh? Well, then, go and tell the kellver
to give you a bottle of Rudesheimer to drink my health
in.'

Fritz touched his hat again, and made way for the Kesters
to pass out. Josef said, as he went away, 'See you to-night,
Fritz; you'll come and smoke a pipe in the old kitchen as
usual.'

Katchen walked home in a state of ill-humour that darkened
her pretty childish face. She was vexed that Fritz should have
come upon her just when he did—vexed to see him touch his
hat like a servant to the man at whose table she had been
dining—vexed with poor Herr Ebner for his good-nature in
treating the kutscher to wine. Why should Fritz accept his
wine? He was able to pay for it. And vexed above all with
her father for inviting the young man to come and 'smoke a
pipe in the kitchen as usual.' As usual! What would the
landlord of the Black Eagle think of them? He never smoked
pipes in the kitchen with a kutscher. This last was a very
unworthy thought, and ungenerous toward Fritz, who would
never have been ashamed of association with her before the
highest in the land. But then I really do believe old Josef had
been right about the moonshine. Still, objecting as he did to
any semblance of love-making between Rosenheim and his
daughter, he should not have encouraged the young man to
come to his house. But this was Josef's way—one of the
many weaknesses in his easy-going nature that had helped to
smooth the down-hill path on which he had slidden so rapidly
from comfort to poverty. He liked Fritz. The young fellow's

cheery talk and pleasant manner, and the news he brought
from the busier world he traversed in his journeys, were very
agreeable stimulants after the sluggish monotony of life at the
Golden Lamb. And, like many inert men, Josef Kester loved
nothing better than to witness and hear of traits of energy and
activity in which he was not expected to participate. As to the
after-consequences of all this familiar intercourse, why, that
would come all right somehow. The young folks would make
love a little—why not?—but it would be all in a wild and
purposeless sort of way that would hurt neither of them very
deeply. He could be very angry when any one took it for
granted that the moonshine meant something real, and spoke
as old Nelbeck had spoken. Not the less angry, perhaps, from
a secret self-reproach in the matter. But the moment Fritz
reappeared he could not resist the temptation of his company,
and, besides, the young man *couldn't* be so desperately in
earnest. In this he was thoroughly mistaken; but it was a
comfortable theory, which lightened his own responsibility,
and therefore Josef Kester clung to it.

CHAPTER THREE

KATCHEN, on reaching home, ran into her own room,
and, having fastened the door, relieved her mortified
feelings by giving loose to a copious flow of tears. They
were childlike tears; an April shower which fell easily, and
gave place to sunshine, without leaving any stormy ground-
swell behind them, as a fit of weeping will do in more passionate
natures. She had made many high resolves that she would not,
by any persuasion, give her company to the smokers in the
kitchen. She would stay up there by herself, and be miserable
without knowing why. But as the afternoon wore on she
repented of her resolution, and at last, about supper-time—
that is to say, between four and five o'clock—she put her head
outside the door to listen to what was going on. She heard

her father's rich bass voice rolling out short, disjointed sentences
between pauses that, she knew, were delightfully occupied by
smoking; and then she heard a ringing laugh that made her
heart beat a little quicker, and, after a farewell glance at the
green mirror, she stole down stairs quietly, and went down
to the kitchen with an assumption of perfect indifference to the
presence of any one there. Besides her father and Fritz there
was another man seated at the table, smoking a long pipe,
which Katchen at once perceived to be a real meerschaum.
The stranger was a singularly ugly man, with flat, blunt
features and a short bull neck; but he looked good-humoured
withal, and intelligent. He was dressed in a frock-coat and
trousers, instead of the peasant costume worn by the usual
frequenters of the Golden Lamb. There was no one else there,
for the one stout serving-maid who, with Katchen, performed
all the indoor work of the house, had leave on Sunday evenings
to visit her friends. So Josef Kester and his two guests had the
spacious kitchen all to themselves. A little table was drawn
up close to one of the open windows, whence a sweet scent
from the woodbine came in with the pure air, but was speedily
choked and stifled by the heavy clouds of tobacco-smoke that
almost hid the smokers from view. Each man had before him a
great glass tankard of foaming amber beer. No one noticed
Katchen at first, and she went and sat down at another window
furthest removed from that where the men were, and, pushing
back the lattice, leaned her elbows on the sill and looked out at
the lake. Presently she felt that some one was standing very
close to her, but she would not turn round; and then Fritz's
voice said in her ear, 'My Katchen, won't you speak to
me?'

'*Your* Katchen, indeed! Not quite. And besides—' Here
Katchen gave a pretty toss of her head in the direction of the
stranger.

'Oh, you needn't mind him', said simple Fritz, delighted to
think that he had discovered the reason of his sweetheart's
show of coolness. 'He's a very good fellow; Johann Laurier, a
Swiss courier. He has come from Ischl with the foreign lady

and gentleman. And he knows—that is, I told him—that you and I——'

'What did you tell him, Herr Rosenheim? How dare you talk about me to a stranger without my permission?'

It seemed fated that whatever Fritz said or did to-day should affront Katchen.

This state of things was not entirely unprecedented; but Fritz always fell into the error of trying to reason about what was quite unreasonable, and, being neither so quick-witted nor so nimble of tongue as his pretty antagonist, he got the worst of the argument, even though he were thoroughly in the right.

'I suppose you're too proud to acknowledge me for a lover, now that you've dined with Herr Ebner, and been rowed in his boat. I heard of it. The folks at the Black Eagle say all sorts of things.'

'The folks at the Black Eagle! And what do I care for them, or for you either, if you are so ignorant as to listen to the gossip of such as them? As to being proud, I can tell you I think father is quite as good as Herr Ebner, even though he may not be as rich. But he was as rich once, and richer, too.'

'Well, Katchen, I'm sorry if I've made you cross——'

'Cross!'

'Well, if I've offended you, then. But it seemed as if you would hardly speak to me to-day when I first saw you, and now you are as cold and stand-offish as you can be; why or wherefore, I'm sure I don't know. I love you with all my heart, Katchen, and I never shall love another girl the same as I do you.'

And Fritz ventured to take up the plump sunburnt little hand that lay on Katchen's lap. He held it lightly in his broad brown palm for a moment, and then the wilful girl jerked it away with a pettish exclamation, and walked off toward her father. 'You tease me', said she, over her shoulder. It was somewhat trying to her lover, that, while Katchen was extremely exacting in her demands on his devotion, she resented any show of tenderness on his part; and sometimes, when he was most earnest in his expressions of love, she would turn all he said into ridicule, and make the house ring with laughter at his protestations. To-night, however, she was not in a laughing mood, but went and sat beside her father, resting her hand on his shoulder, and apparently absorbed in thought. She was conscious, though, of Fritz's rueful puzzled look as he resumed his seat, and absently took long pulls at a perfectly cold pipe; and she was conscious, also, of the admiring gaze that Monsieur Jean Laurier cast upon her flushed face. 'Your daughter, Mr. Landlord?' said he, with a polite bow.

'Yes, Herr Laurier, my little Katerina—Katchen, as she's always called. Child, this gentleman is a great traveller, and can tell you of wonderful places he has seen, and wonderful people too. He speaks all languages——'

'Not quite all, Herr Landlord', modestly put in Laurier.

'Yes, yes, all, I say—all that are worth speaking. You should have come down before, you puss, and you would have heard such things about Rome, and Paris, and Vienna. I've been relating part of my history to the Herr, and he thinks it very hard that a man like myself should have been so ill-treated by fortune. But, lord! I could explain it if I liked. A good deal of it is the fault of others. However, no more on that score. It can't interest a stranger.'

Nevertheless, no stranger was ever half an hour beneath the roof of the Golden Lamb without hearing Josef Kester's version of his own misfortunes.

'What fine hair the Fraulein has!' said Laurier, turning the discourse.

'Our Katchen? Yes, friend, you may say so; and a pretty colour, too; not like the coarse black horse-hair one sees hereabouts. Her blessed mother was a Saxon, and she has her mother's hair.'

'It's long, too, I suppose', pursued the courier. 'It seems all coiled round and round, so.'

'Long! I believe you. Pull that bodkin out, Katchen, and let the Herr see its length.'

And, as Katchen hesitated, he took the pins out with his own hand, and the great silky plaits tumbled down over her shoulders.

'Unplait it, child. It's nearly twice as long when it's all loose. There, Herr Laurier, did you ever see a prettier sight than that in your travels?'

The Swiss got up, and took a long soft tress in his hand, weighing it with a thoughtful look.

'Don't mind me, mam'sell; I've a daughter as old as you, at home in Lausanne. I tell you what, there's a friend of mine, a hairdresser in Paris, who would give you almost any sum you'd like to ask for this hair. It's all the fashion just now, and they can't get enough of it anywhere.'

Katchen jumped back, and hastily twisted up her hair into one great lump, looking meanwhile half in terror, half in indignation, at the courier. But old Josef roared with laughter.

'No, no, thank you. Not to make a wig for our empress herself, God bless her! We're not so poor as that comes to, yet a while. Don't look scared, Katchen. I should like to see the barber who'd put scissors near your head.'

'I'm not scared, father. How stupid you are! But I don't want to make a show of myself any longer, that's all.'

Laurier was more a man of the world than poor Rosenheim, and had lived in it some twenty years longer, so instead of apologizing, or arguing, or retracting, he began a description of the wonderful head-dresses that the ladies wore in Paris, the fine feathers, and flowers, and jewels which adorned their borrowed locks. And in listening to this topic of feminine interest Katchen had time to recover her composure, and even put in a few questions of her own. Before the evening was over, Laurier had established himself in the good graces of both father and daughter.

'Whenever I come this way I shall certainly pay you a visit, Herr Kester', said the courier. They parted with many good wishes on both sides, and Fritz was well pleased to receive a tolerably gracious farewell from his capricious lady-love.

CHAPTER FOUR

THE NEXT day things resumed their old monotonous course at the Golden Lamb. Fritz and the friendly courier were far away on their road to Salzburg. Laurier had said that if he chanced to travel in their direction next year he should certainly come and see the Kesters; but meanwhile, there was all the autumn, and winter, and spring to get through. Gradually—Katchen could scarcely trace how—it came to be no unusual thing for Caspar Ebner to drop into the Golden Lamb of an evening, and before long it was quite an established custom for the Kesters to be taken to and from the church at Hallstadt in his boat. Little presents of flowers, and fruit, and choice cheese, or a bottle of fine Rudesheimer, were sent from the Black Eagle to the Golden Lamb; and once Herr Ebner brought out from his pocket a pair of bright gold earrings, which he begged Katchen to accept. But these she refused. And the refusal brought on an argument which ended in a formal offer of Caspar Ebner's hand and heart. 'Herr Ebner', said Katchen with a gasp, 'you can't be in earnest!'

'Not in earnest, Katerina! Is it possible that you have been blind to my feelings all this time? Can you honestly say so?'

'Well, I fancied, perhaps, that you liked me a little, and—and—thought me pretty; but I never believed that you really—really—' And Katchen began to cry. Why *would* people be so tiresome, and serious, and in earnest? Ebner was terribly distressed at sight of her tears.

'My child, my child', said he, 'pray don't cry in that way. I wouldn't grieve or vex you for more than I can tell. Try to think seriously of what I have said to you. I love you, Katerina, better than I believe you will ever be loved again.'

'But I d-don't love you', sobbed Katchen.

'I don't expect you should, all at once. Indeed no. I am twenty years older than you, my child, and staid and dull in your eyes. But I will be kind to you—oh, Katchen, if you will let me, I will be so kind to you! You shall be mistress of everything I possess, and your father shall have a home with us while he lives. I have plenty.'

'But I am quite, quite poor. I have not a kreutzer of dowry. Perhaps you didn't know?' And the blue eyes looked up into Herr Ebner's spectacles with a naive expression of wonder. The spectacles flashed all over their unmeaning surface as he shook his head, but the eyes behind them were very soft and tender when he answered:

'I did know, I do know; but, my child, no riches could make you more dear to me.'

Katchen had a heart, in spite of her frivolity, and it was touched by the generosity and disinterested affection of her middle-aged suitor. But to marry him! Ah, that was another thing! And then there was Fritz. No, it couldn't be. But Ebner refused to take her answer at once. He would give her a week to consider of his proposal, and meanwhile would not obtrude himself on her in any way. 'Only', said he, as he went away, 'do try to be good to me, my child—*try* to be good to me.'

When old Josef Kester heard of the proposal he was elate with joy and pride.

'Ain't you astonished, father?' said Katchen.

'Astonished? Not a bit of it. I saw, long ago, that the man was desperately in love with one of us two, and I naturally supposed it to be you.'

But his pleasure was suddenly quenched when his daughter protested that, though she felt deeply grateful to Herr Caspar Ebner, and proud of his good opinion, she could never consent to be his wife. At first Josef treated this as mere childish folly that meant nothing. But the more he argued, and the angrier he grew, the more obstinate became Katchen's opposition. So at last he took refuge in his old system of letting her take her own way—for the present.

Two or three days of the week went by, and Katchen had by no means made up her mind as to the answer she should give Caspar Ebner. Her father's tactics of non-opposition were beginning to tell. She thought of the grandeur that lay at her feet, ready to be picked up. The fine clothes, the servants, the importance, the chance of travel, perhaps even of seeing Vienna—all these temptations crowded through her mind pell-mell. And then, duty to her father. Ought not *that* to weight with her? In the midst of her indecision came a letter from Fritz. That is to say, a letter written by some friend at Fritz's dictation, for his own calligraphic powers extended only to the crooked signing of his name. A letter from Fritz! She had never received one from him before.

'MY OWN KATCHEN—I am right glad that I can send you this letter. A trusted friend here at Salzburg writes it down, but the words are all my own. You seemed somewhat cold when I saw you last; but I fear I was to blame. To confess the truth, I was jealous of the landlord of the Black Eagle. Yes indeed. Was I not a fool? Just as if you would think of him! But true love is always kin with jealousy, they say. I know your worth, my angel, and feel sure of your fidelity. But only I would advise, go not too often to Herr Ebner's house. Folks will talk else. I shall see you, please Heaven, early in the year. Meanwhile, forget me not.

'Thine, ever loving,

'FRITZ ROSENHEIM.

'Greet thy father heartily for me.'

Katchen was as uncertain as the sea in her moods; and this unlucky letter sent her into a most hard-hearted and contemptuous frame of mind. 'He is sure of me, is he? Could he say more if we had been betrothed before the whole village? And why *shouldn't* he be jealous, indeed? As if it were impossible to love anyone better than him! Advises me not to go to the Black Eagle! It's downright insolent. I know very well what I'm doing.' And so she worked up her wrath to boiling-point. On a sudden she crushed the offending letter in her hand, and ran down to the water's brink, where her father was pottering about the old boat, trying to mend it in an awkward, unworkmanlike way. He looked tired and aged, and conscious of waning strength and failure in his attempt. His clothes were very threadbare and shabby. His broad placid forehead was puckered up into ignoble cross lines. The down-hill path was getting steeper and steeper; the downward pace quicker and quicker. Tears came into Katchen's eyes as she looked at him, and, with an impulse born of many mingled emotions, she ran to him, and putting her hands on his shoulders, said, 'Father, would you really like me to marry Herr Ebner? Would it make you happy?'

'Child! it is as if you had dropped from heaven! I was just brooding over a tangled web of troubles, and thinking that there was but one way to unravel them, and that you wouldn't take that way, when behold, you come with the welcomest words on your lips that I've heard this many a long year.'

'Would it really and truly make you happy, father?'

'Happy! More happy than I thought ever to be again, child.'

'Then I will', said Katchen, in a low voice.

Josef kissed his daughter, and blessed her, but repressed any exuberant demonstrations of joy, although he could have leaped and shouted aloud. Thought he: 'If I say too much, she'll begin to argue on the other side, and change her mind altogether.' Josef was growing cunning.

CHAPTER FIVE

NOT TO be tempted to break his word to Katchen, Herr Ebner had gone away from Gossan, thus leaving her quite free and unmolested for her week of consideration. Had Ebner been on the spot, Josef Kester would have stolen up to the Black Eagle to give him the good tidings secretly. As it was, he had no choice but to wait until the end of the week. The days passed slowly with him, but to Katchen they seemed to fly past with unwonted rapidity. She sat idly dreaming from morning to night, scarcely making a pretence of turning the great spinning-wheel, before which she sat nearly all day. The servant girl was indignant, and complained that all the work fell on her shoulders; but old Josef bade her hold her tongue,

and gave hints of some grandeur that was shortly to befall
the family, to which Liese listened open-mouthed. At length
dawned Saturday morning. The year was well advanced now.
Cold winds, chilled by the mountain snows, rushed across the
lake and whistled in the scanty foliage, stripping the boughs
barer and barer at every gust. The early morning hours weres
raw and comfortless, although toward mid-day the sun gained
power and brightness. When Katchen arose that Saturday
morning she felt as though a tight hand was pressing on her
heart. 'I must decide—I must decide!' These words rang in her
ears as if another had spoken them aloud, but they were only
uttered by her own anxious thoughts. She came down to
prepare breakfast so pale and heavy-eyed that even slow-
witted Liese perceived there was something wrong, and bluntly
asked her young mistress what was the matter with her, for
which attention Liese received a sharp snubbing. Old Kester
noticed Katchen's wan looks, but said nothing. In truth, he was
a little anxious himself. She had promised to marry Herr
Ebner, and that was well; but he did not wish his child to be
unhappy.

'It is cold', said Katchen, turning from the table to cower
over the great cooking-stove in the kitchen. 'I'm so cold, I
can't eat.' There she sat all the morning, idly clicking her
knitting-needles now and again. Slowly the day wore on.
Dinner-time came, but Katchen was still too cold to eat, she
said, though the sun was high in the heavens. She tasted a few
spoonfuls of soup, and then wrapped a warm cloak around her
and went out. It was impossible, she said to herself, to sit there
any longer, fancying every step to be Ebner's, and expecting
to see him each time the latch clicked. Katchen wandered
down to the lake's brink, where a pile of fuel was stacked, and
sat down on some logs, just as she had done that Sunday at
Hallstadt. She thought of that day, and of the many subsequent
days when she had received kindness from Caspar Ebner, and
she remembered the high character he bore, and his reputation
for honour and honesty. She summed up his good qualities
in her mind one by one, and asked her heart—so she phrased it

mentally—could she consent to be his wife? and something, which I too must call her heart for want of a better word, answered, 'No!'

'He is far better than I—far, far better. He is true and gentle and generous. Can't I marry him?' 'No!'

'He is a learned man compared to ignorant little me, and rich and well thought of. Can't I marry him?' 'No!'

'He offers a home to father, and will smooth his last years, and will be a son to him. *Can't* I marry him?' 'No!'

Katchen was aghast. She had fancied there was nothing to be done but for her to say unconcernedly, 'I will have this man for my husband.' To bring herself to this point might be difficult, but the point once reached, all would be settled. And now, behold, when she said 'I will', some voice in her bosom answered 'I *won't*!' All this time, too, the image of Fritz was was haunting her brain. She tried not to think of him, and even thought she was not thinking of him; but there was his face, looking sadly and fondly at her, if she but closed her eyes an instant in her efforts at reflection. Truly this 'self' of hers was a most incomprehensible and unmanageable antagonist, and Katchen at last resolved to give up the struggle and float with the tide. Just as she had arrived at this philosophical decision a footstep crushed the pebbles on the beach, and Caspar Ebner stood before her. He advanced with outstretched arms, but Katchen jumped up with a start and made quite a leap backward.

'Did I frighten you, Katerina?' said Ebner, a little crestfallen.

'No, only you came sudden like.'

'Are you not cold here, sitting still? The air blows chill from the lake. Will you walk a little way with me?'

Katchen's knees trembled as she complied with his request. She was in a nervous fever of apprehension, but Ebner did not at once broach the important topic. This was a respite; but then she almost wished he would plunge boldly into the subject, waiting was so dreadful. She had not to wait long, however.

'Katchen', said Ebner, when they had walked a few yards side by side, 'have you thought of what I said to you?'

'Yes', said Katchen, in a faint little voice.

'I kept my word, did I not? I went away and left you quite free.' No answer.

'Katchen, may I hope you have a kind word to say to me? It will be easy for you, but oh, how precious to me!'

'It—it isn't easy', said Katchen, with a childlike catching of her breath.

'Well, no; perhaps not quite easy for a young maiden to say; but you will say it, eh, Katchen? You will tell me that you will be my wife, my treasure, my darling, the mistress of my home?' And he caught her two cold little hands in his, bending down his tall form so as to look into her face. The action roused Katchen into energy. She wrenched away her hands, though he held them in a strong grasp, and clasped them before her tearful eyes.

'No, no, no, I can't. Indeed—indeed I can't. Don't be angry with me; I am grateful indeed. You are very kind and very generous, but I can't marry you.' And she sobbed as though she would choke. Ebner stood and looked at her. A hundred thoughts rushed through his mind, but he could find only one word.

'Why?' he said, jerking the syllable dryly out of his throat.

'Because I—I can't', sobbed Katchen.

It did not sound logical, but it was true.

'You can. If you choose to say yes, you can, unless there is someone else that you love.' Ebner's throat seemed to get dryer and dryer, and the words came huskily. Katchen caught at them. They seemed to offer a tangible reason.

'There is someone who loves me very much—' she began, and then stopped short. Ebner's brow darkened into a frown, and he looked sternly at the weeping girl.

'You have deceived me, then', said he at last. 'I trusted in you. I saw you were childish, but I did not think you dishonourable.'

'Dishonourable! Oh dear, oh dear, what makes you say such things, and look like that?'

'Yes, dishonourable. I repeat it. Cruel and heartless. You have been playing with me; drawing me on; and all the while you were the promised wife of another man. Why did you not tell me so at once, honestly?'

'But I'm not', retorted Katchen, roused to anger in her turn. She was in the wrong, but that did not make her the less angry. 'I'm not his promised wife, and how dare you say so? I'll never have him. I don't love him, nor you, nor anybody. I wish I had never been born, I do. You're all cruel and unkind, and I hate you, everyone!' Katchen wrapped her cloak over her head, and ran off sobbing, with her apron at her swollen, tear-stained eyes. Ebner was astounded. Was this his sweet, bright, good-humoured Katchen? This pettish, passionate, unreasonable girl? Caspar Ebner was in love, it was true, but then he had just been refused; and that, perhaps, helped to make him clear-sighted. At all events he did not perceive that Katchen had been strangely wayward, capricious, and, he thought, deceitful. When a man seriously means to ask a girl to be his wife it is difficult to persuade him that she is not fully aware of his intention. He could not but believe that Katchen had understood his feelings from the first, and now she cast him off and told him of someone else who loved her. His amour propre was deeply hurt. In truth, Ebner had not been at all unconscious of the advantages which Katchen would have derived from his alliance. She was penniless, burdened with a shiftless old father, and in a humble rank of life; but if she had consented to marry him he would never have made her feel these things by word or deed. Now they came vividly before his mind. He had been willing to give up his easy, selfish, bachelor life to raise this ignorant little peasant girl to be the mistress of his home; more than willing—eager to do so, but now under the shock of her unreasonable behaviour he said to himself that it would have been a sacrifice. And so he walked slowly home, scorching out the pain of disappointed love with the heat of his angry resentment. But alas! the anger would soon pass, and leave the wounded heart still smarting.

CHAPTER SIX

IT WOULD be impossible to describe Josef Kester's anger and consternation when Katchen confessed to him the result of her interview with Ebner. He stormed and raved in one—the ungovernable and rare fits of fury which now and then broke the calm of his phlegmatic nature. And then, when his passion had spent itself, he tried to coax his wayward daughter. She had changed her mind once, and might change it again. But it was in vain.

'He spoke so harshly to me', said Katchen, taking refuge in an air of being injured.

'Harshly? And no wonder!'

'But he said such shameful things; called me cruel, and heartless, and dishonourable. If ever I could have made up my mind to have him, his words to-day would have cured me of such a notion.'

This was not quite ingenuous on Katchen's part, seeing that she had found herself obliged to refuse him long before he had spoken those harsh words. I am sorry to have to record it, but I am trying to describe her as she really was. Besides, in her blind perversity, she actually began to think herself ill-used. Her father fell into the snare, and, dropping his attitude of attack, assumed the defensive, and commenced to excuse and justify Ebner.

'Why, it's natural enough, too. What do you think the man's made of? Angry! If a girl had treated *me* so, after drawing me on——'

'I did *not* draw him on, father. I never had any idea he wanted to marry me until he spoke. Why, had you yourself?'

'I told you I had. Of course I had. It seems odd to me that you could be so blind. You're quick enough generally. But all that is nothing to the purpose. What I go upon is, that you told me you would marry him. Told me so of your own will; and now you say "No", without rhyme or reason. But I understand well enough that that underhand fellow, Fritz Rosenheim, is at the bottom of it.'

And then he subsided into a growling, half-audible tirade against Fritz; and Katchen sat silent and sullen by the stove, giving little heed to her father's words, but brooding over her own troubles.

The next day, Sunday, neither father nor daughter went to Hallstadt to church. Ebner's boatmen rowed up to the landing-place at the Golden Lamb, but were thanked and dismissed. Their master was not in the boat, but he was above forbidding his servants to go for the Kesters as usual. It was a dreary day within and without the Golden Lamb. That grimy quadruped creaked and moaned in the autumn blast. A dry choking dust blew in clouds over the empty desolate high-road, and the lake wore a livid hue, and broke with a dull splash on the shore. Dusky and dreary the day had dawned, dusky and dreary still it went down, with one lurid line of crimson in the western sky. Josef lit his pipe, and sat puffing cloud after cloud, until the glow of the burning tobacco in his pipe-bowl was the only thing visible in the dark kitchen, except such streaks of light as penetrated through the chinks of the stove. Katchen had taken out a hymnbook, and had read in it mechanically while the daylight lasted, but now she sat staring at her father's glowing pipe, and letting her thoughts go whithersoever they listed. And a wild dance they had of it, flying off to the unlikeliest things and places, but under all, like a pedal bass in a piece of music, was the drowning sense of pain and unrest.

'Hulloa! Are you all asleep here? No light? No welcome for a cold traveller?'

The cheery voice rang through the room, startling its inmates as if a bombshell had burst in their midst. Katchen, whose nerves were unstrung, gave a sharp squeak like a frightened mouse. Old Josef started up, nearly oversetting his chair.

'Who's there?' said he. But he had known the voice well enough.

'Who but I, Herr Landlord? Fritz Rosenheim, at your service. Shall I light the lamp? And where can I find a lantern? for I must stable my beast. He's warm, and the breeze from the lake cuts like a scythe'.

Without waiting for permission, Fritz lit the great old-fashioned oil-lamp that stood ready trimmed on the dresser, and proceeded to search for the lantern, like one who knew the house well.

'Stable your beast!' echoed Josef, recovering himself a little. 'Ay, you may stable him, and that's all, for the deuce a bit of provender you'll find to fill his belly with. There's mighty little entertainment at the Golden Lamb now for either man or beast.'

'Don't fret about that, Herr Kester. I've brought the piebald's supper along with me from Altenau. I thought how it might likely be. Here's the old horn lantern at last, and here's an end of candle ready to put into it'. And honest Fritz bustled out to see to his horse.

'Are you going to stay here, then?' asked Kester, who had been staring open-mouthed at these proceedings. But Fritz was already unharnessing the piebald, and did not hear the question.

'Well, that's cool', said Josef, turning sullenly to his daughter. 'He must mean to stay here. Then there are no travellers with him. Small thanks for his coming. If he had had any rich foreigners to convoy, it's the Black Eagle and not the Golden Lamb that would have been honoured by Herr Rosenheim's presence tonight.'

'Of course it is!' answered Katchen, sharply. None quicker than she to detect unreason and injustice in other people. 'How could we entertain rich travellers? Haven't you just told him that you hadn't even a mouthful of hay for his one horse? How would it have been if he had brought the team?'

'Hold your tongue, saucebox. It's my belief you knew he was coming, and that it was all settled between you'.

'You know you don't really believe that, father', she answered. But the accusation scarcely angered her. It was rather soothing to feel that, in this instance, she was blamed quite wrongfully. Katchen did not mind being a victim up to a certain point, but she resented a merited rebuke with all the temper of a spoiled child. By-and-by Fritz's voice was heard shouting something; but the wind carried the words away.

'What is it?' asked Kester, standing shivering at the house door, and peering out into the night.

'Have you never a key to this outhouse where the cart stands?' bawled Fritz.

'A key? Thou dear Heaven! No; people don't want keys when they've nothing to lock up'.

'Aye, but I *have* something to lock up, as it happens. See!' And he held the flickering lantern within the outhouse door, so as to show a light cart laden with luggage.

'How did you get the cart in?' asked Kester.

'Why made the piebald back it in, before I unharnessed him. The door's wide enough. But I can't leave these things like this all night. They must be secured somehow'.

'Oh', sneered Josef, 'they're so very precious, are they?'

'Yes, that they are', replied Fritz, simply. 'Whatever is in trust is precious. And these things are in trust to me. If you can't lock the door, I must sleep here all night along with them, that's all.'

Kester began to relent. His sulky fits seldom lasted long, they gave him too much trouble, and he was yielding to the fascination of his old liking for Fritz, and the young fellow's pleasant straightforward manner.

'Nay, nay, we'll manage better than that', he said. 'You would be found dead of cold in the morning. What are the things? Are they too heavy to be moved?'

'Not a bit too heavy; only I had a thundering long job strapping and packing them all on this morning, and I didn't want to have to do it over again. However', he added, after a glance at old Josef's helpless face, 'its no use standing talking all night, is it? Hang the trouble! A little more, a little less, it won't kill me, I dare say. If you'll just be so good as hold the lantern, that's all I'll ask *you* to do.'

And Fritz set to work energetically, undoing buckles and cords, and soon had the luggage unpacked.

'There! That was easier to undo than to do', said he, laughing, 'and there ain't many things in this world a man can say that of'. The packages consisted of two tolerably heavy trunks, and a small square box covered with leather. With the landlord's help, Fritz dragged them all across the yard, and piled them in one corner of the kitchen; and then, after some ablutions performed in an adjoining back-chamber, he returned to sit down to whatever supper might be forthcoming. It was a better one than might have been expected from old Josef's cry of poverty; and over the meal Fritz Rosenheim related how and why he happened to be making that mountain journey so late in the year, with but one horse and no travellers. The foreign lady and gentleman with whom Laurier had travelled as courier, and whom Fritz had driven to Salzburg, had there met with some country-people of their own, and had given them a glowing account of the lake and mountain scenery on the route. So charmed were the ladies of the party with the description that they resolved on going by the same way to Ischl.

'They had too much luggage for a carriage to take', said Fritz, 'so they wanted part of it sent on by carrier. They were not staying at the Golden Cross in Salzburg, or I dare say I should have got the job of driving them to Ischl; but I know the kutscher employed by their landlord, he's one Hans Koch, a good sort of fellow. He came to me one night, and said that if I liked to undertake it the landlord of the Archduke Charles, where these foreigners were staying, would employ me to convey the heavy boxes to the hotel at Ischl. Of course I said 'Yes'. It don't do to let a chance of a job slip; especially as these are about the last travellers we shall see till next summer. The roads are getting very bad, as it is. I thought I never should pull up that last hill just before you come to Altenau, and my load's none so heavy, either. However, here I am, safe and sound, and the worst is over. You see I was a little anxious, because they specially warned me that that little leathern box had valuables in it, and of course—'

He stopped abruptly. Happening to look up, he had caught Liese's lacklustre eyes fixed unwinkingly on his face. She was drinking in his words in her dull slow way, but with an eager interest apparent in her heavy countenance.

'Good-evening, Liese', said Fritz. 'I didn't see you before.'

'No; I've only just come in. Just this minute I was up at the saw-mill with Heinrich Amsel's mother. You were talking, and didn't hear me come in. I don't know what you were saying.'

The last sentence was a piece of characteristically clumsy cunning. Rosenheim laughed.

'Well, then', said he, 'you must have grown deaf since I saw you last, Liese. However, I was not talking any great secrets'.

But he did not resume the subject he had been speaking of; and presently, when supper was over, and the two women had washed and put by the plates and dishes, Liese went off to bed, saying she was tired; and her broad, heavily shod feet were heard making the old wooden staircase creak beneath their tread.

'I think our Liese is a great fool', said old Josef, without taking his pipe from between his teeth.

Fritz looked up with an amused smile, and knocked the ash off the end of his cigar against the stove, as he answered, 'Well, I don't just think she's the wisest woman in the world myself'.

'No; but she's a great fool in one special thing. She's always with those Amsels up at the saw-mill. They're a bad lot, mother and son. Heinrich is a wood-cutter by trade, but four days out of six he is not at work in the forest at all. He just hangs about here and there and every where, skulking like a fox; and Liese is with him every spare moment she has'.

'But I thought she was betrothed to him', said Fritz.

'Didn't I *say* she was a great fool?' retorted the old man.

Then he bade Katchen get to bed, and hung his smoked-out pipe by its green cord on a nail—an infallible signal of his being ready to go to rest. Katchen took up her little copper lamp with its wick floating in oil, and said, 'Good-night!' tripping up stairs with a step which her love-troubles had not yet robbed of its spring.

'What a light footfall she has!' said Fritz, listening.

But Josef only grunted. He declined to say a word having his daughter for its subject. He never would speak of her to Fritz. In truth, he knew that if once led into that topic, the young man would openly avow his love, and ask him to sanction his wooing. It would doubtless have been the right course for old Kester to speak frankly to Fritz Rosenheim, or at least, if he would not do that, to have kept his daughter out of the young fellow's way. But the right course is seldom quite an easy one; and Josef Kester never voluntarily faced a difficulty, mental, moral, or physical. So he grunted, as aforesaid, and was in a mighty hurry to see the lights out, and get to his bed. Fritz shouldered the little leather-covered case to carry it to his sleeping-room.

'The big trunks', said he, 'would not be easy to walk off with in the night, but I shall feel better pleased to have this small box by my bedside'.

'Pooh!' said Kester, 'what whim has bitten you? Did you ever hear of anything being walked off, as you call it, hereabouts?'

'No; but it's as well to be on the safe side. If the things were my own I wouldn't be afraid to leave them out there in the shed. Goodnight'.

'I suppose you'll be starting early, Fritz?'

'As early as I can. The daylight doesn't last long now'.

'Good-night, lad'.

And the two separated, each to his rest.

CHAPTER SEVEN.

THE FOLLOWING morning was dull and cloudy, and there was a feeling in the air, and a look in the sky, that betokened a fall of snow before long. Katchen dressed herself almost in the dark, and groped her way downstairs to the kitchen. There was no fire in the stove, and no preparation for breakfast. 'That lazy, hulking Liese', said Katchen to herself; 'to think of her not being down yet! I'll rouse her to some tune in a minute'. But, even as she spoke, she perceived that the house door had been unbolted, and was partly open. 'Why, she's gone out, then!' exclaimed the girl, in a startled tone.

'Where can she be?' She was advancing towards the door when it was opened from without, and Liese entered, followed by Fritz. 'Where have you been at this hour?' asked Katchen, in the imperious way habitual to her.

'Don't you see? To get wood. There wasn't enough to fill the stove.'

Liese spoke sullenly, and threw down a great log with a bang on the stone floor. She was panting, and her shoes were covered with dust.

'You've been running yourself out of breath, I declare', said Katchen, gazing at her in astonishment. 'You don't usually do things in such a hurry. However, it's as well that you are in a humour to make haste this morning. Be quick with breakfast'.

Fritz, meanwhile, had been busied in putting on a new lash to his whip, glancing furtively at Katchen whenever he thought she did not observe him. 'I am early too, this morning', said he, coming forward when Liese had lit the fire, and was making a great clatter of preparation in the scullery. 'I went to have a look at the piebald. He's all right.'

'Oh!' said Katchen languidly. 'Yes; he's all right.'

Katchen was absorbed in measuring out the coffee. Fritz came close to her, and she felt his arm enfold her waist. 'Won't you give a pleasant word to a fellow?' said he, piteously.

'How dare you do that?' exclaimed Katchen, turning to transfix him with a haughty stare which would have done credit to a duchess.

Fritz dropped his arm as if Katchen's little waist had been red hot. 'Dare!' said he, and the blood rushed up into his brown face. 'I did not mean to offend you, Mam'sell Katerina, but it seems that we can't get together at all. When I am away from you I long for nothing so much as the moment when I shall see you again; and yet when we do meet, somehow it's all wretched. It does seem hard.'

Now Katchen had not meant to be taken quite *au pied de la lettre* when she asked Fritz how he dared to put his arm round her. It was simply a piece of coquetry. She had been feeling quite lofty with a sense of the sacrifice she had made of Herr

Ebner on Fritz's behalf. She had persuaded herself that she had given up wealth and station all for his sake, and had meant to dazzle him, by-and-by, with a glimpse of her magnanimous behaviour. And now, here he was beginning by being aggrieved and hardly treated. Fritz was always so provokingly in earnest, and though he could not be aware that Katchen had refused Ebner's offer, she was as perversely angry with him as though he had already known all about it.

'Indeed!' said she, coldly. 'Then if it's all wretched, as you say, I think it a pity that we do meet at all.'

'Oh, don't say that, Katchen! Why *should* it be all wretched? It need not be if you would only—'

'Oh, thank you. Of course it's my fault. I am sorry that I happen to be so disagreeable in your eyes, but really I don't know how to help that'.

'Disagreeable in my eyes! But you know that's just nonsense, Katchen. I've told you how much I love you often enough to make you believe me, if telling would do it; but I think—I do think it shouldn't be quite all on one side. If you care for me I have a right to say that much, Katerina.'

'All on one side! Thou dear Heaven! Ungrateful, insensible creature! What do you endure for my sake in comparison with the sacrifices I make on your account? The greater fool I!'

'You make sacrifices for me, Katchen? I know I'm not your equal in many things; but I know, too, that a real, honest heart is worth something to any woman who knows how to prize it.'

'And do you think yours is the only heart in the world? I can tell you, Mr. Modesty, that I could have had a heart perhaps as honest as yours, if I hadn't been a fool and thought more of you than you merit.'

'What do you mean, Katerina? You *must* tell me now'. Fritz's voice trembled, and his sun-burnt cheek grew pale with the strong effort to preserve his self command. 'Are you thinking of that man at the Black Eagle? Do you believe that he would marry you?'

'Believe it! I know it. He implored me to be his wife. I

might have been rich—a lady— and father would have been provided for; but I said no.'

'And why did you say no?' asked Rosenheim, with his teeth set and his chest heaving.

'Why did I say no?' Katchen was furious. Was this the reception due to the announcement of her noble conduct? She did not reflect how she had been goading and irritating her lover into anger.

'I said no because I was absurd enough to think it would make you happy; but I see now how foolish I have been.'

There was a minute's pause. The two young people stood opposite each other, she flushed excited, he pale, stern, deeply hurt. At length he spoke:

'Well, Katchen, I am truly sorry that I have been the obstacle in your path. I'm too sincere in my feelings toward you to say that I wish you to marry another man. I ought to, perhaps, but I fairly can not. Only I'm grieved to the heart that you should ever have been hampered with a poor clumsy fellow like me, that has neither money nor land to offer you. And since— since you seem to repent what you have done, I'll leave you at liberty now and forever. You shall not have Fritz Rosenheim to blot out the sunshine from you'. Katchen was now standing at the window which looked on the lake, and had her head turned away from her lover. 'Of course if you cared for me— ever so little', pursued Fritz, 'that would alter the case; but you don't; I can see that'. A pause. 'You don't care for me', repeated the poor young fellow, with so wistful a look that, if Katchen could have seen it, her obstinate perversity must surely have melted away. But she did not see it. She kept her head turned from him toward the lake, and vouchsafed no answer. And in another minute it was too late to give any, for old Kester came hurrying down, and the breakfast was hastily set on the table.

The meal was taken almost in silence. Fritz was usually full of talk and mirth, but his light-heartedness had been effectually subdued; and Kester was dull and preoccupied. At last Fritz

rose up with a great sigh, which came out unawares, and
made him colour the moment afterward.

'I must see to putting the luggage up', said he. 'Will you
mind giving a lift with the boxes, Liese?'

Liese's help was very different from old Kester's. She
swung up one end of the great trunks as easily as Fritz himself
carried the other, and the boxes were soon placed in the cart.
Then came the strapping and cording. Fritz had had plenty of
experience in such matters, but it nevertheless took some time
to accomplish; for he was careful and anxious. The large
trunks were put in first, and the small square box strongly
secured on the top of them. Fritz went into the house to pay
his score, and looked eagerly round the kitchen to see if
Katchen would not vouchsafe one word, even one look, to
soften his regret. No, she was not to be seen. There was no
one but old Kester, in one of his most depressed moods. When
Fritz brought out the piebald from the stable to harness him,
he found Liese still busy about the cart, giving some finishing
touches to the cords and straps.

'Let be—let be, Liese', said he. 'It's all right and safe enough.
I'll warrant any knot of my tying to hold fast'. And he tossed
her a piece of money as he mounted into his seat. 'Goodbye,
Herr Kester!' he cried out, and the old man came to the door.

'Oh, you'll be passing back again soon, Fritz Rosenheim.'

'Well, no; I think not. It's likely I shall go from Ischl by the
Traun-see to Grunnden, and then—who knows?—perhaps even
to Vienna. You won't see me again very soon I'm thinking.'

'Well, take care of yourself. I hope we shan't have snow
before nightfall. You have a heavy load.'

'Ay', said Fritz, as he drove out of the little yard and urged
his horse along briskly; 'ay, a heavy load, as you say. Not
that the boxes are so much of a load, but I can understand
now what folks mean when they talk of being heavy-hearted.
My heart feels such a weight in my breast that I almost wonder
the piebald can drag it behind him'.

CHAPTER EIGHT

MORE THAN a week passed away, uncomfortably enough, at the Golden Lamb. Kester's prediction about the snow had been verified. It had begun to fall on the evening of the day on which Fritz went away. But inside the house things looked yet more chill and dreary. Josef had accused his daughter of indulging in more 'moonshine' with Rosenheim. He suspected that that hour they had been together in the early morning had been spent in love-making. But, to his amazement, Katchen informed him that she and Fritz were thenceforth to be as strangers; that it was clear he did not really love her; that she cared nothing for him; and that so it was best that they each go their separate ways, and forget any absurd love-passages which might have taken place between them. Katchen spoke with a flippant laugh and an assumption of her old spoiled-child manner; but the effort was visibly a hard one. Josef was dumbfounded. All along, since the final rejection of Ebner, he had had a secret conviction that he should have at last to accept Fritz for a son-in-law; and, though he grumbled, his easy-going nature had begun to accustom itself to the idea. He liked Fritz. He had done his best for Katchen. If she would be headstrong, was he to make himself miserable about it? But now the news he heard fairly bewildered him.

'Good Heavens above us!' said he, 'who ever heard the like? Why I believed in my soul that you refused Ebner mainly on that young fellow's account'.

'So I did', said Katchen, quickly.

'You did? You own that you did; and after giving up the best prospect ever girl had on account of this lover you go and throw *him* over as well! It's madness. Just stark staring madness, that's all I can say. God help you when I'm gone, my lass; for, as true as I'm a living man, I believe you'll never have such another chance.'

And that was all the comfort Katchen got from her father. But her own conscience said yet harder things to her. And these she had to listen to day by day, at all hours. In the dull grey mornings, amidst her household work, and mixed up with the whirr of the great spinning-wheel, or the click of the knitting-needles, she had to listen to these harsh truths, and to confess her faults with bitter self-upbraiding. For now that Fritz seemed gone forever, she knew that she loved him, and that he had loved her a thousand times better than she deserved. Perhaps, poor, perverse, spoiled child that she was, there needed some such grief and some such parting to open her eyes to the truth. In spite of her vanity, and frivolity, and coquetry, she had a heart, as I have said before, and she suffered very really. She had not the relief of speaking of her sorrow. A remnant of wilful pride prevented her from confiding in her father; for she believed that Fritz must be wearied out with her caprices, and that his love would not be able to survive her unreasonable cruelty.

'Of course he will forget me in time', she said to herself, 'and he will fall in love with some other girl, who will know how to value him. But I know how to value him now, and I love him too, only it is too late. Too late'.

It must not be supposed that Ebner had resigned all hope of winning Katchen from the result of that one interview by the lake. His anger had gone, but his love remained. He came down to the Golden Lamb two days after Fritz's departure, and found Katchen alone. She was pale and weary, tired in body after a hard day's work, and she sat by the stove in the winter twilight, while great hot tears kept falling every now and then on the coarse worsted stockings she was knitting. Ebner could not see her distinctly in the dim light, but the tone of her voice, as she greeted him, betrayed that she was not herself.

'Are you not well, Mam'sell Katerina?' asked Ebner, anxiously.

'Oh yes; quite well, only a little tired.'

And then by degrees Caspar Ebner began to renew his suit, accusing himself of having been harsh and hasty, and pleading for forgiveness. Katchen answered straightforwardly enough now. She was made sympathetic to another's sorrow by the pain in her own heart.

'Oh, Herr Ebner, you were only too good to me. I am not worthy of it. But I want you to believe that I didn't mean to deceive you.'

'I am sure of it, Katchen. And now can't you think better of it, and say that one kind word that shall make me so happy.'

But this Katchen could not do: and the refusal was more difficult to her now than it had been before. Ebner pleaded as best he could, asking not for love such as he offered, only for kindness and confidence. He would wait for the rest. Then Katchen took a resolution.

'Herr Ebner', she said, firmly, though her pale face grew scarlet from brow to chin, 'I have no love to give you. I love someone else with all my heart'.

'Katchen', said he, after a moment's silence, 'when you spoke to me before you told me you were beloved, but you did not say you loved. Am I to believe you false-tongued after all?'

'I didn't know it myself then', answered the girl, simply. Many more words passed between them, but Ebner seemed to lose the hope he had held fast by from the first. Katchen's feeling was too real and strong to be simulated. He perceived that she was in earnest now, whatever might have been her former giddiness. Strange to say, it never recurred to him to guess who the favoured lover might be. There was not a servant about the Black Eagle but could have given him the information, but Caspar Ebner was not a man to talk to his servants on such a matter. So he went out from Katchen's presence that evening, unwillingly convinced that his suit was hopeless, but ignorant of the name of his rival. After all, what did it matter? If Katchen were determined not to love *him*, what did anything matter? Before the end of the week, however, came news which caused a great deal of excitement in Gossan, and even Caspar Ebner found that his misplaced attachment had by no means deprived daily life of its interest and savour. There came a message to Josef Kester from Fritz

Rosenheim, importing that a great misfortune had befallen the latter. The leather-covered box had been lost or stolen, and search and inquiry were to be made for it all along the road. It was an unusual, almost unprecedented circumstance, and made a great stir in the village. Everyone knew, and most people liked, Fritz Rosenheim, and the tale flew like wildfire. The peasant—a rough carter—who had brought the message to Kester was lionized and cross-examined all day long. The demand for beer at the Golden Lamb was greater than it had been for years past, and in spite of his sympathy with Fritz's trouble old Kester enjoyed the bustle and importance of his position.

'How was it, then, Hans!' asked a neighbour, making the twentieth time the question had been put that morning.

'Nobody knows. If they did, no need of all this bother', was Han's sententious answer.

'But I mean, how does he *think* it happened? There are no thieves hereabouts, and anything lost would be sure to be given back to the owner.'

'Oh, *would* it?' said Hans. 'Then it's all right.'

In this laborious way—but, surely if vanity feels no pain, curiosity heeds no trouble—bit by bit, the story was dragged from Hans; and this was his account. Fritz Rosenheim had reached Ischl after nightfall, on the evening of the day on which he left Gossan. The snow had been falling for some hours, and man and horse were stiff and cold and weary. Fritz had driven into the courtyard of the inn, and dismounted, leaving his horse and cart to the care of a friendly hostler. But it was not long before, being revived by warmth and meat and drink, he had visited the stable to look first at his beast, and then gone to the great room next to the porter's lodge on the ground-floor, where the luggage was deposited. Picture his consternation at finding only two packages; the leather-covered box was gone. All inquiries and examination elicited the same statement from the servants. There had been but the two black trunks on the cart when Fritz arrived. The testimony of the waiters, the porter, and the hostler, was positive on this point.

'Indeed', said the man who had helped Fritz down, and afterward unharnessed the piebald, 'I did notice that the top cord was very loose, and seemed a deal too long; but the boxes were secured by straps, so I thought it was all right enough'.

Poor Rosenheim was like one distracted. The travellers to whom the luggage belonged had not yet arrived at Ischl, but they were expected daily, and how should he face them? How face the landlord of the Archduke Charles at Salzburg, who had trusted him? The people of the inn at Ischl tried to cheer him. The box had most likely dropped on the road, and been unheard falling on the soft snow. In that case it would be restored as soon as possible. The people were mostly honest enough in those parts. Every inquiry should be made. But, up to the time of Hans's arrival at Gossan, no tidings had been heard of the missing box. Caspar Ebner had come down to the Golden Lamb when the rumour reached him, and stood listening to Hans with the rest. There was a chorus of comments, suggestions, and exclamations. All at once Liese muttered:

'Perhaps Fritz himself knows more about the box than anyone else. He was mighty careful of it when he was here.'

'That's a lie, whoever said it', exclaimed Ebner, turning quickly round. 'Fritz Rosenheim, whom I have known from a child, is as honest in word and deed as the honestest man in Gossan. I wonder anybody should have the heart to cast a stone at him in his trouble.'

If he had but known how near Katchen came to loving him at that moment! Liese scowled, and launched what she thought to be a poisoned arrow in reply:

'Oh, I know one mustn't say a word against him here', said she. 'I forgot he was Katchen's sweetheart.'

That was the first revelation Ebner had as to who was his rival. But he answered staunchly and almost instantly.

'Not a word shall be said against him here or anywhere else, while I am by to defend him. I have known and employed Fritz Rosenheim for years and, I repeat, he is incapable of dishonesty in word or deed.'

Katchen walked up to him before them all, with streaming
eyes, took his hand and kissed it. It is a common mark of
respect in that country from inferiors to superiors. 'You're a
good man', said she, with a great sob. This little scene made a
hush in the crowded kitchen. All eyes were fixed on Katchen,
but she did not seem to heed them. She was not thinking of
herself at all. Presently the neighbours began to disperse. Not
that they had by any means satiated their curiosity; but it
seemed that Hans was becoming more and more hopelessly
laconic under the influence of the vast potations of beer to
which they had treated him with the idea of making him talk.
And, besides, they had now fresh food for gossip, which could
not be discussed there. It was a memorable day for the scandal-
mongers of Gossan.

CHAPTER NINE

AT LAST the kitchen was cleared of all save the Kesters,
Hans, and Ebner.
'Oh, Herr Ebner, what will they do to him?' asked
Katchen, in a pleading voice.
'Ah, Katchen, Katchen', said he, with a sad smile and a
shake of the head, 'ought *I* to care what they do to him?'
Katchen blushed, but answered eagerly: 'But you do care,
Herr Ebner, because you're good and true, and can't endure
than anyone should suffer unjust suspicions. What can they
do to him?'
'I don't rightly know how far he was responsible, but I
suppose the owners will put a value on their property, and he
will have to make good the loss.'
'Oh, and it might be worth Heaven knows how many
gulden! These foreigners are so rich! What will he do? What
will he do?'
'Well, Katchen, as to the value of the box, I can give you
some good news; and indeed I came down to the Golden Lamb

to-night partly to say something that I wouldn't say before the idle, chattering folk who were here all agape for gossip. There's a man at my house who has come over from Ischl about this business. He is a courier in the service of the people who own the box, and is going with them to Vienna. A Swiss named——'

'Not Laurier?' interrupted Kester.

'Yes, truly; his name is Laurier', returned Ebner.

'Ah, I know him! He's a friend of mine', said Kester.

'Is he? Well, he seems to be a friend of Rosenheim's also. He says the poor fellow is terribly cut up, and vows he will sell everything he has in the world to make up the value of the stolen goods rather than rest under any shade of suspicion if they can't be traced. But, at any rate, Laurier thoroughly believes in Fritz's honesty.'

'Yes, yes, yes; of course he does. He spent an evening with him here, in this very kitchen', said Josef, with a touch of importance in his manner, and omitting, with characteristic inaccuracy, to state that it was Fritz who had brought the courier to the Golden Lamb.

'But, Herr Ebner', said Katchen, timidly, 'please what is the good news about the value of the box?'

'The good news, Katchen, is, that the box, which, it appears, was a dressing-case, contained only a few trinkets of trifling value, and a sum of money in napoleons—French gold coin, you know. The lady removed the rest of her jewels at the last moment, being unwilling to trust them out of her sight.'

Then Ebner went on to explain that Laurier had left the travellers with whom he had journeyed as far as Salzburg, and had been engaged by the owners of the missing box to accompany them to Vienna. It had been his own proposition to come over to Gossan for a day and make inquiries.

'I fancy', said Ebner, 'that he has got scent of something that may lead to discovery. But he's a shrewd, close fellow, and keeps his tongue between his teeth; and it's as well to follow his example in this matter.'

Caspar Ebner had seen enough of the landlord of the Golden Lamb to be quite aware that there was but one chance of

insuring Kester's being discreetly silent on any subject—
namely, to keep him as ignorant of it as might be. Otherwise,
it is possible Ebner could have been more communicative had
he so chosen. Katchen had been sitting silent and attentive.
Suddenly, when Ebner, looking at his big silver watch,
declared that it was time for him to go, she jumped up and
asked, anxiously: 'Then how much do you think Fritz will
have to pay if the box is not found after all?'

'Tut, tut', said her father, testily; for he had been a little
annoyed at the reserved tone which Ebner had assumed.
'Women's curiosity is never satisfied. Do you think we are
going to give you the particulars at full length, just that you
may run all over Gossan to-morrow with your tongue going
like a mill-clack? You'll know all that's needful for *you* to
know in good time, my lass.'

Under other circumstances this speech would have elicited
a tart retort, and possibly an unpleasant and unfilial display
of temper; but now Katchen only turned her large blue
eyes on Ebner with an eager, questioning gaze, and made
no reply.

'I think we might venture to trust Mam'sell Katchen with an
answer to her question', said Ebner, quietly; 'but as far as I am
concerned it is impossible. I don't know the amount of the
sum contained in the dressing-case'.

Then he took his leave, and went away with a sorrowful
conviction at his heart that Katchen never would love him,
and that she did love Fritz Rosenheim very dearly. And yet
Ebner felt a glow of pleasure at the recollection of the way she
had kissed his hand and praised his goodness, and he drew in
his inmost mind that he had never before stood so high in
Katchen's estimation as he did that night.

'I've conquered her in one way, if I can't in another', thought
he. 'She'll never *laugh* at me again, at all events.' Caspar
Ebner had never admitted to himself the possibility of his love
appearing ridiculous in Katchen's eyes so long as he retained
any hope of winning her. But now he confessed that she *had*
laughed at him; so I suppose he must have known it all along.

As to Katchen, she went into her own little room, and, wrapping her cloak around her, sat down on the side of her bed, and meditated on many things. She sat quite still for more than an hour, until the oil in her lamp was nearly exhausted and the wick began to splutter. She roused herself with a start, and knitting her flaxen eyebrows sternly, said aloud: 'I will. Yes; I will; I'm determined.' Katchen had evidently taken a great resolution. Then she lay down, and fell into a deep and childlike slumber.

The wintry sun was faintly struggling to pierce a heavy mass of snow-laden clouds, when, on the following morning, Laurier, who was up betimes, issued forth from the hostelry of the Black Eagle. The clue, whatever it was, which the courier had got as to the fate of the leather-covered box, led him to climb to a very considerable height among the pine woods behind Gossan, and to spend the greater part of the forenoon in hanging about the saw-mills and watching a couple of charcoal-burners loading a miserable pony with canvas sacks. About one o'clock Laurier went back to his inn to dinner, and then, having lighted his meerschaum, strolled leisurely down to Kester's house. The courier could afford to walk leisurely despite the keen air, for he was comfortably wrapped in a fur-lined coat, and wore a travelling-cap with side-flaps coming over his ears, and altogether looked very thoroughly protected from the inclemency of the season. But the protection served also in a great measure as a disguise; so that when Laurier entered the kitchen of the Golden Lamb, where Kester was sitting, the latter did not at once recognize his visitor, but stood up and saluted him as a stranger, with such measure of respect as appeared due to the fur-lined coat and the travelling-cap. Before making himself known to his host Laurier glanced sharply round the large room, as though to assure himself that there was no other person present. Then he unfastened the flaps which nearly covered his face, threw open the heavy coat, and held out his hand to Kester with a friendly gesture. Old Josef was somewhat taken aback on recognizing the courier, and put an extra touch of patronage into his greeting to make up for the low bow he had been cheated into giving him at first. But it was not long before they were seated side by side near the stove, each with a tall glass tankard of beer at his elbow; and the landlord prepared to enjoy a good gossip about the great event of the lost dressing-case. To a certain extent he was gratified. Laurier spoke fluently enough, for he possessed an art of which it may be presumed that Caspar Ebner was ignorant—namely, the power of talking copiously on any subject without telling any essential particular whatever respecting it. So that, though the conversation went briskly on, and Laurier never appeared to be exercising any caution in framing his answers, yet when Kester thought over it afterward, he could not recall having learned one circumstance from the courier which had been unknown to him before. On the other hand, Laurier, by a series of well-directed questions, drew a good deal of information from Josef respecting the events of the morning on which Fritz Rosenheim had left Gossan for Ischl. When somewhat more than an hour had been passed in this way, and the two men were still alone in the kitchen, Laurier asked if he should not have the pleasure of seeing Mam'sell Katerina before he went away.

'Oh, Katchen? Yes, surely, you shall see her if you will. I've hardly set eyes on her myself to-day', answered Kester, in a grumbling tone.

'I hope she's quite well', said Laurier.

'Well, yes, I suppose so. She came down this morning with her head muffled up in a black silk handkerchief after the Bohemian fashion. I asked if there was anything the matter, but she said no; she was only cold. Lord, what queer cattle these women creatures be! The ugly ones bedizen themselves with all manner of finery, while the pretty ones—well, they *mostly* bedizen themselves too!' said Josef, bringing his speech to an abrupt termination from inability to find an antithetical climax. 'Katchen!' he bawled, 'Katchen! Oh, now I think of it, she must be gone down to the wood-stack for fuel.'

'Surely that's rather rough work for her at this time of year', said Laurier. 'What's that strapping wench about that I saw here in the autumn?'

'Ah', rejoined the old man, 'there's another of my plagues! That Liese is the most cross-grained, contrary creature! She can work for six when she has a mind; but if she's as strong as a horse she's as obstinate as a mule, and she has taken herself off, the Lord knows where.'

'Taken herself off!' echoed Laurier, quickly.

'Yes; a message was sent down here about a quarter of an hour before you came, from Heinrich Amsel's mother—Heinrich is Liese's sweetheart, more fool she—and the selfwilled jade said she must leave to go out for the afternoon, and, when I refused, she coolly went, whether I liked it or no.'

Laurier was busy fastening on his cap by this time. 'Well', said he, 'I must be off too. I wish I had known before about—' He checked himself abruptly.

'About what?' asked Kester.

'Oh, nothing, nothing; only I must really be going now. There's a deal to do, and I've lost a good hour here already.' And with a hurried shake of the hand the courier took leave of his host and left the kitchen, setting forth into the gathering shades of the early twilight with a quick, resolute step.

Kester stood for a minute at the door watching him. 'Not too civil, our friend the courier', grumbled the old man, with his pipe between his teeth. 'Lost a good hour here, has he? Sappermint! And *my* time? I suppose he thinks that is of no value, because I sat so good-naturedly listening to his chat! Well, a landlord has a good deal to put up with in the way of business.'

Then Josef returned to his beer and his tobacco, and fell asleep comfortably before the warm stove.

CHAPTER THE LAST

As Laurier walked rapidly toward the Black Eagle he thought over all the circumstances which had come to his knowledge relative to the missing box, and the result of his thinking was so thoroughly to confirm his preconceived suspicions, that he resolved to confide his view of the case without loss of time, to Caspar Ebner, in order to consult with him as to what method had best be taken to bring the guilty parties to justice and clear Fritz's character; for that the dressing-case had been, not lost, but stolen, was to Laurier now no longer a matter of doubt. As he approached the inn his eye lighted on the space of garden-ground in front of the house. Something he saw there appeared to startle him, for he stood still and peered straight before him, straining his gaze in the uncertain light. Almost as he stopped a dark figure, crouching under the garden wall, moved and advanced a few steps so as to be well in Laurier's view. 'Dear Heaven!' exclaimed he, 'I was not mistaken, then! It is you, Mam'sell Katchen.'

'Hush!' said the girl, softly, with one cold, red finger peeping forth from the folds of her cloak and raised warningly. 'Hush! I want to speak to you, Herr Laurier. I've been waiting here for more than half an hour, because I didn't want anyone else to know.'

'What! waiting here? You must be frozen! Will you come into the great kitchen? There'll be a roaring fire there.'

'No, no, thank you; but if you wouldn't mind going in first and opening the back door that leads into the stable-yard, I will come into the little parlour. We shall find nobody there at this hour, and I do so want to speak to you.'

Laurier looked at her with a puzzled expression, but said he would do as she wished, and forthwith proceeded into the house, leaving her to take her way through the stable-yard. When he reached the back-door and opened it, there stood Katchen wrapped in her thick blue cloak, the hood of which was drawn over her head down to the eyebrows. Her round cheeks were pale, her little nose pinched with the cold, and her eyelids red and swollen. And yet Laurier fancied, as he looked at her, that, in spite of the disadvantageous circumstances, there was a beauty in the childlike face which he had not seen there before. 'Come in, mam'sell', said he, holding a light and leading the way into the parlour, 'but I wish there was a bit of fire for you. It's mortal cold in here.'

'I don't mind it', said Katchen, as she entered the room, and shut the door behind her. And then she stood opposite the courier, looking at him with a wistful, timid glance.

Laurier, who was a good-natured fellow, tried to help her to disclose the business on which she had come, but she seemed unable to speak to him. Her lips moved and trembled, but no sound came forth. 'I see how it is', said he, 'you're just petrified with the cold. Let me go and fetch you a bowl of hot coffee.'

'No, no; pray don't!' she cried, with an effort at self-command. 'I don't want anyone to know I am here, and I am not cold. I—I will speak, indeed, in a moment.' She put one hand on the lock of the door to stay him from opening it, and then, with her head partly turned away, said, tremulously, 'Do you remember that night you were at our house, Herr Laurier, when father made me show you the length of my hair?'

'Remember it? To be sure I do! And how angry the Herr Landlord was when I talked of having it cut off for a wig! Ha, ha!'

'You said, that night', pursued Katchen, with deepening colour and a nervous twitching of the hand which still rested on the handle of the door—' you said that you knew someone —that there was a friend of yours in Paris who—I mean you thought that he would—that he might, perhaps—buy it!'

The last words were brought out with a jerk, and her colour deepened and deepened until her whole face was burning red.

'Buy it! Buy what, mam'sell? You don't mean—'

'Yes; I do. My hair. I mean to sell it if I can', said Katchen, whose firmness seemed to return, now that the first plunge was over. 'I should be so grateful to you, if you would try for me. I know I am asking a great, great favour; but I have no

other way. And—and—I can't explain it, Herr Laurier; but
when I thought of the way you spoke of your own daughter
at home, somehow, that gave me courage to come and beg you
to help me in this thing.'

'My child', said Laurier, kindly, taking her hand, 'you're right
in thinking that I am willing to help you; but as I am a father myself, you know, I must say that I shouldn't like *my* lass to shear off
all her pretty locks for the sake of gaining money by 'em.'

'It is not only for the sake of the money, indeed', cried the
girl, eagerly.

'You'd best think of it well beforehand, at all events,
Mam'sell Katchen. Do nothing rashly.'

'Ah, it is too late to warn me. I was afraid you might advise
me not to do it, so—look!' She drew a bundle from under her
cloak, and in so doing displaced the hood, which fell back,
disclosing a little round flaxen head cropped quite closely, and
evidently by inexpert fingers. There was something at once
ludicrous and touching in her aspect, as she stood there looking
so baby-like and simple, and yet with a womanly light shining
out of her blue eyes. Laurier gave a long whistle, and stood
silent for a minute or two staring at her.

'Well', said he, at last, 'it's done, I see; and there's no use in
crying over spilled milk. But I think it's a great pity. And,
now, how much do you expect to get for all this?' As he spoke
he took up the rich coils of plaited hair which Katchen had
produced from beneath her cloak, and weighed them thought-
fully in his hand.

'Ah, that's just what I don't know, Herr Laurier. I want to
get as much as ever I can.'

'I suppose so', said the courier, dryly. It was evident that
Katchen's eagerness about the money revolted him a little.

'How much do you think, Herr Laurier, I shall get?'
pursued Katchen, unheedful of his altered manner.

'Well, I can really hardly tell to a kreutzer', returned
Laurier. 'I'm sorry if anything *I* said has induced you to do
this, for I fear I may have raised false hopes, and you may
happen to be disappointed.'

Katchen's face fell. 'Could you guess anywhere near the sum, please, Herr Laurier?' said she, with a trembling lip.

'Well, perhaps—mind, I can't be answerable to a fraction— I say perhaps, if I got my friend in Paris to buy it, he might go as high as a hundred and fifty or two hundred francs. That's a fancy price for the raw material; but then the hair is something out of the common.'

'Oh, thank you, thank you! Two hundred francs is a great deal of money, isn't it?'

'It all depends, mam'sell. It's a good deal to some people, and very little to others. But it's a great pity, as I said before, that you should have been in such a hurry, for I shan't have an opportunity of seeing my friend at Paris before next spring at soonest; and you might have kept your pretty yellow locks on your head all the time between this and then.'

'Herr Laurier', said Katchen, after an instant's hesitation, 'I thought of that too. I hope you won't have a bad opinion of me for what I'm going to ask. You wouldn't, I believe, if you knew all. Can you—will *you* let me have the money? I don't care if you give me a little less than you think the hair may be worth, only pray do let me have the money now at once! I cut off my hair before I came', she added, naively, 'because I fancied if you saw it was done and couldn't be undone you might be more likely to consent to buy it.'

Laurier was completely puzzled. There was a single-minded, simple earnestness in the girl's manner which seemed incompatible with mere selfish greed of gain. As he looked attentively in her face a light seemed all at once to dawn on him which made him instantly soften his manner.

'My good child', said he, 'I'm not at all sure that I *can* do what you wish. It is possible that I might manage to advance a hundred francs or so; but I am not a rich milord, Mam'sell Katchen, who has but to put his hand in his pocket and bring it out full of gold napoleons. I work hard, and have others to think of besides myself. Look here. If you will go and sit by the fire in the billiard-room—there isn't a soul there, I'll answer for it—I'll just think over how my money matters stand and give you an answer. I won't keep you long.'

Katchen suffered him to take her cold hand and lead her along the stone passage until they reached the door of the billiard-room. It was empty, as he had promised, and he placed her by the stove and was about to leave her when she called him back.

'Herr Laurier, Herr Laurier! You won't tell anybody', said she, gravely, 'because it is a secret.'

'Oh, as to that, Mam'sell Katerina', returned the courier, with a queer glance over his shoulder as he left the room, 'make your mind easy.'

But nevertheless he betook himself forthwith to Caspar Ebner's private apartment, and remained closeted with the landlord for some time. Meanwhile Katchen sat by the stove in the great bare billiard-room, enjoying the warmth in a half-unconscious way. She had let the hood—which she had drawn up on leaving the little parlour—slip back from her head, and every now and then she passed her hand softly over the short silky hair, as though to assure herself that the long luxuriant tresses were really gone. She had sat musing and almost dozing for nearly three-quarters of an hour, when Laurier returned, and, walking straight up to her, put a roll of very dirty Austrian bank-notes into her hand.

'Oh, Herr Laurier!' exclaimed Katchen, looking nervously at the little parcel; 'is this——?'

'Yes, mam'sell; the price of these', answered Laurier, as he held out the long thick plaits of hair at arm's-length. 'I have made an exact calculation, and I find I can afford to give the full price I named. There's eighty-five gulden in that roll.'

Katchen's face beamed with joy, although her eyes were brimming over with tears. She caught Laurier's hand and pressed it between both hers. Suddenly a shadow passed over the childlike joy which lit up her countenance.

'I hope', said she, anxiously—'I do hope you are not doing this merely out of kindness and generosity. You won't be a loser by your goodness, will you?'

'No, no, my little maiden', answered the courier; 'no fear of that. I am quite safe. And listen, Katchen; I beg you not to be grateful to me in the matter, because—because it hurts me. And now, child, I must see you safely within your own home. It is pitch dark outside, and I can't let you go alone.'

But Katchen protested she felt no fear and needed no escort, and before Laurier could remonstrate she had pulled her hood over her head, and run out of the room, and out of the house, leaving him with the soft mass of glistening yellow plaits in his hand.

The next day all Gossan was ringing with the news that the officers of justice had been making perquisitions in the Amsels' cottage up in the pine-woods behind the village, and that old Lotte, Heinrich Amsel's mother, had been arrested. All sorts of stories were flying about. Some said that a band of robbers had been discovered, who had their headquarters at the saw-mills. Others declared that Heinrich Amsel had singly performed exploits which surpassed the most desperate deeds of Schinderhannes. But as the afternoon wore on something like a consistent story was currently accepted. It was known that Liese, Kester's servant, was in custody as well as the old woman. Heinrich Amsel had disappeared from Gossan, and gone no one knew whither; but search was being diligently made for him. The excitement was intense, and the Golden Lamb once more became the focus of interest and news. Again and again did Kester, speaking as one who had private and mysterious means of information, relate to eager listeners the circumstantial evidence which appeared to inculpate the Amsels. And as the customers' thirst for beer was in accurate proportion to the keenness of their curiosity the landlord of the Golden Lamb was in a high state of fuss and satisfaction. It was, perhaps well for Katchen that his attention should have been thus occupied just at this time, for it diverted his mind from the consideration of what he termed her undutiful behaviour. There had been a stormy scene between father and daughter when, at last, Josef had discovered the fact of Katchen's shorn locks. He had gone into one of his ungovernable fits of rage—which were, fortunately, as brief as they were violent—and

had stormed incoherently for ten minutes. But then, curiosity
getting the better of anger, he had insisted on learning the
reason of this sacrifice on Katchen's part. When, after much
hesitation, and with many tears and blushes, Katchen confessed
that she had sold her beautiful hair in order to help Fritz
Rosenheim to make up the value of the lost dressing-case,
Josef Kester was stricken dumb with amazement. He sank
down in the great chair, and stared at his daughter for some
minutes in profound silence. At last, leaning his head back and
folding his arms with an air of superhuman calmness and
resignation, he said, slowly:

'No, no; I can't call it anything else but madness. The girl's
just mad with the spirit of contradiction. It's like my luck. I
oughtn't to be surprised. There's not a man in all the father-
land who's had such troubles to bear as I have.'

'Oh, father', murmured Katchen, with tearful eyes, 'don't
say so! I know I have often been undutiful and self-willed, but
I mean to try to be better; and if you will only forgive me, I
will be a good child to you—indeed I will'.

Kester closed his eyes to intensify the expression of resignation he had thrown into his countenance, and repeated,
nodding his head gently up and down, 'Mad with the spirit
of contradiction. I can't call it anything else but madness.
Look at the case. Here's a girl carrying on all manner of
moonshine with a young fellow who's not worth a kreutzer
in the world. I say nothing against him, but he's as poor as
Job. Her father objects to the moonshine, and exerts himself
to find her a husband worth having in every respect. The man
is found, comes forward in a thoroughly satisfactory way, and
offers to the girl. The girl tells her anxious father, of her own
free-will, that she will accept the offer—an offer, mind you,
which any other lass in Gossan, or for twenty leagues about,
would go down on her knees and thank Heaven for—and,
then, in the next breath, turns round and declares she can never,
never consent to marry him. Her father is naturally angry and
disappointed, but, being a fond parent, is beginning to forgive
her, and even to be reconciled to the idea of letting her choose

for herself, when—piff, paff!—one fine day she informs him that she has quarrelled desperately with lover number one, that she can on no account be induced to think of him any more, and has sent him packing in the footsteps of lover number two. This is another trial to a father's feelings, but it isn't the worst yet. No sooner does lover number one, who has hitherto borne a high character, get into a scrape—no sooner, in short, does he lie under suspicion of theft and breach of trust—than my fraulein, who professed before not to care a snap of the finger for him, coolly cuts off her beautiful hair, that there isn't the like of in the district, and sends him the price of it to help pay his forfeit! I tell you what, my wench, you've only made one mistake after all. Instead of shearing your head, you ought to have shaved it!' Kester had talked himself almost into a good humour by this time, and repeated, complacently, with his eyes still shut and his head thrown back, 'Shaved it. Yes, that's what you ought to have done'.

Katchen took all this with unwonted meekness, and busied herself silently in attending to the household duties, which fell heavily on her shoulders in the absence of Liese. But what helped her to be patient, and even cheerful, was the hope, almost amounting to certainty, that now Fritz's character would come out spotless from the investigations which were being made. 'Not', said Katchen to herself—'not that anyone who knows him could ever suspect him of a dishonest action, but I want all the world to be convinced that his conscience is as clear in this matter as the sun at noonday'.

The course of justice is proverbially tardy, and she puts on no special shoes of swiftness in the Austrian Empire. It was therefore a long time before the legal proceedings necessitated by Laurier's accusation against Liese and the Amsels resulted in the disclosure of any important facts. The strongest circumstance against Heinrich Amsel was the discovery of some fragments of a box, with a broken lock adhering to them, hidden under a heap of pine chips in the sawmills. The lock had evidently resisted the clumsy attempts made to pick it, and the box had been smashed to pieces with some blunt instrument.

A broken woodman's axe was found near the fragments, but could not be proved to have belonged to Heinrich Amsel. As regards this man, it may as well be stated at once that he was traced as far as Hamburg, where it was supposed he got on board an emigrant ship bound for the United States, the sum of ready money contained in the dressing case having doubtless facilitated his escape. The two women, Lotte and Liese, though more than suspected of complicity in the robbery, were finally released, it having been found impossible to elicit any evidence which should amount to legal proof of their guilt. Liese persisted, with dogged obstinacy, in denying all knowledge of the loosened cord, which she was strongly suspected to have purposely untied when packing the boxes on the cart. She also aroused much popular indignation by throwing out stupidly malevolent hints that Fritz Rosenheim, and he alone, was the culprit. As soon as she was set at liberty she went away, no one knew whither, with old Lotte Amsel. Some conjectured that they had gone to join Heinrich in America; others supposed them to have made their way to Vienna where Liese had relatives, not of the most reputable character. However that may have been, it is certain that they disappeared from Gossan, and were heard of there no more.

Fritz Roseheim's conduct in the affair had won the warm approbation of the owners of the lost dressing case. And as soon as the circumstances brought to light on the trial were made known to them they not only restored to Fritz the sum he had insisted on paying to them as the first instalment of the full value of their property, but made him a handsome present into the bargain. But all this, even the preservation of his good name, which was dear to Fritz's honest pride, gave him not one half the joy that filled his heart on learning, as he did from Laurier, the name of the anonymous friend who had forwarded him two hundred francs in Austrian notes.

'I couldn't for the life of me puzzle out who it could be', said he; 'but at last I guessed it might possibly be Herr Ebner. He was always very kind to me, and I knew him to be a good, charitable man. Still, of course, I thought it strange. And I resolved to ask him point-blank. Because, of course, I meant to scrape and strive to pay it all back, some day. But to think of its being my Katchen! The darling! And her pretty, precious golden hair, that was worth more than all the money that ever was coined—just to think of the little angel cutting it all off for *my* sake! There never was anybody in the world like her, and I feel as if I wasn't worthy to fasten her shoe-tie'.

However, as modest as he was, Fritz in course of time screwed up his courage to the point of resolving once more to ask this angel to share his earthly lot. The first meeting between the lovers since that gloomy parting in the grey autumn morning was a somewhat constrained one: Katchen was shy and silent, Fritz timid and anxious. He hesitated for a choice form of words in which to tell her that he knew of the sacrifice she had made for his sake, and was filled with gratitude for it. And at last, after long deliberation and painful mental framing of a fitting speech, he suddenly fell down on his knees before her, and, taking her hands in his, blurted out:

'Oh, Katchen, how good it was of you, and how I love you!'

And I really believe that Katchen found those few words quite as eloquent as anything else he could possibly have said.

'I am very angry', she whispered; but she didn't look so. 'Herr Laurier is a traitor; he ought not to have told you.'

'Not told me!' echoed Fritz, rising up, but still keeping the little hands in his. 'I shall be grateful to him to my dying day for telling me. And, I say, Katchen, you ain't really sorry in your heart that he did tell me, are you? Because, if it hadn't been for that, I should never again have plucked up courage to-to—'

The speech was never finished; but perhaps Fritz meant he should not have had courage to take Katchen in his arms and kiss her. That, at all events, is what he assuredly did.

Old Kester's consent to his daughter's marriage with Fritz Rosenheim was obtained without much difficulty. He was thankful, he said, that she had made up her mind at last; though he persisted in asserting that until he saw Katchen come out of the church a wedded wife, all due forms and ceremonies having been complied with, he should never feel secure that she would not disappoint every one's expectations by some new caprice.

'As long as there was the least chance of your being suspected of robbery, my boy', said the old man to his future son-in-law, 'you were right enough with Katchen. But now that the world agrees to acknowledge you an honest man, why you'd best look sharp after her, that's all!'

But he accepted the new state of things very well, on the whole; and allowed all trouble and toil about the inn to slip from his own hands into Fritz's with much complaisance. Caspar Ebner, when he heard that Katchen's wedding day was fixed, discovered that about that period business would call him away from Gossan for some weeks. He did not come to take leave from Katchen in person, but wrote her a kind little note, and sent with it a box which he wished should not be opened until her marriage morning. It contained, he said, a nuptial wreath and veil, and he begged she would accept and wear them for his sake. When, on the morning of her wedding-day, Katchen opened this box, she found in it a pretty gold cross and chain for the neck, and underneath, covered with a white veil, a thick plaited coronet made of glistening yellow hair. There was also a slip of paper with these words written on it: 'A golden marriage crown for Katchen'. The bride's blue eyes brimmed over with tears as she looked at it.

'My hair!' she exclaimed. 'Then it was he who—How good he is! How good everybody has been except me! But now I mean to try to be good for Fritz's sake'. And she knelt down to say one last prayer by her little bed, with a heart very full of gratitude and humility. Katchen wore the wreath of hair as her bridal head-gear; and though many Gossan people thought a gilt paper tiara covered with ornaments would have been more becoming, yet Fritz then and always declared that no wife had ever worn so beautiful and honourable a marriage crown as his Katchen.

The Golden Lamb, freshly gilt and painted, showed his meek face with a new and pleasant expression on the sign-board. So meek and pleasant was his altered aspect that one might almost have said he smiled. The young couple took up their abode at the old inn, and by energy, thrift, and cheerful civility so extended its trade, that by-and-by Fritz had to relinquish his carriage and team of horses and devote himself to the business of a landlord. Old Kester was very proud and happy when his first grandchild was put into his arms; but the little idol—who was in due time succeeded by sundry brothers and sisters—had no such faithful adorer as Caspar Ebner. He was her god-father, and chose her name. They suggested that the child should be called Katerina after her mother; but he said no, he liked better the name of Margarethe, and so she was called. He often told her the story of her mother's wedding crown; and used to say, looking into the child's clear eyes, and stroking her plump fresh cheeks:

'Ay, my little maid, you've a sweet face and a pleasant, but you'll never be so pretty as your mother. No, no, there is but one Katchen, and there never can be another.'

And I suppose he was sincere in saying so, for he remained a bachelor to the end of his days. Fritz and his wife lived together in faithful and fond companionship; and, notwithstanding old Josef's predictions, the sacrifice of her beautiful hair was the very last of Katchen's caprices.

THE TURKISH
BATH

IT WAS in the month of August. The world had gone to the moors and the Rhine, but we were still kept in town by the exigencies of our position. We had been worked hard during the preceding year, and were not quite as well as our best friends might have wished us and we resolved upon taking a Turkish bath. This little story records the experience of one individual man; but our readers, we hope, will, without a grudge, allow us the use of the editorial 'we'. We doubt whether the story could be told at all in any other form. We resolved upon taking a Turkish bath, and at about three o'clock in the day we strutted from the outer to the inner room of the establishment in that light costume and with that air of Arab dignity which are peculiar to the place.

As everybody has not taken a Turkish Bath in Jermyn Street, we will give the shortest possible description of the position. We had entered of course in the usual way, leaving our hat and our boots and our 'valuables' among the numerous respectable assistants who throng the approaches; and as we had entered we had observed a stout, middle-aged gentleman on the other side of the street, clad in vestments somewhat the worse for wear, and to our eyes particularly noticeable by reason of the tattered condition of his gloves. A well-to-do man may have no gloves, or may simply carry in his hands those which appertain to him rather as a thing of custom than for any use for which he requires them. But a tattered glove, worn on the hand, is to our eyes the surest sign of a futile attempt at outer respectability. It is melancholy to us beyond expression. Our brother editors, we do not doubt, are acquainted with the tattered glove, and have known the sadness which it produces. If there be an editor whose heart has not been softened by the feminine tattered glove, that editor is not our brother. In this instance the tattered glove was worn by a man; and though the usual indication of poor circumstances was conveyed, there was nevertheless something jaunty in the gentleman's step which preserved him from the desecration of pity. We barely saw him, but still were thinking of him as we passed into the building with the oriental letters on it, and took off our boots, and pulled out our watch and purse.

We were of course accommodated with two checked towels; and, having in vain attempted to show that we were to the manner born by fastening the larger of them satisfactorily round our own otherwise naked person, had obtained the assistance of one of those very skilful eastern boys who glide about the place and create envy by their familiarity with its mysteries. With an absence of all bashfulness which soon grows upon one, we had divested ourselves of our ordinary trappings beneath the gaze of five or six young men lying on surrounding sofas—among whom we recognised young Walker of the Treasury, and hereby testify on his behalf that he looks almost as fine a fellow without his clothes as he does with them—and had strutted through the doorway into the bath-room, trailing our second towel behind us. Having observed the matter closely in the course of perhaps half-a-dozen visits, we are prepared to recommend that mode of entry to our young friends as being at the same time easy and oriental. There are those who wear the second towel as a shawl, thereby no doubt achieving a certain decency of garb; but this is done to the utter loss of all dignity; and a feminine appearance is produced—such as is sometimes that of a lady of fifty looking after her maid-servants at seven o'clock in the morning and intending to dress again before breakfast. And some there are who carry it under the arm—simply as a towel; but these are they who, from English perversity, wilfully rob the institution of that picturesque orientalism which should be its greatest charm. A few are able to wear the article as a turban, and that no doubt should be done by all who are competent to achieve the position. We have observed that men who can do so enter the bathroom with an air and are received there with a respect which no other arrangement of the towel will produce. We have tried this; but as the turban gets over our eyes, and then falls altogether off our brow, we have abandoned it. In regard to personal deportment, depending partly on the step, somewhat on the eye, but chiefly on the costume, it must be acknowledged that 'the attempt and not the deed confounds us'. It is not every man who can carry a blue towel as a turban, and look like an Arab in the streets of Cairo, as he walks slowly down the room in Jermyn Street with his arms crossed on his naked breast. The attempt and not the deed does confound one shockingly. We, therefore, recommend that the second towel should be trailed. The effect is good, and there is no difficulty in the trailing which may not be overcome.

We had trailed our way into the bath-room, and had slowly walked to one of those arm-chairs in which it is our custom on such occasions to seat ourselves and to await sudation. There are marble couches; and if a man be able to lie on stone for half an hour without a movement beyond that of clapping his hands, or a sound beyond a hollow-voiced demand for water, the effect is not bad. But he loses everything if he tosses himself uneasily on his hard couch, and we acknowledge that our own elbows are always in the way of our own comfort, and that our bones become sore. We think that the marble sofas must be intended for the younger Turks. If a man can stretch himself on stone without suffering for the best part of an hour —or, more bravely perhaps, without appearing to suffer, let him remember that all is not done even then. Very much will depend on the manner in which he claps his hands, and the hollowness of the voice in which he calls for water. There should, we think, be two blows of the palms. One is very weak and proclaims its own futility. Even to dull London ears it seems at once to want the eastern tone. We have heard three given effectively, but we think that it requires much practice; and even when it is perfect, the result is that of western impatience rather than of eastern gravity. No word should be pronounced, beyond that one word—Water. The effect should be as though the whole mind were so devoted to the sudorific process as to admit of no extraneous idea. There should seem to be almost an agony in the effort—as though the man enduring it, conscious that with success he would come forth a god, was aware that being as yet but mortal he may perish in the attempt. Two claps of the hand and a call for water, and that repeated with an interval of ten minutes, are all the external signs of life that the young Turkish bather may allow to himself while he is stretched upon his marble couch.

We had taken a chair—well aware that nothing godlike could be thus achieved, and contented to obtain the larger amount of human comfort. The chairs are placed two and two, and a custom has grown up—of which we scarcely think that the origin has been eastern—in accordance with which friends occupying these chairs will spend their time in conversation. The true devotee to the Turkish bath will, we think, never speak at all; but when the speaking is low in tone, just something between a whisper and an articulate sound, the slight murmuring hum produced is not disagreeable. We cannot quite make up our mind whether this use of the human voice be or be not oriental; but we think that it adds to the mystery, and upon the whole it gratifies. Let it be understood, however, that harsh, resonant, clearly-expressed speech is damnable. The man who talks aloud to his friend about the trivial affairs of life is selfish, ignorant, unpoetical—and English in the very worst sense of the word. Who but an ass proud of his own capacity for braying would venture to dispel the illusions of a score of bathers by observing aloud that the House sat till three o'clock that morning?

But though friends may talk in low voices, a man without a friend will hardly fall into conversation at the Turkish Bath. It is said that our countrymen are inapt to speak to each other without introduction, and this inaptitude is certainly not decreased by the fact that two men meet each other with nothing on but a towel apiece. Finding yourself next to a man in such a garb you hardly know where to begin. And then there lies upon you the weight of that necessity of maintaining a certain dignity of deportment which has undoubtedly grown upon you since you succeeded in freeing yourself from your socks and trousers. For ourselves, we have to admit that the difficulty is much increased by the fact that we are short-sighted, and are obligated by the sudorific processes and by the shampooing and washing that are to come, to leave our spectacles behind us. The delicious wonder of the place is no doubt increased to us, but our incapability of discerning aught of those around us in that low gloomy light is complete. Jones from Friday Street, or even Walker from the Treasury, is the same to us as one of those Asiatic slaves who administer to our comfort, and flit about the place with admirable decorum and self-respect. On this occasion we had barely seated ourselves, when another bather, with slow, majestic step, came to the other chair; and, with a manner admirably adapted to the place, stretching out his naked legs, and throwing back his naked shoulders, seated himself beside us. We are much given to speculations on the characters and probable circumstances of those with whom we are brought in contact. Our editorial duties require that it should be so. How should we cater for the public did we not observe the public in all its moods? We thought that we could see at once that this was no ordinary man, and we may as well aver here, at the beginning of our story, that subsequent circumstances proved our first conceptions to be correct. The absolute features of the gentleman we did not, indeed, see plainly. The gloom of the place and our own deficiency of sight forbade it. But we could discern the thorough man of the world, the traveller who had seen many climes, the cosmopolitan to whom East and West were alike, in every motion that he made. We

confess that we were anxious for conversation, and that we struggled within ourselves for an apt subject, thinking how we might
begin. But the apt subject did not occur to us, and we
should have passed that half-hour of repose in silence had not
our companion been more ready than ourselves. 'Sir', said he,
turning round in his seat with a peculiar and captivating grace,
'I shall not, I hope, offend or transgress any rule of politeness by
speaking to a stranger'. There was ease and dignity in his
manner, and at the same time some slight touch of humour
which was very charming. I thought that I detected just a hint
of an Irish accent in his tone; but if so the dear brogue of his
country, which is always delightful to me, had been so nearly
banished by intercourse with other tongues as to leave the
matter still a suspicion—a suspicion, or rather a hope.

'By no means', we answered, turning round on our left
shoulder, but missing the grace with which he had made his
movement.

'There is nothing', said he, 'to my mind so absurd as that two
men should be seated together for an hour without venturing
to open their mouths because they do not know each other.
And what matter does it make whether a man has his breeches
on or is without them?'

My hope had now become an assurance. As he named the
article of clothing which peculiarly denotes a man he gave a
picturesque emphasis to the word which was certainly Hibernian. Who does not know the dear sound? And, as a chance
companion for a few idle minutes, is there anyone so likely to
prove himself agreeable as a well-informed, travelled Irishman?

'And yet', said we, 'men do depend much on their outward
paraphernalia'.

'Indeed and they do', said our friend. 'And why? Because
they can trust their tailors when they can't trust themselves.
Give me the man who can make a speech without any of the
accessories of the pulpit, who can preach what sermon there is
in him without a pulpit'. His words were energetic, but his
voice was just suited to the place. Had he spoken aloud, so that
others might have heard him, we should have left our chair,

and have retreated to one of the inner and hotter rooms at the moment. His words were perfectly audible, but he spoke in a fitting whisper. 'It is a part of my creed', he continued, 'that we should never lose even a quarter of an hour. What a strange mass of human beings one finds in this city of London!'

'A mighty maze, but not without a plan', we replied.

'Bedad—and it's hard enough to find the plan', said he. It struck me that after that he rose into a somewhat higher flight of speech, as though he had remembered and was desirous of dropping his country. It is the customary and perhaps the only fault of an Irishman. 'Whether it be there or not, we can expatiate free, as the poet says. How unintelligible is London! New York or Constantinople one can understand—or even Paris. One knows what the world is doing in these cities, and what men desire.'

'What men desire is nearly the same in all cities', we remarked —and not without truth, as we think.

'Is it money you mane?' he said, again relapsing. 'Yes; money, no doubt, is the grand desideratum—the "to prepon", the "to kalon", the "to pan!"' Plato and Pope were evidently at his fingers' ends. We did not conclude from this slight evidence that he was thoroughly imbued with the works either of the poet or the philosopher; but we hold that for the ordinary purposes of conversation a superficial knowledge of many things goes further than an intimacy with one or two. 'Money', continued he, "is everything, no doubt; rem—rem; rem, si possis reste, si non—; you know the rest. I don't complain of that. I like money myself. I know its value. I've had it, and—I'm not ashamed to say it, sir—I've been without it'.

'Our sympathies are completely with you in reference to the latter position', we said—remembering, with a humility which we hope is natural to us, that we were not always editors.

'What I complain of is', said our new friend, still whispering, as he passed his hand over his arms and legs, to learn whether the temperature of the room was producing its proper effect, 'that if a man here in London have a diamond, or a pair of boots, or any special skill at his command, he cannot take his article to the proper mart, and obtain for it the proper price'.

'Can he do that in Constantinople?' we inquired.

'Much better and more accurately than he can in London. And so he can in Paris!' We did not believe this; but as we were thinking after what fashion we would express our doubts, he branched off so quickly to a matter of supply and demand with which we were specially interested, that we lost the opportunity of arguing the general question. 'A man of letters', he said, 'a capable and an instructed man of letters, can always get a market for his wares in Paris'.

'A capable and instructed man of letters will do so in London', we said, 'as soon as he has proved his claims. He must prove them in Paris before they can be allowed'.

'Yes—he must prove them. By-the-bye, will you have a cheroot?' So saying, he stretched out his hand, and took from the marble slab beside him two cheroots which he had placed there. He then proceeded to explain that he did not bring in his case because of the heat, but that he was always 'muni'— that was his phrase—with a couple, in the hope that he might meet an acquaintance with whom to share them. I accepted his offer, and when we had walked round the chamber to a light provided for the purpose, we reseated ourselves. His manner of moving about the place was so good that I felt it to be a pity that he should ever have a rag on more than he wore at present. His tobacco, I must own, did not appear to me to be of the first class; but then I am not in the habit of smoking cheroots, and am no judge of the merits of the weed as grown in the East. 'Yes— a man in Paris must prove his capability; but then how easily he can do it, if the fact to be proved be there! And how certain is the mart, if he have the thing to sell!'

We immediately denied that in this respect there was any difference between the two capitals, pointing out what we believe to be a fact—that in one capital as in the other, there exists, and must ever exist, extreme difficulty in proving the possession of an art so difficult to define as capability of writing for the Press. 'Nothing but success can prove it', we said, as we slapped our thigh with an energy altogether unbecoming our position as a Turkish bather.

'A man may have a talent then, and he cannot use it till he have used it! He may possess a diamond, and cannot sell it till he have sold it! What is a man to do who wishes to engage himself in any of the multifarious duties of the English Press? How is he to begin? In New York I can tell such a one where to go at once. Let him show in conversation that he is an educated man, and they will give him a trial on the staff of any newspaper—they will let him run his venture for the pages of any magazine. He may write his fingers off here, and not an editor of them all will read a word that he writes'.

Here he touched us, and we were indignant. When he spoke of the magazines we knew that he was wrong. 'With newspapers', we said, 'we imagine it to be impossible that contributions from the outside world should be looked at; but papers sent to the magazines—at any rate to some of them—are read'.

'I believe', said he, 'that a little farce is kept up. They keep a boy to look at a line or two and then return the manuscript. The pages are filled by the old stock-writers, who are sure of the market let them send what they will—padding-mongers who work eight hours a day, and hardly know what they write about'. We again loudly expressed our opinion that he was wrong, and that there did exist magazines, the managers of which were sedulously anxious to obtain the assistance of what he called literary capacity, wherever they could find it. Sitting there at the Turkish bath with nothing but a towel round us, we could not declare ourselves to a perfect stranger, and we think that as a rule editors should be impalpable—but we did express our opinion very strongly.

'And you believe', said he, with something of scorn in his voice, 'that if a man who had been writing English for the Press in other countries—in New York say, or in Dublin—a man of undoubted capacity, mind you, were to make the attempt here, in London, he would get a hearing'.

'Certainly he would', said we.

'And would any editor see him unless he came with an introduction from some special friend?'

We paused a moment before we answered this, because the question was to us one having a very special meaning. Let an editor do his duty with ever so pure a conscience, let him spend all his days and half his nights reading manuscripts and holding the balance fairly between the public and those who wish to feed the public, let his industry be never so unwearied and his impartiality never so unflinching, still he will, if possible, avoid the pain of personally repelling those to whom he is obliged to give an unfavourable answer. But we at the Turkish bath were quite unknown to the outside world, and might hazard an opinion, as any stranger might have done. And we have seen very many such visitors as those to whom our friend alluded; and may, perhaps, see many more.

'Yes', said we. 'An editor might or might not see such a gentleman; but, if pressed, no doubt he would. An English editor would be quite as likely to do so as a French editor.' This we declared with energy, having felt ourselves to be ruffled by the assertion that these things are managed better in Paris or in New York than in London.

'Then, Mr. ——, would you give me an interview, if I call with a little manuscript which I have, tomorrow morning?' said my Irish friend, addressing us with a beseeching tone, and calling us by the very name by which we are known among our neighbours and tradesmen. We felt that everything was changed between us, and that the man had plunged a dagger into us.

Yes; he had plunged a dagger into us. Had we had our clothes on, had we felt ourselves to possess at the moment our usual form of life, we think that we could have rebuked him. As it was we could only rise from our chair, throw away the fag end of the filthy cheroot which he had given us, and clap our hands half-a-dozen times for the Asiatic to come and shampoo us. But the Irishman was at our elbow. 'You will let me see you tomorrow?' he said. 'My name is Molloy—Michael Molloy. I have not a card about me, because my things are outside there.'

'A card would do no good at all', we said, again clapping our hands for the shampooer.

'I may call, then?' said Mr. Michael Molloy.

'Certainly—yes, you can call if you please'. Then, having thus ungraciously acceded to the request made to us, we sat down on the marble bench and submitted ourselves to the black attendant. During the whole of the following operation, while the man was pummelling our breast and poking our ribs, and pinching our toes—while he was washing us down afterwards, and reducing us gradually from the warm water to the cold—we were thinking of Mr. Michael Molloy, and the manner in which he had entrapped us into a confidential conversation. The scoundrel must have plotted it from the very first, must have followed us into the bath, and taken his seat beside us with a deliberately premeditated scheme. He was, too, just the man whom we should not have chosen to see with a worthless magazine article in his hand. We think that we can be efficacious by letter, but we often feel ourselves to be weak when brought face to face with our enemies. At that moment our anger was hot against Mr. Molloy. And yet we were conscious of a something of pride which mingled with our feelings. It was clear to us that Mr. Molloy was no ordinary person; and it did in some degree gratify our feelings that such a one should have taken so much trouble to encounter us. We had found him to be a well-informed, pleasant gentleman; and the fact that he was called Molloy and desired to write for the magazine over which we presided, could not really be taken as detracting from his merits. There had doubtless been a fraud committed on us—a palpable fraud. The man had extracted assurances from us by a false pretence that he did not know us. But then the idea, on his part, that anything could be gained by his doing so, was in itself a compliment to us. That such a man should take so much trouble to approach us—one who could quote Horace and talk about the 'to kalon',—was an acknowledgment of our power. As we returned to the outer chamber we looked round to see Mr. Molloy in his usual garments, but he was not as yet there. We waited while we smoked one of our own cigars, but he came not. He had, so far, gained his aim; and, as we presumed, preferred to run the risk of too long a course of hot air to risking his object by seeing us again on that afternoon. At last we left the building, and are bound to confess that our mind dwelt much on Mr. Michael Molloy during the remainder of that evening.

It might be that after all we should gain much by the singular mode of introduction which the man had adopted. He was certainly clever, and if he could write as well as he could talk his services might be of value. Punctually at the hour named he was announced, and we did not now for one moment think of declining the interview. Mr. Molloy had so far succeeded in his stratagem that we could not now resort to the certainly not unusual practice of declaring ourselves to be too closely engaged to see anyone, and of sending him word that he should confide to writing whatever he might have to say to us. It had, too, occurred to us that, as Mr. Molloy had paid his three shillings and sixpence for the Turkish Bath, he would not prove to be one of that class of visitors whose appeals to tender-hearted editors are so peculiarly painful. 'I am willing to work day and night for my wife and children; and if you will use this short paper in your next number it will save us from starvation for a month! Yes, sir, from—starvation!' Who is to resist such an appeal as that, or to resent it? But the editor knows that he is bound in honesty to resist it altogether—so to steel himself against it that it shall have no effect upon him, at least, as regards the magazine which is in his hands. And yet if the short thing be only decently written, if it be not absurdly bad, what harm will its publication do to any one? If the waste—let us call it waste—of half-a-dozen pages will save a family from hunger for a month, will they not be well wasted? But yet, again, such tenderness is absolutely incompatible with common honesty—and equally so with common prudence. We think that our readers will see the difficulty, and understand how an editor may wish to avoid those interviews with tattered gloves. But my friend, Mr. Michael Molloy, had had three and sixpence to spend on a Turkish Bath, had had money wherewith to buy—

certainly, the very vilest of cigars. We thought of all this as
Mr. Michael Molloy was ushered into our room.

The first thing we saw was the tattered glove; and then we
immediately recognised the stout middle-aged gentleman
whom we had seen on the other side of Jermyn Street as we
entered the bathing establishment. It had never before occurred
to us that the two persons were the same—not though the impression made by the poverty-stricken appearance of the man
in the street had remained distinct upon our mind. The features
of the gentleman we had hardly seen even yet at all. Nevertheless we had known and distinctly recognised his outward gait
and mien, both with and without his clothes. One tattered glove
he now wore, and the other he carried in his gloved hand. As
we saw this we were aware at once that all our preconception
had been wrong, that that too common appeal would be made,
and that we must resist it as best we might. There was still a
certain jauntiness in his air as he addressed us. 'I hope thin',
said he as we shook hands with him, 'ye'll not take amiss the
little ruse by which we caught ye'.

'It was a ruse, then, Mr. Molloy?'

'Divil a doubt o' that, Mr. Editor.'

'But you were coming to the Turkish Bath independently of
our visit there?'

'Sorrow a bath I'd 've cum to at all, only I saw you go into
the place. I'd just three and ninepence in my pocket, and says I
to myself, Mick, me boy, it's a good investment. Three and
sixpence for them savages to rub me down, and threepence for
the two cheroots from the little shop round the corner. I wish
they'd been better for your sake'.

It had been a plant from beginning to end, and the 'to kalon'
and the half-dozen words from Horace had all been parts of
Mr. Molloy's little game! And how well he had played it!
The outward trappings of the man as we now saw them were
poor and mean, and he was mean-looking too, because of his
trappings. But there had been nothing mean about him as he
strutted along with a blue-checked towel round his body. How
well the fellow had understood it all, and had known his own

capacity! 'And now that you are here, Mr. Molloy, what can we do for you?' we said with as pleasant a smile as we were able to assume. Of course we knew what was to follow. Out came the roll of paper of which we had already seen the end projecting from his breast pocket, and we were assured that we should find the contents of it exactly the thing for our magazine. There is no longer any diffidence in such matters—no reticence in preferring claims and singing one's own praises. All that has gone by since competitive examination has become the order of the day. No man, no woman, no girl, no boy, hesitates now to declare his or her excellence and capability. 'It's just a short thing on social manners', said Mr. Molloy, 'and if ye'll be so good as to cast ye'r eye over it, I think ye'll find I've hit the nail on the head. "The Five-o'clock Tay-table" is what I've called it.'

'Oh—"The Five-o'clock Tea-table".'

'Don't ye like the name?'

'About social manners, is it?'

'Just a rap on the knuckles for some of 'em. Sharp, short, and decisive! I don't doubt but what ye'll like it.'

To declare, as though by instinct, that that was not the kind of thing we wanted, was as much a matter of course as it is for a man buying a horse to say that he does not like the brute's legs or that he falls away in his quarters. And Mr. Molloy treated our objection just as does the horse-dealer those of his customers. He assured us with a smile—with a smile behind which we could see the craving eagerness of his heart—that his little article was just the thing for us. Our immediate answer was of course ready. If he would leave the paper with us, we would look at it and return it if it did not seem to suit us. There is a half-promise about this reply which too often produces a false satisfaction in the breast of a beginner. With such a one it is the second interview which is to be dreaded. But my friend Mr. Molloy was not new to the work, and was aware that if possible he should make further use of the occasion which he had earned for himself at so considerable a cost. 'Y'il read it—will ye?' he said.

'Oh, certainly. We'll read it, certainly.'

'And ye'll use it if ye can?'

'As to that, Mr. Molloy, we can say nothing. We've got to look solely to the interest of the periodical.'

'And, sure, what can ye do better for the periodical than print a paper like that, which there is not a lady at the West End of the town won't be certain to read?'

'At any rate we'll look at it, Mr. Molloy', said we, standing up from our chair.

But still he hesitated in his going—and did not go. 'I'm a married man, Mr. ——', he said, We simply bowed our head at the announcement. 'I wish you could see Mrs. Molloy', he added. We murmured something as to the pleasure it would give us to make the acquaintance of so estimable a lady. 'There isn't a better woman than herself this side of heaven, though I say it that oughtn't', said he. 'And we've three young ones'. We knew the argument that was coming—knew it so well, and yet were so unable to accept it as any argument! 'Sit down one moment, Mr. ——', he continued, 'till I tell you a short story'. We pleaded our engagements, averring that they were pecu-liarly heavy at that moment. 'Sure, and we know what that manes', said Mr. Molloy. 'It's just—walk out of this as quick as you came in. It's that what it manes'. And yet as he spoke there was a twinkle of humour in his eye that was almost irresistible; and we ourselves—we could not forbear to smile. When we smiled we knew that we were lost. 'Come, now, Mr. Editor; when you think how much it cost me to get the inthroduction, you'll listen to me for five minutes any way.'

'We will listen to you', we said, resuming our chair—remembering as we did so the three-and-sixpence, the two cigars, the 'to kalon', the line from Pope, and the half line from Horace. The man had taken much trouble with the view of placing himself where he now was. When we had been all but naked together I had taken him to be the superior of the two, and what were we that we should refuse him an interview simply because he had wares to sell which we should only be too willing to buy at his price if they were fit for our use?

Then he told his tale. As for Paris, Constantinople, and New York, he frankly admitted that he knew nothing of those capitals. When we reminded him, with some ill-nature as we thought afterwards, that he had assumed an intimacy with the current literature of the three cities, he told us that such remarks were 'just the sparkling gims of conversation in which a man shouldn't expect to find rale diamonds'. Of 'Doblin' he knew every street, every lane, every newspaper, every editor; but the poverty, dependence, and general poorness of a provincial press had crushed him, and he had boldly resolved to try a fight in the 'methropolis of litherature'. He referred us to the managers of *Boyne Bouncer*, the *Clontarf Chronicle*, the *Donnybrook Debater*, and the *Echoes of Erin*, assuring us that we should find him to be as well esteemed as known in the offices of those widely-circulated publications. His reading he told us was unbounded, and the pen was as ready to his hand as is the plough to the hand of the husbandman. Did we not think it a noble ambition in him thus to throw himself into the great 'areanay', as he called it, and try his fortune in the 'methropolis of litherature?' He paused for a reply, and we were driven to acknowledge that whatever might be said of our friend's prudence, his courage was undoubted. 'I've got it here', said he. 'I've got it all here'. And he touched his right breast with the fingers of his left hand, which still wore the tattered glove.

He had succeeded in moving us. 'Mr. Molloy', we said, 'we'll read your paper, and we'll then do the best we can for you. We must tell you fairly that we hardly like your subject, but if the writing be good you can try your hand at something else'.

'Sure there's nothing under the sun I won't write about at your bidding'.

'If we can be of service to you, Mr. Molloy, we will'. Then the editor broke down, and the man spoke to the man. 'I need not tell you, Mr. Molloy, that the heart of one man of letters always warms to another.'

'It was because I knew ye was of that sort that I followed ye in yonder', he said, with a tear in his eyes.

The butter-boat of benevolence was in our hand, and we proceeded to pour out its contents freely. It is a vessel which an editor should lock up carefully; and, should he lose the key, he will not be the worse for the loss. We need not repeat here all the pretty things that we said to him, explaining to him from a full heart with how much agony we were often compelled to resist the entreaties of literary suppliants, declaring to him how we had longed to publish tons of manuscript—simply in order that we might give pleasure to those who brought them to us. We told him how accessible we were to a woman's tear, to a man's struggle, to a girl's face, and assured him of the daily wounds which were inflicted on ourselves by the impossibility of reconciling our duties with our sympathies. 'Bedad, thin', said, Mr. Molloy grasping our hand, 'you'll find none of that difficulty wid me. If you'll sympathise like a man, I'll work for you like a horse'. We assured him that we would, really thinking it probable that he might do some useful work for the magazine; and then we again stood up waiting for his departure.

'Now I'll tell ye a plain truth', said he, 'and ye may do just as ye please about it. There isn't an ounce of tay or a pound of mait along with Mrs. Molloy this moment; and, what's more, there isn't a shilling between us to buy it. I never begged in my life—not yet. But if you can advance me a sovereign on that manuscript, it will save me from taking the coat on my back to a pawnbroker's shop for whatever it'll fetch there'. We paused a moment as we thought of it all, and then we handed him the coin for which he asked us. If the manuscript should be worthless the loss would be our own. We would not grudge a slice from the wholesome home-made loaf after we had used the butter-boat of benevolence. 'It don't become me', said Mr. Molloy, 'to thank you for such a thrifle as a loan of twenty shillings; but I'll never forget the feeling that has made you listen to me, and that too after I had been rather down on you at thim baths'. We gave him a kindly nod of the head, and then he took his departure. 'Ye'll see me again anyways?' he said, and we promised that we would.

We were anxious enough about the manuscript, but we could not examine it at that moment. When our office work was

done we walked home with the roll in our pocket, speculating
as we went on the probable character of Mr. Molloy. We still
believed in him—still believed in him in spite of the manner in
which he had descended in his language, and had fallen into a
natural flow of words which alone would not have given much
promise of him as a man of letters. But a human being, in
regard to his power of production, is the reverse of a rope.
He is as strong as his strongest part, and remembering the effect
which Molloy's words had had upon us at the Turkish Bath,
we still thought that there must be something in him. If so
how pleasant would it be to us to place such a man on his legs—
modestly on his legs, so that he might earn for his wife and
bairns that meat and tea which he had told us that they were
now lacking. An editor is always striving to place someone
modestly on his legs in literature—on his or her—striving, and
alas! so often failing. Here had come a man in regard to whom,
as I walked home with his manuscript in my pocket, I did feel
rather sanguine.

Of all the rubbish that I ever read in my life, that paper on the
Five-o'clock Tea-table was, I think, the worst. It was not only
vulgar, foolish, unconnected, and meaningless; but it was also
ungrammatical and unintelligible even in regard to the wording
of it. The very spelling was defective. The paper was one with
which no editor, sub-editor, or reader would have found it
necessary to go beyond the first ten lines before he would have
known that to print it would have been quite out of the question.
We went through with it because of our interest in the man;
but as it was in the beginning, so it was to the end—a farrago
of wretched nonsense, so bad that no one, without experience
in such matters, would believe it possible that even the writer
should desire the publication of it! It seemed to us to be impossible that Mr. Molloy should ever have written a word for
those Hibernian periodicals which he had named to us. He had
got our sovereign; and with that, as far as we were concerned,
there must be an end of Mr. Molloy. We doubted even whether
he would come for his own manuscript.

But he came. He came exactly at the hour appointed, and

when we looked at his face we felt convinced that he did not
doubt his own success. There was an air of expectant triumph
about him which dismayed us. It was clear enough that he was
confident that he should take away with him the full price of
his article, after deducting the sovereign which he had borrowed. 'You like it thin', he said, before we had been able to
compose our features to a proper form for the necessary
announcement.

'Mr. Molloy', we said, 'it will not do. You must believe us
that it will not do'.

'Not do?'.

'No, indeed. We need not explain further—but—but—you
had really better turn your hand to some other occupation.'

'Some other occupa-ation!' he exclaimed, opening wide his
eyes, and holding up both his hands.

'Indeed we think so, Mr. Molloy.'

'And you've read it?'

'Every word of it—on our honour.'

'And you won't have it?'

'Well—no Mr. Molloy, certainly we cannot take it'.

'Ye reject my article on the Five-o'clock Tay-table!' Looking
into his face as he spoke, we could not but be certain that its
rejection was to him as astonishing as would have been its
acceptance to the readers of the magazine. He put his hand up
to his head and stood wondering. 'I suppose ye'd better choose
your own subject for yourself', he said, as though by this great
surrender on his own part he was getting rid of all the difficulty
on ours.

'Mr. Molloy', we began, 'we may as well be candid with
you——'

'I'll tell you what it is', said he, 'I've taken such a liking to
you there's nothing I won't do to plaise ye. I'll just put it in
my pocket, and begin another for ye as soon as the children
have had their bit of dinner'. At last we did succeed, or thought
that we succeeded, in making him understand that we regarded
the case as being altogether hopeless, and were convinced that
it was beyond his powers to serve us. 'And I'm to be turned

off like that', he said, bursting into open tears as he threw himself into a chair and hid his face upon the table. 'Ah! wirra, wirra, what'll I do at all? Sure, and didn't I think it was fixed as firm between us as the Nelson monument? When ye handselled me with the money, didn't I think it was as good as done and done?' I begged him not to regard the money, assuring him that he was welcome to the sovereign. 'There's my wife'll be brought to bed any day', he went on to say, 'and not a ha'porth of anything ready for it! 'Deed, thin, and the world's hard. The world's very hard!' And this was he who had talked to me about Constantinople and New York at the Baths, and had made me believe that he was a well-informed, well-to-do man of the world!

Even now we did not suspect that he was lying to us. Why he should be such as he seemed to be was a mystery; but even yet we believed in him after a fashion. That he was sorely disappointed and broken-hearted because of his wife, was so evident to us, that we offered him another sovereign, regarding it as the proper price of that butter-boat of benevolence which we had permitted ourselves to use. But he repudiated our offer. 'I've never begged', said he, 'and, for myself, I'd sooner starve. And Mary Jane would sooner starve than I should beg. It will be best for us both to put an end to ourselves and to have done with it'. This was very melancholy; and as he lay with his head upon the table, we did not see how we were to induce him to leave us.

'You'd better take the sovereign—just for the present', we said.

'Niver!' said he, looking up for a moment, 'niver!' And still he continued to sob. About this period of the interview, which before it was ended was a very long interview, we ourselves made a suggestion the imprudence of which we afterwards acknowledged to ourselves. We offered to go to his lodgings and see his wife and children. Though the man could not write a good magazine article, yet he might be a very fitting object for our own personal kindness. And the more we saw of the man, the more we liked him—in spite of his incapacity. 'The place is so poor', he said, objecting to our offer. After what had passed between us, we felt that that could be no reason against our visit, and we began for a moment to fear that he was deceiving us. 'Not yet', he cried, 'not quite yet. I will try once again—once again. You will let me see you once more?'

'And you will take the other sovereign', we said—trying him. He should have had the other sovereign if he would have taken it; but we confess that had he done so then we should have regarded him as an impostor. But he did not take it, and left us in utter ignorance as to his true character.

After an interval of three days he came again, and there was exactly the same appearance. He wore the same tattered gloves. He had not pawned his coat. There was the same hat—shabby when observed closely, but still carrying a decent appearance when not minutely examined. In his face there was no sign of want, and at moments there was a cheeriness about him which was almost refreshing. 'I've got a something this time that I think ye must like—unless you're harder to plaise than Rhadhamanthus'. So saying, he tendered me another roll of paper, which I at once opened, intending to read the first page of it. The essay was entitled 'The Church of England—a Question for the People'. It was handed to me as having been written within the last three days; and, from its bulk, might have afforded fair work for a fortnight to a writer accustomed to treat of subjects of such weight. As we had expected, the first page was unintelligible, absurd, and farcical. We began to be angry with ourselves for having placed ourselves in such a connection with a man so utterly unable to do that which he pretended to do. 'I think I've hit it off now', said he, watching our face as we were reading.

The reader need not be troubled with a minute narrative of the circumstances as they occurred during the remainder of the interview. What had happened before was repeated very closely. He wondered, he remonstrated, he complained, and he wept. He talked of his wife and family, and talked as though up to this last moment he had felt confident of success. Judging from his face as he entered the room, we did not doubt but that he had been confident. His subsequent despair was unbounded, and we then renewed our offer to call on his wife. After some

hesitation he gave us an address in Hoxton, begging us to come
after seven in the evening if it were possible. He again declined
the offer of money, and left us, understanding that we would
visit his wife on the following evening. 'You are quite sure
about the manuscript?' he said as he left us. We replied that we
were quite sure.

On the following day we dined early at our club and walked
in the evening to the address which Mr. Molloy had given us
in Hoxton. It was a fine evening in August, and our walk made
us very warm. The street named was a decent little street,
decent as far as cleanliness and newness could make it; but
there was a melancholy sameness about it, and an apparent
absence of object which would have been very depressing to
our own spirits. It led no whither, and had been erected solely
with the view of accommodating decent people with small in-
comes. We at once priced the houses in our mind at ten and
sixpence a week, and believed them to be inhabited by piano-
forte tuners, coach builders, firemen, and public office messen-
gers. There was no squalor about the place, but it was
melancholy, light coloured, and depressive. We made our way
to No. 14, and finding the door open entered the passage.
'Come in', cried the voice of our friend; and in the little front
parlour we found him seated with a child on each knee, while
a winning little girl of about twelve was sitting in a corner of
the room, mending her stockings. The room itself and the
appearance of all around us were the very opposite of what we
had expected. Everything no doubt was plain—was, in a
certain sense, poor; but nothing was poverty-stricken. The
children were decently clothed, and apparently were well fed.
Mr. Molloy himself, when he saw me, had that twinkle of
humour in his eye which I had before observed, and seemed to
be afflicted at the moment with none of that extreme agony
which he had exhibited more than once in our presence.
'Please, sir, mother ain't in from the hospital—not yet', said
the little girl, rising up from her chair; 'but it's past seven and
she won't be long'. This announcement created some surprise.
We had indeed heard that of Mrs. Molloy which might make

it very expedient that she should seek the accommodation of
an hospital, but we could not understand that in such circumstances she should be able to come home regularly at seven
o'clock in the evening. Then there was a twinkle in our friend
Molloy's eye which almost made us think for the moment that
we had been made the subject of some, hitherto unintelligible,
hoax. And yet there had been the man at the Baths in Jermyn
Street, and the two manuscripts had been in our hands, and the
man had wept as no man weeps for a joke. 'You would come,
you know', said Mr. Molloy, who had now put down the two
bairns and had risen from his seat to greet us.

'We are glad to see you so comfortable', we replied.

'Father is quite comfortable, sir', said the little girl. We
looked into Mr. Molloy's face and saw nothing but the twinkle
in the eye. We had certainly been 'done' by the most elaborate
hoax that had ever been perpetrated. We did not regret the
sovereign so much as those outpourings from the butter-boat of
benevolence of which we felt that we had been cheated. 'Here's
mother', said the girl, running to the door. Mr. Molloy stood
grinning in the middle of the room with the youngest child
again in his arms. He did not seem to be in the least ashamed of
what he had done, and even at that moment conveyed to us
more of liking for his affection for the little boy than of anger
for the abominable prank that he had played us.

That he had lied throughout was evident as soon as we saw
Mrs. Molloy. Whatever ailment might have made it necessary
that she should visit the hospital, it was not one which could
interfere at all with her power of going and returning. She was
a strong hearty-looking woman of about forty, with that mixture in her face of practical kindness with severity in details
which we often see in strong-minded women who are forced
to take upon themselves the management and government of
those around them. She curtseyed, and took off her bonnet
and shawl, and put a bottle into a cupboard, as she addressed us.
'Mick said as you was coming, sir, and I'm sure we is glad to
see you—only sorry for the trouble, sir.'

We were so completely in the dark that we hardly knew how

to be civil to her—hardly knew whether we ought to be civil to
her or not. 'We don't quite understand why we've been brought
here', we said, endeavouring to maintain, at any rate, a tone of
good-humour. He was still embracing the little boy, but there
had now come a gleam of fun across his whole countenance,
and he seemed to be almost shaking his sides with laughter.
'Your husband represented himself as being in distress', we said
gravely. We were restrained by a certain delicacy from informing the woman of the kind of distress to which Mr.
Molloy had especially alluded—most falsely.

'Lord love you, sir', said the woman, 'just step in here'. Then
she led us into a little back-room in which there was a bedstead,
and an old writing desk or escritoire, covered with papers. Her
story was soon told. Her husband was a madman.

'Mad!' we said, preparing for escape from what might be to
us most serious peril.

'He wouldn't hurt a mouse', said Mrs. Molloy. 'As for the
children, he's that good to them, there ain't a young woman in
all London that'd be better at handling 'em'. Then we heard
her story, in which it appeared to us that downright affection
for the man was the predominant characteristic. She herself
was, as she told us, head day nurse at Saint Patrick's Hospital,
going there every morning at eight, and remaining till six or
seven. For these services she received thirty shillings a week and
her board, and she spoke of herself and her husband as being
altogether removed from pecuniary distress. Indeed, while the
money part of the question was being discussed, she opened a
little drawer in the desk and handed us back our sovereign—
almost without an observation. Molloy himself had 'come of
decent people'. On this point she insisted very often, and gave
us to understand that he was at this moment in receipt of a
pension of a hundred a year from his family. He had been well
educated, she said, having been at Trinity College, Dublin, till
he had been forced to leave this university for some slight, but
repeated irregularity. Early in life he had proclaimed his
passion for the Press, and when he and she were married was
absolutely earning a living in Dublin by some use of the

scissors and paste-pot. The whole tenor of his career I could
not learn, though Mrs. Molloy would have told us everything
had time allowed. Even during the years of his sanity in
Dublin he had only been half-sane, treating all the world
around him with the effusions of his terribly fertile pen. 'He'll
write all night if I'll let him have a candle', said Mrs. Molloy.
We asked her why she did let him have a candle, and made
some inquiry as to the family expenditure in paper. The paper,
she said, was given to him from the office of a newspaper which
she would not name, and which Molloy visited regularly every
day. 'There ain't a man in all London works harder', said Mrs.
Molloy. 'He is mad. I don't say nothing against it. But there
is some of it so beautiful, I wonder they don't print it'. This
was the only word she spoke with which we could not agree.
'Ah, sir', said she; 'you haven't seen his poetry!' We were
obliged to tell her that seeing poetry was the bane of our existence.

There was an easy absence of sham about this woman, and
an acceptance of life as it had come to her, which delighted us.
She complained of nothing, and was only anxious to explain
the little eccentricities of her husband. When we alluded to
some of his marvellously untrue assertions, she stopped us at
once. 'He do lie', she said. 'Certainly he do. How he makes
'em all out is wonderful. But he wouldn't hurt a fly'. It was
evident to us that she not only loved her husband, but admired
him. She showed us heaps of manuscript with which the old
drawers were crammed; and yet that paper on the Church of
England had been new work, done expressly for us.

When the story had been told we went back to him, and he
received us with a smile. 'Good-bye, Molloy', we said. 'Good-
bye to you, sir', he replied, shaking hands with us. We looked
at him closely, and could hardly believe that it was the man
who had sat by us at the Turkish Bath.

He never troubled us again or came to our office, but we
have often called on him, and have found that others of our
class do the same. We have even helped to supply him with the
paper which he continues to use—we presume for the benefit
of other editors.

MARY GRESLEY

W^{E HAVE} known many prettier girls than Mary Gresley, and many handsomer women—but we never knew girl or woman gifted with a face which in supplication was more suasive, in grief more sad, in mirth more merry. It was a face that compelled sympathy, and it did so with the conviction on the mind of the sympathiser that the girl was altogether unconscious of her own power. In her intercourse with us there was, alas! much more of sorrow than of mirth, and we may truly say that in her sufferings we suffered; but still there came to us from our intercourse with her much of delight mingled with the sorrow; and that delight arose, partly no doubt from her woman's charms, from the bright eye, the beseeching mouth, the soft little hand, and the feminine grace of her unpretending garments; but chiefly, we think, from the extreme humanity of the girl. She had little, indeed none, of that which the world calls society, but yet she was pre-eminently social. Her troubles were very heavy, but she was making ever an unconscious effort to throw them aside, and to be jocund in spite of their weight. She would even laugh at them, and at herself as bearing them. She was a little fair-haired creature, with broad brow and small nose and dimpled chin, with no brightness of complexion, no luxuriance of hair,

no swelling glory of bust and shoulders; but with a pair of
eyes which, as they looked at you, would be gemmed always
either with a tear or with some spark of laughter, and with a
mouth in the corners of which was ever lurking some little
spark of humour, unless when some unspoken prayer seemed
to be hanging on her lips. Of woman's vanity she had absolutely
none. Of her corporeal self, as having charms to rivet man's
love, she thought no more than does a dog. It was a fault with
her that she lacked that quality of womanhood. To be loved
was to her all the world; unconscious desire for the admiration
of men was as strong in her as in other women; and her instinct
taught her, as such instincts do teach all women, that such love
and admiration was to be the fruit of what feminine gifts she
possessed; but the gifts on which she depended—depending on
them without thinking on the matter—were her softness, her
trust, her woman's weakness, and that power of supplicating
by her eye without putting her petition into words which was
absolutely irresistible. Where is the man of fifty, who in the
course of his life has not learned to love some woman simply
because it has come in his way to help her, and to be good to
her in her struggles? And if added to that source of affection
there be brightness, some spark of humour, social gifts, and a
strong flavour of that which we have ventured to call humanity,
such love may become almost a passion without the addition of
much real beauty.

But in thus talking of love we must guard ourselves somewhat from miscomprehension. In love with Mary Gresley,
after the common sense of the word, we never were, nor
would it have become us to be so. Had such a state of being
unfortunately befallen us, we certainly should be silent on the
subject. We were married and old; she was very young, and
engaged to be married, always talking to us of her engagement
as a thing fixed as the stars. She looked upon us, no doubt—
after she had ceased to regard us simply in our editorial
capacity—as a subsidiary old uncle whom Providence had
supplied to her in order that, if it were possible, the troubles of
her life might be somewhat eased by assistance to her from

that special quarter. We regarded her first almost as a child, and then as a young woman to whom we owed that sort of protecting care which a greybeard should ever be ready to give to the weakness of feminine adolescence. Nevertheless we were in love with her, and we think such a state of love to be a wholesome and natural condition. We might, indeed, have loved her grandmother—but the love would have been very different. Had circumstances brought us into connection with her grandmother, we hope we should have done our duty, and had that old lady been our friend we should, we trust, have done it with alacrity. But in our intercourse with Mary Gresley there was more than that. She charmed us. We learned to love the hue of that dark grey stuff frock which she seemed always to wear. When she would sit in the low arm-chair opposite to us, looking up into our eyes as we spoke to her words which must often have stabbed her little heart, we were wont to caress her with that inward undemonstrative embrace that one spirit is able to confer upon another. We thought of her constantly, perplexing our mind for her succour. We forgave her all her faults. We exaggerated her virtues. We exerted ourselves for her with a zeal that was perhaps fatuous. Though we attempted sometimes to look black at her, telling her that our time was too precious to be wasted in conversation with her, she soon learned to know how welcome she was to us. Her glove—which, by-the-bye, was never tattered, though she was very poor—was an object of regard to us. Her grandmother's gloves would have been as unacceptable to us as any other morsel of old kid or cotton. Our heart bled for her. Now the heart may suffer much for the sorrows of a male friend, but it may hardly for such be said to bleed. We loved her, in short, as we should not have loved her, but that she was young and gentle, and could smile—and, above all, but that she looked at us with those bright, beseeching, tear-laden eyes.

Sterne, in his latter days, when very near his end, wrote passionate love-letters to various women, and has been called hard names by Thackeray—not for writing them, but because

he thus showed himself to be incapable of that sincerity which
should have bound him to one love. We do not ourselves
much admire the sentimentalism of Sterne, finding the expression of it to be mawkish, and thinking that too often he
misses the pathos for which he strives from a want of appre-
ciation on his own part of that which is really vigorous in
language and touching sentiment. But we think that Thackeray
has been somewhat wrong in throwing that blame on Sterne's
heart which should have been attributed to his taste. The love
which he declared when he was old and sick and dying—a
worn-out wreck of a man—disgusts us, not because it was
felt, or not felt, but because it was told—and told as though the
teller meant to offer more than that warmth of sympathy which
woman's strength and woman's weakness combined will ever
produce in the hearts of certain men. This is a sympathy with
which neither age, nor crutches, nor matrimony, nor position
of any sort need consider itself to be incompatible. It is
unreasoning, and perhaps irrational. It gives to outward form
and grace that which only inward merit can deserve. It is very
dangerous because, unless watched, it leads to words which
express that which is not intended. But, though it may be
controlled, it cannot be killed. He, who is of his nature open
to such impression, will feel it while breath remains to him.
It was that which destroyed the character and happiness of
Swift, and which made Sterne contemptible. We do not
doubt that such unreasoning sympathy, exacted by feminine
attraction, was always strong in Johnson's heart—but Johnson
was strong all over, and could guard himself equally from
misconduct and from ridicule. Such sympathy with women,
such incapability of withstanding the feminine magnet was
very strong with Goethe—who could guard himself from
ridicule, but not from misconduct. To us the child of whom
we are speaking—for she was so then—was ever a child. But
she bore in her hand the power of that magnet, and we admit
that the needle within our bosom was swayed by it. Her story
—such as we have to tell it—was as follows.

Mary Gresley, at the time when we first knew her, was

eighteen years old, and was the daughter of a medical prac-
titioner, who had lived and died in a small town in one of
the northern counties. For facility in telling our story we will
call that town Cornboro. Dr. Gresley, as he seemed to have
been called, though without proper claim to the title, had been a
diligent man, and fairly successful—except in this, that he
died before he had been able to provide for those whom he
left behind him. The widow still had her own modest fortune,
amounting to some eighty pounds a year; and that, with the
furniture of her house, was her whole wealth, when she found
herself thus left with the weight of the world upon her
shoulders. There was one other daughter older than Mary,
whom we never saw, but who was always mentioned as poor
Fanny. There had been no sons, and the family consisted of
the mother and the two girls. Mary had been only fifteen
when her father died, and up to that time had been regarded
quite as a child by all who had known her. Mrs. Gresley, in
the hour of her need, did as widows do in such cases. She
sought advice from her clergyman and neighbours, and was
counselled to take a lodger into her house. No lodger could
be found so fitting as the curate, and when Mary was seventeen years old, she and the curate were engaged to be married.
The curate paid thirty pounds a year for his lodgings, and on
this, with their own little income, the widow and her two
daughters had managed to live. The engagement was known
to them all as soon as it had been known to Mary. The love-
making, indeed, had gone on beneath the eyes of the mother.
There had been not only no deceit, no privacy, no separate
interests, but, as far as we ever knew, no question as to prudence in the making of the engagement. The two young
people had been brought together, had loved each other, as
was so natural, and had become engaged as a matter of course.
It was an event as easy to be foretold, or at least as easy to be
believed, as the pairing of two birds. From what we heard of
this curate, the Rev. Arthur Donne—for we never saw him—
we fancy that he was a simple, pious, commonplace young man,
imbued with a strong idea that in being made a priest he had

been invested with a nobility and with some special capacity beyond that of other men, slight in body, weak in health, but honest, true, and warm-hearted. Then, the engagement having been completed, there arose the question of matrimony. The salary of the curate was a hundred a year. The whole income of the vicar, an old man, was, after payment made to his curate, two hundred a year. Could the curate, in such circumstances, afford to take to himself a penniless wife of seventeen? Mrs. Gresley was willing that the marriage should take place, and that they should all do as best they might on their joint income. The vicar's wife, who seems to have been a strong-minded, sage, though somewhat hard woman, took Mary aside and told her that such a thing must not be. There would come, she said, children, and destitution, and ruin. She knew perhaps more than Mary knew when Mary told us her story, sitting opposite to us in the low armchair. It was the advice of the vicar's wife that the engagement should be broken off; but that, if the breaking-off of the engagement were impossible, there should be an indefinite period of waiting. Such engagements cannot be broken off. Young hearts will not consent to be thus torn asunder. The vicar's wife was too strong for them to get themselves married in her teeth, and the period of indefinite waiting was commenced.

And now for a moment we will go further back among Mary's youthful days. Child as she seemed to be, she had in very early years taken a pen in her hand. The reader need hardly be told that had not such been the case there would not have arisen any cause for friendship between her and us. We are telling an Editor's tale, and it was in our editorial capacity that Mary first came to us. Well, in her earliest attempts, in her very young days, she wrote—heaven knows what; poetry first, no doubt; then, God help her, a tragedy; after that, when the curate-influence first commenced, tales for the conversion of the ungodly—and at last, before her engagement was a fact, having tried her wing at fiction, in the form of those false little dialogues between Tom the Saint and Bob the Sinner, she had completed a novel in one volume. She was then seventeen, was engaged to be married, and had completed her novel! Passing her in the street you would almost have taken her for a child to whom you might give an orange.

Hitherto her work had come from ambition—or from a feeling of restless piety inspired by the curate. Now there arose in her young mind the question whether such talent as she possessed might not be turned to account for ways and means, and used to shorten, perhaps absolutely to annihilate, that uncertain period of waiting. The first novel was seen by 'a man of letters' in her neighbourhood, who pronounced it to be very clever—not indeed fit as yet for publication, faulty in grammar, faulty even in spelling—how I loved the tear that shone in her eye as she confessed this delinquency, faulty of course in construction, and faulty in character—but still clever. The man of letters had told her that she must begin again.

Unfortunate man of letters in having thrust upon him so terrible a task! In such circumstances what is the candid, honest, soft-hearted man of letters to do? 'Go, girl, and mend your stockings. Learn to make a pie. If you work hard, it may be that some day your intellect will suffice to you to read a book and understand it. For the writing of a book that shall either interest or instruct a brother human being many gifts are required. Have you just reason to believe that they have been given to you?' That is what the candid, honest man of letters says who is not soft-hearted—and in ninety-nine cases out of a hundred it will probably be the truth. The soft-hearted man of letters remembers that this special case submitted to him may be the hundredth; and, unless the blotted manuscript is conclusive against such possibility, he reconciles it to his conscience to tune his counsel to that hope. Who can say that he is wrong? Unless such evidence be conclusive, who can venture to declare that this aspirant may not be the one who shall succeed? Who in such emergency does not remember the day in which he also was one of the hundred of whom the ninety-and-nine must fail— and will not remember also the many convictions in his own mind that he certainly would not be the one appointed? The man of letters in the neighbourhood of Cornboro to whom poor Mary's manuscript was shown was not sufficiently hard-hearted to make any strong attempt to deter her. He made no reference to the easy stockings, or the wholesome pie—pointed out the manifest faults which he saw, and added, we do not doubt with much more energy than he threw into his words of censure—his comfortable assurance that there was great promise in the work. Mary Gresley that evening burned the manuscript, and began another, with the dictionary close to her elbow.

Then, during her work, there occurred two circumstances which brought upon her—and, indeed, upon the household to which she belonged—intense sorrow and greatly increased trouble. The first of these applied more especially to herself. The Rev. Arthur Donne did not approve of novels—of other novels than those dialogues between Tom and Bob, of the falsehood of which he was unconscious—and expressed a desire that the writing of them should be abandoned. How far the lover went in his attempt to enforce obedience we, of course, could not know; but he pronounced the edict, and the edict, though not obeyed, created tribulation. Then there came forth another edict which had to be obeyed—an edict from the probable successor of the late Dr. Gresley—ordering the poor curate to seek employment in some clime more congenial to his state of health than that in which he was then living. He was told that his throat and lungs and general apparatus for living and preaching were not strong enough for those hyper-borean regions, and that he must seek a southern climate. He did do so, and, before I became acquainted with Mary, had transferred his services to a small town in Dorsetshire. The engagement, of course, was to be as valid as ever, though matrimony must be postponed, more indefinitely even than heretofore. But if Mary could write novels and sell them, then how glorious would it be to follow her lover into Dorsetshire! The Rev. Arthur Donne went, and the curate who came in his place was a married man, wanting a house, and not lodgings. So Mary Gresley persevered with her second novel, and completed it before she was eighteen.

The literary friend in the neighbourhood—to the chance of whose acquaintance I was indebted for my subsequent friendship with Mary Gresley—found this work to be a great improvement on the first. He was an elderly man who had been engaged nearly all his life in the conduct of a scientific and agricultural periodical, and was the last man whom I should have taken as a sound critic on works of fiction—but with spelling, grammatical construction, and the composition of sentences he was acquainted; and he assured Mary that her progress had been great. Should she burn that second story? she asked him. She would if he so recommended, and begin another the next day. Such was not his advice. 'I have a friend in London', said he, 'who has to do with such things, and you shall go to him. I will give you a letter'. He gave her the fatal letter, and she came to us.

She came up to town with her novel; but not only with her novel, for she brought her mother with her. So great was her eloquence, so excellent her suasive power either with her tongue or by that look of supplication in her face, that she induced her mother to abandon her home in Cornboro, and trust herself to London lodgings. The house was let furnished to the new curate, and when I first heard of the Gresleys they were living on the second floor in a small street near to the Euston Square station. Poor Fanny, as she was called, was left in some humble home at Cornboro, and Mary travelled up to try her fortune in the great city. When we came to know her well we expressed our doubts as to the wisdom of such a step. Yes; the vicar's wife had been strong against the move. Mary confessed as much. That lady had spoken most forcible words, had uttered terrible predictions, had told sundry truths. But Mary had prevailed, and the journey was made, and the lodgings were taken.

We can now come to the day on which we first saw her. She did not write, but came direct to us with her manuscript in her hand. 'A young woman, sir, wants to see you', said the clerk, in that tone to which we were so well accustomed, and which indicated the dislike which he had learned from us to the reception of unknown visitors.

'Young woman! What young woman?'

'Well, sir; she is a very young woman—quite a girl like.'

'I suppose she has got a name. Who sent her? I cannot see any young woman without knowing why. What does she want?'

'Got a manuscript in her hand, sir.'

'I've no doubt she has, and a ton of manuscripts in drawers and cupboards. Tell her to write. I won't see any woman, young or old, without knowing who she is'. The man retired, and soon returned with an envelope belonging to the office, on which was written, "Miss Mary Gresley, late of Cornboro." He also brought me a note from 'the man of letters' down in Yorkshire. 'Of what sort is she?' I asked, looking at the introduction.

'She ain't amiss as to looks', said the clerk; 'and she's modest-like'. Now certainly it is the fact that all female literary aspirants are not 'modest-like'. We read our friend's letter through, while poor Mary was standing at the counter below. How eagerly should we have run to greet her, to save her from the gaze of the public, to welcome her at least with a chair and the warmth of our editorial fire, had we guessed then what were her qualities! It was not long before she knew the way up to our sanctum without any clerk to show her, and not long before we knew well the sound of that low but not timid knock at our door made always with the handle of the parasol, with which her advent was heralded. We will confess that there was always music to our ears in that light tap from the little round wooden knob. The man of letters in Yorkshire, whom we had known well for many years, never had been known to us with intimacy. We had bought with him and sold with him, had talked with him, and, perhaps, walked with him; but he was not one with whom we had eaten, or drunk, or prayed. A dull, well-instructed, honest man he was, fond of his money, and, as we had thought, as unlikely as any man to be waked to enthusiasm by the ambitious dreams of a young girl. But Mary had been potent even over him, and he had written to me, saying that Miss Gresley was a young lady of exceeding promise, in respect of whom he had a strong presentiment that she would rise, if not to eminence, at least to a good position as a writer. 'But she is very young', he added. Having read this letter, we at last desired our clerk to send the lady up.

We remember her step as she came to the door, timid enough then—hesitating, but yet with an assumed lightness as though she was determined to show us that she was not ashamed of what she was doing. She had on her head a light straw hat, such as then was very unusual in London—and is not now, we believe, commonly worn in the streets of the metropolis by ladies who believe themselves to know what they are about. But it was a hat, worn upon her head, and not a straw plate done up with ribbons and reaching down the incline of the forehead as far as the top of the nose. And she was dressed in a grey stuff frock, with a little black band round her waist. As far as our memory goes, we never saw her in any other dress, or with other hat or bonnet on her head. 'And what can we do for you—Miss Gresley?' we said, standing up and holding the literary gentleman's letter in our hand. We had almost said, 'my dear', seeing her youth and remembering our own age. We were afterwards glad that we had not so addressed her; though it came before long that we did call her 'my dear'—in quite another spirit.

She recoiled a little from the tone of our voice, but recovered herself at once. 'Mr.—— thinks that you can do something for me. I have written a novel, and I have brought it to you.'

'You are very young, are you not, to have written a novel?'

'I am young', she said, 'but perhaps older than you think. I am eighteen'. The for the first time there came into her eye that gleam of a merry humour which never was allowed to dwell there long, but which was so alluring when it showed itself.

'That is a ripe age', we said laughing, and then we bade her

seat herself. At once we began to pour forth that long and
dull and ugly lesson which is so common to our life, in which
we tried to explain to our unwilling pupil that of all respectable
professions for young women literature is the most uncertain,
the most heart-breaking, and the most dangerous. 'You hear
of the few who are remunerated', we said; 'but you hear
nothing of the thousands that fail.'

'It is so noble!' she replied.

'But so hopeless.'

'There are those who suceed.'

'Yes, indeed. Even in a lottery one must gain the prize;
but they who trust to lotteries break their hearts.'

'But literature is not a lottery. If I am fit, I shall succeed.
Mr. —— thinks I may succeed'. Many more words of wisdom
we spoke to her, and well do we remember her reply when we
had run all our line off the reel, and had completed our sermon.
'I shall go on all the same,' she said. 'I shall try, and try
again—and again.'

Her power over us, to a certain extent, was soon established.
Of course we promised to read the MS., and turned it over,
no doubt with an anxious countenance, to see of what kind
was the writing. There is a feminine scrawl of a nature so
terrible that the task of reading it becomes worse than the
treadmill. 'I know I can write well—though I am not quite
sure about the spelling', said Mary, as she observed the glance
of our eyes. She spoke truly. The writing was good, though
the erasures and alterations were very numerous. And then
the story was intended to fill only one volume. 'I will copy
it for you if you wish it', said Mary. 'Though there are so
many scratchings out, it has been copied once'. We would
not for worlds have given her such labour, and then we promised
to read the tale. We forget how it was brought about, but she
told us at that interview that her mother had obtained leave
from the pastrycook round the corner to sit there waiting till
Mary should rejoin her. 'I thought it would be trouble enough
for you to have one of us here', she said with her little laugh
when I asked her why she had not brought her mother on with

her. I own that I felt that she had been wise; and when I told her that if she would call on me again that day week I would then have read at any rate so much of her work as would enable me to give her my opinion, I did not invite her to bring her mother with her. I knew that I could talk more freely to the girl without the mother's presence. Even when you are past fifty, and intent only to preach a sermon, you do not wish to have a mother present.

When she was gone we took up the roll of paper and examined it. We looked at the division into chapters, at the various mottoes the poor child had chosen, pronounced to ourselves the name of the story—it was simply the name of the heroine, an easy-going, unaffected, well-chosen name— and read the last page of it. On such occasions the reader of the work begins his task almost with a conviction that the labour which he is about to undertake will be utterly thrown away. He feels all but sure that the matter will be bad, that it will be better for all parties, writer, intended readers, and intended publisher, that the written words should not be conveyed into type—that it will be his duty after some fashion to convey that unwelcome opinion to the writer, and that the writer will go away incredulous, and accusing mentally the Mentor of the moment of all manner of literary sins, among which ignorance, jealousy, and falsehood, will, in the poor author's imagination, be most prominent. And yet when the writer was asking for that opinion, declaring his especial desire that the opinion should be candid, protesting that his present wish is to have some gauge of his own capability, and that he has come to you believing you to be above others able to give him that gauge—while his petition to you was being made, he was in every respect sincere. He had come desirous to measure himself, and had believed that you could measure him. When coming he did not think that you would declare him to be an Apollo. He had told himself, no doubt, how probable it was that you would point out to him that he was a dwarf. You find him to be an ordinary man, measuring perhaps five feet seven, and unable to reach the standard of the

particular regiment in which he is ambitious of serving. You
tell him so in what civillest words you know, and you are at
once convicted in his mind of jealousy, ignorance, and falsehood! And yet he is perhaps a most excellent fellow, and
capable of performing the best of service—only in some other
regiment! As we looked at Miss Gresley's manuscript, tumb-
ling it through our hands, we expected even from her some such
result. She had gained two things from us already by her
outward and inward gifts, such as they were—first that we
would read her story, and secondly that we would read it
quickly; but she had not as yet gained from us any belief that
by reading it we could serve her.

We did read it—the most of it before we left our editorial
chair on that afternoon, so that we lost altogether the daily
walk so essential to our editorial health, and were put to the
expense of a cab on our return home. And we incurred some
minimum of domestic discomfort from the fact that we did
not reach our own door till twenty minutes after our appointed
dinner hour. 'I have this moment come from the office as
hard as a cab could bring me', we said in answer to the mildest
of reproaches, explaining nothing as to the nature of the cause
which had kept us so long at our work.

We must not allow our readers to suppose that the intensity
of our application had arisen from the overwhelming interest
of the story. It was not that the story entranced us, but that
our feeling for the writer grew as we read the story. It was
simple, unaffected, and almost painfully unsensational. It contained, as I came to perceive afterwards, little more than a
recital of what her imagination told her might too probably
be the result of her own engagement. It was the story of two
young people who became engaged and could not be married.
After a course of years the man, with many true arguments,
asked to be absolved. The woman yields with an expressed
conviction that her lover is right, settles down for maiden life,
then breaks her heart and dies. The character of the man was
utterly untrue to nature. That of the woman was true but
commonplace. Other interests, or other character there was

none. The dialogues between the lovers were many and tedious, and hardly a word was spoken between them which two lovers really would have uttered. It was clearly not a work as to which I could tell my little friend that she might depend upon it for fame or fortune. When I had finished it I was obliged to tell myself that I could not advise her even to publish it. But yet I could not say that she had mistaken her own powers or applied herself to a profession beyond her reach. There were a grace and delicacy in her work which were charming. Occasionally she escaped from the trammels of grammar, but only so far that it would be a pleasure to point out to her her errors. There was not a word that a young lady should not have written; and there were throughout the whole evident signs of honest work. We had six days to think it over between our completion of the task and her second visit.

She came exactly at the hour appointed, and seated herself at once in the armchair before us as soon as the young man had closed the door behind him. There had been no great occasion for nervousness at her first visit, and she had then, by an evident effort, overcome the diffidence incidental to a meeting with a stranger. But now she did not attempt to conceal her anxiety. 'Well', she said, leaning forward, and looking up into our face, with her two hands folded together.

Even though Truth, standing full panoplied at our elbow, had positively demanded it, we could not have told her then to mend her stockings and bake her pies and desert the calling that she had chosen. She was simply irresistible, and would, we fear, have constrained us into falsehood had the question been between falsehood and absolute reprobation of her work. To have spoken hard, heart-breaking words to her, would have been like striking a child when it comes to kiss you. We fear that we were not absolutely true at first, and that by that absence of truth we made subsequent pain more painful. 'Well', she said, looking up into our face. 'Have you read it?' We told her that we had read every word of it. 'And it is no good?'

We fear that we began by telling her that it certainly was good—after a fashion, very good—considering her youth and necessary inexperience, very good indeed. As we said this she shook her head, and sent out a spark or two from her eyes, intimating her conviction that excuses or quasi praise founded on her youth would avail her nothing. 'Would anybody buy it from me?' she asked. No—we did not think that any publisher would pay her money for it. 'Would they print it for me without costing me anything?' Then we told her the truth as nearly as we could. She lacked experience; and if, as she had declared to us before, she was determined to persevere, she must try again, and must learn more of that lesson of the world's ways which was so necessary to those who attempted to teach that lesson to others. 'But I shall try again at once', she said. We shook our head, endeavouring to shake it kindly. 'Currer Bell was only a young girl when she succeeded', she added. The injury which Currer Bell did after this fashion was almost equal to that perpetrated by Jack Sheppard, and yet Currer Bell was not very young when she wrote.

She remained with us then for above an hour—for more than two probably, though the time was not specially marked by us; and before her visit was brought to a close she had told us of her engagement with the curate. Indeed, we believe that the greater part of her little history as hitherto narrated was made known to us on that occasion. We asked after her mother early in the interview, and learned that she was not on this occasion kept waiting at the pastrycook's shop. Mary had come alone, making use of some friendly omnibus, of which she had learned the route. When she told us that she and her mother had come up to London solely with the view of forwarding her views in her intended profession, we ventured to ask whether it would not be wiser for them to return to Cornboro, seeing how improbable it was that she would have matter fit for the Press within any short period. Then she explained that they had calculated that they would be able to live in London for twelve months, if they spent nothing except on absolute necessaries. The poor girl seemed to keep back nothing from us. 'We have clothes that will carry us through, and we shall be very careful. I came in an omnibus—but I shall walk if you will let me come again'. Then she asked me for advice. How was she to set about further work with the best chance of turning it to account?

It had been altogether the fault of that retired literary gentleman down in the north, who had obtained what standing he had in the world of letters by writing about guano and the cattle plague! Divested of all responsibility, and fearing no further trouble to himself, he had ventured to tell this girl that her work was full of promise. Promise means probability, and in this case there was nothing beyond a remote chance. That she and her mother should have left their little household gods, and come up to London on such a chance, was a thing terrible to the mind. But we felt before these two hours were over that we could not throw her off now. We had become old friends, and there had been that between us which gave her a positive claim upon our time. She had sat in our armchair, leaning forward with her elbows on her knees and her hands stretched out, till we, caught by the charm of her unstudied intimacy, had wheeled round our chair, and had placed ourselves, as nearly as the circumstances would admit, in the same position. The magnetism had already begun to act upon us. We soon found ourselves taking it for granted that she was to remain in London and begin another book. It was impossible to resist her. Before the interview was over, we, who had been conversant with all these matters before she was born; we, who had latterly come to regard our own editorial fault as being chiefly that of personal harshness; we, who had repulsed aspirant novelists by the score—we had consented to be a party to the creation, if not to the actual writing, of this new book!

It was to be done after this fashion. She was to fabricate a plot, and to bring it to us, written on two sides of a sheet of letter paper. On the reverse sides we were to criticise this plot, and prepare emendations. Then she was to make out skeletons of the men and women who were afterwards to be clothed with flesh and made alive with blood, and covered with cuticles. After that she was to arrange her proportions; and at last, before she began to write the story, she was to describe in detail such part of it as was to be told in each chapter. On every advancing wavelet of the work we were to give her our written remarks. All this we promised to do because of the quiver in her lip, and the alternate tear and sparkle in her eye. 'Now that I have found a friend, I feel sure that I can do it', she said, as she held our hand tightly before she left us.

In about a month, during which she had twice written to us and twice been answered, she came with her plot. It was the old story, with some additions and some change. There was matrimony instead of death at the end, and an old aunt was brought in for the purpose of relenting and producing an income. We added a few details, feeling as we did so that we were the very worst of botchers. We doubt now whether the old, sad, simple story was not the better of the two. Then, after another lengthened interview, we sent our pupil back to create her skeletons When she came with the skeletons we were dear friends and learned to called her Mary. Then it was that she first sat at our editorial table, and wrote a love-letter to the curate. It was then mid-winter, wanting but a few days to Christmas, and Arthur, as she called him, did not like the cold weather. 'He does not say so', she said, 'but I fear he is ill. Don't you think there are some people with whom everything is unfortunate?' She wrote her letter, and had recovered her spirits before she took her leave.

We then proposed to her to bring her mother to dine with us on Christmas Day. We had made a clean breast of it at home in regard to our heart-flutterings, and had been met with a suggestion that some kindness with propriety be shown to the old lady as well as to the young one. We had felt grateful to the old lady for not coming to our office with her daughter, and had at once assented. When we made the suggestion to Mary there came first a blush over all her face, and then there followed the well-known smile before the blush was gone. 'You'll all be dressed fine', she said. We protested that not a garment would be changed by any of the family after the decent church-going in the morning. 'Just as I am?' she asked. 'Just as you are', we said, looking at the dear grey frock, adding some mocking assertion that no possible combination of millinery could improve her. 'And mamma will be just the same? Then we will come', she said. We told her an absolute falsehood, as to some necessity which would take us in a cab to Euston Square on the afternoon of that Christmas Day, so that we could call and bring them both to our house without trouble or expense. 'You shan't do anything of the kind', she said, However, we swore to our falsehood—perceiving, as we did so, that she did not believe a word of it; but in the matter of the cab we had our own way.

We found the mother to be what we had expected—a weak, ladylike, lachrymose old lady, endowed with a profound admiration for her daughter, and so bashful that she could not at all enjoy her plum-pudding. We think that Mary did enjoy hers thoroughly. She made a little speech to the mistress of the house, praising ourselves with warm words and tearful eyes, and immediately won the heart of a new friend. She allied herself warmly to our daughters, put up with the schoolboy pleasantries of our sons, and before the evening was over was dressed up as a ghost for the amusement of some neighbouring children who were brought in to play snapdragon. Mrs. Gresley, as she drank her tea and crumbled her bit of cake, seated on a distant sofa, was not so happy, partly because she remembered her old gown, and partly because our wife was a stranger to her. Mary had forgotten both circumstances before the dinner was half over. She was the sweetest ghost that ever was seen. How pleasant would be our ideas of departed spirits if such ghosts would visit us frequently.

They repeated their visits to us not unfrequently during the twelve months; but as the whole interest attaching to our intercourse had reference to circumstances which took place in that editorial room of ours, it will not be necessary to refer further to the hours, very pleasant to ourselves, which she spent with us in our domestic life. She was ever made welcome when she came, and was known by us as a dear, well-bred, modest, clever little girl. The novel went on. That catalogue of the skeletons gave us more trouble than all the rest, and many were the tears which she shed over it, and sad were the misgivings by which she was afflicted that a girl of eighteen should portray characters such as she had never known. In her intercourse with the curate all the intellect had been on her side. She had loved him because it was requisite to her to love someone; and now, as she had loved him, she was as true as steel to him. But there had been almost nothing for her to learn from him. The plan of the novel went on, and as it did so we became more and more despondent as to its success. And through it all we knew how contrary it was to our own judgment to expect, even to dream of, anything but failure. Though we went on working with her, finding it to be quite impossible to resist her entreaties, we did tell her from day to day that, even presuming she were entitled to hope for ultimate success, she must go through an apprenticeship of ten years before she could reach it. Then she would sit silent, repressing her tears, and searching for arguments with which to support her cause.

'Working hard is apprenticeship', she said to us once.

'Yes, Mary; but the work will be more useful, and the apprenticeship more wholesome, if you will take them for what they are worth.'

'I shall be dead in ten years', she said.

'If you thought so you would not intend to marry Mr. Donne. But even were it certain that such would be your fate, how can that alter the state of things? The world would know nothing of that; and if it did, would the world buy your book out of pity?'

'I want no one to pity me', she said; 'but I want you to help me'. So we went on helping her. At the end of four months she had not put pen to paper on the absolute body of her projected novel; and yet she had worked daily at it, arranging its future construction.

During the next month, when we were in the middle of March, a gleam of real success came to her. We had told her frankly that we would publish nothing of hers in the periodical which we were ourselves conducting. She had become too dear to us for us not to feel that were we to do so, we should be doing it rather for her sake than for that of our readers. But we did procure for her the publication of two short stories elsewhere. For these she received twelve guineas, and it seemed to her that she had found an El Dorado of literary wealth. I shall never forget her ecstasy when she knew that her work would be printed, or her renewed triumph when the first humble cheque was given into her hands. There are those who will think that such a triumph, as connected with literature, must be sordid. For ourselves, we are ready to acknowledge that money payment for work done is the best and most honest test of success. We are sure that it is so felt by young barristers and young doctors, and we do not see why rejoicing on such realisation of long-cherished hope should be more vile with the literary apirant than with them. 'What do you think I'll do first with it?' she said. We thought she meant to send something to her lover, and we told her so. 'I'll buy mamma a bonnet to go to church in. I didn't tell you before, but she hasn't been these three Sundays because she hasn't one fit to be seen'. I changed the cheque for her, and she went off and bought the bonnet.

Though I was successful for her in regard to the two stories, I could not go beyond that. We could have filled pages of periodicals with her writing had we been willing that she should work without remuneration. She herself was anxious for such work, thinking that it would lead to something better. But we opposed it, and, indeed, would not permit it, believing that work so done can be serviceable to none but those who accept it that pages may be filled without cost.

During the whole winter, while she was thus working, she was in a state of alarm about her lover. Her hope was ever that when warm weather came he would again be well and strong. We know nothing sadder than such hope founded on such source. For does not the winter follow the summer, and then again comes the killing spring? At this time she used to read

us passages from his letters, in which he seemed to speak of
little but his own health. In her literary ambition he never
seemed to have taken part since she had declared her intention
of writing profane novels. As regarded him, his sole merit to
us seemed to be in his truth to her. He told her that in his
opinion they two were as much joined together as though the
service of the Church had bound them; but even in saying that
he spoke ever of himself and not of her. Well—May came,
dangerous, doubtful, deceitful May, and he was worse. Then,
for the first time, the dread word, Consumption, passed her
lips. It had already passed ours, mentally, a score of times. We
asked her what she herself would wish to do. Would she
desire to go down to Dorsetshire and see him? She thought
awhile, and said that she would wait a little longer.

The novel went on, and at length, in June, she was writing
the actual words on which, as she thought, so much depended.
She had really brought the story into some shape in the arrangement of her chapters; and sometimes even I began to hope.
There were moments in which with her hope was almost
certainty. Towards the end of June Mr. Donne declared himself to be better. He was to have a holiday in August, and then
he intended to run up to London and see his betrothed. He
still gave details, which were distressing to us, of his own
symptoms; but it was manifest that he himself was not despon-
ding, and she was governed in her trust or in her despair
altogether by him. But when August came the period of his
visit was postponed. The heat had made him weak, and he
was to come in September.

Early in August we ourselves went away for our annual
recreation—not that we shoot grouse, or that we have any
strong opinion that August and September are the best months
in the year for holidaymaking—but that everybody does
go in August. We ourselves are not specially fond of August.
In many places to which one goes a-touring mosquitoes
bite in that month. The heat, too, prevents one from walking.
The inns are all full, and the railways crowded. April and May
are twice pleasanter months in which to see the world and the

country. But fashion is everything, and no man or woman will stay in town in August for whom there exists any practicability of leaving it. We went on the 10th—just as though we had a moor, and one of the last things we did before our departure was to read and revise the last-written chapter of Mary's story.

About the end of September we returned, and up to that time the lover had not come to London. Immediately on our return we wrote to Mary, and the next morning she was with us. She had seated herself on her usual chair before she spoke, and we had taken her hand and asked after herself and her mother. Then, with someting of mirth in our tone, we demanded the work which she had done since our departure. 'He is dying', she replied.

She did not weep as she spoke. It was not on such occasions as this that the tears filled her eyes. But there was in her face a look of fixed and settled misery which convinced us that she at least did not doubt the truth of her own assertion. We muttered something as to our hope that she was mistaken. 'The doctor, there, has written to tell mamma that it is so. Here is his letter'. The doctor's letter was a good letter, written with more of assurance than doctors can generally allow themselves to express. 'I fear that I am justified in telling you', said the doctor, 'that it can only be a question of weeks'. We got up and took her hand. There was not a word to be uttered.

'I must go to him', she said, after a pause.

'Well—yes. It will be better.'

'But we have no money'. It must be explained now that offers of slight, very slight, pecuniary aid had been made by us both to Mary and to her mother on more than one occasion. These had been refused with adamantine firmness, but always with something of mirth, or at least of humour, attached to the refusal. The mother would simply refer to the daughter, and Mary would declare that they could manage to see the twelvemonth through and go back to Cornboro, without becoming absolute beggars. She would allude to their joint wardrobe, and would confess that there would not have been a pair of boots between them but for that twelve guineas; and indeed she seemed to have stretched that modest incoming so as to cover a legion of purchases. And of these things she was never ashamed to speak. We think there must have been at least two grey frocks, because the frock was always clean, and never absolutely shabby. Our girls at home declared that they had seen three. Of her frock, as it happened, she never spoke to us, but the new boots and the new gloves, 'and ever so many things that I can't tell you about, which we really couldn't have gone without', all came out of the twelve guineas. That she had taken, not only with delight, but with triumph. But pecuniary assistance from ourselves she had always refused. 'It would be a gift', she would say.

'Have it as you like.'

'But people don't give other people money.'

'Don't they? That's all you know about the world.'

'Yes; to beggars. We hope we needn't come to that'. It was thus that she always answered us—but always with something of laughter in her eye, as though their poverty was a joke. Now, when the demand upon her was for that which did not concern her personal comfort, which referred to a matter felt by her to be vitally important, she declared, without a minute's hesitation, that she had not money for the journey.

'Of course you can have money', we said. 'I suppose you will go at once?'

'Oh yes—at once. That is, in a day or two—after he shall have received my letter. Why should I wait?' We sat down to write a cheque, and she, seeing what we were doing, asked how much it was to be. 'No—half that will do', she said. 'Mamma will not go. We have talked it over and decided it. Yes; I know all about that. I am going to see my lover—my dying lover; and I have to beg for the money to take me to him. Of course I am a young girl; but in such a condition am I to stand upon the ceremony of being taken care of? A housemaid wouldn't want to be taken care of at eighteen'. We did exactly as she bade us, and then attempted to comfort her while the young man went to get money for the cheque. What consolation was possible? It was simply necessary to admit with frankness that sorrow had come from which there could be no present release. 'Yes', she said. 'Time will cure it—in a way. One dies in time, and then of course it is all cured'. 'One hears of this kind of thing often', she said afterwards, still leaning forward in her chair, still with something of the old expression in her eyes—something almost of humour in spite of her grief; 'but it is the girl who dies. When it is the girl, there isn't, after all, so much harm done. A man goes about the world and can shake it off; and then, there are plenty of girls'. We could not tell her how infinitely more important, to our thinking, was her life than that of him whom she was going to see now for the last time; but there did spring up within our mind a feeling, greatly opposed to that conviction which formerly we had endeavoured to impress upon herself— that she was destined to make for herself a successful career.

She went, and remained by her lover's bedside for three weeks. She wrote constantly to her mother, and once or twice to ourselves. She never again allowed herself to enter- tain a gleam of hope, and she spoke of her sorrow as a thing accomplished. In her last interview with us she had hardly alluded to her novel, and in her letters she never mentioned it. But she did say one word which made us guess what was coming. 'You will find me greatly changed in one thing', she said; 'so much changed that I need never have troubled you'. The day for her return to London was twice postponed, but at last she was brought to leave him. Stern necessity was too strong for her. Let her pinch herself as she might, she must live down in Dorsetshire—and could not live on his means, which were as narrow as her own. She left him; and on the day after her arrival in London she walked across from Euston Square to our office.

'Yes', she said, 'it is all over. I shall never see him again on this side of heaven's gates'. We do not know that we ever saw a tear in her eyes produced by her own sorrow. She was possessed of some wonderful strength which seemed to suffice for the bearing of any burden. Then she paused, and we could

only sit silent, with our eyes fixed upon the rug. 'I have made
him a promise', she said at last. Of course we asked her what
was the promise, though at the moment we thought that we
knew. 'I will make no more attempt at novel writing.'

'Such a promise should not have been asked—or given', we
said vehemently.

'It should have been asked—because he thought it right', she
answered. 'And of course it was given. Must he not know
better than I do? Is he not one of God's ordained priests? In
all the world is there one so bound to obey him as I?' There
was nothing to be said for it at such a moment as that. There
is no enthusiasm equal to that produced by a death-bed parting.
'I grieve greatly', she said, 'that you should have had so much
vain labour with a poor girl who can never profit by it.'

'I don't believe the labour will have been vain', we answered,
having altogether changed those views of ours as to the futility
of the pursuit which she had adopted.

'I have destroyed it all', she said.

'What—burned the novel?'

'Every scrap of it. I told him that I would do so, and that he
should know that I had done it. Every page was burned after
I got home last night, and then I wrote to him before I went
to bed.'

'Do you mean that you think it wicked that people should
write novels?' we asked.

'He thinks it to be a misapplication of God's gifts, and that
has been enough for me. He shall judge for me, but I will not
judge for others. And what does it matter? I do not want to
write a novel now.'

They remained in London till the end of the year for which
the married curate had taken their house, and then they returned
to Cornboro. We saw them frequently while they were still
in town, and despatched them by the train to the north just
when the winter was beginning. At that time the young clergyman was still living down in Dorsetshire, but he was lying in
his grave when Christmas came. Mary never saw him again,
nor did she attend his funeral. She wrote to us frequently then,

as she did for years afterwards. 'I should have liked to have stood at his grave', she said; 'but it was a luxury of sorrow that I wished to enjoy, and they who cannot earn luxuries should not have them. They were going to manage it for me here, but I knew I was right to refuse it'. Right, indeed! As far as we knew her, she never moved a single point from what was right.

All these things happened many years ago. Mary Gresley, on her return to Cornboro, apprenticed herself, as it were, to the married curate there, and called herself, I think, a female Scripture reader. I know that she spent her days in working hard for the religious aid of the poor around her. From time to time we endeavoured to instigate her to literary work; and she answered our letters by sending us wonderful little dialogues between Tom the Saint and Bob the Sinner. We are in no humour to criticise them now; but we can assert, that though that mode of religious teaching is most distasteful to us, the literary merit shown even in such works as these was very manifest. And there came to be apparent in them a gleam of humour which would sometimes make us think that she was sitting opposite to us and looking at us, and that she was Tom the Saint, and that we were Bob the Sinner. We said what we could to turn her from her chosen path, throwing into our letters all the eloquence and all the thought of which we were masters; but our eloquence and our thought were equally in vain.

At last, when eight years had passed over her head after the death of Mr. Donne, she married a missionary who was going out to some forlorn country on the confines of African colonisation; and there she died. We saw her on board the ship in which she sailed, and before we parted there had come that tear into her eyes, the old look of supplication on her lips, and the gleam of mirth across her face. We kissed her once—for the first and only time—as we bade God bless her!